D1506377

Mothers and Lovers

MOTHERS AND LOVERS

Elizabeth Wood

A GROLIER COMPANY

Franklin Watts
New York / Toronto / 1987

Library of Congress Cataloging-in-Publication Data

Wood, Elizabeth.
Mothers and lovers.

I. Title.
PS3573.O593M6   1987   813'.54   87–10468
ISBN 0–531–15062–3

*I wish to thank
Ruth Sullivan, Jane Isay
and Jeanne Vestal
for their invaluable help*

For Sarah and Sandy,
Kirsten and Kate

Mothers and Lovers

PART I

Much Madness is divinest Sense—
To a discerning Eye—
Much Sense—the starkest Madness.
'Tis the Majority
In this, as All, prevail—
Assent—and you are sane—
Demur—you're straightway dangerous—
And handled with a Chain.

Emily Dickinson

CHAPTER ONE

My mother had intended to call me Meghan, but when Harry, my father, filled out the forms at the registry, he spelled my name Morgan Evans. I never knew if that was because he was excited, or wanted a son, or whether the slip was due to his unfulfilled longing for a vintage motorcar, but the name stuck. My only sister Cicely was named three years before me for the goddess of music. I should have liked a goddess. In my private diary, I signed myself Princess Margaret Elizabeth of Morgana, a cross between a royal flush and a Welsh witch that a decent fairy might have bestowed on me at birth, had I been lucky enough to have a godmother at all. Dilys, my mother, didn't believe in them.

Cicely and I played the secret game at night under the sheets. We took turns drawing codes, names, maps, and narratives of adventure on our backs underneath our pajamas. The trick was to communicate without speaking, a skill like primitive cave painting. Elaborate stories grew into sagas, stroked across the entire back region toward more ticklish borders of underdeveloped breasts and rounded bottoms near the thighs, past the neck and ears and across expanses of young and listening flesh.

Our graphic, wordless confidences were very comforting whenever there was a storm outside our upstairs sleepout that shook the veranda on its four slender pillars and flashed electric signals through the louver windows. Then we snuggled tightly together and our fingers pressed alarm, and sometimes terror, onto each other's trembling skin.

When we were older and our parents occasionally left us alone in the upstairs flat, we took the game farther afield. We tiptoed through the dark house. Because I was the bravest, I led the way, holding Cicely's hand behind me, down the front stairs, across the tiled entrance hall, past Miss Clayton's rooms, and up the back stairway to our kitchen. At the threshold to each door, the rules let me snap on the light switch briefly to check for burglars or pirates. Our final destination was Mother's bedroom. While Cicely shivered in her nightdress, I had to touch the black marble mantelshelf and count to ten before we could begin a new chapter of the game. I believed there were mythical bunyips buried inside the marble, whose ghostly shapes patterned the stone and inspired our adventures.

I was always the leader. It may have had something to do with being left-handed. Mother blamed my rebellious streak on that. She said that was another accident at birth, like my name. I was convinced that my right side, the clumsy, powerless, self-conscious side, was liable to make the wrong decisions, wrong in the eyes of the world. As soon as I could be independent, my left side and I would conquer the sinister odds of the right.

The Dalcroze System was my first elated experience of independence. When I was five, I was chosen. I dangled my skinny legs and bare feet over the edge of the huge platform of the Adelaide Town Hall, ready to leap to the music and dance to its beautifully logical beat with fifty other children to whom the new method was to be demonstrated. A radiant Isadora, with expressive arms, pleated tunic, and bare feet, showed Leonora Skinner and me our first dance. Leonora's father was an artist. Leonora was artistic as well. She was my first friend. We told stories in tandem; I'd begin, and at a dramatic point Leonora took up the thread, surrounded by a circle of rapt children in the Westall kindergarten. Peggy Daye, our first teacher, encouraged Leonora and me in our storytelling. I loved Miss Daye so deeply that once, when Leonora and I were on opposite sides of an easel to paint sunsets drenched in orange and scarlet and indigo blues, I deliberately hit my elbow on the chair behind me.

"Ouch, Miss Daye!" I cried. "I feel funny. I think I am going to die."

She rushed toward me and rubbed my arm softly until it tickled. I closed my eyes and went limp. Gently she laid me on a little stretcher, covered me with her pink cardigan, and whispered to the children to be quiet. I smelled her perfume among the crimsons on Leonora's painting.

The five-year-olds had compulsory rests on stretchers after lunch every day. Wearing our bloomers and singlets, under regulation gray school blankets on which the mothers had embroidered our initials in red cotton, we closed our eyes and listened to each other's breathing until Miss Daye blew her silver whistle for the next lesson. I dreamed I was Princess Margaret on twenty feather mattresses and Miss Daye was a lady-in-waiting. Once, I pretended really to fall asleep.

"Sh, children, Morgan is sleeping. Everyone dress as quietly as you can. We'll leave her to wake up when she is ready."

I lay for what seemed an eternity, it was so hard to keep my eyes absolutely still under my eyelids and to breathe slowly. I longed to peep to see if Miss Daye was watching over me, but I didn't dare to break the spell.

Rest time was my favorite until the terrible day when I wet the bed. There was no disguising it. Miss Daye took me behind the cupboard where she kept the musical instruments to give me a pair of ugly yellow bloomers several sizes larger than my sodden ones, which she rinsed out and hung to dry on the carob tree that overhung our sandpit. I blushed at the indignity. From that moment, I vowed never to pretend when it wasn't true.

From the Dalcroze exercises, I graduated to be chief conductor of the kindergarten band. I had to stand with my back to the long windows of the classroom, baton at the ready, and face the full orchestra. I swept an imperious eye over triangles and castanets, xylophones and a choir of clapsticks on my left, and then the tambourines, gongs, and finger bells on my right. Symmetrically in the middle, right in front of me, were Leonora Skinner and Bridget Baddeley (*her* father was a bishop) on the two bass drums. I waited for all eyes to meet mine. I raised my stick.

Out of the corner of my left eye, I saw Miss Daye on her revolving piano stool, fingers above the keys, and the music for "The Toy Symphony" on her stand. I marked four beats, the last an upbeat, then down! Begin! When we neared the final bars, my zest, my happiness was so intense that I swung the baton in a Dalcroze arabesque clean across the windows, smashing the stick into three uneven bits. Wretched Bridget lost her beat and I heard a titter from the triangles and the music began to sound like a record running down. But the mothers applauded, we stood and bowed, and prepared to file out of the room at the end of the concert.

"Ssst! Idiot!" I hissed at Bridget, and flicked her plait viciously with the remains of the baton. Miss Daye was talking with the parents; I'd seen my mother's worried frown sideways as we marched past. Bridget turned, raised her hand to hit me, and Miss Daye swooped me into her arms.

"Wonderful, Morgan! It was Sir Bernard Heinze's baton that he presented to the school, but it was an accident, in the power of music, and you mustn't mind." I squeezed back hot and furious tears.

Until I was given a bicycle, I walked to Westall on my own because Cicely hated to be late. I memorized every inch of the route. The path was tarred, but because all the suburban gardens and streets grew jacaranda trees, the entire surface was rutted and bumpy with fissures and potholes that could snare shoelaces or trip me up if I didn't watch my feet. I also kept my head down ready to duck low-flying branches to avoid being smothered in a confetti shower of the fine, sticky purple blossoms, twigs, seed pods, and dried leaves that jacarandas always seem to shed.

Mrs. Rundle had three across her front and a pepper-tree on one corner of Navarro Street. Going past Mrs. Rundle's was like running through a sugar and spice and pepper spray and I went as fast as I could but mainly because I did not want to say hello to Rosalind Rundle. She was retarded. Her lips were not made to fit so that dribble seeped from one corner down to her chin. She always waited on the veranda to wave to the Westall girls, drooling with excitement whenever she saw a navy school hat bobbing along Navarro Street. The three Kelly girls lived a few doors down from the Rundles, which was how we all knew everything there was to know about Rosalind and more than enough to make me want to hurry past rather than say hello and risk an unlucky start to a school day.

I devised rules for rapid transit along Navarro Street. I couldn't step on any crack, I had to jump to avoid a bump, and I had to hum. Like Pooh of Pooh Corner, I hummed as I breathed in and out to the rhythm of whatever tune happened to be in my head that day. Sometimes I made up my own tune, but mostly it was "Für Elise," which I was learning on the piano—a perfect piece for the hopping, skipping, and running necessary to navigate Navarro Street without breaking my rules or arriving too late for morning prayers. Beethoven must have composed while bustling along extremely uneven streets in Vienna. Years later, when I turned fifteen, Nat "King" Cole better suited my stride because I could simultaneously conjure the divinely handsome face of Jack Fry while I walked and hummed my way to school to the tune of

Oh how I love you, honey-hush!
Oh how you're giving me the rush!
I'm saving my dimes,
I hear wedding chimes,
My sweet and lovely honey-hush!

That tune could waltz or swagger or simply float, depending on my mood when I awoke. I made it last, with improvisations, all the way to the Westall gate, on foot, on bicycle, come rain, come shine.

When the crowns of my front teeth wore thin, Cicely said it was because I ground my teeth in my sleep. Privately, I thought it was caused by excessive mouth-music. I could click out the rhythms of entire symphonies with my musical nutcracker jaw; my breathing like a woodwind, my lips the reed, my teeth the percussion for my tongue which orchestrated everything and kept the beat. Once, in Ancient History, Miss Chase accused me of chewing forbidden gum when in fact and absentmindedly I was performing the "Consecration of the House" inside my mouth. Miss Chase was not at all musical and gave me a detention for cheekiness. Short of cutting out my tongue and vocal cords, I scowled to myself, You cannot prevent an artist from making art, Miss Chase. I completed the performance by tapping out the rhythm under the desk with my fingernails and hoped she'd think it was raining.

Music at Westall College was limited to piano instruction, but I planned to become a composer. "Music," Miss Chase pontificated while I wrote out one hundred lines of insincere apology, "is not a realistic career. It's an accomplishment, like drawing and embroidery. Besides, Adelaide is not Vienna. It's all very well to dream, but we are too far from the sources of civilization to emulate a genius like Beethoven. We must be realistic about what we can and can't accomplish here, especially when we're young, and especially in our history class. Realism, Morgan, realism."

I sat close by the wireless at home until I could identify all the instruments of the orchestra. I covered my mother's glory box with layers of soft green felt and thumped her wooden spoons upon it to accompany the timpani in broadcast concerts. I pestered my piano teacher to show me how to write down melodies remembered, and spent hours at the piano coaxing from my fingers the sounds I heard inside my head. All too often what emerged were the unremitting falterings of Miss Chase's realism in a tattoo of defeat.

My composition fires flickered until our junior Westall class was taken to the Theatre Royal to see Dame Judith Anderson as Medea. Dizzy with the resonance of her thrilling voice and hypnotized by her eyes, I had to steady myself against the red velvet balustrade of the dress circle for fear and longing that I'd tumble over into the pit and land, stunned, entranced, at Dame Judith's sandalled feet. When Medea entered with the bodies of her sons, some children in the audience began to giggle. I looked around the darkened theatre. Here was my heart at breaking point and Medea awash with blood—and people could find that funny? I'd show them. I'd show them what was real. One day I'd stand there, on that stage, and, like Medea, command them with my fury and my passion and my flesh and flaming words until they quaked.

After that performance, I devoted every spare moment to plays and acting. The day an actor and producer from the Elizabethan Theatre Trust visited the junior drama club and told me I had talent, I rushed home to tell my parents. Harry and Dilys were usually proud if Cicely or I won prizes, yet this dramatic news brought only tepid applause at the dinner table.

Later, when I was trying to finish my homework at the sewing table behind the sleep-out door, Mother and Dad settled on my bed for a "serious family discussion." It was futile to look for privacy in our small flat. No matter where I set down my work, my parents staked their claim to the area. My desk was a repository for Harry's newspapers, a depot for Dilys's sewing boxes, a meeting place for cups of tea and telephone conversations, the choicest route to the bathroom and the laundry. It never mattered which destination, or which errand, gave my parents an excuse to interrupt my private study.

"Of course we care about success," Harry began. "You can't think your mother and I have scrimped and saved and made our sacrifices all these years to give you the best start in life—a private school—not to take some pride in your accomplishments, but you can't make a career on the stage, my girl. You'll have to choose something more reliable and substantial. You know I may die at any moment. Where would that leave your mother?"

"I don't want to be a nurse or a librarian, Dad. I want to act. I'll study drama at the university if that makes it more substantial."

"And you're not going to university. Nobody in my family—or in your mother's family, either—ever talked about a university. You're getting all the education you will need. When you grow up, you'll have to earn a decent wage, pay board, and get a steady job before you marry. All these years, your mother has gone without for the sake of you girls, and I could go, like this," he said, and clicked his finger and thumb together, "without a minute's notice. Then it's only right that you start taking care of your mother. Your mother, Morgan, is the most precious person in the world." That, he reminded me many times, was that.

"And don't argue with your father. You'll be the death of him," came mother's conclusive refrain. "If it wasn't for your father's pluck, dear, you wouldn't be where you are today." She bent her head closer to my page. "Isn't that sentence too wordy? Oh, you're reading Keats. 'Hail to thee, blithe spirit'—or was that Wordsworth?"

I chose not to correct her but ground my teeth and wrote on. Mother cradled her favorite poets' names as if she pressed a baby to her breast or petals between pages of a little book. She had never finished high school but took secretarial jobs to support her father, a carpenter, who was chronically unemployed during the Depression. Mother told her friends disparagingly that she was hopelessly uneducated, but she read a great many books and always wrote a sonnet for our birthday cards. She had dedicated a small corner of family life to constant self-improvement.

Harry was suspicious of Dilys's private interests in case they should exclude him. When I was eight, and he spent two years in the hospital with a heart disease, Mother took on the task of reorganizing the office at Westall to reverse decades of amateur administrative disorder into an efficient streamlined business. When Harry recovered enough to return to the bank, he was too proud to have her earn and insisted she resign. Instead, she became honorary secretary of the parents' association at Westall and opened a small office in the grounds where she called her weekly meetings and kept an eye on my progress.

Harry resented her unpaid work, too, and the demands the school made on his family life. "That job's beneath you, Mother," he would chide. "You're too fine for secretarial duties. You should be Madam President and give the orders. Let somebody else take a turn as General Dogsbody. After all we've paid to put two girls through Westall, that school owes us a thing or two," he grumbled, jealous of the time she gave to others.

Each year, at the end of the Westall term, parents were invited to the prize-giving. The poetry, prose, and reading competitions were followed by a short play, sometimes in French, and "moments musicale" from selected pianists in the senior music club, before final prayers and two-part anthems sent the students crashing loudly and exuberantly through the double doors of the Memorial Hall and out to the schoolyard free, free, free.

I'd pretend not to recognize my parents at break-up. Harry looked so like a choirboy, alert and chaste when he sang the hymns, his face polished, collar starched. He sang a half pitch too high and a decibel too loud and I wished he'd simply be anonymous like the other gray-suited fathers. When he craned his neck to look for me among the choir, I'd hunch down or blow my nose or study the gold-lettered honor boards hung above the stage and pretend I was an orphan. If I was a prize winner, his head bobbed up and down like a buoy at sea, a beacon to steer by, or a marker to warn me of perils ahead, to protect me from the shoals of failure. Mother bobbed beside him, pink, proud, and tense. They might have been the only parents in that hall. Their applause always came a second early, their smiles a shade too bright, when they mouthed the passages I read, which they knew by heart down to every comma and exclamation point, the pitch and pace of every phrase.

"A good education is the only way up in the world" was Dad's weekly sermon.

He knew. He was a scholarship boy. His own father, Reginald, had never learned to read. There was always a droplet on the end of Reginald's pitted, tuberous nose as he cut and measured lengths of worsted for men's business suits at Montgomery's haberdashery store. Harry's mother, Minnie Maud, was a milliner who stitched at home. He was the youngest of three sons and younger than his sister by three years. They lived near the docks at Port Adelaide. Harry worked his way up after local bullies taunted him and called him Snowy because he was skinny and blond with flapping ears and refused to collaborate in their petty larceny and larrikin pranks.

Dad's older brothers left the Port public school as soon as legally possible. Dick went into the Farmers Union as a milk packer. Max was apprenticed to a boiler maker. His sister, Irene, spent her Post Office wages on nylons and nail polish and waited for the right man. Harry studied at the scrubbed kitchen table, fair head bent over Latin grammar and arithmetic, while his father smoked a pipe and cleaned his boots by the wood range and silently observed his son's mysterious labors, and Minnie Maud sewed another bunch of artificial violets on another straw brim.

In his fifteenth year, Harry won the open scholarship to All Saints, the Eton of the Antipodes and a richly endowed private college for the sons of the Establishment.

He won no prizes, and never made the First Eleven, and was not invited into other boys' homes, but he knew he had climbed the first rung to success. He steam-pressed his flannel trousers on the kitchen table and spat on his shoes until they shone. When he left school, he started a good job as a bank teller and took night classes in money management. Eager and ambitious, he was the first to volunteer for overtime. He moved quite rapidly up the clerical ladder and was sent to Sydney to be the youngest branch manager. There he joined the Men's Fellowship at Bondi Presbyterian Church, sang tenor in the choir, and met my mother at a church picnic on Pittwater. On the windy drive back to Bondi Beach, in the dicky seat of a friend's Dodge car, he knew that all he wanted now was for Delicia Wells to become his bride.

When he was recalled to the Adelaide head office to organize the Overseas Department, the young couple lived for a while in one room of Reginald's house, but Dilys developed headaches and Harry found an apartment nearer the city. Cicely was born, and they rented the top flat of a two-storied house in the suburbs near Westall College and bought a cocker spaniel. When I was born, Dad gave Dilys their first wireless, a huge cabinet on lions' paws with a carved wooden scroll in front of a lace curtain that protected the speaker. Dad paid cash in full. A banker, he believed all his life that time payment, credit, and borrowing were sins.

Then the bank announced the marvellous news: Harry was appointed to the bank's London branch management. Dilys read Dickens and Galsworthy and memorized London street names on our Monopoly. Harry was measured by Reginald for his first tailor-made, double-breasted suit with waistcoat and a second set of trousers.

Then he collapsed. Structural flaws undermined ambition. Within reach of his one big chance to make it, he was struck down by symptoms of terror. He lost his voice, then found it difficult to breathe. Doctors diagnosed asthma. Then he found he could not walk. They thought it was paralysis. Then he became too weak to feed himself. He baffled medical science. During Harry's second year in the Royal Adelaide Hospital, a specialist discovered an unusual artery malfunction. Harry volunteered to be his fifth candidate for a series of experimental surgical procedures and, to Mother's alarmed discovery, the first survivor.

Everyone said it was only his will that had kept him alive. Harry always insisted it was the thought of Mother. She alone gave him reason to struggle for life. We lived on intimate terms with death. He could go, any minute. Anything we did or said to upset him could kill. Mother put a reminder list of forbidden substances on the door of the icebox: salt, alcohol, smoke, animal fats, exercise, and anger.

I dreaded those hospital visits. I was scared when we had to walk the length of the ward past long slack bodies of adult men under sheets to my father's white face at the far end. "You girls must be very brave and take care of your mother," he whispered. A nurse taught us to spoon liquids from a bowl into his mouth. I worried about how Cicely and I would care for Mother as well.

Cicely vented her own frustrations in the simplest and safest manner. She waylaid me behind doors, grabbed my wrist and Chinese-burned it, hissing like a maddened reptile until I cringed to the floor in painful submission. We both learned to fight wordlessly to avoid causing another heart attack. As soon as Harry was back at daily work, albeit on the bottom rung again, mother had *her* breakdown. She spent several months in bed in a darkened room while we sisters whispered, tiptoed on silent errands, and ran the household while I fretted every night about our family's disintegration.

Mother allotted us chores. I mowed the lawns downstairs on Saturday afternoons, humming cheerful marches like "Yankee Doodle Dandy" and "Soldiers of the Queen" to boost my strength because we had a rotary hand mower with rusty iron blades that needed a speedy run-up with a fast follow-through to make any impression on the clover.

Our clover lawns were covered with long runners that tangled the blades and with white flowers that attracted the bees. I was allergic to bees. They liked my fair hair or my scent. Every Saturday, after hockey, barefoot on the clover lawns, I'd push the heavy mower through a whining, buzzing, droning bomb attack by killer bees. Each time I was stung, I'd get sicker and sicker and have to spend days in bed missing lessons. My legs swelled, my temperature went sky high, my skin seemed infested all over with lethal lumps, and I could hardly breathe.

My worried mother had a special reward for bee stings: a cup and saucer with a yellow wattle pattern of raised fluffballs and green twigs against a white background. Dilys fixed me warm tea with an extra sugar lump, or milk sweetened with chocolate, or a spider of lemonade fizzed into delicious bubbles with a dollop of vanilla ice-cream. It never occurred to her that an obvious remedy was to relieve me of my duties with the mower. It never occurred to me to complain, as I sipped from the wattle cup Mother's reward of sweet nectar for my stings of sacrifice.

By the time Harry came home from the hospital, I could also chop kindling for the chip heater in the shower and fix blown fuses in the cellar wiring. I did think Cicely might have taken more of the danger-zone jobs instead of dusting bannisters and combing out the fringes of the carpets. On the other hand, I was more attracted than my sister to heroism.

Lightheartedly among my school friends, I called my father Prince Hal or Harry Hotspur. The truth was, he was a handicap. Everybody knew my dad had practically died. He never ran or played roughhouse games like other children's fathers. I wished I had a hero for a father: Robert Falcon Scott on an Antarctic sled; Horatio Hornblower shouting "Ready about!" on the poop of his flagship; Napoleon galloping over Russian steppes; Beethoven thrusting a fist to the skies. I longed to stride over paddocks and deserts and oceans in seven-league boots. I craved a uniform and medals like my uncle Max wore in the war. I'd polish his service medals for the Anzac Day parade, when all the Australian heroes from El Alamein, Tobruk, Singapore, Burma, and Gallipoli marched through the city to the Cross of Sacrifice. Uncle Max, in digger's slouch hat and batman's khaki, might have worn the Victoria Cross as far as my dazzled eyes could see.

One weekend, the cellar fusebox presented inspiration. The room was a dank prison hung with cobwebs and smelling foul from salt damp in the bluestone walls. I fixed the fuse, then set to with broom and pan to clean it thoroughly. I scrounged a glass jam jar, arranged some fresh geraniums on the windowsill, and stole one of Mother's old tea-towels. A broken table and empty fruit crates, upturned, would do for seats. Then I called Leonora.

"Come over as soon as you can get away, will you? I have an announcement to make. Bring an old school blazer and your sewing kit and any ribbons—anything gold—you can find. And hurry!"

Leonora's home was like a white elephant stall. Because her mother had been on the vaudeville stage in the West End of London, and her father was an artist, between the two they'd filled their house with perfect props for every conceivable game. Leonora and I often dressed up in her mother's costumes. Mrs. Skinner had absolutely wonderful legs. She could kick up her heels and do the Lambeth Walk like a Gaiety Girl. I envied Leonora for her black and silver Raleigh bicycle; for her fur gloves her mother bought in Harrods that looked exactly like Robert Falcon

Scott's mittens; for having tall slim parents who let us do almost anything we wanted.

I could tell that my mother didn't completely approve of the Skinner family. That made them even more attractive. Through their London stage and sporting connections, the Skinners had living heroes as weekend guests. The English touring cricket team took afternoon tea on the Skinner tennis court. I served lemonade to Denis Compton and Len Hutton, tall in white flannels, tanned from their Australian tour, and smiled adoringly at their elegant gestures and masculine jokes. When the Stratford Players visited for a late-night supper while I was staying over at the Skinners' place, Anthony Quayle gave us fencing lessons on the staircase. Leonora and I hung over the balustrade to watch Laurence Olivier and Vivien Leigh arrive. When Mrs. Skinner spotted us, as we planned she would, we came down in our pajamas to serve them cupcakes on a silver tray.

Leonora had another asset called Uncle Peter, a real sea captain in the merchant navy. He let us have the freedom of his ship when it anchored at Port Adelaide. Uncle Peter was our Nelson; Leonora and I stood on his bridge like boys on the burning deck, heirs to the best of British history, wearing Uncle Peter's naval caps. Leonora was an unstintingly generous friend, as happy to let me lead as she was to provide authentic contexts.

On this particular day, from my perch in the pine tree, I heard Leonora's bicycle bell as she rounded Navarro Street and sailed high into the wind of Hyde Park Road toward my crow's-nest lookout.

"Ahoy! Lay to, landlubber, and avast there! I'm coming down the mast with news for you!"

She braked at the foot of the tree and wheeled her bike through the open gate. Arm in arm, we marched down the cellar steps, and by the light of a dusty lamp bulb, spent the afternoon cutting material and sewing ribbons to make Napoleonic epaulettes and officers' golden loops on our cast-off navy school blazers. I painted the buttons gold, and Leonora had brought a box of gold satin ribbons to make stripes up the sleeves. We borrowed Mother's iron to steam our navy felt hats into tricorns edged with more gold braid and topped with a magpie feather for a cockade. The sun was setting by the time we emerged into the garden resplendent in full admiralty uniforms. I had the four bands and double stripe of the admiral of the fleet; Leonora wore four for a captain. Cream jodhpurs and Harry's cast-off dancing gloves complemented our rig. We paraded around the vegetable plots and, on the end of the clothesline, raised and lowered the tea-towel for a flag until it was time for dinner.

Next school day, I whispered to Leonora when Miss Adair turned her back to write up our French homework on the blackboard, "We need a crew—deckhands—who?"

Leonora pondered. She had a thin, rather plain face, with slightly greasy plaits that dangled from a centre part. She chewed on her pencil, then scribbled a note in the margin of her French grammar: "Bridget Baddeley, Pip Whittle, and Mary Kelly."

"Bridget tells, Whittle no bike, Kelly childish," I wrote back.

"Whittle definite. Asset: one farm."

"Roger. First mate: Pip Whittle. Over and out."

We formally saluted one another just before Miss Adair turned back to her desk. Now we had a ship: the Whittle farm. We had our operations headquarters: my cellar. We had uniforms and a crew. The British Commonwealth Women's Navy was incorporated.

For the remainder of that school term, we prepared top-secret strategies in the cellar and, under cover of washing on the line, surreptitiously drilled on the garden deck until we were perfectly synchronized. Since Pip Whittle was a weekly boarder at Westall, my mother was not too surprised when I invited Pip home on weekend exeats. Pip helped embroider the fleet flag, a yellow pillowcase, with *H.M.A.S. Amazon* and the letters *B.C.W.N.*

in gold inside a shield. That was the only time I'd enjoyed sewing. On deck, between rows of sweet corn and broad beans and around the nasturtium and iris beds, we wheeled, turned, and slow marched to Leonora's mouth organ and my commands, and longed for the coming holidays.

Mrs. Whittle let us bivouac on their farm at Mount Pleasant during the May school holidays. At last we had a full ship's complement: the Whittle hens. Our subordinates cackled, flapped, and clucked with a maddening lack of discipline when we drilled in the chook yard. Fortified by Mrs. Whittle's almond macaroons and cream butterfly cakes for sea rations, we hiked over the hills with a compass and supplies, following the sheep tracks across an ocean of wheatfields toward a treasure island that looked like a haystack. A few neighborhood boys turned into enemy savages when they threw stones at us. In our first major naval battle, we managed to rout them. Mrs. Whittle said we must have scared the daylights out of them.

After the school term resumed, Whittle, who was now much taller than me and modestly refused to change out of her shorts in front of the rest of the hockey team, said she didn't want to come and stay at my place anymore. For no reason that I could see, Leonora began to wash her hair regularly. I wrote a new three-act play with an Arthur Ransome adventure plot for my classmates, but Whittle drew me aside at a rehearsal and said, "Look here, Morgan, you're acting like a bloody admiral again. I think you ought to know I'm resigning my rank. Frankly, I'm bored having to be first mate in this play, too. I want to play a girl, but you never write good girls' parts."

I was baffled at losing cast and crew simultaneously. I gave my next play a Gilbert and Sullivan style, with a soppily romantic heroine, Princess Esmeralda, to please Pip Whittle, but she turned the part down.

I had other problems. It was the year that Queen Elizabeth was crowned in Westminster Abbey and I was chosen to portray her in the Westall Pageant. The little princess had to grow up. My plaits were permed. My mother sewed a gold brocade evening gown from our old dining-room curtains and made a glass tiara from a cornflakes box. I thought I looked hideous. Harry's dancing gloves reappeared, miraculously white, from his lowboy. Everyone said that I looked just like the Queen and that Harry was the spitting image of Prince Philip, the Duke of Edinburgh and a real admiral of the fleet, but by the time the pageant was over and I'd managed to brush out most of the frizz, I'd lost interest in royalty and military heroics, in spite of a gilt-edged letter on Buckingham Palace notepaper to congratulate me on my impersonation. It was signed by a lady-in-waiting.

At lunch, while my classmates sat on suitcases munching sandwiches and giggling about boys they knew, the younger kids and I dribbled a ball around the tennis court with hockey sticks. A girl in the grade below mine began to follow me around like a faithful basset hound. I didn't mind; I was preoccupied with my own severe and unrequited crush on my house prefects, the languid and inseparable Leighton twins.

I usually rode the long way home after school in the forlorn hope that either Josephine or Natasha, but preferably both, would happen to be in their front garden. I left anonymous poems in duplicate in their mailbox. The Basset Hound knitted a sweater for me and inside wrapped a shakily written note: "This is Exactly the same model that Audrey Hepburn wore in *Roman Holiday* that I copied from her photo in *The Women's Weekly*. You look Exactly like her, size 8, Please say if it doesn't fit as I have a spare ball of wool, with Undying Affection." I had to split the neck open, but it would have been heartless to tell her. I begged the Hound to teach me to knit, and soon I had two identical scarves ready for the Leighton mailbox—scarves that looked more like the narrow neckties worn by teddy boys.

My legs were so thin, there were chasms all the way between my shins when I put my knees together. My nose was far too long for the rest of my face. Whittle, growing meaner by the day, started to call me Cyrano, which only made me try harder than ever at Latin to wallop her. Still not a word, not one encouraging sign, from the Leighton twins.

I threw myself passionately into drama and wondered if I should become a nun.

The only private hiding place where I could dream of loveless orphanages and repressed desires was my large unruly pine tree in the front garden, overhanging Hyde Park Road. From its branches I could watch the tram cars clank along their tracks to and from the city and imagine foreign places. I took Helen Waddell into the innermost branches to read aloud her medieval Latin lyrics, awaiting like an Heloise my Abelard's passionate embrace. I copied my three-act plays in a gothic script and packed an overnight bag with a pair of old pajamas and some underwear. I plotted my escape.

I began organ lessons with Father John, the handsome young curate of St. Augustine's Church where the Westall girls worshiped. He couldn't help noticing me in the annual Passion Play when I played Saint Veronica and had to wipe his face at one of the Stations. He eyed me keenly and thought hard when he heard me confess that I might be destined for the religious life. Then he suggested I should make a start with sacred music.

In preparation, I was confirmed by Bridget Baddeley's father, who laid his hands on me while I examined his black slippers under the heavily embroidered robes and mitre and watched, in vain, for a signal from the Holy Ghost.

After Friday organ lessons, Father John always came along home for family dinner. Mother admired Father John. He and I played through all the Bach *Passions* together, his sweet sherry balanced on the piano lid next to his bicycle clips, our four hands side by side, his right foot on the soft pedal, my left foot on the sustaining one. His aftershave smelled of crushed pine. Mother listened and nodded with a sanctimonious smile when we harmonized chorales, but my father left the room until dinner was served. Harry said it was premature for me, at fifteen, to be entertaining any kind of spiritual calling.

At St. Augustine's, Father John sat in a front pew to hear me practice Bach's *Little Preludes and Fugues*. He said our lessons helped him pray more meaningfully. Before long, we devised a ritual to conclude them. I'd pull out the trumpet stop and open the swell while Father John climbed up to join me in the organ loft where the silver pipes vibrated to the chords of his favorite hymn. His light baritone warbled feelingly in the final verse:

> *Breathe through the heats of our desire*
> *Thy coolness and thy balm;*
> *Let sense be dumb, let flesh retire;*
> *Speak through the earthquake, wind, and fire,*
> *O still small voice of calm . . .*

Canon Drake must have said something to my father, because Dad told me I had to give up organ lessons.

"Why, Dad, why? You know how much I love it."

"Don't answer back. We can't afford it. God knows we spend enough on you, and what thanks do we get? All you do these days is argue with your mother. Who have you been seeing? Who are you copying? Who's making you so moody and difficult?"

"I'm not copying anyone, Dad. I'm only being me. Please don't stop the organ—that's not fair! I'll get a job and earn enough to pay for the lessons if that's the problem."

"You'll do nothing of the kind." Mother sat on the end of my bed, ignoring the obvious fact that I was trying to conjugate Latin verbs for tomorrow's test.

Cicely jeered from her bed under the window, "You couldn't keep a job even if you had one. You get up too late." Cicely was leaving school in a few months to take a secretarial job with the Hyde Park Council. "I bet you haven't asked anyone yet to the school ball, have you? Bet you haven't anyone to ask!"

"Leave me alone, all of you!" I threw my pillow at her head, but Dad began to go red in the face and Mother screamed at us to stop fighting. It was true. I'd been in a panic wondering who I could ask to the Westall Ball, a compulsory end-of-year rite for all senior girls. I'd give anything to leave school right now and take the veil, but Father John had sounded positively off-putting when I tried to talk to him about my religious vocation. I couldn't discuss that at home now. Nor could I discuss my agony over the ball.

Pip Whittle had been going steady with Jack Fry, the captain of the All Saints tennis squad, but she threw him over for a country boy who lived on the farm next to hers at Mount Pleasant. On one of those Saturdays when you begin to think there really is a god, Jack Fry rang up to ask me to the All Saints Blues, his end-of-year school dance. Jack was a genuine catch. Not only was he a bronzed tennis champ, he'd spent a year in Oklahoma on student exchange which made him doubly glamorous. He was an officer in the cadet corps and wore a real army uniform, and—best of all—he had his driver's license. Since the Leighton twins were evidently too exalted to notice that I'd dedicated a new verse tragedy to them, I tore it up, and accepted.

I expected that none of my Westall friends would believe that Jack Fry liked me, but suddenly I was quite popular. Whittle became positively charming, and Leonora, asked to the All Saints dance by one of Bridget's brothers, offered to lend me her best kid gloves. On my birthday, a week before the dance, Jack Fry rode over to my place on his bicycle and handed me a tiny box. Inside, I found a thin silver chain. Jack put it around my neck and kissed me on my nose with a sly grin. I wore the chain to school, hidden under my collar, and dreamed through lessons, gazing through the windows at the tennis court, fingering the silver chain, trying hard to visualize a perfect tango clinch.

Between dances, one of the boys sang "Honey Hush," and I thought I'd simply melt away. Like every Westall senior, I'd learned ballroom dancing on wet days in the lunch hour in the Memorial Hall with Mr. Cecil Flood. Mr. Flood, who wore black patent leather pumps, sucked musk Life Savers, and had a gold tooth, had consented to let me lead. With Jack, there was no need to lead. There were none of Mr. Flood's effeminate clasps. Jack laid his cheek alongside mine and held me like a trophy, tight around the waist, while I worried myself sick about the sweat on my hands inside Leonora's gloves.

Jack drove me home in his father's Rover in time to make my midnight curfew. With the gearstick jambed between our knees, Jack groped for my face and kissed me on the lips. My first cramped kiss smelled of leather, automobile oil, and Jack's father's cigar butts in the dashboard ashtray, but I didn't mind. I had fallen, desperately, in love.

Under the sheets that night, where Cicely couldn't see, I began a new column in my Letts Schoolgirl Diary next to my hockey scores and the picture of the 1956 English women's cricket team. It read:

KISSED:
1. *Philip Baddeley x*
2. *Father John x*
3. *Jack Fry xxxx*

and in brackets underneath:

(*but P.B. doesn't really count because x was Bridget's dare, and with Father John, x was the one and only*).

Then it was the Westall Ball. Whittle took the farmer's son who'd left school to study winemaking at an agricultural college. Leonora took Phil Baddeley who still had acne and bad breath but was going to be a priest like his father so it wouldn't matter in the long run. And I took Jack Fry.

The mournful Hound watched us circle the dance floor. We all had little cards attached by silk cords to silver pencils for us to write in the name of our partner before every dance. The Hound's was almost empty. I winked at her, and made Jack ask her for a tango because I knew the Hound was good at that, and I was rewarded by her radiant smile when she and Jack swooped past me. I could afford to be generous because I was feeling quite sick with excitement. Just before the last dance, Jack and I walked outside to see the Westall garden by moonlight, but Miss Butler, the Headmistress, had left the school gardener on duty by the tennis court and he'd trained the sprinklers on all the benches so that nobody could sit down to do anything indecent.

That night, Jack parked under my pine tree at the front gate. Between kisses, I kept my eye on the rear window and Jack kept his on the front in case my parents tried a pincer probe. My parents had an uncanny nose for sex. I think they stayed awake to listen for the sound of the Rover engine. Once, to fool them, Jack turned it off and idled to a stop on our corner where we pushed the car to the pine tree, but Harry must have heard our giggles because there he was, as usual, in his tartan flannel dressing gown on the front veranda.

"Morgan, late again! Go inside at once. Your mother is worried to death. Jack, I'll have a word with you, my boy."

"Dad, it's all my fault," I said, blushing with furious and unspent passion. "Don't take it out on Jack—we were only talking, Dad." I climbed the stairs with a heavy tread, expecting the usual interrogation from Mother, hoping to hear the Rover speed away safely from Harry's sermon. I patted my hair flat, dried my lips, and called out, "Coming, Mum."

I knew it couldn't last. Jack left school a year ahead of me to study pharmacy at the university. I rarely saw him. When I called, he made excuses about having too many laboratory reports to do. One day, when I arrived home hot and sweating from a hockey match, he was waiting for me under the pine tree, peeling pine nuts from the cones. I beamed at him. He shuffled from one foot to the other.

"Listen, Morgan, Mum says I've got to keep my head down—no more girls and flings and stuff—just work work work from now on. You're too—well, you're a bit serious for me, y'know? What with exams, the lab, experiments—well, I reckon I haven't the time to go steady."

"Jack, I'd rather, if there's someone else, you . . ." For once I was glad of Harry's perfect timing.

"Dinner's served, Morgan," he called from the upstairs balcony. "Come in at once. That you, too, Jack? Hang on a minute—I'll ask Mother if there's some to spare."

"Don't bother, Dad. Jack was just leaving." I picked up my schoolbag and slumped up the stairs without a backward glance. I leant against the sleep-out door and waited to hear the Rover start, wishing he'd called after me to say it was all a mistake. But the only noise was Mother's pressure cooker, whistling to tell us the stew was cooked.

I had to talk with somebody. There was only one person at school who could be trusted. Miss Gordon taught physics at Westall. My best subjects were English, Latin, and history; I'd never had the slightest interest in science. Miss Gordon was young and sympathetic. Her smile was like Mona Lisa's, remembering how it felt to be a teenager. I decided to take physics with her in my final year.

The year began badly. Princess Margaret announced her tragic decision to forsake Peter Townsend for her country, and Miss Butler forbade us to talk about it because divorce was a sin. Leonora left school early to study at the Royal College of Art in London. Bridget Baddeley also had to leave prematurely, but that was because she was pregnant and had disgraced the bishop and the school and we were forbidden to talk about that as well. I was elected head girl as I'd hoped, but developed a curious distaste for the leadership expected of me. Being the judge of rules and punishments made me sick with worry about fair play. I did not feel particularly suited—or worthy—to practice power over junior girls.

Thinking it might comfort me, Miss Gordon suggested I join St. Augustine's Christian Mission. I rose with unaccustomed punctuality to say my morning prayers. Father McLeod, Father John's replacement curate, reacted enthusiastically to my renewed missionary fervor by inviting me on a weekend of conversions among the heathen who lived along the banks of the River Murray.

I decided to go because Miss Gordon was coming too.

I was billeted with a Renmark family who met our midnight bus. The younger daughter, Ellen, an effortlessly beautiful and supple girl, chewed bubblegum incessantly and wore bed socks with sinuous silver threads. I'd never tried gum before. My worn old slippers, packed in the bottom of my bag, were dowdy lambswool. I stared at feet that rippled like fascinating fish under water, at cheeks blowing bubbles like elastic gills. Mine, I feared, were blushing, for Ellen examined me too, with candid curiosity.

She took me to the room where we were to share a three-quarter bed. Her walls and ceiling were completely papered in magazine posters of Elvis Presley. This was a shrine to sex and sin. It went far beyond *my* salvation. I should have to ask Miss Gordon for help in the morning with the kindling of Ellen's delinquent faith.

I placed my copy of Bishop Fulton Sheen's *Life of Christ* with the Dali crucifixion cover on top of Ellen's pillow when she left to clean her teeth. Quickly, while she was gone, I scrambled into my nightgown, slid into my side of the bed, tucked tight my share of the sheet, and crossed myself, prepared to resist the smouldering stares of Elvis. Ellen, I saw with a thrill, wasn't wearing anything.

I lay very still, stiff with the knowledge of other limbs

so casually close to mine, tormented by the mocking, sultry Presley smile. It was impossible to avoid his eyes. I closed my own and prayed for a sign of grace.

Ellen turned off the light. Her body heat was stifling.

Ellen's leg grazed mine. She must surely be asleep.

In an exploratory gesture like a novitiate's first benediction, I stretched out my hand in the gap between us and it touched what I imagined was a hip. Ellen tucked it between her legs to rock it like a cradle, and then she took my other hand to suck on my fingers, one by one, wriggling like an eel until both hands were slithery. I thought my chest would burst like a diver with the bends.

"Gee, Morgan, you're cool." Ellen licked the inside of my ear. Then, as if it were a very natural thing to do, she kissed me. Her lips tasted at first like hot spearmint gum but inside the shell of her mouth was the scent of musk or attar of roses, a breath as sweet and aromatic as I'd always imagined the smoke of myrrh and frankincense might be. I'd never known such strange sensations with Jack Fry. I wanted to discover more, but Ellen, with a shudder, and a sigh, had flipped on her side to sleep.

I awoke burdened by a long confusing dream about chastity, blasphemy, anatomy, and sin and an urgent need to see Miss Gordon.

She found me first. "Your mother just called. She wants you to go home on the bus today. Your father's apparently had a mild heart attack. It's alright, don't cry— he'll live."

I did cry, not only because I thought something I'd done must have made Harry ill in some obscure and irresponsible way, but because I'd come to Miss Gordon for comfort and understanding, and, if she were only to hold me, maybe the troubled feelings aroused by Ellen and Elvis would clear away. Yet this no longer seemed the right moment to confess. I didn't want to risk losing Miss Gordon as well.

When Harry came home, he made it clear there was to be no more talk of further education. Since the idea of living in a chaste nunnery cell seemed claustrophobic now, and I'd have to pay my way through a drama degree, my only hope was to work very hard for an acting scholarship.

The University Drama Guild came to school to see my last performance there. Miss Gordon said I made a devilish handsome Mr. Darcy, but the Guild insisted for their auditions that I'd have to play female roles. I chose Lady Macbeth. They offered me the maid in a Feydeau farce with a loan to cover tuition when classes began in February. I'd hoped my parents would applaud this first step to freedom, but home was now a silent, solitary prison where the warders refused to discuss my case at all.

In my final weeks at Westall, having banished all personal responsibility for Ellen or the mission, I slept late every morning. I felt guilty about the poor loyal Hound, especially on Prize Day when we met to say good-bye. She'd made a pair of angora gloves for me, trimmed with fur. I shared my first cigarette with her outside the Westall gate and wished she wouldn't cry. I'd never made anything for her. Nothing I'd ever done deserved her kind of devotion.

CHAPTER TWO

"They complain I'm not normal because I refuse to be like Cicely and bring home weekly pay from an office typing pool. I can't stand their constant disapproval, treating me like a schoolgirl still—at seventeen! Dad thinks I'm only play-acting, just pretending to be different. My mind's rambling like an overgrown vine—don't know if I'm Arthur or Martha."

Miss Gordon put a comforting arm around my shoulders. We were sitting on her bed drinking coffee. I'd called her toward the end of May to say I was running away from home. "I'll come and get you" was all she said. When her car arrived, I was waiting under the old pine tree.

"Drink this, dear. It's not surprising that you feel confused, with all the medication you're taking. Why did you get in touch with Jack Fry again and ask him for sleeping pills and purple hearts? That's a crazy combination for a start." Miss Gordon poured another cup of strong black coffee.

"Dad got them from Jack, not me. Dad says it's a nervous breakdown. Feels more like sleepwalking to me. All through the term I've been falling asleep—over night lectures, at work in the university bookstore, cramming between play rehearsals—I forget all my lines and forget to eat. Life adds up to zero when you can't tell day from night, doesn't it? I suppose you think I'm pretty crazy, too."

"No, I think you need to get away from home before you can sort out who you are or what you want to do.

You're having to spend too much energy and will on simple survival, on resisting your parents' narrow minds."

"They're so anxious, so restrictive—I'm tied up inside their straitjacket, slowly choking to death. They never did understand me."

"You scare them. You *are* different. How do you feel now?"

"Dizzy. Murky. Scared of myself."

"Let's walk up and down some more. You have to keep awake until the effects wear off. Poor old thing. Damn Jack Fry! Damn your father's hypochondria!"

The one thing I needed just then was Miss Gordon. I wanted her to hold me, walk me, support me. I couldn't manage even that on my own. I didn't know how to tell her how much I needed her. "What am I going to do?"

"You can stay here, but I've a better idea. I know a couple on a sheep station near the Flinders. Collins." Miss Gordon turned me around at the end of the passage and marched me along while she pondered the problem. "A bush cure with bush hospitality. Think you could handle a trip to the bush?" I couldn't answer. I was close to tears. "Look, while your head clears, let me place a trunk call to Ethel Collins right away. I'll tell her you need a break, see if she can put you up. Now whatever you do, don't sleep— keep walking, Morgan. Shan't be long."

She was gone. I yawned. Her bed looked so inviting. I sat down. My head swam. I'd been to the bush before. Did I really want to run away so far, all the way to the Dreamtime? I rested back on Miss Gordon's pillow to wait for her, and closed my eyes. . . .

My first trip north, five years ago . . . I was twelve then, a little kid, a townie. Today, a bushman would diagnose my problem as temporary insanity. "She's got kangaroos in her top paddock and white ants in the attic." Even my parents think I'm nuts . . .

A Walkabout. So much space, some people get lost in

it, disappear forever, perish from abandoned hope, dry up like parchment, and simply blow away as dust . . .

Things disappear in the bush before you can make them out. You lose track of time, of place. The sky is clear with a perfect light, but there's a haze over the land that obscures people—white people like me, that is. Not the Aborigines. The bush and the Dreamtime belong to them. Did I really want to go back?

When I was twelve, I wanted terribly to belong there, as naturally as old Johnny the horse-breaker who worked in the home paddocks. When Johnny sat cross-legged on the earth, he could feel in his fingertips, all the way to his scalp, the vibrations of his tribe when they began a Walkabout as far away as three hundred miles. Townies don't survive out there on their own.

Johnny didn't tease me for being a townie, but Debbie Palm did. She was a Westall boarder who'd invited me to spend the September holidays on her sheep station. It was on the southern edge of Lake Eyre, a vast basin which, for much of the time, is asbestos-baked by the sun into a flat, bone-dry, and glistening saltpan.

I'd pretended I was Alice in Wonderland stepping into a mirage that actually materialized like an unknown planet. It took all of two days to drive there. We slept overnight in the Port Augusta Hotel on the northern extremity of Spencer Gulf—of civilization as I'd known it. I'd never been in a hotel before. We'd eaten fish with giant butter knives, served by a man in black bow tie and white shirt— an elegant penguin washed ashore on the rim of a shallow ocean that stretched beyond the horizon. Only, instead of water like the gulf, this sea swirled with red dust, criss-crossed dirt tracks, dead and spiny bushes, and listless gum trees, their colors rinsed by a sky of the same brilliance and clarity as the cube of Reckett's Blue my mother dissolved in our laundry tub.

The farther north we drove, the more the land seemed to brood upon its own immense and haunting destiny. It was often miles between sightings of a single tree or a leaping kangaroo in that graveyard where dead animals far outnumbered the living. Sightless sheep and cattle heads, their skin and hair intact, gaped up in agony at the unforgiving sun like Trojan masks, their skeletal bones stuck casually in the sand like the ribs of once-proud rowing boats, their useless hooves the cleats from a disintegrated mast.

The desert was never utterly barren. Its drab patches of drought-resilient mulga and grassy knolls would awaken, when rare rains fell, to multicolored wildflowers and the scarlet and black runners of Sturt's desert pea. The atmosphere was pervaded by dust and blowflies and the constant choral hark of crows. Up close, in miniature formations or in unexpected movements, there were subtle changes in the landscape: shadows of mauve and purple cast by a dead tree on claypans cracked by erosion to resemble large discarded dinner plates; intricate entrances and labyrinths beneath the pockmarked, scrotal skins of anthills, some as tall as nine feet, that colonize the northern plains like cairns from some prehuman plague; a gaudy shock of wild budgerigars, strung out against the sky in green, gold, and scarlet bunting, as they flew south from the Territory.

I'd begun to adjust to a new sense of scale, wondering how I'd ever learn to recognize or remember my direction when one dirt track or empty paddock looked exactly like the next. I saw tracks narrow once they began to follow the natural contours of the land; paddocks were more closely fenced the nearer we came to the station homestead. Unlike cozy farms on the outskirts of the city of Adelaide, there was no sign of livestock until we reached outlying home paddocks, where an occasional flock of sheep and horses stood patiently near water troughs or browsed together on bare earth in the scanty shade of a tree.

Debbie took turns with me to open the heavy barbed-wire gates that frequently crossed the track. Another deterrent for straying animals were the cattle grids, laid over trenches like flat pipe racks, that rumbled under our wheels. We stopped the car at one of these to watch an athletic family of emus lope alongside. Debbie waved a red towel above her head to attract them to us, but they were running too fast to be interested and soon escaped among a line of red gums that etched the meandering bed of a dry inland creek.

Suddenly, there was the homestead, a cool, two-storied stone house sprawling with rooms and surrounded by galvanized iron sheds and outbuildings filled with machinery and equipment. Debbie's bedroom was larger and grander than the hotel room we'd shared, with heavy Victorian walnut furniture and a marble washstand with a pitcher of warm water pumped from the homestead bore—water the color of amber, with a brackish, stale smell like the bottom of my Port Adelaide grandmother's millinery chest where she kept her felt blocks and straws.

Debbie's brother, Craig, had left boarding school in the city to gain management experience as a jackaroo on his father's property. He offered to take us up the back country overnight on a hunt for dingoes, a type of wild wolf-dog. He packed the Land-Rover with food and water, and we drove some hundred miles to a small stone shepherd's hut, part of its tin roof missing, empty but for a stone fireplace and an iron bedframe without a mattress.

Craig taught me how to load and use his shotgun, and set a blackened billycan on a fence post for me to aim at, but the repercussion in my ears and against my shoulder made me drop the gun in pain. We walked a mile or two, following the barbed wire fence so we wouldn't lose our way back, until Craig found a wombat hole and then the wombat itself, a sleeping mound of tough brown fur. He loaded; fired; the heavy bundle slouched deeper in the dirt, and I turned away squeamishly when Craig kicked it over to examine the hole behind its tiny ear. Just as well we hadn't spotted any dingoes, I thought in the night, in my sleeping bag beside the dying fire, terrified by the sound of their harrowing cries, appalled at the thought of destroying living things where only the strongest could survive.

Everything seemed frightening at first. We were woken one morning by a heavily built woman in a sackcloth apron, hands on rollicking hips, who bawled at us from the corridor, "Tucker's up! Jeez, ain't youse dames niver gittin up? Struth! Yer flamin brekfists cold. Shake a leg, youse."

When the fearsome apparition left, I asked Debbie what she meant. "That's Jessie, our cook, and we'd better hurry or she'll chuck our breakfast to the sheepdogs." I flung on shorts, a cotton shirt, and ankle boots with thick socks, and ran after Debbie to the dining room. Craig greeted me with a mouthful of fried sausages and potato chips. "Snags and spuds," Debbie translated, "and lots of dead orse. Help y'self, Morgan."

"What's dead horse?" I eyed the plate dubiously.

"Tomato sauce, silly. Don't you know nothin?"

I'd have to stop asking dumb townie questions and keep my eyes peeled and my ears to the ground, if I wanted to learn my way around this native language.

Only Johnny seemed to understand what it felt like to be a stranger. I'd hang on the wire fence in the stockyards to watch Johnny break in a pony or work with the dogs. His nonchalant authority bordered on cruelty yet was instantly obeyed. Johnny, I thought, could teach me every thing I'd ever need if only I belonged—things that weren't in books or classrooms, things I hadn't known I would need as long as I was a townie.

When a willy-willy spiralled through the paddocks, kicking up a torment of dust on its erratic corkscrew way across the desert, I ran to the veranda and cowered with my back to the wind. Then I realized Johnny was speaking to me. "Him's divil's dust." It sounded as if he assumed I already knew. His eyes were liquid with fear, but mine stung, and I rubbed them hard. . . .

"Morgan! Hey, wake up—you look like a ghost. You must have been dreaming." Miss Gordon was shaking me and pulling me upright again. "Good news. Ethel Collins says fine, she'll take you in for as long as you want. They need a governess for their two little girls—not so much to teach as to mind them. Frank, her husband, is driving a load of wool bales down to the Port next week. You can hitch a ride back on his trailor. By then, Jack Fry's pills and your parents' poisons should be flushed out of your system. Come on, stand up straight. Left, right, left . . . and, Morgan, if it doesn't work out, you can always come back here. Left, right . . ."

"I'll find out now if I'm mad or not, won't I?"

Miss Gordon said nothing, merely pecked me on the cheek—a fleeting kiss that didn't reassure. It felt more like a bruise.

Ethel and Frank Collins lived fifty miles from the nearest town and within sight of the arc-shaped Elder Range, a towering and rugged backdrop to the low blue hills of Arkaba that gently undulated at its feet. At that considerable distance, the southern Flinders Ranges, with their blue depths and ochre fissures, looked like vertical waves about to break on the dazzling pale gold plain below.

The station home was a low stone bungalow with wide and shady verandas on three sides, a vegetable garden out the back, and buffalo grass planted as a prickly lawn to hold down the dust inside a stone wall where two imported palm trees struggled against the heat and dryness, with a few stout agapanthus in their shade for company. Outside the walls, on every side, was a familiar vista—the parched and glaring paddocks of the Collins property.

Behind the homestead were assorted shearing sheds, garages, stables, mustering yards, and, some yards away from a long galvanized iron hut where shearers and itinerants bunked down in the shearing season, a manager's cottage. To the right of these, a dam with a windmill and dripping pump provided the homestead's bore water supply. To the left, hidden by a saltbush hedge, was a green-tiled swimming pool.

This was no mirage: olympic-sized with a diving board and steps at one end and lily pads floating on the surface and slime and frogs underneath. And as far as the eye could see, red dust.

The two girls slept every afternoon. During their siesta, I'd walk up into the hills to sit on a rock and write a letter to Miss Gordon. Whenever I turned the page or moved my head, what I'd taken for other rocks turned out to be euros, the small gray rock wallabies that grazed in that area. They'd stare at me, sniff, wait for stillness, then settle back into Stone-Age meditation. In the distance, crows signalled another dead sheep somewhere out on the plain.

My work with the children was undemanding. In the mornings, after breakfast together, I taught them numbers and the alphabet through games and stories and wheeled them for walks along homestead tracks, usually accompanied by a pack of border collies, the dogs Frank trained for sheep control. A switch on the end of a riding crop warded off both the dogs and the incessant flies. I wasn't bored. There was a piano to play and books to read— *Moby-Dick, Oliver Twist, The Jungle Book,* and old volumes of *The Readers' Digest.* There were tubs of indoor ferns, hydrangeas, and African violets to water twice a day; a cow to milk and fresh cream to be separated and pasteurized; a pedal wireless receiver and transmitter to listen in to isolated outback children receiving daily lessons from the Port Augusta School of the Air, or to country women sharing recipes, home remedies, station-to-station news, and gossip.

A highlight of the week was a Friday drive down the Willochra Plain for groceries and implement supplies in Orroroo, with a stop en route at Carrieton to pick up our mailbag. The postmistress ran her office and all-purpose store on the bitumen strip that sealed the dirt for a hundred yards between a narrow-gauge railway station at one end, where the train from Adelaide to Hawker called twice a week, to the Carrieton pub at the other end of town. Other buildings that shared the bitumen were a Methodist church, whose pastor serviced four more missions on the plain, and the Returned Soldiers' League Hall, formerly a Mechanics Institute in the 1890s, now doubling as a monthly movie theatre and a parking site for the travelling caravan of the Country Lending Library who'd begun to supply me with local history books and bush novels.

It was hard to believe that a few fallacious rainy seasons in the 1870s had enticed pastoralists to journey northward to grow wheat on the Willochra Plain. Theirs was a dismal experiment, for the annual rainfall averages less than ten inches and is unpredictable at that. All that remained now of an abundant saltbush ground cover that wheat croppers ignorantly stripped away were the ruins of farms, mills, and small communities on a plain vulnerable to drought, dust storms, and freakish flooding. Only a handful of hardy sheep squatters like Frank Collins held on. A few small townships like Carrieton had managed to survive through tourism; the larger towns were transport centers on road and rail connections with the northern lines to the Territory or far east to Broken Hill.

Orroroo was one of those luckier towns. It boasted a bank, a police station and district hospital, silos and wool barns, bakery and saddlery; stores with old-fashioned mannikins and yesterday's fashions in their windows; and shady, secretive hotels where men tethered their horses and dogs to the veranda rails, lounged all day at the bar, and regarded all women as unwelcome intruders or suspicious strays.

Nobody could tell me the meaning of *Orroroo*. Some landmarks sounded familiar, named by the first white explorers and settlers to chart their terrible journeys in a strange new land: from Mount Remarkable in the pastoral south; Mount Deception in the northwest, where mountains abruptly met the desert; to Mount Hopeless, a far-north outpost of the Flinders in the sacred Gammons, where the Arkaroo, a giant snake of the Dreamtime, was said to rumble down its deep, impenetrable gorges.

Many other place names were derived from musical Aboriginal words that evoked both a physical texture and the mythical presence of the region: Wirrabara, Wooltana, Parachilna, and Arkaba; or sounded like invocations to running water and clear natural springs: Moralana, Utan-ouna, Bunbinyunna, and Wilpena. *Orroroo* sounded like a bird call across a windswept plain. When I recited these names to myself on solitary walks, their incantation transposed my personal and present troubles to another more mysterious plane that gave me a kind of peace.

Indoors, especially at night, my life with Ethel also had a tranquil, detached quality that resembled an early colonial daguerreotype of two women, quite unlike, side by side on a drawing-room settee. One, country born and bred, measured and pinned dress materials on paper patterns bought from the Orroroo haberdashery to be made up on a Singer treadle sewing machine. The other, tanned and sleepy from too much sun, pondered the meaning of her life while she wrote a letter or darned a man's torn bush shirt and listened to the rustlings of tissue paper and the busy click of scissors and the quiet shrinking sounds of the earth as it cooled. Outside, the dogs lay watchfully on their paws, and rowdy cockatoos and mag-pies perched placidly at last on corners of the verandas; a frog gargled in the pool; a little lisping breeze shuffled the palm leaves momentarily in the garden, until all the plain was still.

Then Frank would return from days in the saddle, smelling of leather and sweat and grease and swearing like a trooper and waking the babies and barking dogs. We'd abandon Ethel's formal front room and adjourn to the kitchen to hear Frank's racy descriptions of dipping, mustering, shearing, or droving, of the men who worked with the sheep. I'd put away my book and pen, prop my feet in the plate-warming oven, and watch Ethel prepare the Boss's homecoming feast.

There are one hundred and one ways to cook a sheep. Ethel knew them all. She grilled mutton chops for breakfast. She made cold leftover mutton loaf or a scalding Shearer's Curry for lunch. When Frank went out mustering with the station hands, she packed a saddlebag of mutton sandwiches for their journey. There'd be boiled mutton or baked Colonial Goose for dinner.

Ethel never tired of imitations and imaginations in her ways with legs, shanks, haunches, shoulders, ribs, sides, and saddles. Had her worn copy of John and Barbara Hays's mutton cookbook not lacked pages 87 through 109, she would have done wonders with heads, necks, trotters, cheeks, tongues, and brains as well. After we worked through the rehashes, made-overs, and barbecued whole sheep, the ultimate treats, ultimate horror—the "lights," as she called them—were thrown raw to the sheepdogs.

On feast days, Gigot Epicure was mutton dressed as haute cuisine à la bush. First, Ethel soused a battered baking pan with lamb drippings accumulated from earlier roasts and placed that in the oven to heat. Next, she took oil, crushed garlic, and rosemary sprigs from her kitchen garden, made a lotion, and massaged the massive leg of dark-colored husky flesh, made dark and gamey from its three-day suspension, upside down, in the shade of the outdoor meatsafe. Its deep reddish hue came also from the creature's daily ingestion of saltbush, a diet that distinguished Frank's autumnal rams from those pale pink cuts called spring lamb that I'd known and loved in the city.

Then Ethel gashed the leg in several places to insert slivers of garlic and cloves into its wounds until the limb resembled Saint Sebastian in punctured ecstasy. She popped it in the sizzling fat where it chuckled and gurgled to itself for three hours. When its final hour approached, she tossed a handful of treacly brown sugar on the crest, cushioned it around and about with a victor's garland of parsnip, potato, and carrot strips, and splashed it shiny with its bubbling juices. The kitchen seemed to sweat and groan with marathon rich and pungent smells and the sounds of blistering skins.

When at last the mutton was taken out to rest on the carving board, Ethel poured its fats into a billycan, leaving just enough to thicken with flour and mull with a pint of boiling broth kept over from the previous night's Drovers' Stew to make a galloping gravy.

My job now was to prise the wax seal off a jar of home-preserved peaches for the dessert course to follow; to ladle fresh cream off the top of the morning's milk; and to place both bowls on the sideboard and veil them from the blowflies with little nets weighed down by beads sewn into the hems.

Then I placed in the middle of the table a heavy silver condiments tray that Ethel's grandfather had brought all the way from London to an outback kitchen in 1896 and, at Ethel's instruction, piled it with glass castors and cruets of pepper, salt, mint vinegar, tomato sauce, Worcestershire sauce, mustard, mango chutney, and Madeira wine, in case our epicurean hero demanded additional flavors or tenderizers.

Now Ethel called for Frank to come and do his bit. He rolled up his sleeves. I could see where his ablutions had reached by the soap ring just below the elbows. He licked his lips while he sharpened the carving knife to a lethal point. He sliced the leg in thick vertical and demo-cratic chunks. My father had always carved in thin hori-zontal slices so that only one person, himself, got to eat the outer crackling skin. Frank flicked away the cloves with the point of his knife and, on the same blade, tasted a bite near the bone for doneness. Then he tucked his napkin under his chin while Ethel smothered his plate in vegies and gravy. Then he said grace.

"For these and all thy gifts oh lord we thank thee amen"—a voice sincere with anticipation.

I'd been a working visitor to the station for two mutton months before I encountered Ethel's Everest.

I observed her cut and bone a forequarter of sheep, and casually mentioned that it looked remarkably like a wild duck in flight. She laughed.

"Dead right. We call it Mock Duck." She showered it in orange sauce.

"Enough!" I said. I couldn't look the poseur in the eye, nor contemplate another morsel of poor spread-eagled sheep upon another plate. Heretically munching a raw carrot, I cut a chunk of cheddar and scooped a serving of apricots and custard into a bowl. Frank eyed this modest rebellion incredulously.

"Cripes! That stuff won't grow no hair on yer chest, Midge." He shook his head. Frank had called me Midget from the moment we met, when he'd had to lift me up to reach the truck cabin. Now he balanced a compensatory load of minced lamb's fry on toast (Mock Pâté de Foie Gigot) that Ethel had served for starters, and conveyed the sacred wafer to his lips.

I turned my head away. "Look here, Frank, I'll die if I take another bite of your sheep. I'm counting them in my sleep. I've started to bleat, for heaven's sake. You won't have to lead another little lamb to slaughter on my account, thanks a lot."

He downed a glass of beer in one gulp to swill down the last mouthful of lamburger, wiped his lips with the back of his hand, and burped.

"Ter water, yer mean, Midge—take a lamb ter water." He snickered. "But yer gotta be jokin, doncha? Jeez, Midge, I mean seriously, I'd reckoned you for one of us red-blooded types, not a flamin bluestockin." Frank frowned. "Yer not another bloody city slicker, one of them bloody veginatariums, are youse, Midge?"

Ethel sat down and nudged his elbow. "Now come on, Frank, that's enough cheek from you. Leave a girl alone. She'll come round. She'll be hungry enough for meat when she's got a man for herself to feed. Nothing comes between a man and his mutton, I say. She'll make the best of it, won't you, Midge? It's no bad bargain too. Now, Frank love, how about some breast? Make a bit of room there for me, dear."

Come September and the lambing season and my eighteenth birthday, I began to wonder how to fill the months until February and a new university year. I'd need to make some money. Miss Gordon was mailing live-in job advertisements. I wouldn't have to go back to my parents, but there was still no place I could call home. Much as I liked the Collins children and my work around the homestead, I missed the theatre. I'd have to go back, soon, to pick up my career.

I'd become less of a talker, more accustomed to silence. The quiet ease I had with Ethel, and Frank's rare spurts of conversation, were companionable. I might not belong to the bush quite as they did, but I certainly had survived. Dilys and Harry had been temporarily disarmed. Their warring voices inside my head had disappeared. They hadn't written or called me once. At school, when we were cruel and ganged up on an unpopular child, our torture technique was to refuse to speak to her or acknowledge her existence. That's what my parents had done; they'd sent me to coventry. I much preferred abandonment to their nagging choruses of don'ts and can'ts.

I think it was the bush that had worked a kind of truce. I could hear my own small voice at last. It sounded lonely.

It helped when Brian arrived. A mission padre asked Frank to take him on as a rouseabout for a few weeks. Brian was recuperating from two years in a city mental hospital after he'd run amuck and threatened his mother with a knife. He was scrawny and scared. Institutional care had softened his muscles; he couldn't hold his body straight, as if it had taken beatings that he'd held down, forbidden, in his flesh. Although he was twenty, he had no skills and was in far worse shape than I had been two months before. I realized how strong I'd become—deeply tanned, my hands calloused from the hard bore water, my body lean and agile.

He slept alone in the shearers' quarters. He was too frightened, at first, to walk alone there in the dark, so I offered to take his hand and lead him to the shed. "I've learned to see in the dark up here," I said. "Your eyes develop a night sight out in the open, where the stars are as bright as silver beacons." He liked that. We sat on fence posts to trace the Southern Cross, the Saucepan, and all the pointers of the Milky Way until he felt brave enough to go to bed. One night, he clumsily tried to kiss me, but I held him off.

"You might be afraid of the dark, but I'm afraid of that," I said, surprising myself because I liked him. He was attractive in a vulnerable way. Kissing a boy hadn't alarmed me before, had it? Kisses in secret under the pine tree while Dad patrolled the balcony upstairs seemed safer than here on an empty plain, canopied by millions of stars and with only the sheep for sentries. The vastness of the space around us was more perilous to me than Dad's front veranda because it gave a greater significance and intimacy to the slightest human contact.

So why the impulse to withdraw? Had I erected a barrier between us by devising a theatrical panorama to protect myself while I burrowed like a wombat underground? Or was it to project myself, a dingo howling for the open? Perhaps there was a simpler explanation. Here in the bush I'd been free to roam. I wanted no restraining hands on me. "Sorry, I've got into the habit of talking to myself." Brian was staring dejectedly at his feet. "I forget to say things out loud." To change the subject, I told him about Miss Gordon.

On those tentative nights with Brian, trying to understand him, sharing his fears, I couldn't decipher which of us was the crazier or if both of us would survive when we had to move on alone.

Frank and Ethel invited Brian and me to join them at the annual picnic races and rodeo at Hawker, a town in the Flinders Ranges.

Light rain had fallen that week, enough to settle the dust, more than enough for the foothills to bloom with wild red hops and Salvation Jane, a pretty purple weed the farmers called Paterson's Curse because it played havoc with sheep's digestive systems. Rodeo day was sunny and clear. We parked under a gum on the bank of a dry creek in which the Country Women's Association members had set up their trestle tables and portable gas rings. The urns already bubbled with boiling water for the tea.

I'd never seen so many cream cakes and lamingtons and pies and pasties and Anzac biscuits; or as many country women in aprons over cotton frocks, chattering gaily as they spread the food on doilies and white linen tablecloths and laid out china cups and saucers, sniffing admiringly each other's rainbow cake, Napoleon slice, date loaf, sultana and fruit cake, gem scones, pikelets, and meringues, and buzzing over the food like worker bees around a hive. Ethel introduced me to this one and that as outback women darted up with another tray or emerged red-faced from a car boot with bundles of teaspoons and boxes of paper plates.

The men had already positioned themselves around the perimeter of the dirt track to cheer or jeer at the events. In the center ring, riders erupted from wooden chutes on wild unbroken horses, competed in bulldogging events, and gave speed demonstrations of mustering five or six sheep through an obstacle course with a dog trained to obey a whistled command or a flick of a finger.

I stood behind one of the urns, ready to pour tea and to endure the young men who gathered at my table like buyers vying at an auction ring: "Good on yer, Sheila"; "Where's the keg, sport?" "She's a bit of orright"; "She's a little beaut, mate—where'd Frank dig this'n up?" until Ethel sent them scuttling with her "Chuck it in, boys! Mind your p's and q's around the ladies!"

I looked around for Brian, but he'd wandered off alone somewhere, probably into the crowd at the saddling enclosure.

We all stopped work to watch the races. It was a motley crew: professional jockeys in garish silks; squatters' sons slick from city boarding schools; bareback Aboriginal riders who'd driven their dented Holdens from humpy settlements on the edge of town; and sun-creased stockmen from miles around, relaxed and leathery from a life in the saddle.

The Hawker town clerk, in tweed jacket, bow tie, white shirt, and khaki shorts, his hair greased flat with Brylcreem and cheeks blotched by sun and spirits, stood on the roof of a truck to fire the starting gun. Hooves pounded along the track and choked the air with dust. It was Rafferty's rules: riders jostled for the lead with ruthless spurs, flailing whips, and bloodcurdling shouts. Even while the race was run, onlookers yelled their bets to on-track bookies who held wads of money high above their heads. When the town clerk's flag came down at the finish, disgusted punters tossed empty beer bottles over their shoulders. The creek bed already resembled a bottle dump swarming with flies, sulphur-crested cockatoos, and inquisitive galahs.

Shadows from the red gums had crept into long splinters by the time I rugged up two sleepy little girls on the back seat of the car and helped Ethel retrieve our belongings.

"No sign of Brian. Where's he got to?" Ethel asked Frank when he sauntered up, hat at a rake on the back of his head.

"Wouldna have a clue. Prob'ly hitched a ride." He sounded unconcerned. "Be seein you. Hooroo!" he called to his friends as he turned the car's engine. His breath reeked of beer.

Brian wasn't at the homestead. He hadn't appeared by sundown. Ethel called up the neighboring stations, and word went out on the bush telegraph. A decision was made. If he hadn't shown up by dawn, a search party would form. I went to bed uneasily. The still night air gave warning of a scorching day to come.

Early in the morning, Frank drove back to the Hawker area with all the station hands while Ethel and I waited by the wireless.

They found him very late that day, twenty miles north of the racetrack, almost hidden in a gully, nowhere near a road or track, and still walking. He didn't recognize Frank. He'd not worn a hat or protective clothing, and of course he carried no water. From the footprints, Frank saw he'd been circling his own tracks without realizing it. His teeth chattered, but his temperature was high, and huge blisters were rising on the raw skin of his neck and shoulders.

Ethel at once called up the hospital. "Burnt to a crisp," I heard her tell Doc Hyde. "We'll bring him in on the flatbed. No, I'll stay, but Morgan can come—couple of hours, then."

We laid Brian on a mattress in the back of the truck, and I knelt next to him to shade him with my body and to hold his hand because he was still disoriented and making incoherent sounds like a dry throat gargling. Doc Hyde was waiting for us at the Orroroo hospital entrance. As we carried Brian inside, Doc glanced at me and said, "You seem like a sensible lass. We're short-staffed here. Want a job?" I looked at Frank, who nodded. "Well, you can start by packing that young fellow in ice."

And so I became a nurse in a hospital with twenty beds, a trained nursing sister, and three other inexperienced local girls as aides. I was given a uniform of starched collar, cuffs, and a long white apron with a perky white cone to pin on my hair. The duty roster called for ten hours of daily labor, six days on, earning one full day off each week. I had a small room of my own in the nursing quarters, a tin-roofed bungalow at the rear of the kitchen. Doc Hyde put me in charge of my first patient, Brian.

"Why did you have to wander off?" I asked as soon as he was well enough to recognize me. "You gave me the fright of my life. Who did you think you were, Burke and Wills, you bloody fool? Don't you know you never go off alone in the bush without water or a hat, a hello or a good-bye?" I took the thermometer out of his mouth.

"I didn't think—" he whispered, tears in his eyes. "I don't understand it like you do, Morgan—the sun, the heat, going around and around inside my head looking for you . . ."

"Well, I'm here now, and I'll stay. Frank said you were lucky to be found at all." I marked his temperature on a clipboard at the foot of the bed.

"I wanted to show you I wasn't afraid," he said.

"Afraid of what? Dying of thirst, for pity's sake? Having your carcass picked clean by the crows?"

"Of the dark," he said. At least I had made him smile.

"You must be stark raving mad! You don't have to prove anything to me." I tucked in the corner of his sheet, pleased with my new-found efficiency. It felt good to be needed; good to be somebody useful in a practical way. I'd been very afraid of hospitals when I was a little girl visiting my father every week, but now I had a job to do. "That's my bell—back soon."

"Nurse Evans, you're wanted in number three. Take Pop to the bathroom." Matron was waiting for me in the corridor. "As the newest nurse, you're in charge of Pop's rodeo."

Pop had Parkinson's disease. I had to lift him off the bed, prop him up from behind, and kick his quaking legs forward to propel us in tandem across highly polished linoleum floors. Pop, much taller than me, had devised a way of making the journey spectacular. He should have been in motley because, halfway across the passage, he wobbled and went limp in my arms like a sack of flour and managed to drag me down beneath him.

"Giddy-up, me beaudie," he wheezed excitedly, and whacked my behind as if he rode a bush brumby. I desperately struggled to untangle my legs from his, looked up, and saw the nursing staff doubled up with laughter.

"Had your fun, cowboy?" I dug Pop in the ribs and he let me go with a *youch*. "Try that again, and I'll leave you here," I warned. He smiled as if to say I'd passed with honors.

Pop had spent his long life on the plains working at odd jobs mending tack, repairing wire fences, clearing the scrub. When he couldn't manage on his own any longer, like a modern swagman he parked his battered utility van in the hospital yard, made a tidy bundle of his blanket and billycans, tethered his dog to the bumper bar, emptied out the canvas waterbags that hung from the radiator, and admitted himself as a patient. The name and address he gave was "Pop, Back of the Black Stump." The hospital was his first home. Nobody ever came to visit him, but he was a favorite among the nurses and had ruled the men's ward for seven years before I arrived in Orroroo. The cook saved scraps from patients' plates to feed Pop's dog, and every night, when I finished my chores, I sat on the end of his bed, rubbed his back with mentholated spirits, and listened to his bush yarns and shaggy dog stories.

I soon became addicted, too, to another story, the longest running radio play, called *Blue Hills*. All work stopped, and every radio in the hospital was tuned, promptly at noon, to listen to the latest episode around the lives of characters who might have come straight off Main Street, Orroroo.

An even more intimate and thrilling drama was played out in our delivery room and operating theatre. Doc Hyde let me assist at childbirths. I held a leg and watched a baby's head emerge, its crown a round stone veined with wet strands of hair like fossil markings. I learnt to time the cycles of contractions to anticipate the moment of birth.

Once a baby was delivered by Caesarian section, blue and cold, and all our efforts to revive her failed. I helped to lay her out. Brian came to the funeral with me, shortly before he returned to the city. He was robust now, and the scars had healed. I envied him, partly, going back

—50—

home again. We held hands at the cemetery a few miles outside town; a desolate paddock; the father, a fettler on the railway, in his tight navy-blue Sunday suit; the mother in a bluebell dress and a white straw hat; a processional line of straggling tea-trees the only other mourners. It was their first baby. Tenderly, they placed the tiny box into a shallow grave while the Methodist minister read a short service. It took such a little time. The mother's tears evaporated where they fell in the hot red sand.

I missed Brian's friendship. I had little in common with the nurses who all had boyfriends in the area or sauntered home down the dirt track from the hospital when they went off duty. I hadn't finished, yet, with the bush, with its formidable solitude and space. Brian, when we parted in late November, said the vastness and the emptiness still frightened him. Before long, I thought I was the foolish fearful one. It was 117 degrees outside. Once the temperatures top the century, heat feels much the same, but that day was particularly vicious because of the dry northerly winds that blasted the plain like a slipstream exhaust.

I went to the water tank to fill a bucket of water. I thought someone should cool the horses down. I could feel the earth burn through the soles of my leather shoes. The handle on the bucket felt iron-hot. I wore only my stiffly starched wraparound apron, as it was too hot for underwear or materials that cling to the skin. The blood vessels in my brain were throbbing, and I wondered, idly, if blood could literally boil. And then I screamed.

There were three large and very venomous brown snakes crawling up the corrugated iron sides of the tank and another swimming in the water. I screamed louder. Matron came running. When she saw the snakes, she grabbed a length of fencing wire, whisked it around her head, and cracked it across the back of one, breaking it, and then another, and another, until they lay in querulous coils dead in the dirt. Using the wire like a coathanger, she fished the last one out of the water and whipped it twice until it, too, writhed into a grotesque pose and lay still at her feet. I put my hand on my mouth like an idiot. I'd been screaming all that time.

Pop expertly skinned the snakes and Matron hung the casings on the fence like prize ribbons. Within days they'd shrivelled in the sun to paper-thin, transparent, harmless things.

The sheer hardship country people suffer was depressing. I was with a young farmer's wife when she died. She'd been flown in from a distant station by the Flying Doctor Service. I was the only nurse she permitted to touch her. I'd sing to her and bathe her and stroke her forehead but she wouldn't eat. She could scarcely lift her head from the pillows and couldn't tolerate light. After two weeks, Doc Hyde said in a curiously detached voice that there was nothing more he could do. I found Matron wringing her hands in the corridor outside the room after the young woman died. We should have called for a second opinion, she was repeating to herself. The nearest hospital is hundreds of miles away, I reasoned with her. He shouldn't have lost her, she sobbed; he shouldn't try to do everything on his own.

I took her a cup of tea after Doc Hyde had gone home to sleep.

"Forget what I raved about, will you, Nurse?" she asked.

"Of course, Matron."

"We simply follow doctor's orders." I turned the doorknob, waiting to be dismissed, but she shook her head. "He was wrong, terribly wrong. I knew it was meningitis, but he stuck to his damned theories about psychosomatic illness and depression, and what could I do? Who was I to disagree with his diagnosis? But I knew, I knew—" She noticed me standing in the doorway. "Don't say a word to anyone, Nurse, or we'll both be sacked. That's an order. I'm tired, or I wouldn't say such things. Will you have a cuppa with me?"

"No thanks, Matron. And I shan't say anything."

"Sit here by me, will you, just for a moment, till I finish my tea. Then you can take the cup back to the kitchen. Gets lonely, doesn't it. Don't you feel it? Hollow, bitter, like a draught around your bones. That was an unnecessary death, Nurse. We should have saved her. I should have argued, made a scene—" She began to cry.

I didn't know what more I could do except to keep my mouth shut. Intimacies between trained staff like Matron and aides like myself were strictly off-limits in hospital tradition. Since Orroroo made no exception, I was surprised when Doc Hyde handed me a formal note of thanks for my care and comfort for a dying patient. I wondered if Matron had put him up to it.

At Doc's suggestion, I began to visit his wife on my off-duty nights to play duets with her. Joy Hyde confided that she hated the bush and was starved for civilization after twenty years in Orroroo. She was a townie like myself, a perpetually tired woman, her face eroded by worry lines. After we read through two albums of Classical Favorites, and before I walked back to my quarters, we'd share a cup of tea in the kitchen while Doc saw private patients in his consulting room at the front of their house.

Doc was an oddball and a loner, too, a thin and wiry man, intensely serious and secretive about his work. One Sunday, he came into Joy's kitchen with a bundle of papers and asked me if I could type. The notes, he explained, represented a decade of research into his use of hypno-therapy in stress-related illness. He wanted to put them into shape in a professional paper for the Northern Chapter of the Australian Medical Association. He had an old Remington manual he didn't know how to use. I said I'd think about it. He gave me some pages to take home to read.

It was fascinating material. Doc Hyde had had spec-tacular results among farmers in outlying districts who came down like flies with appendicitis whenever there was a drought. When I accompanied him on the ward rounds as duty nurse, I told him how interesting I'd found his research. I asked him more questions about stress and depression, wondering privately if hypnotherapy might have helped my father's heart condition, but at first he answered desultorily, as if abstract questions bored him. We stopped at Miss Wilson's bed and I lifted the sheet for him to inspect her gangrenous toe. He pressed her foot for a moment, lost in thought, then turned to me with a sweet smile as if something had just caught his imagination.

"A cause of depression," he said quickly, "is your inability fully to appreciate yourself. You feel that your body is an alien territory that you carry around like a shell."

Miss Wilson was extremely deaf. Doc pressed my hand under his on the iron bed rail. He smelled of antiseptic. He wore rubber surgical sandals and khaki shorts under a green apron. I withdrew my hand and tidied Miss Wilson's sheet. He continued more urgently, "I want you to explore the regions of yourself that seem so foreign to you. The body, Nurse, is like the virgin bush—rich in wonder and precious delights—caves and waters, ferns, mosses, mounds, and valleys of unending pleasure. Your body, Nurse," and again he took my hand in his, "is a blessed land, the source of life. We nourish life by knowing its secrets. Here at the hospital, you have come close to the source of life as well as death, haven't you? You *are* a virgin, aren't you?"

I drew back in embarrassment and some repulsion. "I don't feel depressed, Doctor, or at least not really, not since I came to Orroroo. I don't think I . . ."

"You *do* want to know. At heart, you are an explorer." Miss Wilson coughed, and I turned away. "You'll see," he called after me encouragingly.

I had to admit I was curious. Hypnotherapy treatment wasn't only for the sick. The mothers giving birth under hypnosis—their dilated pupils, their preoccupation with their bodies, the deep relaxation of their muscles even after the most convulsive spasms and contractions—did impress me with a sense of otherness, as if they had become explorers of frontiers I could not imagine existed. Three months of solitude and another three of hard manual work at the hospital had made my previous experiences seem chaotic and unimportant. I'd even entertained the thought that someday I too might like to give birth.

"Do your patients know exactly what is happening to them? I mean, are they conscious?" I asked him cautiously on another day.

"Naturally. You will be fully aware of everything you say and discover about yourself at the same time you descend into the dark unconscious. Trust me. We will approach it together, in stages, and if you want to stop, anytime you want, you merely have to ask me. Then I wake you up and everything will seem as it was before. Only you yourself will know a difference."

I decided I was ready for a new adventure when I ended my first stint as night nurse—a fortnight on duty alone in the darkened wards. Old Pop had sworn at phantasmagorical bullock teams in his dreams; babies had woken in the early dawn yawning and yowling for the breast. After I'd eaten a light breakfast of poached eggs, I strolled down to the town, whistling, still wearing my uniform.

A boy in overalls was swabbing down the hotel veranda. He leaned on his mop to watch me pass. I swung my arms and breathed deeper the delicate morning scents of wattle and oleander. It was going to be a lovely day.

The milko's bottle crates clinked together like cowbells on the tray of his horsedrawn cart. He winked and whistled suggestively when I waved; I crossed the road to pat his horse, whose head was buried in a nosebag of chaff and oats. Maybe I'd go for a ride afterward, on one of the hospital nags. Take the Pekina track. Maybe call Ethel for lunch next time she drove in for supplies.

Shutters were still closed on the shop fronts in Main

Street; the smell of oven-fresh bread wafted from the bakery; and down at the railway yards men worked a conveyor belt bringing bags of wheat from the silo to a goods train across the tracks.

"Morning, Nurse Evans! You're an early bird!" Mr. Gale, the minister, greeted me when I turned the corner off the bitumen onto the dirt road that led past the church where he was opening the door to prepare for Sunday services. "Will we be seeing you at the service?"

"I've just come off night duty." I shook my head. He nodded understandingly. I swung past the Returned Soldiers League Hall, where Saturday night moviegoers had left the usual mess of empties and torn sweets papers, and opened Doc Hyde's gate.

The front door was unlatched. Doc's three young sons were sound asleep in a wire-enclosed veranda. I guessed that Joy was still in bed, and tiptoed to the surgery to wait for Doc.

In half-light, he came softly into the room in a yellow gown and slippers. He looked childishly sleepy. He carried a tray with a glass of milk.

"Drink this, Nurse."

I gasped. The milk burnt my throat. It must have been laced with rum. I forced it down with loathing. He watched me.

"I'm going to turn around while you undress. Lie on that table under the blanket. You can cough when you are ready. Don't be afraid."

I most certainly would not be. My heart thudded so loudly, I expected he could hear it. I folded my uniform and laid it on a chair before wrapping myself in the gray blanket as if I were a corpse. I cleared my throat.

I heard the clink of the milk glass on the tray when he put it down. The ceiling swam a little tipsily like a pearl-green ocean. He was so quiet, I wondered if he was preparing an injection. Then he came to the table and held an ordinary silver fountain pen in a steady hand in front of my face. Behind it, I could sense rather than see the blurred shape of his gray-green eyes, the graying tufts of hair behind his ears.

"Keep your eyes on this pen. I am slowly counting to ten, and you will look only at the tip of this pen, and at the stroke of ten you will fall asleep. Your eyes will feel heavy. You will close them when I say so, but you can open them at any time you wish even though you will feel deeply, comfortably asleep. You feel perfectly warm and safe and comfortable. You are warm. You are very safe. You are watching the tip of the pen. All you can see is its silver tip. Your eyes are blinking and the lids are so heavy that you want to let them fall. Your eyes are closing. You are very warm. The warm milk inside you is falling safely and comfortably inside you, deep inside you. You are sinking into a slow deep sleep. One. Two. Three. You are looking at the pen and you can see its silver tip."

He repeated the formula in many transformations and my eyes quivered and fell shut, as he insisted they would, when he calmly reached the stroke of ten.

I believed I was still looking at the silver pen under closed eyelids. I knew I did not have the strength to open them yet I imagined I could see. I felt his hands on me draw the blanket down to my feet and toes, like the shedding of an outer skin. I felt lighter. He began to stroke my arms and thighs, speaking quietly to me as if he wanted to blanket me with words under the soft strokes of his hands. I did feel warm and safe.

"What is the first memory you are having?" he asked.

"I am in bed, in a little cot. A woman has come into the room with my mother. Mother comes over to my cot and looks down at me, and I close my eyes, pretending to sleep. Mother says to the other woman, 'It's alright, she's asleep,' and the other woman uncovers her breast and feeds a baby."

"Very good. How are you feeling?"

"I feel like a baby."

"You are. You are that baby." I felt him part my legs, and I felt the rhythmic strokes of his hands, first upon my breasts, then up the crevice between my thighs. His voice gently penetrated the warm air that stroked my body.

"You are still looking at the pen. Your eyes are too heavy to open. You want the pen to enter you. It is rising toward you." He opened wider my legs and drew my knees up and apart and I felt the cool thin shape of the pen slide along my pubic crest like a gentle beak. I felt his hands holding the pen, enclosing its coolness in feathery warmth. My legs opened farther apart involuntarily, tentatively at first, and then with a longing that took me by surprise.

"Good. You are very warm and safe and you want the pen to come deep inside you. You feel the milk is filling you with warmth and security." He began to suck on my nipples that felt to me like eager mouths that rose and swelled on his tongue. He eased himself on to me, a featherless weight as smooth and as sliding and as silvery as the pen, and his penis entered me more thickly and more silkily than the pen before it. Fat and firm, it slowly pushed inside me, keeping time with his stroking tongue and lips upon my breasts, and at first I lay very still as if I, too, had entered a warm interior space, as if I would swoon beneath the lips of sleep itself.

His quiet commands continued. Now he covered me completely but the sensation was oddly light. I felt myself float and fall simultaneously with the thrust of his tongue in my mouth and the thrust of the penis inside me. Slowly and rhythmically, I now desired his weight and solidity to enter every opening of my body: my ears, my eyes, the penis pulsing in my vagina, the tongue inside my mouth, and silently I called on him to complete and enclose me as fluently and insistently as he had begun. I felt my body open as if river banks parted to let in the sea, but at that moment he withdrew and I felt him stand beside me. I was instantly lonely.

"Good girl. You are flowing with milk and warmth

and safety. Now you can drink your mother's milk. You want to drink, you are thirsty for her milk."

The penis was in my mouth. In place of his tongue, I felt the strong round head of the penis on the back of my tongue. Semen spurted down my throat and I wanted, at first, to gag, but I swallowed the globs of thick hot fluid conscious only of his commands and my helplessness to alter anything. Then he covered me once more in the smooth gray blanket. I lay, breathing heavily, my body as immobile and passive as if weighted with warm stones.

"You are going to wake soon. Your body will rest under the blanket while I count from ten and back to one again, and then you will open your eyes and find yourself awake. You will remember that you wanted to drink your mother's milk and she gave it to you and when you drank you felt safe and comforted. You have bathed in her womb and your belly has filled with her milk. Whenever you want it, she will fill you with warm milk and you will drink. Now I will begin to count and you will begin to wake."

It happened as he said it would, and when I blinked my eyes, he was seated in his office chair in his yellow gown, his slippered feet on a footstool, his face turned away from me.

I raised my head cautiously and saw that I was covered. My body still felt strangely numb. I wanted to check it for signs that it was mine. The details of my recent sleep felt folded inside my flesh like a map of a journey. I wondered why I felt so reluctant to shed this heavy passivity and resignation.

Then he spoke reassuringly and smiled cheerfully across at me.

"Good. You are an excellent subject for hypnosis. I think we will be able to discover a great deal about you. You may come again tomorrow. At six. Good girl."

When I went outside, I still felt completely dazed. He hadn't even called me by my name: Morgan Evans. I said it, twice, aloud. It did sound strange. I'd been a good subject? I should wash, take a shower, but my uniform felt protective. I didn't want to take it off again. Good girl, good nurse—a cipher, privy to something secret that I'd never be allowed to reveal.

The sun was up. The air was hazy now. I walked back to the hospital, thankful that nobody saw me. I didn't recognize the horses who came up to the sliprail at my approach. Then one of them pawed the ground and whinnied. That jolted me wide awake.

"Goddammit, the bastard! How dare he, that creep, sneak up on me when I was asleep! He betrayed me, the animal! When I was helpless, he took advantage of me. Good subject indeed!"

I marched into Matron's office. Thank God she wasn't there. I mustn't say anything to anyone. Doctor's orders. I unhooked the telephone on the switchboard. It was almost too heavy to hold, as if it had grown larger than life. I stared at it; the hand that held it shrank into the shape of a dead bird, a carcass on the plain. Where did I belong now? What did I want now? Oblivion and domination, alone out there, in the bush? Should I quietly go Walkabout like Brian and hope they'd never find me? An unnecessary death, Matron had said. No one need ever know.

Panic surged over me. I called the operator with a trembling voice.

"Get me . . . area code 8 . . . 505-7259. Collect, please. Person to person. The name's—just say Morgan. Yes, I'm waiting. Miss Gordon? I'm so sorry if I woke you but I have to come back. Today. You said to call if any—can I stay with you? No, I'm fine, but I must come home."

CHAPTER THREE

"I don't like papal choirs much." I lay on cushions in Annie's bedsitter at Robe Terrace and helped myself to another handful of nuts and raisins.

"Too nasal," Annie agreed. "Who wrote these madrigals?"

"Gesualdo, a mad Italian monk who killed his wife between voluptuous verses. Strange how often monks and madness go together."

Annie nuzzled my ear. "You, with your own monkish cell at the Infirmary! Yes, there's a touch of divine madness here!" I feigned a grotesque expression, turned over onto my back, and Annie fell on top of me to pummel me, and we both rolled over and over the carpet toward the bed.

We'd met a week before, chatting backstage in a student production of Purcell's *Dido*. Annie sang with the contraltos in the chorus while I was the second witch. Annie Christiansen was taking psychology. She said she'd invite me home for dinner as soon as Dido died.

I needed a friend. I'd just lost a lover. Rather, I'd shaken one free. For almost a year since I returned to university from Orroroo, I'd been a glorified room-service lover to Rod Cross.

Initially, that had been with my partial, because ignorant, consent. After Orroroo, Rod was a snuggly comfort. He was popular, slightly older than most students, a close friend to some of the junior arts faculty men, smart, witty, with laugh lines around his eyes. I knew his reputation as a campus pioneer of the Free Love movement. Paradoxically, he also led the wave of intellectual conversions to Catholicism that swept the student halls in the late fifties. That acted on me like a mystical charm.

I had been perched on a ladder at work to sort paperbacks into alphabetical order in their sections under Puffins, Pelicans, Classics, and Crime, when a deep, amused voice at knee level said, "I'm looking for *The Ladder of Perfection*." It was wedged ambivalently between Saint Teresa and *The Song of Roland,* and I handed it down without looking at him. He opened it at random, or so I thought, and read aloud,

"On page one sixty-three we have a general remedy against the evil influences of the world, the flesh, and the devil—'If you have some mundane duty to do for yourself or your neighbor, get it finished as soon as possible, so that it does not preoccupy your mind.' Now, what shall we make of that, Miss—?" When I didn't reply, he continued from the book, " 'Focus your mind on this desire—' Look, when are you going to cease your mundane duties to focus on me, Miss—?"

"Evans, Morgan Evans." I moved the stepladder briskly to the Peregrine section. "Excuse me, mundane or not, I have to finish this by five."

He flattened himself against the books. "I know, you're thinking, 'Just another cheeky student—Honors English no doubt—' But will you permit me, Miss Evans, to browse at your feet?"

"Feel free." I brushed past him, my arms filled with books. I had plenty of unpacking to do instead, in the back room. I knew about Rod Cross. I knew when to be on my guard.

He was waiting for me outside when I locked the staff door.

"I've seen you, haven't I," he smiled winningly, "in *Arms and the Man.* Raina, a lovely name, with a yen for chocolate creams."

"A chocolate soldier. Perhaps you saw me in the same play at Westall when I was a schoolgirl. I played Captain

Bluntschli then." Touché, I thought. That'll puncture Mr. Cross's inflatable romance. I began to walk down the brick steps to the student center and he hurried after me.

"Where are you off to now?"

"A pie and coffee in the cafeteria before my next job."

"Allow me to accompany you. Aren't you overdoing it?" he puffed behind me. "Two jobs, *and* two roles in the same play? What are you, a Shavian Superwoman?"

"No, I'm broke. I sell paperbacks by day in the University Bookstore, I do night duty at the Old Folks Mission Infirmary, and I read Drama in the cracks between. Don't you work too?"

"At many things, my dear: all work and play, and play. I've read *Ulysses* twenty-three times, should you need proof of my diligence. And yes, I am in Final Honors English, and you do have quite the finest scholar's nose I've ever kissed." The compliment was the loveliest I'd ever received.

Rod had rooms in one of the residential male colleges. I thought him terribly profound. He invited me over, poured me my first glass of red wine, a memorable Coonawarra Estate Bin 1952, and read me passages from his first, unpublished, novel that he'd tentatively titled *Circe,* above the melancholy sounds of a Max Bruch string quartet on the gramophone.

Rod was a very hairy man. When he undressed, he exuded a very strong smell, an earthy smell, and his back was covered with silky black hairs like a water spaniel. His legs were short and muscled and strong, and even his hands were hairy. Only his tongue and the tip of his penis were pink and moist and strangely naked. In the candlelight, I imagined I was mating with a satyr.

With Rod, I entered bohemia. I wore my hair in a loose chignon and trousers long before they became fashionable with undergraduate women. Rod was adept at coitus interruptus because he didn't want to get me pregnant, although at first I assumed it was his sophisticated way of making love.

"Did you get there?" he'd pant when he drew away

from me to lie on his face on the bed, humping up and down with concentrated frenzy. "Don't worry, you will, you will," he'd reassure me afterward, pulling the kangaroo fur rug up to his ears. Then I'd kiss him lightly on his beard, blow out the last candle, climb out of the window, tiptoe down the fire escape, and pad around the side path to the street like an endangered nocturnal possum. It was strictly forbidden to have women in men's colleges overnight. With all its imposed restrictions, our lovemaking did have a certain undercover ferocity that kept it, temporarily, alight. Its fuel was solely Rod's desire, its flint my determination to erase the secret memory of Doc Hyde, to cure myself with Rod, there, and then, in that resplendent bower, among brass candlesticks, darkly faded crimson curtains, pewter wine goblets, and, on the walls, the dingy reproductions of Byzantine icons hung to hide the stains of legendary orgies. Every available nook and cranny overflowed with books, except for one corner where Rod kept a gleaming copper basin raided from the college laundry, complete with Bunsen burner and wooden stirring stick, in which he mulled wine according to venerable habits.

My room at the Infirmary was small and white with bricks and boards for bookshelves and a narrow stretcher with two regulation flannel blankets. Leonora Skinner's watercolor sketch of Eros in Piccadilly Circus hung over my bed. I rarely slept there. When I wasn't dutifully curled up under Rod's kangaroo fur, I was on night call, listening to old women's tales of their youth and marriages and joking gaily with them to cover their needs, their modesty, while I changed sheets, lifted frail bodies off commode chairs, sponged faces and withered feet, and remembered to give the right pills at the right times. The work was simpler than at Orroroo Hospital. My patients didn't need nursing skills; they needed affection.

I couldn't invite friends there and was surprised one evening when Rod dropped in to lend me some books.

"My god, dearest girl, you're pale as a nun. I haven't seen you for days. Are you retreating from the world?" He gazed around the sitting room while I poured him coffee from the metal jug where we normally kept thermometers. He recited the names and ailments of all my sleeping patients in the duty book until I stopped him. It sounded too much like invasion of privacy. Each of us was marking time, waiting to see if the other would make a move.

He looked out of place and I wished he hadn't come. I think he realized that, because he suddenly made a lunge for me, his eyes glittering and his voice husky with impatience as he tried to push his hands up under my apron. "Morgan, I want you, right now, right here on the floor."

"Don't, Rod, you can't." The empty jug clattered to the floor. "I don't want to be touched. Please leave me alone. Don't ask why, but I don't feel like sex these days."

"What's happening to you? Dear girl, you aren't going celibate, I hope. What a wicked waste. Or is it me—don't I please you? Ah, I know what it is. You're sick of having to be the one who always comes to me. Come, let me remind you how wonderful I make you feel—"

"Stop, Rod. I'm on duty."

He looked puzzled, but he released me. I opened the door and motioned with my head for him to leave. "I won't come. You have to go."

"There's something wrong with you, Morgan. Something very peculiar."

"No one ever really deals with it." Annie stared at the fire.

"With what?"

"Rape. They all think they do, but they mostly skirt around it, pretend it isn't violence, and call it frustrated sex."

During that first night together at Robe Terrace, Annie and I had been telling each other the story of our lives backward and in tandem, while Annie's Melanesian folk-songs, and my Italian madrigals, took turns on the radio-gram and the kedgeree got colder and colder in a casserole dish on the hearth. Every now and then, Annie threw another stick of sandalwood incense on the fire.

Her room was in a boarding house that she shared with Terry O'Reilly, an Irish architect, and their landlady, Miss Mowbray, who'd been left the house and a small pension by her dead brother, a former Liberal Party whip. Miss Mowbray honored his memory by haunting the visitors' gallery when Parliament was in session. She took down in shorthand all the Labor opposition speeches and mailed off daily broadsides to the *Advertiser* editor with a style so scurrilous, a content so libelous, that she never appeared in print. At home, she spied on her tenants in much the same manner.

Terry had dined with us earlier. Her contribution to the collective meal was a flagon of cheap red plonk. Mine, relatively cheaper, was a rockmelon. Terry came alone, withdrew after the fish course, and had hung on the telephone ever since. A quick-tempered and mercurial fox, she had a retinue of gay young men to prance attendance and keep her constantly amused. She styled her hair on Robert Helpmann's: a blunt black fringe and pageboy clip thatched waspish green eyes and upturned nose. My mother would have described Terry as a shrew had they met. After my introduction that evening to the inmates of Robe Terrace, I determined that they never would.

Annie was poor like me and had to teach high school boys to pay her way through part-time psychology. She was my height, medium; my type, bohemian; my age, nineteen. The only way to tell us apart, sniffed Miss Mowbray disapprovingly, was by hair: mine was blond and meager while Annie's was long, thick, and burnished with Botticelli's auburn tones.

Her room was furnished with six large cushions and six wooden fruit crates for tables and books. There was a single, luxurious focal point: a brass double bedstead with two mattresses. Because Annie was still in her ethnic phase, her walls were hung with batik sheets and oriental ink sketches on rice paper with willows and bridges and occasional strutting peacocks. Underneath the cedar mantelpiece and on the hearth were rows of beautiful turquoise ceramic tiles. The Robe Terrace house must have once belonged to an affluent colonial family; now it was draughty, the walls were crumbling away with salt damp, and the plumbing and wiring were inadequate and dangerous.

Annie was entrancing. I couldn't take my eyes off her. The room was deliciously warm, her soft voice a spell. She'd been telling me how she overthrew her last boyfriend when she smiled and said, "You've been very quiet. It's your turn again."

I'd reached into the very recent past and produced Doc Hyde.

"The bastard!" she exploded now, her brown eyes glinting in the firelight. "I call that the worst kind of exploitation. I call that rape, premeditated rape. You should have reported him."

"But to whom, Annie? I've never told a soul. My parents wouldn't know how to handle something like that. There's a teacher from school I almost told, but, well, who would believe me?"

"I do."

"It seems like a dream to me, something that happened in my sleep. I've wondered—Did it, in fact, really happen at all? Quite possibly I dreamt the whole thing up."

"You couldn't have. From what I know of psychology, those reactions of yours are a normal way of blocking the harm he did."

"Well, afterward, when I thought about it, I wondered if I had led him on. I mean, I did ask for hypnosis, didn't I? I was willing to go along and try it."

"But, Morgan, you had no idea what you were getting into. God, I could kill him! How much sexual experience had you had before?"

"Not much. Not the real thing. Oh, Annie, I'm embarrassed. I really am an inexperienced prude when it comes to sex. Sex spells trouble as far as I'm concerned."

"What do you mean, trouble?" She handed me a tiny glass of ruby port.

"Well . . ." Warmed with the glow inside me and the nearness of Annie, I rushed headlong into an account of Jack Fry, and then Rod Cross, and we laughed and laughed together until I added, "Then there was Ellen," and stopped short, and stared into the fire.

"Go on," she said quietly.

"There's nothing to say. That's like a dream, too. I've never told this to anyone before. Why am I blurting it out to you?"

"I can think of at least one good reason. You are attracted to me."

"What does that mean, Annie? What does it say about me?"

"Don't you know what Terry's mates are? Think about it, Morgan. As Miss Mowbray says, 'They're a blooming lot of fairies, a field of bloody pansies,' to coin her charming phrase. They're homosexuals, Morgan darling. Didn't you know?" When I didn't reply, she added, "You may be like that, too."

We stared at one another. Terry chose that moment to barge in uninvited.

"Baby dolls, come see what I've just found. Quick! There's a real nocturnal orgy in my room, for our eyes only."

I looked at Annie, nonplussed, but she put a finger to her lips and Terry withdrew her head from the doorway. I whispered, "What does that word mean? Does Terry know? About—?"

"I don't know. Come on. We'll talk about this later." Annie took my hand and led me down the passageway to Terry's front room.

"Look at that!" Terry opened her closet door. All I

could see was row upon row of smart shoes on top of a pile of books. Terry lifted up one of the stacks and pointed. "See, there they are, the little vermin." She turned one book over, and on the underside we saw a gaping hole. When she separated the volumes, we could see a jagged tunnel boring upward through each book.

"Repulsive! What are they?" asked Annie.

"White ants. They've wormed their way through all my old architectural textbooks. What a comedy: *Man and Materials*; *Design and Structure*; and—best of all—*Building Better Homes*! Amusing, eh? Can't wait to show Dennis and Larry and Rich and the boys. The termites are coming, hurrah, hurrah! They'll take over the world. What's underneath this rambling derelict we live in? Think. America." Terry broke into a soft shoe routine, tapping her feet across the fallen books. "They're munching their way to New York. But not before I sue Miss Mowbray. She probably planted them here to undermine my career."

The ants, exposed to sudden light, had burrowed back under the pine floorboards to the foundations.

"Look, they're allergic to light, the darlins. The queen is probably hiding somewhere in the garden. Unless she's hunted down and destroyed, her minions will multiply in droves. She's the only one who breeds. All the others serve her, feed her, fuck her—and all on my architectural materials. That's so endearing, don't you agree?"

"They're probably chewing tunnels the length of this house. Hell, Morgan, there's a loose and squelchy floorboard under my bed. I bet it's them. Come quick."

We raced back to Annie's room. I took her penknife and prised up the pine board. Sure enough, in its rotting seams, a colony of white ants scuttled out of sight. I threw the board back in disgust and Annie covered it with a cushion to smother them.

"What shall we do?" I closed the door to the passage gingerly.

"They'll eat down through the foundations. The whole

house must be near collapse. I don't want to wake Miss Mowbray tonight. In the morning, we can all look through the yellow pages for a Big White Hunter, if there is such a thing." Annie put her arm around my shoulder. "I have a hunch in any case that it's time I looked for somewhere else to live. There's not enough privacy here. Now that I've met you, I feel like moving out, starting up afresh. Shall we?"

"Live together? We hardly know each other. How do we know if we'll be compatible?" Suddenly I felt very shy.

Annie gently pushed me on the bed. She lay beside me and began to unbutton my shirt, and then, with a short exasperated sigh, pulled it off and hers as well. She looked down at my breasts. The silver chain she wore around her neck hung across my lips and I opened them and she lowered her nipple into my mouth and said very softly in my ear, "Sh, we're about to find that out."

At some time during the night, I must have dropped into a shallow sleep, tucked into her shoulder, our legs entwined like gloryvine, our flesh autumnal in the dying firelight. I dreamed that wormlike and translucent creatures burrowed down her hair into my hair and down my body until they found their queen, swollen, and white, and invisible. Her very secrecy disgorged a swelling appetite, ravenous and powerful, but then the house she built began to swell within her, and it tottered as if she were destroying it and herself inside it, and I wrestled myself against her into wakefulness, thinking, at first, to bury the dream somewhere deep, somewhere no one could ever see, where no one could uncover it. Then Annie awoke, too, and I whispered to her my dream and she took me in her arms and crooned to comfort me and to dispel the dream, and we lay together quietly until I wanted her to come with me again and I traced the marvelling narrative of my passion with my hands and lips to taste the sweetness of her, and to blow upon her, like a golden trumpet, a thrilling trembling fanfare.

And in the morning, early, Annie gave Miss Mowbray notice.

The flat that Annie and I found and made our home was an old schoolhouse converted into ten apartment warrens. Lost hearts and initials were carved in the cedar mantelpiece above the fireplace. Rent was only four pounds ten a week for a large living room, a bedroom in a closed-in veranda, a spacious bathroom, and a tiny, claustrophobic kitchen in a boarded-up section of the entrance hall. Our garden was a dirt path that led to other flats at the back, past an old dishevelled jacaranda tree where we parked our bicycles.

I planted mint and parsley, marjoram and thyme in one of Annie's fruit crates under the veranda. Together, we spent all our savings on a set of saucepans with copper bottoms. Miss Gordon lent us other items of necessary furniture to augment the brass bed and the bricks and boards. I'd taken Annie immediately to meet Miss Gordon. I felt that was a declaration of independence. Miss Gordon smiled and pecked me on the cheek and suggested it was, rather, a declaration of love. Only then did I realize Miss Gordon had been a kind of godmother all along.

I didn't want to tell Dilys or Harry yet. They'd never forgiven Miss Gordon for taking me away, or me for going. Mother had cancelled my scholarship while I was in the bush; I didn't want to reactivate her wrath. Annie was an outcast too. Her father was in weapons research, which Annie couldn't approve; her mother refused to speak with her after she left home. It was maybe just as well. Neither of us knew how to introduce the other, or how to describe our new living arrangements. We tried out various titles—flatmates—rentmates—just mates—then let it drop.

Word did get out to other students about our hospitality. When Terry guessed what had happened between us, she threw a housewarming party and brought all her boys around to meet what she called the "terrible perverts." We found ourselves the center of unusual friends who mostly lived at home with parents but gravitated, by some osmotic diffusion, to our flat on Sundays.

Gayle and Winifred were regulars, both undergraduates in the politics department, notorious drinking partners, and student agitators. Winnie was the tall, ebullient daughter of an evangelical preacher, and Gayle was our first Marxist. We sat around a roaring fire while she lectured us on class and consciousness, pudgy arms circled behind her head in Miss Gordon's yellow butterfly chair, thick brown tufts of hair luxuriant in her armpits.

Our informal Sunday soirées included psychology and drama students, a few unmarried tutors from the arts faculty, Winnie and Gayle, and whichever current men Annie and I happened to be dating.

For whilst we were passionate lovers by night, we both quite naturally continued to meet and go out with men.

Rod Cross renewed our friendship. He told me I'd become even more attractive as an untouchable, as Annie's lover. For Rod, too, had changed. As usual, he was ahead of his times.

He'd begun a new partnership with a dentist called Philip who drove a Porsche and collected Puccini. Once, but rather ineffectually, Rod and Philip and Annie and I tried making love all in a raffle together on the brass bed with the sobs of *Madama Butterfly* turned up to deafening shrieks to drown the sounds of an orgy. The landlord's violent rapping on the door brought to a flustered denouement our experimental overtures. Everything, we all agreed, was game in liberated love; anything could happen at the start of a new decade, the start of the sixties.

It wasn't always a carefree time. When Annie thought she might be falling in love with Jonathan, a tutor in animal husbandry, I unleashed a raging torrent of jealousy and burnt the precious lamb shoulder chops that neither of us could really afford. When faced with my protests and a choice between Jonathan or starvation, Annie lost Jonathan, and I gained nothing but a guilty ache and a lonely bed for a week on the living room couch.

On another wintry night, we were taking turns to read aloud with Winnie and Gayle from *The Second Sex,* which had just appeared in the bookstore where I worked, when Annie's mother paid us an unexpected visit.

We were so absorbed in the text, delivered by Winnie in a revivalist's tone of high moral indignation and punctuated with the sounds of chestnuts splitting their skins on hot coals, that we didn't hear the door open. Mrs. Christiansen burst in, her hair wet and her mouth awry. There was a gin bottle in her fist.

"Christ, Annie, she's dead drunk. Let's get her out of here fast," I muttered, but I wasn't fast enough. Mrs. Christiansen swayed, then lumbered toward Annie, who was still kneeling on the hearthrug, and raised the bottle over her head. Gayle moved with extraordinary alacrity and caught her arm.

"What's wrong, Mother?" Annie asked.

Her mother stared at us, then spat on Annie's head.

"Filthy bitches, all of you." She spat again. "You think I haven't heard what goes on here? Filthy dirty bloody bed of bloody filthy lesbians and *my* daughter. Flesh of my flesh and bone of my bloody bones, you're coming home with me, miss, out of this filthy bloody whorehouse. Home." She blazed and crackled like the chestnuts. Annie had told me her mother was an alcoholic who threw knives across the kitchen when she drank herself into a rage—the main reason why Annie left home when she was only sixteen—but she usually kept herself under control. Now she swayed again, lurched, and vomited over Annie.

We three rose at once, took her arms, and marched her, half pushing, half shoving, to the door and into the air outside. I returned to help clean Annie up and to comfort her as she wept in the bathroom. In a little time the others returned.

"Where is she? She wasn't in a fit state to go very far," I said.

"No, we put her in a cab." Even Winnie was subdued. "I gave the driver the Salvation Army address. She can damned well sleep it off with the hoboes tonight. How are you, Annie?"

We huddled close together. "Okay, I guess, but I feel sick, too." I squeezed her shoulder and looked around our living room; it seemed to have tilted; something had upset its equilibrium.

"This proves something to me." Gayle took charge of us. "We can't be on our own, in twos or fours or couples anymore, in little soirées hidden away where the world can ignore or slander us. We have to set up a protective group. We're going to need to band together. This is war. It's on, it's started."

"What do you mean by war, Gayle? That was one drunk woman, one drunk mother, one drunken act."

"Wrong, Morgan. We're not normal daughters talking about abnormal mothers. We're lesbians, and that, to the world as a whole, not only to our mothers, is vomit."

"I don't exactly think of myself as a lesbian. I'm not even sure I know what it means." I frowned. "Annie and me, we're kind of hermaphrodites, I think."

"Sweetheart, whether you play Robin or Maid Marian, whether you think you are Romeo or Juliet, you're a lesbian and you may as well accept what that means. You do not exist. That's all. There's no such thing as far as the law and politics and civil rights and Queen Victoria are concerned. Face it, whatever you want to call yourself, outside this group of four you simply don't exist. That's why we have to join together. It's an act of pure terrorism— us four against society. Come. We have to exorcize them now, our persecutors. I'm going to make a ritual."

Gayle pulled Annie to her feet. We drew into a tight circle by the fire. I found it hard to breathe. Gayle yanked the poker from the grate, strode to the door, and we followed in a unison line behind her.

On the pavement, under our jacaranda, Gayle raised the poker and pointed above the park trees to the city lights in the distance.

"Death! Death to the fathers who defile us! Death to the old men whose whores are our mothers! Death to parental power! Death to capitalist swine! Death, death, death!" She hurled the poker like a lance straight and true across the road, where it fell into a hedge, quivered, and clanked on the wet concrete below. Gayle and Winnie began to circle the spot where it fell, chanting Annie's mother's name like shocking infidels.

"Christiansen, Christiansen, Christiansen, Christiansen."

Annie held my hand. She was shivering. I wished we were back by the warm fire.

"War!" Winnie shouted to the treetops. "War, comrades, sisters, into battle against society." She linked her arm in Gayle's and began to march off down the road.

I glanced at Annie. She hadn't moved.

I retrieved the poker. Still Annie didn't say anything.

Together, we watched the two bold warriors stride into the night as rain began to fall. Slowly, reluctantly, Annie and I returned to our flat.

"I won't touch you again, Morgan. Not after this. She always wins, my mother. Whatever I believe in, she destroys. One by one she destroys my friends, she defiles my ideas. And now she'll send you away from me, too."

"Annie darling, I'm still here. I'm not afraid of your mother. I'm here with you. I shan't leave."

"They'll never leave us alone. Don't you see? They won't let go. Mummy won't melt. Dilys won't disappear. We will never be free of them. We are the daughters who will never do."

"We are daughters who dare, Annie, who have dared to be different," I said with a courage I didn't quite feel. I held Annie tightly. Perhaps, I thought, I should have fought her mother off with my bare hands. Perhaps we should have marched off down the road. Perhaps Winnie and Gayle were right about us, and we were simply fooling ourselves.

Annie met Ivan on the same night I met Duncan.

I was playing Lady Teazle in a university production of *School for Scandal*. I adored the part. At thirteen, with Leonora, I'd seen Vivien Leigh play Lady Teazle at the Theatre Royal. Elegant, vulnerable, and bored: that's how I would be.

Ivan Goodall was our lighting designer and an undergraduate fixture. He had a certain notoriety derived from his enormous height and girth, the number of years he was taking to finish a degree, and the privilege of owning a battered black MG sports car when few students could afford cars. Ivan even had a set of keys to the main university gates. He idled his way through courses and clubs, never seriously attached to anything or anyone. We'd met in the Drama Guild in my first year, his tenth, in arts. Ivan was thirty then, unremarkable unless behind his racing wheel, like Toad of Toad Hall, in checked cap, goggles, and leather gloves. Heads turned when he cruised the campus. On his own two feet, he looked about as glamorous as an oversized schoolboy.

During rehearsal breaks, he hovered around our dressing rooms. He told me I smoked too many Camels. He brought samples of his mother's baking to fatten me. I took very little notice of him until the first dress rehearsal. I was memorizing my lines for the screen scene when he stooped under the curtain in my doorway and knocked on the mirror.

"Lady Tease, er, I wonder, er, have you ever gone bush?"

Eyes on my script, I waggled the ostrich fan at him. "Forsooth, sir, confuse me not. Pray do explain yourself." I looked up into the mirror, which reflected his smooth pleased countenance, and continued speaking in my normal voice. "If by going bush you mean spending time in the wilderness, in the great Australian outback, yes, I have, in Orroroo. Know it?" He nodded with interest, but I had no intention of telling Ivan about Orroroo or my rebirth in the bush that year. My mind was meant to be on Richard Brinsley Sheridan. "That was in another life, pre-Restoration comedy. I'm no bushwacker from back of the black stump, if that's what you mean. I'm pure unadulterated suburban like the rest of us." I returned to the script.

Ivan, who rarely looked directly at people, skirted behind me, grabbed my fan, spread it, and peeped coyly in the mirror like a grotesque soubrette, only his eyes and balding head visible above the feathers. When he saw he'd caught my attention again, he snapped the fan shut.

"I wanted to invite you to join us on a trip to the bush. We have an old army truck. Make our own tracks, camp out, a bit rugged. Some girls like it. I think you would."

"Who are we and where and when? Ivan, be specific. You've interrupted me." What sort of a woman does he think I am? I arched one eyebrow to the mirror.

"Sorry. There's about a dozen, mostly students in medicine and engineering. One of them rebuilt the truck— Duncan Ross, do you know him?" I shook my head. "We drive up north beyond the Flinders Ranges every Easter. The play will be over then. Do you want to come?"

"Only if I can bring my flatmate. We do everything together. Except acting. And camping, come to mention it, unless that applies to our rugged flat. She's in psychology—Susannah Christiansen. Annie, actually; that's the edited version."

Ivan was looking puzzled. Whenever I mentioned Annie to people who didn't know us, I found myself stalling. I wondered what she'd think of Ivan's scheme. Better discourage him.

"Rare as it is, Ivan, we both smoke, wear trousers, and wish our parents were dead. Don't be shocked, Ivan dear. We're the flotsam from the fifties; the bold new breed who've run away from home to our sixties squalor: baked beans, cabbages, and Camels. Come up and see our slum some time. I don't imagine you'd approve, but we're absolutely penniless." Ivan had never left home. I pictured his country mother stirring soup and shaking her head at our bohemian ways, our skinny bones, our unpredictable hours. Quite recently, I'd been featured in a newspaper article on young women who lived and worked away from home. My mother, Dilys, took one look at the photograph—my cigarette in a long black holder, my sunken Camille-like eyes, my books on Brecht and Hieronymous Bosch—and hurriedly folded the article and tucked it away in her glory box under new sheets and tea-towels. I was positive Ivan's mother wouldn't approve of Annie and me.

"Oh, don't worry about money, that's no trouble. I'd really like to meet her, too, and get to know you better," Ivan's reflection was saying. "Come to Duncan's house, Friday fortnight, around seven. That's the last house in Edinburgh Square. Kenilworth. Terrific. Here, so you can't forget it." He picked up my number-nine makeup stick and scrawled *Kenilworth* in bold letters over the mirror.

I could no longer see my Vivien Leigh expression. Annie would be sure to refuse. We'd get out of it somehow. I closed my eyes and settled down comfortably to repeat my lines.

"Stop sulking, Morgan. Remember, this was your idea," Annie said cheerfully. We were walking toward the rear stables of Kenilworth, where, we'd been told, the truck would be waiting. The house loomed darkly above us. It looked uninhabited. In a tower window, a dim light showed behind flounced ivory curtains.

"Grim," I muttered irritably.

"It's certainly a novel way to choose to recover from a flop."

"Idiot!" I tried to stifle giggles. "I wasn't talking about the damned play or the camping trip. I meant this awful castle. It's straight out of Brothers Grimm. Can't wait to meet the resident prince. He probably looks like a frog. Here, take my train."

Annie took the tail of my secondhand army shirt as we swaggered round the last corner and bumped into Ivan.

I introduced them. Several men were loading crates of food, cooking gear, and jerrycans of water into the back of the truck. In the semidarkness, Ivan pointed to Duncan Ross. All I could see was a gash of white skin indefinite between hair, brows, beard, and black turtleneck. Duncan slung our bag under the tarpaulin and came over to shake hands. Then, without a word, he returned to the darkness.

I marched to the truck, climbed up, and perched on our duffle bag to await the others. Some I vaguely knew: Claudia from history; her husband, Ian, in classics; and James, an engineering graduate and tenor in the university choir. Ivan introduced Bob, a general practitioner, and his girlfriend Janice, a stubby nurse with a nasal whine and peephole eyes. Three other men were employees, Ivan explained, of Duncan's computer factory.

My mood had not improved when we got underway, Ivan at the wheel, Duncan beside him in the cabin, the ten of us bouncing uncomfortably on bags and boxes in the back. Whenever the nurse cracked jokes about bumps and bruises, I scowled at Annie.

We parked eventually a few miles south of Hawker, the last town before the mountains, to make camp for the night. We'd come to rest in a dry creek bed edged by tall river gums and dead bushes that crackled underfoot.

Ivan built a fire to boil a billy for tea and cocoa and produced one of his mother's square fruit cakes, which he doused with brandy before cutting it into twelve generous chunks. I walked a little way off with my steaming tin mug to watch the others unroll sleeping bags and prepare their beds, their silhouettes black against the firelight. Annie had settled next to my pack, and I saw Duncan crouch on the other side. Damn. I'd planned on a private gossip with Annie. A bat bleeped like radar as it flew past. I felt it brush my hair, and stifled a scream. Its eerie sound echoed off ghostly trees, then disappeared. Reluctantly, I returned to the camp and wriggled into my bag.

Duncan snored. He was like a dark and downy bush animal rolled alongside me, a species I hadn't met before. All my close friends were in the arts, the garrulous, argumentative, and articulate arts. This was a silent, self-sufficient, separate creature. I turned over to keep him at my back.

The sandy creek cradled my hip bone and shoulder like a suit of soft armor. When the fire died, stars above, in a cloudless sky, exploded with a stunning clarity. I stared up into them until they seemed to detonate on my eyelids.

We awoke stiff and cold just before dawn. It was a crisp and lovely morning, when the scent of gum trees has a subtle sweetness. Duncan was up first to revive the fire and break eggs for breakfast. He'd slept in his clothes. In daylight, his movements were neat and purposeful.

"You snore," I called.

"Well, move your bed." He laughed. His face was handsome when he smiled, with regular features that resembled the bearded sea-dog on a packet of Capstans. Annie unzipped her bag and joined him at the fire. Once she'd warmed her face and hands, she whisked the eggs while Duncan sliced bacon. They looked attractive: Annie slim, amused, her dark hair glowing bronze in the light; Duncan with his broad hands and untidy curls and peppery beard. His nails were bitten down to half-moons and there were fine hairs on the backs of his fingers. Although the others were dressing, I stayed curled in my cocoon to watch them and to listen to Annie's conversation and Duncan's short and muffled responses.

That day we drove through well-made mountain paths on the tourist route to St. Mary's Peak, the highest point of Wilpena Pound which forms a natural stockade around a sheep pasture, then followed a track to the source of the Edeowie River. Here, we made our second camp in another bone-dry sandy creek, mountains at our backs and the long, empty plain stretching endlessly before us. Dead tree branches festooned the living like ancient wreaths. Ivan told us stories about the floods that gather, after heavy rains fall hundreds of miles away on barren plains, and swell into mile-wide torrents that tear down the creeks and rip whole trees, fences, sheep, and unsuspecting obstacles in their path, bearing the land itself on a twelve-foot shoulder of water.

Near our campsite, we found the remains of a small community. Hand-hewn foundation slabs, a stone fireplace, a chimney, and crudely carved tombstones were all that a flood had not destroyed. The tombs marked deaths by drowning, in childbirth, from drought, or by spear in Aboriginal attacks during the tribal displacements caused by the advance of the Great Northern Telegraph from Adelaide to Darwin. At dusk, the ruins protected wildlife; in the long red shadows lurked an emu, kangaroos, and sleepy lizards, who stopped and stared when they heard our footsteps. The farther inland we travelled, the fewer human signs we found.

"It would be easy to get lost here," Annie said to Ivan and me on a walk up the Edeowie Gorge before dinner.

"One young boy, son of my art master at school, has never been found. The family went camping near the Pound, the boy disappeared on a walk, and although search parties combed the area, nothing was found, not a trace of his clothing, not even his bones."

I shivered. "It's haunted." The rocks around me were scarred by natural erosion, as if a giant's teeth had been left to decay. "We could be annihilated if we stay too long." We all jumped at the crack of gunshot. Duncan had wandered off on his own in search of rabbits or a fox, and in the receding echo of the blast, I heard his footsteps in the underbrush. He wasn't carrying a carcass but was smiling to himself.

"Please don't shoot. They belong here, to the bush. They deserve to live," I pleaded, but Ivan and Duncan both laughed as if I were a child. As schoolboys, they'd come here on scouting bivouacs, then on undergraduate mining expeditions, before they'd bought the disused army truck for camping trips. Every morning before choosing the route for the day, they studied army ordnance maps and listened on a portable battery-powered radio receiver to outback station transmissions which reported on local road and weather conditions.

"They're veteran campers, Morgan. They know what they're doing," Annie reminded me. She joined me on the walk back to camp, and we loitered behind the others to talk.

"*Annie Get Your Gun,*" I mocked. "It suits you. I didn't know you had hunting instincts, too. While you defend the killers, I'll protect the wildlife."

"Oh, and I'd hoped you were cheering up. Well, I'm having fun. What do you think of him?" she asked.

"Who, Duncan? A bit unapproachable. I don't know if I like him. Not at first sight. But there's something attractive about him, I suppose. Seems like a survivor." But of what? I wondered. What walls had rushed down and closed on him, or stranded him high and dry out of reach of other people? "A primitive, very much at home in this setting. Remember, I know the bush, too," I added.

"He's not domesticated like Ivan. I like your Ivan a lot. At least he belongs to the common herd. Duncan seems rather sinister to me. He alerts my sense of self-destruction in a peculiar way." Annie slung her arm around my shoulder.

"What do you mean, destruction, Annie? I think he's rather sensitive and gentle. I feel sorry for him."

"The gentle hunter? Who smiles behind his teeth? He has about as much gentleness as a dingo. But he's on to your scent, I can tell. Better take cover or he'll track you down."

I stopped. I looked around for a perfectly round,

smooth stone, rubbed it, then threw it far behind us. It hit a rock with a loud, resonant clang.

"I can take care of myself. As for Ivan, he's too obvious for my liking, too obsequious, with a kind of false bravado. There's too much of him altogether. I prefer the tall, mysterious stranger with the disappearing act. I'd like to get to know him better. Thanks for the advice." I picked up another stone and gave it to Annie. She threw it in the same direction as mine, but it fell short and thudded in the sand.

"It was actually a warning. You should have had brothers like me. That's the trouble with you—no realism, all romance." Annie threw a handful of pebbles at the nearest gum tree, then another, and another. When I did not reply, she added more sharply, "Surely you don't imagine either Ivan or Duncan could be candidates for *our* way of life, do you? In your technicolor fantasies, can you picture either one of them at our Sunday evening parties at the flat? Duncan, sans tongue, sans nails, sans charm of any kind. Ivan, perhaps. At least he knows Vivaldi from Marconi. But Duncan? Morgan, darling, he's an engineer. You'd be bored in a week."

"Computers, Annie. That's delicate and intricate. He's probably brilliant. He just doesn't brag like most of our friends." I ran through a stream of clichés, like "Still waters run deep" and "Let the better man win" but chose not to risk any, given Annie's skepticism.

"You'd better stick with me." Annie kicked away another stone and walked ahead. I caught up and squeezed her quickly.

"There's never been any suggestion of leaving you, Annie. No one is going to intrude on our life together. I want things just as they are. Now—race you!" I dashed forward, my feet raising a white dusty smokescreen behind me.

On the following day, when we'd driven to the edge of the ranges where the last vegetation met gibber plains that stretched as far as one could see toward a hazy horizon, and to where the mountains receded in a purple mirage behind us, we found a waterhole with cold fresh water. We all washed and played there before dinner. Only Duncan didn't undress for a swim. He sat on the surrounding rocks to watch us. When Janice lay down to dry, he tickled her toes and it turned into a game of chase which looked very juvenile to me—the chubby nymph nurse cavorting with a shaggy shepherd in the wilderness. Janice blushed and squealed as if she'd been hoping for this all along until Duncan suddenly stopped teasing her and disappeared. Ivan led the others back to camp to stir the stew and bake potatoes in their jackets, but Annie and I decided to have another swim.

I sat on marbled rocks pitted with fine fossil tracings. The water was clear but too deep to touch bottom. Annie held to the sides of the pool. Her body shone like an iridescent stone. Then she splashed and coiled away from the sides, drawing a handful of reeds along her legs. Her thighs looked disembodied under the water. She called out when she reached the other side, "Sing, sweet siren of the rock!"

She began to climb out, so I dived in and swam after her. "Sing!" she called. I flipped over on my back, my breasts above water. Annie laughed. "Don't be so provocative." And then I saw him. His face was in shadow. He'd been watching us from the pathway behind the white rocks where I had been sitting. Then he left, as suddenly and silently as he had come.

"Sing, siren!" Annie was calling to me. I couldn't. Water bound my throat and arms in an icy grip. I scrambled out and covered my breasts with my shirt.

"Duncan was here, watching us," I shivered.

Annie turned crossly away. "Why are you quaking, then? He's been staring at you the whole weekend. Go on then, if you want to be with him. I'm going to swim."

I looked down at her, at the way she moved easily through the water while I felt caught in an eddy of contrary currents, as if a fierce undertow were drawing us apart. "Come over here. Please." Annie swam closer. "Remember our pact? That we will never go after the same man? That we shan't compete? Well, let's drop the subject of Duncan Ross, shall we?" I leaned down, wanting to touch her, and she looked up and smiled.

"No bid, Morgan. He's all yours, take it or leave it. I'm not in the running for this one."

She climbed out and wound herself inside a towel. I wanted to talk about Duncan. I'd expected her to discourage me, to banish him, or to raise some kind of poignant but resolute objection, but she didn't seem interested. Or concerned for us. It was all most confusing. I didn't understand the feelings that had surfaced, let alone those too deep, too buried, too dark to be seen. I had rather hoped that Annie would clarify everything for me as she usually did.

In my sleeping bag that night, our last night in the bush, I made up my mind not to see Duncan again. Ivan was more adaptable. And Ivan clearly liked us both. But Annie was right—Duncan simply didn't fit. I would not be attracted to him. If we couldn't agree on Duncan, well then, I'd simply forget him. Simple. Pff. That was that. Anyway, I loathed men who snored.

Ivan said he'd come to see me, but he spent the whole visit on the end of our brass bed talking animatedly with Annie, who was nursing a heavy cold she'd caught after our swim in the Flinders Ranges waterhole.

On the following night, he brought Duncan along, too, since our flat was only a short distance from their factory and they were both en route to work. I made coffee for everyone. They stayed for only half an hour.

Their visits became weekly, then nightly, after-dinner calls. Duncan brought us a bottle of Drambuie to improve the taste of our instant coffee. When I thanked him for being so generous, he admitted he'd lifted it from his father's cellar, freshly stocked from a family trip abroad.

"Didn't you loathe having to tag around Europe with

parents? I can't imagine anything more boring than the back seat behind my parents. I hate the view from the back. Not that my father even has a car."

"Father never let me drive."

"Let you! I'd have insisted."

"You don't know Father."

"I'm not sure I want to." I'd just bought my own car. It had belonged to Miss Gordon's brother, a 1932 Ford the color of cucumbers, with thousands of miles on the clock and minimal brakes. When I'd driven it home with a pile of laundry, Dilys was aghast.

"Don't you dare tell your father you bought a bomb! He'll have a fit. It isn't safe."

"Mother, it means I'm mobile—free—can't you imagine how wonderful that feels?"

"We've managed without a car; I don't see why you need one. How did you scrape up seventy pounds for a motorcar when you always complain you haven't any money?"

She reminded me of Edith Sitwell, talking gibberish through a megaphone behind a screen. "Why don't you come right out and say it, Mum? Admit you're jealous."

"What's that, what's that—do I hear Morgan?" Harry called out from the bathroom.

"Not a word, understand?" Mother glared. "Yes, dear, she says she can't stay long."

"Dad—come on out! I've got a surprise." I glared right back. Independence hadn't improved some relationships. I'd always be their problem child. At least Duncan understood my passion for cars. He'd even offered to repair my brake rods.

Now Duncan rubbed his hands together, put the cork back on the liqueur, and checked his wristwatch.

"Ivan, old man, time for work."

Ivan pulled his cap over the balding spot on his head and groped for Annie's hand. "Actually, Duncan, I thought I'd take Annie for a spin, maybe up the Windy Point

Road, give the MG a burn, see the city lights. I'll join you at the Shed later."

Duncan shrugged and sat down again. When the others left, I put a record on and made a fresh pot of coffee.

"I'm tone deaf when it comes to music," he said.

"Nobody's really tone deaf. Given time, and a certain willingness on your part, I could teach you to sing." He laughed. "Truly! And you could teach me the mathematical theory behind your digital designs. I could even teach you to dance."

"Never! I have no sense of rhythm, no feel for it at all. I think you'd find me a dead loss."

"I could, I promise you. The major hurdle is your willingness to learn. You'd have to put yourself into my hands. Of course you have rhythm. I can see that in the way you move."

"Really?" He was taken aback. "I hadn't noticed anything different."

I changed the record to a waltz. I held out my arms. He stood up awkwardly.

"No, really Morgan, I can't—" he began.

"Try." I took him in my arms. "Sorry, that's backward, I always try to lead. Here, you lead. Ach, you feel like a stuffed bear. One, two, three—put your arm around me— tighter—One, two, three—no, Duncan, like this—" I drew apart and waltzed alone around the couch. I hummed the tune as I danced and let my arms sway and curve to the rhythm of my feet. I caressed the music as if that would help him hear it. I danced toward him. He grabbed my arm, pressed me against him, and kissed me. I pulled back to look up at him and smiled directly into his eyes.

"Well, there's music in your bones after all." I put my lips up for another kiss. As I held him, he found himself beginning to move, clumsily at first, as if his feet and legs were trying to attach themselves to me, as if he were afraid of falling were I to release him, as if he could not stand alone. I wound myself around his body as a clef clings to the stave, and slowly, tentatively, we began to dance.

CHAPTER FOUR

The house where Duncan was born, where he was living when I first met him, was an imposing castle called Kenilworth. It reminded me of a colonial Australian stage setting for a nineteenth-century Scottish melodrama. The outsides were expansive in scale, in disproportion to the interiors where the decor was domesticated, perhaps to illustrate the homely tastes and pursuits of the players, Duncan's parents, Donald and Constance Amy Ross.

The family's indoor actions revolved around a dimly lit billiard room. Other occasional excursions were made to other smaller rooms for specific scenes of social inter-action. In the smokeroom, on a leather couch, Donald was served after-dinner coffee. He took his pre-dinner Scotch in the library, where glass-fronted mahogany cabinets preserved complete sets of Sir Walter Scott and A.J. Cronin and his collection of fishing rods, pistols, and gaudily feathered homemade fishing flies. Bottom shelves hid clusters of crystal decanters, whose contents were identi-fied on engraved silver collars hung from little silver necklaces.

On my first formal invitation to dinner at Kenilworth, a month after I'd met Duncan, Constance Amy led me on a tour of the castle. The outside grounds were Donald's domain; the house, she proudly explained, was her special theatre of responsibility.

"It must look rather stuffy to your modern eyes," she apologized as she presented her collection of art in the downstairs gallery just inside the front doors. I'd come face to face with a herd of highland cattle. Some nuzzled grassy banks; others looked out warily from heavy gilt frames. More cattle grazed up along the marble staircase. Birds of paradise with pinioned plumage perched stuffily on silken screens. Cheviot sheep stared in pensive silence from their oily canvas fields.

"Did Mr. Ross kill that?" I pointed to a massive buffalo head on top of a mantelshelf.

"Goodness no, that was Gammy's, his mother—Mrs. Ross senior. Donald bags only birds nowadays. An excellent shot. If the stock market fluctuates, his ulcer perforates and he takes to a wheelchair. Nurse wheels him to the orchard where he can practice on the blackbirds. It soothes him so; they're such a pest with the fruit."

I sipped my dry sherry. We were entering the drawing room.

"We don't use this now. I've forgotten the color scheme." Drapes covered the furniture. Green felt gaitors strapped in leather buckles clad the legs of a grand piano to protect it from the dust. "Let me take you upstairs now to the bedrooms." She gestured for me to follow, and as I mounted I imagined I was the bride Lucia on a page of a Waverley novel, except I had no fear of her fatal fall.

"There's gray for my room and a view across the roof; red for the master; green for the son," Constance Amy chanted brightly. "And here are the guest suites—mauve, blue, and gold—only we don't really have guests to stay. During the last war, we took in two London waifs from the battles—for the duration, you know—but since peace was declared, we've become rather reclusive." She walked briskly down a corridor toward the back of the house. "These are the maids' rooms. I wonder—don't you?— what servants do off duty in their spare time. It was Donald who suggested the military scheme. Gunmetal floors, clotted cream walls—they blend with personal belongings and won't clash with *our* tastes. Silly, isn't it, how that distant war affected us! It bothers me that no one ever managed to strip all the blackout paper off these skylight windows. And it came so close. Darwin bombed . . . such a terrible war. Now we shall go downstairs to the service rooms."

The kitchen recalled a farmhouse filled with antiquated implements. I admired its immaculately scrubbed surfaces. "Red and white oilcloth is very effective, Morgan. It exposes accidental spots and stains. I've kept the same theme through all the pantries, larders, the flower-arranging room, and Cook's sitting room. Oh, we've had some dreadfully dirty cooks."

"You have a large . . . cast of servants, Mrs. Ross?"

"A substantial number over the years. Good, clean, reliable staff are hard to find now. Donald had his own chauffeur and valet, but oh dear, everyone had to cut back after the war. So many good things have gone. We never forgave the way the English treated Churchill, you know. There's no loyalty left."

"Did you actually buy this place?" I hoped my curiosity wouldn't offend her, but she seemed to enjoy tutoring me in family history.

"It was my dowry, from Daddy. Donald will show you the grounds after dinner." She led me back to the library talking all the way. "Oh, goody, the men have disappeared. We can sneak another sherry." She giggled and sat down on the edge of a large leather armchair. "Duncan was born after three miscarriages." She leaned forward eagerly, as if she rarely had the opportunity to confide in another woman. "Thank goodness. Someone to leave the money to at last."

While she'd waited for an heir, her fortune had multiplied. Her younger brother, Thomas Gay, squandered his third of the Gay silver mine inheritance on race horses and bad bets. Her elder brother, Willy, weakened by liquor and a wilful wife, sold his share for a song and died a pauper. When Constance Amy married Donald Angus Burnham Ross, she'd gladly given all her worldly goods into his lawful care.

Donald immediately abandoned his career in insurance

to devote his mind to stocks and bonds. Of course, he paid a price, she said sadly: the recurrent stomach ulcer, the canker that troubled an otherwise painless existence.

Donald took charge of all financial matters. Constance Amy did whatever she was told, and signed. Her assets became his lifetime interest. As a reward, and to please her, he accompanied her on overseas trips along routes identical to those she'd taken with her father, who had believed that the best schooling was the Grand European Tour.

Every alternate year, Donald booked the suite on the boat deck of a Pacific and Orient liner to and from Southhampton via Suez or, after the crisis, the Cape. At disembarkation, a brand-new Daimler, its Mulliner coachwork molded to their personal contours, awaited them on the wharf. London was always first port of call for shopping: gowns from Harrods, a portable gas burner from Army and Navy Surplus for brewing roadside cups of tea or soup, some furs, some jewelry perhaps, then off on a leisurely drive among the watering holes of Western Europe.

Once the first frost began to chill their toes, they'd pack for the return voyage along the same sea route. The Daimler went into the hold with a mileage sufficient to evade import duty. Illicit cuttings of exotic foreign plants, hidden in cellophane envelopes inside Donald's waistcoat, thwarted detection in customs inspections. If the liner should anchor off Aden or Singapore, Donald, like the child with too little who leaves the best for last, bought inexpensive Oriental trinkets for his collection in the library—the latest camera or watch, binoculars or guns— while Constance Amy bargained for embroidered silks and satins to replenish Kenilworth's supplies.

When they docked in Perth, Constance Amy sent a telegram ahead to alert the Kenilworth staff. Housemaids laid out fresh linen. McPhee, the gardener, clipped hedges and border perennials. Dust covers came off the brocades, pianos were tuned, the rituals readied.

Her eyes shining, Constance Amy described for me the climactic duties of her arrival. Valuables had to be exchanged in the strongroom: the emeralds and sapphires worn at sea replaced the crystal, the pearl and ivory inlays, the antique silver and Florentine goblets that were locked away in her absence. Furs went into cold storage. Constance Amy hated ostentation in Australians. She worried about envy, greed, and robbery. Despite the maintenance at Kenilworth of traditional customs and appearances, like formal dress for dinner, she never wore the family jewels on Australian soil.

Then Duncan would be shaken out of boarding school, rescued from his miserable weekends with his grandmother Gammy Ross, and restored to his green bedroom. Mr. and Mrs. Ross resumed their chairs by day beneath the revolving ceiling fans of the billiard room (for their return was at the height of Australian summer heat waves), shivering with relief to have once again escaped the wintry winds of Home.

Kenilworth spelt Romance. As a child, I'd pored over my share of basic fairy tales and scarlet pimpernels, a quantity of powder and patch to glut most avid readers of High Romance. This was the real thing, even if its eclectic conventionality, its atmosphere of stolid Victoriana, slightly disappointed me.

It dawned on me how quiet everything was. Duncan had told me that his father loathed music and believed that no news was good news, so he'd refused to install any radios, or a gramophone, or modern television gadgetry. Cook kept a valve wireless in her sitting room. On clear nights, when he was very young and his parents went abroad, Duncan might sneak into Cook's room to listen to Test cricket scores from Lords. The whole family, once, had gathered there to hear Neville Chamberlain across the waves of static, but that incident only confirmed how right as usual was Donald Ross.

Now Cook appeared in the library doorway to announce that dinner was ready. Duncan and his father were already seated in the dining room—a gentle pink and beige room—at a flawless Louis Quatorze table that could have accommodated at least twelve guests.

Duncan stood to hold out my tapestry chair opposite his. Mr. Ross sat some yards away at the far end from his wife. I studied Mrs. Ross while she served from an electric traymobile. She must have done years of dressage to develop that long straight spine. Knowing little of horses, I adjusted on my knee a white damask napkin and asked, "May I play your piano sometime, Mrs. Ross?"

She nodded vacantly and handed me my plate. The letter R was repeated in gold in interlocking waves around the china rim. Within, two slices of lean beef were marooned on a sea of gravy, and a shoal of watery peas swam toward a flimsy breakwater of carrot strips that fenced a sloppy mound of mashed potato. The plate was scalding hot but the food gave off no warm inviting odors. I waited, knife and fork poised nervously, for the others to be served.

"I have to practice on friends' because I can't afford my own." My words clanged in the silence like unsought penny change on tin.

Mrs. Ross held her napkin to her lips as if to hide dismay. After another long pause, Duncan came to the rescue.

"You'll be the first person in twenty years to play it." He grinned reassuringly. "If the drawing room piano is out of tune, there's a spare grand in the park folly you can try. McPhee keeps hydrangea cuttings on the lid."

"It will be quite a treat to have some Chopin." Mrs. Ross recovered and sat down at the head of the table. No one said grace. In fact, none of us spoke at all during the first course.

Mrs. Ross rang the bell for Cook to collect the trolley and bring the second round. Duncan's beard was mirrored in exact replica upside down on the glassy surface of the table. His somewhat dishevelled reflection among all that silver and polished glass was oddly comforting. I ventured forth again.

"Duncan, we should have a game of tennis soon. It's a shame to see a perfect grass court go unused."

Mr. Ross looked up for the first time.

"Give McPhee a heart attack, that will. Have to give notice if you want extra work from McPhee. God knows he's slowed down. Arthritis, in the joints. Warned him it was time to take on another man. Didn't think much of that." He sounded pleased.

"It hasn't been played on for fifteen years or more, not since the war, Morgan. McPhee would have to roll and mark it," Duncan explained, but his father cleared his throat noisily and glowered at Mrs. Ross.

"One of your damned fundraising fêtes did it. Tent pegs wrecked the turf. Troops Comfort Station indeed! People don't give a damn for *my* comfort. What's the matter, flatulence again?" Mrs. Ross was crushing her napkin against her lips.

"The garden has always been too much for one man, Father," Duncan gallantly bridged the gap. His father turned on him instead.

"Wartime, when McPhee enlisted, had to do the whole damned place m'self." He pointed at me. "Too young to know what hardship is. No petrol for mowers. Near broke my back. Ahha, what's dessert?" Cook smartly wheeled her traymobile back to port, docked at Mrs. Ross's chair, and handed her something white and spongy in a casserole.

"It's Friday, sir. Mr. Duncan's favorite, sir." Cook left the room smugly and Duncan feigned disgust.

"Cook means bread and butter pudding, Morgan. Mother never wastes leftovers from afternoon tea. Pity you didn't come tomorrow. That's always Queen Pudding." I tasted the milky slops and made a mental note to come in future on a different day.

"*Every* Friday, ever since he left the nursery," Constance Amy chanted to herself.

"Baby muck. Tell Cook more brandy." Donald Ross banged his silver spoon on the bowl and held it out for another helping. He cast a cryptic glance at me. "Eat up if you're going to play tennis. Too thin," he chuckled. "If you were a fish, I'd throw you back."

Was that a baited line? I held my breath and took it. After I'd asked a sensible question about flies and rods, we adjourned to the smokeroom for coffee where Mr. Ross continued his discourse on hooks and sinkers. Finally, he proposed a walk around the garden. I hoped Duncan would join us now that I'd found an opening that worked, but he declined.

"I've heard it all before, and anyway, you're well ahead, with flying colors," he whispered. "It'll be my turn to catch you in the billiard room later. Have fun." He was gone.

So, Duncan had noticed and approved. Privately, I thanked my years at Westall and its headmistress, Miss Mary Butler, for my schooling in poise, deportment, and grace. I'd known what to say and when. I'd walked without tripping and eaten without spilling. From an ordinary cockleshell to a peal of silver bells, a more contrary Mary was beginning to feel at home with the litany of Ross family lore and the creed and catechism of Ross family customs. Only one thing seemed unusual: no one had asked any questions about me.

There were four acres of landscaped garden, another acre or two of cunningly wild parkland, massive twin gates at the main entrance, and a cobbled driveway, laid for carriages, that curved around the mansion to rear stables. These now sheltered a Daimler, Duncan's MG and Donald's Bentley, laundry and drying rooms, various gardening sheds, and Donald's tool collection.

He hoarded things that once had worked—disused farm machinery and mechanical implements that he could strip for parts. Parts of what? I wondered. In the back of one shed were the remains of a World War I Rolls-Royce aeroplane engine, its propellers now clogged with greasy dirt. When I asked about it, Mr. Ross told me it had belonged to his mother, Gammy Ross, the flying ace. The way he said it sounded like a curse.

There was no kitchen garden. Herbs made Constance Amy ill. She disliked the disorder of vegetables. Instead, a greengrocer drove a covered van in the tradesman's entrance every week and lowered his portable ladder for Cook to mount and select her scheduled menus. Other suppliers carted meat, fish, milk, bread, rabbit (in a horsedrawn buggy), and whatever small necessities the Ross household required to sustain complete seclusion from surrounding suburbia.

We strolled toward the park behind the tennis court. The folly was shrouded in wistaria. Here, Mrs. Ross used to hold annual balls to introduce Duncan to the local debutantes. As his father now explained with a touch of pride, she'd long ago despaired of his choosing a lifelong partner and had taken down forever the strings of colored lights that once festooned the tennis court marquee. They were stored away with the Scotch in the cellar.

Ivy creeper clad the Kenilworth walls. In winter, it would bear the last of the green because the rest of the garden was planted with imported species that had completely erased all trace of an original Australian environment. No eucalyptus, no acacia bloomed in that transplanted camouflage of camellia, willow, elm, and silver birch. Not one scrawny native bush intruded on the manicured lawns. In the orchard, fish-net curtains fluttered across ripening fruit on plum, quince, peach, and nectarine trees to frighten off the birds. Trespassers were shot.

Mr. Ross now took my arm to steer me toward the boundary wall.

"McBain taught me to poach," he confided. Angus McBain was distantly related on the Burnham side and owned a castle in the Outer Hebrides. Donald and Angus had shared many a hot toddy and a poacher's tale. In fact, Donald told me, he and not Angus should have inherited that castle, had there been fewer ancestral spats.

"Damned good training too. See that house next door? Old Taggart owns it. Bloody-minded fool. Took me to court, he did, over some damned foot of my land he claims is his or ought to be his. Should have known better than to try that on me. Had our eastern wall painted silver on the side facing his bedroom. Damn near blinds him in the morning. Next he goes and cuts down my trees. Said they came over his fence. *His* fence! Next day, got McPhee to plant a row of poplars. Heh, heh. Know what poplars do to plumbing, eh? Heh, it'll cost old Taggart a pretty penny to clear his pipes!"

He squeezed my arm painfully above the wrist and pulled me toward a dividing wall where we bent to peer between bushes at other suffering neighbors.

"This side, the Watterbury lot. Mined Iron Knob down to the ground before the crash. Not a brain among 'em. With a brood of wild daughters. Kept a pack of hounds too. Slobbered and yapped all night, disturbed our sleep. Had McPhee put up an electrified fence along that boundary. Heh, heh. Smelt scorched fur for days. Put paid to Watterbury's hunt club. Nearly made an end of all the daughters, too." Donald sniffed the air appreciatively.

"How many neighbors altogether?" I surveyed the Ross acreage.

"Seven. Every darned one tries, sooner or later, to take something from me. Court actions. Idiots from the Council or Land Titles. Surveyors with new measurements. Lawyers and petitions. Waste of time. No one ever got an inch. Not at my game."

"Well, what do you think?"

"They've been . . . your mother's very kind. Is Mr. Ross always angry?"

"Oh, you haven't seen anything. Just never pick an argument with Father, that's all. He has a habit of winning by pulverizing the opposition into submission. Actually, I think they quite liked you," Duncan said quickly. We'd left his parents in the billiard room and escaped to the lawns under the elm trees.

"Do you really think so? Were *you* pleased? I mean, my gaffe over the piano—I was so embarrassed. Your mother went into shock."

"That wasn't shock. It's chronic indigestion. She's also very shy. She talked more tonight than usual. I was relieved. At least, they didn't dislike you. That would've been obvious. What do you think of Father?"

"You are proud of him, aren't you! Belligerent, to be frank. Underneath, do I detect a sense of humor, a soft spot below the crust? Like you. But you're so—oh dear, I'd counted on you for rescue when needed—why did you leave me all alone with him?"

"You don't need any help from me. You're a seasoned trooper. I enjoyed watching you play your part so well."

"I had stage fright. And you had to prompt me at the table. Tennis! Shall we dare play tennis and risk giving the gardener a heart attack? Honestly, with all the references to war, I felt I was on a firing line, holding a live bomb that could explode in my face any second. That's how nervous I was."

Duncan laughed. "That's what I like about you, Morgan. The feeling that anything can happen. Give old Kenilworth some fire, some excitement at last. Home life is pretty quiet, but you light it up like a shooting star." He playfully lunged at me.

"An incendiary, you mean. Tick, tick, tick, tick . . ." I began to run ahead in the direction of the tennis court. His footsteps sounded like a muffled drumbeat behind me. I ran faster, and as I did so, I felt a twinge of doubt, of foolishness.

Did they like me? I was running short of breath.

Did Duncan? He was not far behind me.

Did I want him to? How much did I want him to?

"Caught you." He held my arms captive behind my back and I tried half-heartedly to squirm free. He held on fast. I felt his breath and then his lips on my neck as he turned me toward him. I closed my eyes and we kissed until I needed to draw air back into my lungs.

"Father's right as usual. You need conditioning."

"Actually, I'm starving—but I was too scared to ask for second helpings—" and I'm breathless from excitement, not the running, not the chase. I raised my face for another kiss.

"Why are you whispering? They can't hear us out here."

"Because I'm hungry—no—I mean because I want you."

He lay on top of me, blanketed me with the whole of his body, but I wore him lightly, pressed back into the grass, feeling his pulse against my thigh. We began to grapple for buttons and zippers and fastenings and groaned in impatience when our hands met and fumbled and quickly tugged and finally found bare flesh, so that we took back our hands forgetfully, almost reluctantly, with momentary calm and measured breathing, with pleasure at the fit, and paused to eye each other, to wait, like gladiators fully armed, for the signal to begin.

Afterward, we lay quietly side by side in the open air and traced with fingers interlocked the patterns of leaves and branches in the elms above our heads as if to map and memorize in the sky the mazes of desire.

"That's the first time I didn't feel secondary." I touched his lips.

"What do you mean?"

"Most men take charge. You didn't. We went together."

"Like a team?"

"Maybe. Unlikely partners, aren't we!" I nestled into him.

"With practice, we could pull it off." He kissed me. Then he whispered in my ear, "I'm not very experienced, you know. This is awfully new. Was—are you? . . . Was it . . . satisfactory?"

"I've already said it, haven't I? What more is there to say." I squeezed his hand reassuringly and closed my eyes.

"Love me," I heard him say. It seemed to come from a great distance across a vast and lonely plain, an echo of an ancient longing calling down to me. I rolled on top of him and held him tight against my breast to take him inside me with an overflowing tenderness.

"I suppose I'm jealous," I said to the bedroom ceiling.

"What?" Annie raised herself on an elbow to look at me. "What did you say?"

"Of Ivan. I didn't want him to like you, or for you to like him so much. Jealous, that's what I said. I'm in a rotten mood. Ivan has complicated everything, now that you're taking him off to meet your parents. Isn't that a bit premature?"

"Don't be silly, it's only a preliminary tryout."

"For what? Do you absolutely have to marry him?"

Annie laughed. "I haven't decided, absolutely, if I want to marry anyone."

"It's no laughing matter. It feels more like a betrayal. Hold me. Please. This will mean the end of us, Annie—as partners, I mean."

"Nonsense, Morgan—you're family. We're so close, nothing can separate us—you know that. Anyway, things are moving between you and Duncan. You'll probably pip us to the post. Don't talk to me about betrayal."

"The only possible reason for me to marry is to have children. Since you and I can't marry, can't conceive each other's child, I guess I don't have too many options."

Annie switched on the bedlight and looked down at me with dancing eyes. "What is this surly face, this little martyred Morgan in my arms? I thought we'd agreed, long ago, that we both want children, that we both intend to make a family of our choice. You know we'll make a better job of it than any of our parents did. Darling, don't you see? This couldn't be more perfect with its amazing symmetry. Duncan and Ivan: business partners, close friends. And you and me: former lovers, closer friends. It's a circle, a magic circle—don't you see?"

I turned back into her arms, wanting them always to be around me as they were now. "A little Victorian love knot," I murmured into her hair; then, longingly, I raised my head to kiss her mouth, to feel for her tongue with mine, but she gently closed her lips and kissed me lightly in return, patting my thigh with a reassuring hand. I held my breath, held back a disappointed sigh, and turned off the light again.

I moved away from her to lie on my back.

I waited for my restlessness to calm, to take my cue from her. My skin felt prickly and hot with distress. I marvelled at her coolness. Ever since her mother's terrible scene, Annie had insisted we should refrain from making love, from even talking about it. I still wanted to. No matter how hard I'd tried to clamp it down, my body refused to conform to our new agreement. It continued to emit unwanted messages of desire. I'd have to develop Annie's strength of mind and switch them off. Switch tracks, rather. That needn't alter the fundamentals.

Damn Mrs. Christiansen! If Annie could, I too would learn self-control. In the circumstances—or as Annie would say, given the time and place—we had to be realistic. Annie was right. We'd still be close. Nothing could separate us.

What was it about Duncan that made attraction different? It would be out in the open. There'd be no need for restraint or pretense, no need for secrecy . . . and yet . . . I couldn't bear to imagine Ivan . . . Did Annie think about Duncan with me, and if she did, wasn't she a little jealous?

Stop—let's think this through more slowly. "Annie—" I shook her shoulder. "Don't go back to sleep again. I need to know why Duncan. I never thought I'd find detachment lovable. Did you?"

Annie yawned and turned over. "He doesn't make

demands on you—sexual demands, that is. That part of you is free."

"I wonder. I'd like it to be." Free. To go on loving Annie? When had that ever been free?

"I think our little love knot will only work if we both tie it, if none of us ever tries to break it. Annie?"

But Annie had fallen asleep.

Fortunately for Duncan and me, novelties never upset the Ross routines. His parents sailed away on schedule within six months of our meeting. Their timing was impeccable, for Annie and Ivan had decided on a trial live-in relationship and had found an unfurnished flat near our old Robe Terrace digs which were being demolished to make way for a new highway. Duncan proposed I move in to Kenilworth with him; it would save me rent, he reasoned, and since Cook had to maintain her usual catering, there seemed little point in staying on alone in a deserted flat.

After I arranged my books and clothes in the gold guest suite, I took the first of many languid baths in the fully imported Marseilles bathroom, where an intricate series of pumps and pressure gauges kept the water at an even temperature for hours.

Duncan was right. A little luxury and pampering were exactly what I needed. I'd finally left the Infirmary to teach drama at two rival girls' colleges, one Catholic, the other run by Anglican nuns. I sped from school to school in Duncan's red MG. When I spun into the driveway of Santa Barbara Convent, the cast for *The Crucible* waited in the cloisters with breathless anticipation. When I braked at the stage door of St. Margaret's College, gravel spewing like foam, the girls auditioning for *She Stoops to Conquer* jumped up and down with envy in the wings.

But the most desirable setting for dramatic inspiration was the intimate and secular stage of the gold guest suite at Kenilworth. There I could indulge in playful fancies cast for two, to captivate an audience of one.

I'd be ready on the marble stairs to greet Duncan after

work, dressed in an Edwardian lace gown and tiara rummaged from Ross closets; or in a yachting cap with brass-buttoned blazer; and once in Mr. Ross's tail coat with the trousers held up by safety pins and a top hat stuffed with tissue paper. Duncan scooped me into his arms and bore me giggling to the dining room, saying that was the only play-acting he could decently accomplish.

Kenilworth's kitchen was presented with a paperback set of Elizabeth David's French and Italian cookbooks, and overnight Cook's mashed potatoes yielded to fettucine alfredo, her soggy English vegetables were transformed into crisp raw strips, and shepherd's pie and Cornish pasties gave way to ossobuco or boeuf bourguignon. I was never served bread and butter pudding. During dinner, we heard Cook humming to music blasting from my portable radio on top of the traymobile.

When Ivan and Annie decided on a trial marriage, Duncan and I held a nuptial supper for them at Kenilworth, since Annie's parents hadn't bothered to attend their civil ceremony. The billiard table was strewn with flowers we'd secretly picked by moonlight after McPhee refused to cut roses without Mr. Ross's permission. I strung colored paper streamers over mounted antlers, from picture frames to chandeliers, then braided down the bannisters, determined to prove to myself that jealousy was nothing but a sentimental tie. Duncan pumped away on the player piano while everybody danced, and Ivan raided Mr. Ross's cellars for the sacred Veuve Clicquot. Cook unexpectedly appeared with a rich rum cake and beamed at the applause. "I swear," she chortled, "this old house has come to life—and about time, too."

"I don't understand this at all." Duncan lay in my lap under the elms one sunny Saturday afternoon while I trimmed his hair with a pair of nail scissors.

"What's 'this'?" Soft hairs ringed the top of his ears. When I stroked them, they flattened like the whiskers of a reticent cat.

"For thirty-three years I've been perfectly happy on my own. Now I can't seem to concentrate on my designs during the day without thinking of you, longing to come home." He turned to face me. "I think perhaps I should give you up."

"Turn around or I'll prick you. Why give me up?"

"My work's always meant more to me than anything."

"Why do you suppose I feel so secure with you?"

"Please put those scissors down. You look dangerous. Or are you angry with me?"

"Not angry. On the contrary. Part of your attraction is the passion you have for your work. When you explain some new design to me—when you show me a microscopic pattern of transistors and conductors through a magnifying glass and tell me how everything works when it's soldered together—it sounds like poetry to me. Not the sort I'm used to, but still creative, still intense. I love that, your passion for what you do best."

"I don't have your words. You're the poet, Morgan; you're so—so dramatic."

"You don't have to talk. I like it that we're so passionately different. I like it best when I come to the Shed at night, when no one else is there, and watch you concentrating at the drawing board in a circle of light with darkness all around." My fingers followed the contours of his scalp and travelled down the ridge of his nose to find his mouth. I felt my womb stir and cramp as if held in a vise. When I withdrew my fingers, my body relaxed again. On impulse, I asked, "Have you ever been in love?"

"There was . . . I knew a girl, Ruth, at university. She came on a camping trip. Ivan invited her. Quiet, clever. We met again at a reunion party. I remember we tickled each other in somebody's strawberry patch and the stains on my clothes never came out in the wash. Mother must have spotted them. Next thing, after my graduation, I was whipped off overseas for a whole year and Ruth went to Queensland. By the time I returned she was married—to some Queensland farmer. I haven't seen her since—no, she called once, the Shed, from the airport, just passing through—but I was out. She sent me a little book: *Pigs Can Fly*—silly title! She's Catholic. I think Father found that out. That was why they took me away, not as a graduation gift. It wasn't really love. Of course, none of us ever spoke about it, not directly. I don't know why I'm telling you now. I haven't thought about her for years, so it couldn't have been love—'in love'—I mean. She probably has a pile of kids by now."

"Probably. Do you want children?"

"I have a picture of her in my rolltop desk. Want to see it?" He began to rise, but I pushed him back on the grass.

"Of course not. Wake up. I asked about you and children. Do you?" He'd scarcely known her, but the Ross shears. . . .

"Someday . . . a daughter . . . I don't think I could handle a son."

"Why not? Competition?" I gently tugged on his hair.

"Ouch." He rolled away and sat up. "I wouldn't know how to bring up a son. Father had nothing to do with me when I was a boy. Mother never put me to bed—we always had a nanny for that sort of thing. I was pretty much left to my own devices. I'd be afraid I might end up in father's shoes."

"You could stand up to him, in a new and uniquely different pair. Fathers aren't always right, you know." I put my arms around him like a cradle.

"What's that? What are you driving at now?"

"You're forgetting there's a new component. Me."

"Is this some kind of proposal, Morgan?"

"You *are* horribly dense. Isn't that up to you?"

"Morgan, seriously, don't ever leave me. I couldn't bear that, not now."

When my sister Cicely became engaged to marry Robert Murray, our mother had consulted the future.

Her timing was propitious. Bunny Wild, wife of the

new general manager at Harry's bank, had invited a soothsayer to entertain the bank wives at their annual bridge and tennis luncheon. Normally, Dilys kept herself aloof from wives' social gatherings. *Her* husband did not encourage fraternizing. He liked to keep home and work distinct, and besides, Harry thought his wife was a cut above the other bank wives. Dilys complied because she never did enjoy games without spouses; they seemed to her like a bridge hand with only half a deck.

Dilys also thought Bunny common because of her broad country accent and the way she wore pants instead of floral dresses. Bunny plastered her face in makeup, not the normal puff of powder with a touch of rouge, but purple eye shadow and mascara. That wouldn't have gone down well in the London branch. Then, it was hard to imagine Phil and Bunny as the bank's representatives in Piccadilly, in the very overseas posting Harry almost won, in the manager's Hampstead house where she and Harry almost lived. Now that Phil Wild had returned to be manager of the head office and Harry's boss, Dilys decided to attend the luncheon after all.

Madame Fortuna chose Dilys first. Maybe she noticed the anxiety and anticipation Dilys betrayed in the way the corners of her mouth twitched; maybe, Dilys thought, she mistakes me for a gullible victim. Dilys obligingly drained her teacup until only the dregs remained at the bottom. Madame Fortuna stared hard and long into the china cup, turned it once or twice in her ringed fingers, sighed, and pronounced, "I see seven steps. I see a young woman in white. She stands on the top step with a dark young man."

Dilys smiled to herself. The other wives crowded round the table to look in her cup.

"It is not so clear now," Madame continued. "I see darkness. I see a great fortune. Much money will come into your life. I read it here. I see letters in the cup. D . . . O . . . N . . ." Madame's sentence trailed away. Dilys waited hopefully for more.

"Do you see anything more? Do you?"

Madame looked up at her and shook her head.

"No. I see a fortune come, and I see it go. Next please."

Dilys moved into a far corner of the living room and gazed out of the bay window at the abandoned tennis court as if cropped blades of grass and chalk-white parallel lines were inspirational. Of course, the bride has to be Cicely, with Robert beside her. There must be some significance to the seven steps. Seven children? Dilys shuddered. But the fortune—how puzzling. She so wanted to believe in that. *D . . . O . . . N.* She tried through the initials of her spinster aunts in Sydney, but Gwendolyn, Ida, and Martha wouldn't fit. She thought ruefully of her own given names: Delicia Swansea Wells. How she hated *Delicia.* Before she married Harry, she'd had that changed by deed poll to Dilys; when she took up calligraphy at the Conservative Club, she adopted the professional name of Dell, a rendering of Dilys and Wells. No, her name did not add up to DON, no more than Harry Edward Evans did. She tracked backward through the Wells and Evans lineage. Was there a great-uncle?—No, how foolish—all the Wells men died decades in advance of their wives, and none made any money in their working-class jobs. She tried Harry's line again. Maybe Harry had neglected to tell her all his forebears.

Of course! This must be for Morgan. Quickly she corrected herself: not *for* Morgan, *through* Morgan. That was it! Morgan would marry a rich man. Morgan's marriage would bring great fortune to the family.

That couldn't be right. Dilys rose, oblivious to Madame Fortuna's sotto voce predictions in other wives' teacups, and chanted like an acolyte: *D . . . O . . . N;* *D . . . O . . . N—Don.* But Madame had pronounced it quite distinctly as *Dun.* Dun. Done. John Donne? Dilys loved poetry. She tried it over and over again,

"When thou hast done thou hast not done for I have more." Suddenly it all connected.

"Madame" she cried, and hurried to the bridge table, "It must be *done.* When I have done something, the great fortune will come. Don't you see, it will be something I *do*?" But Madame nodded curtly and resumed her readings.

Dilys couldn't wait to go home and decided to walk, rather than ride with the others in Beth's car. She bid them all a hasty good-bye, and strode through Bunny's side gate at a smart clip. In bracing rhythm to match her brisk steps, she repeated the magic formulas, *done, done, done,* and *more, more, more,* and wondered, vividly, what the doing might be. Obviously, it would not come through her voluntary secretarial work at Westall, and as for Harry's bank—Madame hadn't mentioned Harry. No, the doing would be hers. Her good works? Hadn't she devoted herself, unstintingly, to unrewarded good works? How silly—to have had that moment of expectation for Morgan! Morgan's boyfriend, when she actually brought one home, was a scruffy writer—Rod somebody. No likely flush of fortunes there. Cicely? But Cicely was already spoken for, and although Robert might be said to have a future, he was only an academic and prone to migraines. Dilys was sure, by the time she opened her own front gate, that she was on the brink of enormous self-discovery. In her fiftieth year, too.

She hugged the prophecy to herself until the night I told her I was dating a man called Duncan, son of Donald Ross.

"Darling, I'm so excited! This fulfills my dreams. Don't put a step wrong now. If he asks to marry you, say yes. It will bring us something we've never had: security. Don and Dun—oh darling, listen to this." She told me her cryptic solution.

Her enthusiasm irritated me. I had assumed parental approval, but the Ross wealth wasn't a major issue. Other Ross virtues had captivated me: Duncan's kindly eyes, the salty streaks in his beard, his shyness, the way he giggled when he begged me to tickle his feet, his poetic passion for his work. I was the first woman Duncan had ever fallen for. That was security enough for me. Money was little more than a scenic backdrop, like splendid antique decor, that added lustre to the romantic drama of our fresh and sparkling love affair. Dilys, as usual, seemed to be reciting from a different script.

Our engagement, however, restored Harry to his best health in decades.

We'd driven out to see my parents one Friday night before Christmas, shortly before the Ross parents were due home again. Their imminent arrival meant I'd leave my Kenilworth suite for a couch in Annie and Ivan's flat, and Duncan dreaded being alone again after nearly a year together. Once decided, we agreed it would be hilarious for Duncan to ask Harry's permission the old-fashioned way. He practiced on bended knee on the Kenilworth stairs, but once we were halfway to Hyde Park Road, the plan no longer seemed amusing.

"We don't have a ring." Duncan swerved to avoid a parked car.

"Let's pretend. I'm sure to have some old stage jewelry at home. While you pop the question, I'll adorn myself in fake diamonds and make an abashed and unsuspecting entrance. Darling, watch out! You're driving like a lunatic!"

"Sorry. What if he says no?"

"I'm nearly twenty-one and anyway, you don't know Dad. He'll be overwhelmed: your name; your address; the old school tie! Only one thing worries me. They'll both have simultaneous heart attacks from sheer relief to have me respectably settled on such a prestigous name and heir. This has to be the first time that something I've done will meet with their approval. Why are we turning round at a stop sign? That's illegal, darling."

"We should have told my father first."

"He's in the Outer Hebrides. We sent a cable, remember? Technically he did know first. Does it matter anyway? It won't be officially announced until their return."

"No—I don't know—I wish I knew the right protocol.

I wish you'd take this initiative instead of leaving it all to me."

"Darling, when you asked me to marry you . . ."

He turned quickly. "Morgan, I didn't ask, you did."

"Look out! Darling, of course you asked. What's this church-door panic about? If you've changed your mind and are jilting me . . . is that what's on your mind? You don't want to go through with it."

"If I didn't . . . Ivan and Annie would never forgive us, would they—but now that we've got this far—oh Morgan, must we?"

"We can go back home to Kenilworth and try again tomorrow if that makes it easier for you, but don't come crawling into my bed tonight unless you have my father's permission. Stop the car."

He pulled into the curb. I noticed we'd stopped opposite a floodlit nativity scene on the steps of St. Augustine's Church, where I'd been confirmed as a Westall schoolgirl; where I'd been a Girl Guide leader; where, in the darkened doorway to the vestry, Father John had kissed me when I was fifteen. Now, bolder than those times and their problematic ghosts would ever recognize, more daring than I'd felt myself to be with any man— and more determined—I took Duncan's head between my hands and kissed him passionately on the mouth until he wilted and his hand abandoned the steering wheel and alighted on my breast. "Which is it to be? Harry, for my hand—or lifelong chastity?"

"Blackmail." He giggled happily. "Even if it kills them." He sat up. "But darling, what should I say if he asks about my expectations? Isn't that what fathers ask?"

"Tell him the truth: that your father keeps you in the dark. Tell him what you've told me: that money doesn't count. Anyway, I'm sure he won't dare ask. Say we've agreed that I shall keep you in a manner you are least accustomed to. Drive on, darling, they go to bed early. They'll be more nervous than you are. If there's any doubt in Harry's mind, I'll tell him I'm your mistress."

"God! Never say that to *my* father—please, Morgan. Never."

They were waiting for us in the front room. Mother had arranged a vase of roses on the coffee table next to the photograph album of Cicely's wedding day. Even though it was ten o'clock at night, Dad wore a new tie and a clean shirt and had brushed what remained of his hair. When he stood to shake hands, he was inches shorter than Duncan.

Dad cleared his throat. "Now, what should Mother and I call you, Mr. Ross . . ." I heard him begin.

I steered Dilys into the kitchen to boil the kettle for tea.

"Well, Mum, are you pleased I'm happy?"

"He's very distinguished, dear. Looks so like the late Duke of Kent. My son-in-law. It's a fairytale!" She fussed over setting the tray with her best china. "Do you think he'd prefer fruit cake to cheese straws, Morgan—or should I offer him peaches and ice-cream? Will these spoons do?—I polished the silver when you called to say today was the big day—I don't want him to think we don't know how things should be done. No, not those paper napkins, Morgan, nothing so tawdry—the Ross family's aristocracy."

"Mum, he won't notice, he has other things on his mind. If Duncan can fall in love with me in a dusty creek bed, you shouldn't have to worry about appearances. Oh, Dad, we were just bringing the tea." That was quick. Had Duncan really asked?

"Wouldn't I like to see Phil Wild's face when he hears this!" Harry chuckled in the kitchen doorway. Phil Wild, the bank manager whose promotions had followed Harry's falls, now lived two blocks east of Kenilworth. Bunny, on the social scale, had gone from two to ten overnight. "It all goes to show, Morgan, that Westall was worth every penny we saved to spend on your betterment. I told you so." He rubbed his hands together.

"We told you so," Mother began sternly, but smiled like sugar frosting when she saw a red-faced Duncan in the doorway. "Shoo! No men allowed in my kitchen. Gracious me, where are your manners, Morgan. Show your *fiancé* to the settee and make him feel he's wanted here."

"Why are you marrying *him?*" Duncan's grandmother looked down her nose at him, but the question was fired at me.

She repeated, "Why? He never speaks, you know. Not a word. Stubborn, too. Silent and stubborn and a Scorpio. Can't imagine why you want to go through with it, girl."

She glared at the family group.

"Mean, too. Mean with words, mean with money. It runs in the family. See?"

Gammy Ross swept the assembled trio of Duncan, his father Donald, and his mother Constance Amy with a bravura beat of her walking stick as if it could mobilize marble. Nobody moved or spoke.

Catherine Ross had broken a leg in a pioneer flying escapade many years ago and still bore a limp. She was tall, bony, brazen, and ninety. Donald, her only offspring, was still afraid of her. So, too, was Duncan, her solitary grandchild. As a young boy, he'd been commanded to kiss her cheek in greeting on the spot she indicated with her ringed finger. He associated her flesh with cold metal. He watched her now with a look of frozen horror.

An hour earlier, I'd been mustered hastily to meet Gammy in the Kenilworth library for afternoon tea. Our official engagement had finally appeared in the morning newspaper. Nobody had thought first to inform Gammy Ross of the event. She called on the family for an immediate inspection.

She stared at me across stuffed brocade as if she were assessing livestock, the cane a whip against her knee. With each staccato question, she jabbed the floor for emphasis.

"Schooling?"

"Westall College from kindergarten to Leaving Honors. I ended up head girl," I responded eagerly.

"Hrmph. Sports? Gels need games more than brains."

I leapt to the challenge. "Hockey, left fullback, won my Blue," I paused, then added lamely, "and softball, and a bit of tennis."

"No softball in my day. That's American." She grimaced as if the word tasted bitter.

"It's a version of baseball. The ball itself is quite hard unless you wear a mitt." My courage was at stake. An aggressive defense seemed best. I looked her in the eye. "I pitched."

"Good" came the reward. Her next throw took me by surprise from my knowledge of Ross rules.

"Church?" Gammy almost shouted. Was this her fast ball? "Do you adhere to a church?"

"No," I risked. "In my childhood, I was first a Methodist, then a Presbyterian. Those were family decisions, not mine. At school, we were automatically confirmed as Church of England. Now, lapsed Christian, I suppose," wisely choosing to omit two years of missionary vocation at the zealous age of sixteen.

Gammy waited edgily for further revelations. When none came, she turned to Donald and nodded. "She'll do."

I relaxed into my padded armchair. I'd passed the stiffest test. Gammy was famous among the senior echelons of Adelaide Society for her own original and sporting triumphs. The first woman to fly solo from Port Adelaide to Mount Gambier in a Moth. The first to ride to hounds like a man; no split-skirt side-saddle femininity for Gammy Ross. The woman who ordered her late husband to cease sexual labors after the birth of a son because she'd intended only to carry daughters like herself. The mother whose contempt for weaklings was turned on that only son when he preferred tickling trout to hunting game. The grandmother whose ivory-handled cane now pointed straight at Duncan.

"That boy," she sneered, "always dropped the ball. Knock-knees. No coordination. No reflexes. How are yours?" She tapped the stick smartly across my knee. I jerked. Again, she roared approval.

Constance Amy, who was standing at full attention beside the tea-table, reacted as if on command. She straightened a row of monogrammed spoons into silver sentries in charge of the sugar pot. Then she polished the silver spout, and marshalled the cups and saucers for parade. She seemed torn between her pleasure at our engagement, which meant that she could once more bring out the silver service from the strongroom, and her terror lest Gammy should notice it was only the second best.

Gammy, however, was whispering loudly in my ear. The two men stood side by side in the bay window, hands clasped behind their backs, and appeared to be studying the elms in the garden.

"I always won, you know. I will never forget the day I walked him home from school. *They* were away on one of their infernal trips. He must have been six or seven. He threw a tantrum. His cap blew off and fell in the gutter. 'Pick that thing up,' I said. He refused. We stood there, on that road, an hour or more. I never relent. He picked it up, of course. In the end. I got my way in the end. Stubborn child."

She leant nearer, flung a bony fist like a gauntlet on my forearm, and raised her voice. "If you want my advice, my girl, get away from here as far as you can fly—Iceland, Greenland, whatever it is—if you want this marriage to last. Off the map. Far enough to be off *their* beaten tracks, and too far for him to come snivelling home."

Donald Ross turned back from the window and scowled at the room. "No one asked you for advice, Mother," he said through clenched teeth. He stumped to his armchair.

My fiancé, who'd winced under Gammy's vicious onslaught, lowered himself gingerly like a fox with wounds to the window seat. Gammy chuckled to herself. Constance Amy clinked a teaspoon on the saucer, flushed, and said to me in a quivering voice, "One lump, or two?"

PART II

I, who was late so volatile and gay,
Like a trade wind must now blow all one way,
Bend all my cares, my studies, and my vows,
To one dull rusty weathercock—my spouse! . . .
And say, ye fair, was ever lively wife,
Born with a genius for the highest life,
Like me untimely blasted in her bloom,
Like me condemn'd to such a dismal doom? . . .
Must I then watch the early crowing cock,
The melancholy ticking of a clock;
In a lone rustic hall for ever pounded,
With dogs, cats, rats, and squalling brats
   surrounded? . . .
Farewell!—all quality of high renown,
Pride, pomp, and circumstance of lively Town!
Farewell! your revels I partake no more,
And Lady Teazle's occupation's o'er!

Epilogue written by Mr. Colman
and spoken by Mrs. Abington as
Lady Teazle in *The School for Scandal*
by R. B. Sheridan, 1777

CHAPTER FIVE

It was typical of April to pour with rain after a fifteen-month drought. Annie, my matron of honor—Mother said it was bad luck not to have a virginal bridesmaid—waited with me on the front porch. Dad had gone back indoors to hunt for an umbrella.

I dabbed at the pimple which had erupted that morning on my top lip. My jaw felt like a nutcracker. The artificial flounces into which the hairdresser had teased my straight hair would probably droop in the rain. I glanced at Annie. She stared straight ahead. I could think of nothing to say.

Harry took his umbrella to wait on the footpath. His head twitched left and right like a pendulum, looking for the limousine. He consulted his watch, then tugged at his hired morning suit and the silver-gray cravat that Mother, through haste or inexperience, had knotted too tightly. I knew what was troubling Dad. The Ross parents had planned the whole affair. Out of doors, in this weather. And goodness knows what it would all cost. The father of the bride with a heart history wasn't in the running when it came to Ross money, but Dad had his pride. A marquee, waiters, caterers—somewhere along the reception line, Harry must be expecting the bill. He'd want to chip in, at the very least, or he'd feel like an ordinary guest. He hitched up his braces. The pants didn't fit. He looked borrowed, old. Suddenly, I wished we'd eloped. I felt sorry for everyone, sorry for the rain.

By the time we assembled outside All Saints Chapel where both Harry and Duncan had been students, our long dresses hung in damp rags. Annie silently adjusted my veil. I heard the organ break into the "Trumpet Voluntary" and smiled encouragement at Annie. At least we'd triumphed over the musical selections in a fight with the doddering school organist. At least we had our way on that score.

Canon Drake, bent double with arthritis, whispered final instructions to Dad and hobbled back along a blue carpet scuffed almost bare by thousands of unwilling school shoes.

"Chin up, ducks," Harry quipped, as we slowly followed Canon Drake up the aisle. To control a wild impulse to laugh, I lowered my eyes demurely and examined the white roses I carried.

My god! Hundreds of tiny aphids were on the march! Determined black termites gushed from the buds! A steady trail had begun to trickle down the rose stems toward the seed pearl buttons of my gloves. Could anyone else see? I held the repulsive nest at arm's length and composed a horrified prayer: Please God, don't let them take a detour inside my gloves or crawl up my arms into my tight and apprehensive bodice.

I hadn't heard a word of the service until, halfway through, Canon Drake lost his balance and dropped his prayerbook. A half-century of marginal meditations and inserted exegeses fluttered down like white confetti. I dropped, too, on my knees to harvest the leaves of prayer, and a titter ran along the pew behind me. Canon Drake, visibly shaken, continued the service from memory.

We'd agreed to jettison obedience, but at the words *love and honor,* and just as Ivan Goodall held out the gold ring, Canon Drake's hands shook in new convulsions and the ring rolled across the carpet toward the altar. Again, obeying instinct, I fell to my knees; again, when I swept the spoiled hearth, a ripple of merriment came from the nave. I sighed for a fairy godmother to produce her transforming wand.

My voice broke on "Come down, oh love divine" when I realized that Duncan had not sung a single word of our chosen hymns. It was a relief, at last, to lead the way to the vestry after the Canon's blessing. The room was too small to accommodate all of us and soon fogged with our breaths. Harry opened the outer door and the rain spattered inside onto my ivory silk dress.

Mr. Ross had brought along his own attendants. Mr. Hands, the retired bank manager, held out a new will. Mr. Longford, the accountant, produced a pen and explained that I must sign before we left the chapel, "in case of accidents." Longford unwrapped a new insurance policy on Duncan's life, and our initials cemented what now appeared to me to be an unexpectedly fragile partnership. After Annie and Ivan had countersigned all the documents, Canon Drake had to remind us all to sign the wedding register as well.

My mother, in a snug ice-blue cloche and satin dress, looking very like a frosty Duchess of Windsor with a smile to match, nodded nervously to Constance Amy, who, during the familiar witnessing of business papers, had seemed to thaw until Donald asked her for the day's date. She stammered, corrected herself, and held the corner of her spotted veil to her lips.

Donald and his men checked and sorted deeds and documents with practiced aplomb. Only Harry had nothing whatever to do. He stood beside the vestry door, hands behind his back, lips pursed, and stared out at the heavy rain. His cheeks were so blotchy that I thought his cravat must be cutting off the blood supply like a tourniquet, so I rubbed his shoulder and gave him an invigorating kiss. Then I realized that Duncan had forgotten to kiss me and the organ was sounding the opening bars to the "Entrance of the Queen of Sheba". So everybody kissed me, too, even Longford, and all the men shook hands.

We were man and wife.

It continued to rain throughout our reception in the Kenilworth garden. Guests in spindly heels sank like golf tees in the grass, their flat-footed escorts leaping like tipsy crickets over soggy bushes and flooded paths. Duncan held tightly to my hand. We visited each table in turn during the hot hors d'oeuvres and made shy conversation with people who looked like strangers. Water droplets shimmered on my satin shoes, and sweat patches spread under my silken armpits.

Ivan toasted us briefly. In Duncan's equally rapid reply, he forgot to include my parents in the rollcall of thanks. Together, we were to cut a three-tiered wedding cake with a Ross ancestral sword, said to have felled a dozen Roundheads in the days of Bonnie Prince Charlie. As the point of the sword descended on the frangipani topknot, I spied a bushy caterpillar curled asleep on the icing. Was I hallucinating? I was beginning to feel like a tropical Titania, captive in a colored tent, while in the forest insects crawled on every leaf and flower. Afraid that I was about to faint, I shut my eyes tightly until roused by Duncan's brisk kiss and cheers from the crowd. There was no sign of the dozing beast.

When the time came, I ran inside to change. Annie sat on Mrs. Ross's bed and lit Camels for us both while I changed into a dry woolen suit. Annie said it all felt strangely like a wake. She and Ivan planned to raid the Ross champagne supply for a cheer-up party once we'd gone away. I'll get smashed, she promised. No regrets, she added. Is that a question? I asked. Don't be silly, Annie, you and Ivan are responsible for this. And then I added quickly, You know I'd much rather stay with you than go away so soon, so immediately after a wedding.

My wedding. There was no turning back. We embraced like sorrowing ruptured twins. I descended the stairs first. On the landing, waiting in front of a flock of ruminating sheep, my old headmistress beckoned me. I scampered down to her.

"You may kiss me, here." Miss Butler pointed to her cheek. I had never so much as touched my headmistress before, but this seemed one of the simpler duties of the day.

"Of course, you have my blessing, but Morgan, it is never enough to marry. Don't hide your talents, my dear. And by the by, I never did like beards. When my brother, the Archbishop, grew a beard in the Great War, I turned his photograph to the wall. Remember, Morgan: remember ambition, honor, and success. Now go forward to the world, and don't ever forget what I've taught you."

Impulsively, I kissed her other cheek. I would have liked to tell her how enthralled I was to be married—how a different kind of recognition dawned for me, that dazzled like an unconstructed Jacob's ladder of dreams and desires—but I'd already caught sight of Duncan pressed against the front door by the waiting and anonymous throng, and it seemed too late for explanations. I called to Duncan, "Let's get out of here," and ran down the last of the stairs.

The army truck in which we'd met in the bush stalled twice. Duncan cursed Ivan for tampering with it, but rain must have wet the sparkplugs because, eventually, festive and incongruous under white paper streamers, we lurched out under the dripping elm boughs, past the outstretched arms of my mother Dilys and of Constance Amy, the waves of relatives and retainers, and through the iron gates to Edinburgh Square. My last sight from under the truck's tarpaulin was of Harry's grave but waterlogged salute.

"Darling, I didn't see Miss Gordon there," I shouted over the engine din. "Why do you think she stayed away?" Gayle and Winnie hadn't come either. Among the Ross menagerie, there'd been few friendly faces from the old bohemian days.

"Perhaps she's sick. Want to drop in to see her? It isn't

too far off our route, and it'll help to kill the time." Duncan looked elated now.

"Let's." Something had been missing, not having her there. "I'm so glad you know how I feel." I smiled across at him. Duncan accepted everything about me. He'd never shown the slightest envy of my other relationships. When I'd told him how Annie and I had been lovers in the pre-Ross phase, he'd simply nodded. "That's alright with me." When I said that Annie was the most important person in my life, he answered that Ivan meant a lot to him, too. "You're wonderful, did I ever tell you that?"

"What?" he yelled back.

"I said, I forgive you for only pretending to sing the hymns." I removed the silly feather hat that Constance Amy had insisted I wear, and leant back against the vibrating metal cabin, flushed with our success. "We made it, darling!" I screamed again as Duncan crashed through third gear on the rise before Burnside Common. "Did you see Gammy when we drove away—roaring like a lion rampant—and your father's smile? We did it, Duncan, we did!" He began to laugh, too. "I never thought we would."

"We'd gone too far to turn back." He peered through the rain for house numbers. "Just as well, perhaps, or I might have got cold feet, or Father might have changed his tune and banished me to the Hebrides. Did you say forty-one?"

"Yes, this is it. We forgot an umbrella." My voice was suddenly too loud.

"Doesn't matter—we've been drenched all day." He lifted me down into the rain and crushed me in his arms. "This will ruin my honeymoon suit, but what the hell, I'm happy," he laughed.

She didn't hear our knock on the front door, so we splashed around to the back. I called up the passage and heard a surprised hello.

She lay on a couch in her study sitting room under a tartan rug.

"You're ill," I said from the doorway. "Is there anything I can do?"

She beckoned me. She looked so pale and alone with her head on one side and the dark curls damp on her forehead that I stroked the edge of her cheek and bent down to kiss it, and when my face was near hers, she turned her head then as if to greet me and our lips accidentally met.

Miss Gordon was blushing.

"I'm sorry . . ." I whispered shakily, "I'm so sorry." I stepped aside and she saw Duncan behind me in the doorway. "This is Miss Gordon."

"I'm sorry, too. That I couldn't be with you." She smiled at him. She turned back to look at me. "I'll be alright. Will you?" I nodded. "Then shouldn't you be going? Your husband is waiting."

It was the first time I'd heard anyone say that.

"That was a shock," I said.

"I know. I am alright," she repeated softly. "It's one of my bad heads. In a day or two . . ."

Unable to say good-bye, unable to stay, I held out my hand for Duncan and he took it and we tiptoed back down the passage and around the side to the street, to where the truck's lamps stared ahead like steadying searchlights.

Duncan slammed my door. "Well, that certainly put a damper on things, didn't it."

I lay across a yellow eiderdown in a motel bedroom. Duncan hunched at the foot of the bed sipping champagne. He'd turned the television on to a replay of *Colonel Blimp*. I felt very hot, as if I had a temperature. My head ached.

I went to the bathroom to take off my suit. My eyes glistened like falling meteorites in the glass.

On the end wall of the bedroom, a full-length mirror reflected my nakedness. My breasts lay pat, like two unrisen lumps on a baking sheet. Duncan's eyes never left the screen.

This is ridiculous, I thought. We've often made love before tonight. This man is no stranger. What's the matter with me?

I stretched out my legs. They looked as slender as ghost gums. My skin felt prickly like arid spinifex. I began to shake from head to toe. In the background, Colonel Blimp shouted orders to his troops over the thud of artillery. Lights shone down from the mirror and fractured across the bed in crystal shards.

While the movie was still showing, Duncan joined me. It was not as it had been before; he ignited like a short, sharp thunderclap, but I felt no soothing response, only a dry disturbance compounded by the heat of my body, the tumult of the old war movie, the flickering light from the screen. Shapes of ordinary things—my foot, his eye—tumbled together in unfamiliar collage. Duncan fell asleep quickly, inert in the twisted sheets and snoring like a satisfied savage.

"I think I have the flu," I announced next morning on our way to the airport. I slept throughout the long flight to Hong Kong. The hotel doctor diagnosed influenza and sent me back to bed. I begged Duncan to do things—shopping, sightseeing, anything—but he was always there when I awoke.

I said that when I was better, we'd climb down the cliff steps to the beach below our hotel room. From my bed, I could see a path wind down through flowering flame trees and poincianas to the bitter blue of Repulse Bay. Duncan seemed listless.

"Humidity makes me lethargic," he agreed. "Can't we cut the trip short and go home? I don't want to do anything without you, and I'm sick of strange smells and crowds and hotel rooms. Are you well enough to fly?"

"I've ruined our honeymoon," I said, but privately I was happy to be going home, even if that had to be Kenilworth until we found one of our own. We'd both go back to work again. There'd be other holidays, other trips away, an ample time ahead to be together and to do whatever we chose. With Annie, too, and Ivan.

Unlike Donald Ross, Constance Amy spoke well of everyone. Her good deeds shied from publicity. In the early months of marriage, when Duncan and I lived at Kenilworth, I learnt that she'd been a trustee of the district orphanage for forty years, that she sent anonymous weekly donations to the local parson, and kept the unnecessary services of a seamstress purely because the poor woman supported a drunkard husband.

Constance Amy's head was small, crowned with sparse but fluffy gray curls. It stored a remarkable ledger of unusual information. She knew by heart the height above sea level of every village in the old Hapsburg Empire. When asked, and often unsolicited, she recited the daily Fahrenheit readings in April 1923 for Nice, or Stavangar, or Skye.

Closer to home and necessity, she could recall with photographic accuracy the day, hour, minute, and weather conditions that then prevailed for the births of all her godchildren. Moreover, on each child's birthday, she dispatched by chauffeur's hand a five-pound note, crisp and freshly minted. When Australia went decimal, she sent five dollars, as crisp and new and punctual as before, if slightly diminished in value. After Donald sacked the chauffeur, she made sure to mail her gifts ahead of time.

Her intellectual inventory extended to all the Ross possessions. She changed tracks with the changing seasons. Winter flannels and wools were promptly exchanged for summer cottons, silks, and linens in mothproofed trunks. Closets with racks of clothing were rotated on a modified Dewey system, for she kept every article of clothing she'd ever bought and, like Queen Mary, rarely wore the same costume twice. While Duncan and I were away on our honeymoon, Constance Amy reorganized the contents of his drawers and shelves in chronological order: from first cap in cradle, to muddy boy scouting, through boarding school and undergraduate gowns, to air squadron greatcoat, yachting blazer, and chalk-white deck shoes. His cast-off clothing was cleaned, pressed, catalogued, and preserved. Constance Amy was said to have numbered the hairs of his head.

Our wedding day had coincided with her fortieth anniversary. The Ross parents began to take stock of their future. On the billiard table after family dinner, Donald unfolded his maps to revise their seventeenth itinerary. Global tracks the travellers had engraved by rights should have been indelible, yet year by year they'd seen the red-colored borders of their beloved British Empire shrink. London, they lamented, was becoming hideously black and white. While surely India would always be India and Rhodesia Rhodesia, the new coinage, *Commonwealth,* had an unfamiliar ring that sounded both precarious and profligate.

"There's Switzerland," Constance Amy reminded Donald comfortingly, "and Holland. They still have a queen. So do the Swedes, don't they? Or was she a commoner? Then Liechtenstein and Monaco, and we can always extend our time in Scotland, dear. You can rely on Scotland not to change."

"Cable McBain. Have the castle ready." Donald stubbed a red pencil on the Hebridean coastline. "Ferry across the Firth from Oban. Show 'em Tobermory, eh?"

". . . near Ben More, longitude fifty-seven, three thousand one hundred and sixty-nine feet . . . they'll need their woollies." Constance Amy passed him his after-dinner mint.

They? I glanced at Duncan, but he was hidden behind the evening paper. I looked at my watch. It was only seven-thirty. "I should go up to our room to study a script. I'm holding auditions next week. Will you excuse me, Mrs. Ross?"

"Auditions? Script?" Donald's fingers jealously drummed

on the map like a general guarding secret troop maneuvers.

Before I could explain, Duncan stood up, stretched, and announced that he was off to the Shed. He kissed the top of my head, dropped the newspaper on the open map, and left the room.

"I'll come with you," I called hurriedly after him. "Darling," I said as we reversed the MG out of the stables, "you mustn't leave me alone every night like this. Surely they don't plan to take us with them?"

"Take us? Where?"

"Oh, how you manage to block your ears! I think they're hinting about a trip abroad."

"Hm. Not a bad idea. You've never been. Get to travel free, plus a bonus—they're better informed than most tourist guides."

"Duncan, that's not how I want to see the world, through your parents' eyes. I'd rather go with you."

"Silly thing, you see enough of me as it is, and you have plenty of time on your hands now that you're a married woman. I doubt if I can take the time, though. The new RG20 model has design snags. I think it's a grand idea."

"I don't." This wasn't how I'd planned to tell him. All evening I'd waited for a moment together, but as usual we were never left on our own at Kenilworth. "Duncan, I can't go unless you come with me."

"What's happened to your remarkable independence, Morgan? You managed very well on your own before you took up with me." Duncan tapped his fingers impatiently on the steering wheel while waiting for the lights to change.

"I had Annie, remember." This wasn't proceeding as it should. "We spent more time together in a week than I have with you these past three months." He accelerated so abruptly that I was jerked back into the seat. "Steady. You'll need to drive more sedately in future." I tried to sound cheerful.

"What's wrong? You've never criticized my driving before," he said crossly. "Look, if it makes you unhappy to go overseas with them, don't go. It's a lost opportunity in my view, but I guess you'll do what you want to do. Better tell them soon, before they take it for granted. They don't like sudden changes. What will you give for an excuse?" After he'd neatly parked next to Ivan's car in the Shed's backyard, he began to climb out.

"I'll tell them I want to be here with you when their first grandchild is born."

He poked his head back through the perspex window. "You'll say *what*?"

"I'm pregnant."

"Morgan, darling," he shouted, and ran around to my side of the car to open the door. "What are you going to do?"

"Have it, of course. Now let me out, and I'll come type those specifications you've been worrying about and make us some coffee, and if you don't mind," I wiped my eyes, "while you tell Ivan, I'll call Annie with the news."

"My god," he said, as his eyes widened incredulously. "A baby."

"Our baby." I grinned up at him.

"Ivan, why must you choose today of all days to make fig jam? The house reeks of it! While you stand there stirring that black tar with your wooden spoon, Morgan and I are doing all the work. Men! Please get rid of those jars and lids on the table—we need the space for cooking and I need the sink to wash the lettuce and—Where is this meant to be?"

Annie had rushed into my kitchen with a full tray of dinner plates balanced on her hip. I took it from her and pushed it under the laden kitchen table. We'd never be ready on time.

Annie stretched and groaned. "Oh, my back. Have you settled the seating arrangements, Morgan?"

"It's a delicate operation." I consulted my list. "We

—130—

have to separate potentially hostile factions. Donald should be isolated down at one end. You, Annie, will hold veto powers to his left, and Ivan's mother, Mrs. Goodall, can keep the peace on his right."

"This is fun. What do you say, Ivan?"

"That's tantamount to handing Mr. Ross the floor, since my mother will be too intimidated to open her mouth at all."

"He'll take it regardless. Ivan, will you play the other superpower down this end?—or should it be Duncan—no—you, Ivan, because then we can have Mrs. Ross and Dilys next to you. No—that's too much of a consensus—let's try me on your left. Dilys can sit on the fence in the middle here."

"So to speak. That places her too near your father, Morgan," Annie straddled the kitchen stool, "with their tied vote dead in the center. It's simpler to do it biblically, like Noah, and pair the species in marital couplings. Come here, Ivan. See how this is shaping." We huddled over the sketch I'd made of our dining room. Drippings from the jam spoon soon made it quite illegible. Ivan drew up a fresh plan. "Five of each pair, Ivan, and separate the sexes," Annie advised. She frowned. "Should we also classify by age and seniority?"

"Or class—it's all in Mrs. Beeton," I offered. "Her banquet settings are in order of merit—the king at the top, then princes, dukes, knights—down to the peasants. Where *is* my new Mrs. Beeton that Duncan gave me?"

"On the stove for the jam," Ivan said. "I need her for my peasants' preserves. This won't work, Morgan. It's your party. Let's have our hostess on the kitchen end orchestrating the food while Duncan keeps the wine flowing at the other. There. How's that?"

"Unfair. You've put me next to Mr. Ross."

"Better get used to it, sweetheart." Annie chuckled until she saw that she was on his other side. "Oh well," she added philosophically, "maybe together we'll neutralize the old buzzard. Where's that wretched lazy Duncan?"

"At the Shed, of course. Annie, while I stuff the lamb, will you lay the table for the fray?"

"With brand-new silver weapons and crystal ammunition. Well, I suppose it is time that we christened the loot. I hope it's sharp."

The Rosses arrived in two cars, hers bearing white satin cushions and a rack of Duncan's baby clothes, his filled with old wicker furniture—Duncan's crib, high chair, and miniature rocking chair. More painting, I sighed to myself. From the boot emerged a dilapidated life-sized dog on wheels, the fur around its neck rubbed bare. I parked the dog in the unfurnished nursery to watch Donald unpack miscellaneous boxes of toys and fancy-dress costumes that Duncan had worn as a child on board ship.

"What a dreadful color for a newborn." Constance Amy gaped at the ceiling. "You'll have to get it painted."

"I just did. It's called Tobacco. I rather like it," I said defensively, trying on a monkey mask.

"Looks like turds," Donald snorted. "Should be blue."

"Pink," said Constance Amy. I left them to fight it out and answered the doorbell.

"How do you do," said Harry with a little bow.

"Dad! It's me, Morgan." I removed the mask, touched to see that he had worn his London suit. Dilys had dressed up, too, in her blue wedding finery. "Hello, Mum. Bring the coats to our bedroom."

"A white carpet! Oh, Morgan dear, white's so impractical." Dilys flung herself backward onto our kingfisher-blue silk bedspread as if she meant to claim the bed as her own. Her hand stroked the pillow, then she shrieked, "What's that moth-eaten rubbish under the curtain?"

"A cat, mother. We've called it Mulligatawny for its curried coat. It was starving when I found it last week at the back door."

"You can't have a cat—they suffocate babies! Put it out, put it out!" Mother chased the cat down the hallway that ran from front to back in typical colonial Georgian style. I was about to follow, thinking this would be a good time to divert our guests with a garden tour—what Duncan would call a wilderness ramble because, with all the interior painting to do, I hadn't found time to work on the weeds—when I smelt a terrible odor coming from the kitchen.

"Ivan—where's Ivan?" I ran through the house. "Ivan!" He was coming up the cellar stairs with bottles of wine. "The jam—my god the jam, Ivan!"

Annie helped clear away the appetizers—lemon halves stuffed with an anchovy mousse that had tasted rather bitter. Constance Amy hadn't touched hers, but Harry, I noticed gratefully, had scraped his clean to the rind. Since Duncan was needed to carve the roast lamb, I went around the table to refill the wineglasses. Judging by her rosy cheeks and sagging eyes, Mrs. Goodall was several glasses ahead of me.

"What's this stuff, anyway?" Donald sniffed distrustfully at the wine.

"South Australian—a Coonawarra '52—our best claret, don't you agree?" I waited while he twirled the glass between his fingers and held it to the light and sniffed again.

"Rotgut" was the verdict. "Should have brought our own. No comparison with Europe. Shouldn't imbibe, you, not in your condition." I left the bottle by his elbow and retreated to the kitchen.

Annie put an arm around my shoulders at the stove. "You're doing just fine, darling. Relax. Don't let him get to you. Here, let me help with that gravy."

"It's a disaster. Everything tastes like burnt fig." I patted my stomach. "Four months without morning sickness, but the Rossling is kicking up a storm inside. And I wanted to do everything right. How's yours?"

"Asleep, like Grandmother Goodall will be if she continues to guzzle the wine. I have this recurring nightmare, Morgan, that I'm breeding a mute like her. Given the grandparent pool, these poor babies . . . do you suppose genetic traits skip a generation?"

"Duncan's afraid the Rossling will resemble Gammy. I wouldn't mind that. At least she's spunky. I wish she were at the controls tonight instead of me, but there weren't enough chairs. Gammy is the only woman alive who can safely pilot Donald Ross. Oh, Annie, I so want to be a success . . ."

". . . and walk on water. Your inaugural guest list is hardly conducive to miracles."

"Not just our first dinner party. I meant as a wife, as a daughter-in-law, as someone who can manage to do everything well."

Ethel Collins's lamb recipe was a triumph, but the dinner deteriorated during salad and cheese. Mr. Goodall reminisced about his war in Gallipoli, waving the stump of his amputated arm and moving the cutlery about with his good one to demonstrate the Anzac retreat. When Constance Amy interrupted to complain about hotel service in postwar Istanbul, Mr. Goodall became very agitated.

"Attaturk, Atta bloody Turk, we should have poisoned those sewer rats!" he shouted, wielding his knife like a scimitar.

"Living in the past, man," said Donald coldly. "Stinking yellow peril, that's the next war. Chinks'll walk in our front door at Darwin and pour straight down." He shifted the gorgonzola to a commanding position inside Mr. Goodall's fork battalions and planted a knife flat across the melting cheese. "Darwin up here, Adelaide there. Damned fool Yanks laid a sealed highway clean across the desert. Open invitation. Walk right in. Obvious to any fool."

"Ah yes, but don't forget the Yanks saved us from the Nips," Harry interposed in a reasonable tone of voice. "If it hadn't been for the Coral Sea . . ."

"Japanese subs came right into Sydney Harbor," Dilys piped up, "two of them, miniature submarines, under the net, past the cannon at South Head, almost up to Circular Quay—I saw them myself."

Mr. Goodall snorted so loudly that Constance Amy clutched the tablecloth. "Fat lot of use those old cannon. Rusty junk from the Boer War. It was Churchill what saved us from the Asiatics."

"Another humiliating defeat," Harry persisted. "It was your Churchill who put your lot into Gallipoli the first time around, and it was your same Churchill who abandoned the Aussie fighting man in Singapore and stranded you on the Kokoda Trail. We lost some good mates. Mind you, they came in far too late for my liking, but if America hadn't finally entered the war . . ."

"I wouldn't say a word against Churchill in present company," Duncan quietly warned Harry. I could see he was too late. We had to stop them. I signalled across the table to Annie.

"The only good thing anyone can claim for the slaughter at Gallipoli is that it made a nation of us." Harry stuck to his guns, averting his eyes from Mr. Goodall's gesticulating stump. "Tell that to your Churchill." He nodded to Duncan.

Oh dear, Annie hadn't noticed me. I clapped my hands vigorously. "Bravo! This may be a good time to ask if you'd like your coffee with dessert, or later . . ."

"Nation?" Donald Ross ignored me. "Call that Irish Catholic convict scum a nation? And all these refugees— can't even talk the Queen's English—anarchists, communists, criminals . . ."

"We don't know what the world is coming to," murmured Mrs. Ross.

"I'd hardly call today's New Australians criminals, Mr. Ross. Menzies had the right idea on immigration. We need skilled labor," Ivan chipped in, but Mr. Ross cut him down at once.

"Mingies!" The Scottish pronunciation made all heads turn. "Don't give me Mingies—he's the Queen's man. It was Evatt and his damned socialists opened those floodgates . . ."

"What *is* for dessert, Morgan?" Annie interrupted at last.

"Peach Melba." I flashed her a smile.

"Ah, there's a loverly voice, old Nellie Melba." Mrs. Goodall sloughed off her torpor, raised her head from Harry's shoulder where it had lain snoozing, and spoke up for the first time. "I 'member 'er farewell 'ome sweet 'ome. A real 'omegrown star, that one, such a game old girl."

"Drunk." Donald was curt. "A sodden drunk."

"Well, at least she left us our national dish," said Dilys consolingly. I sprinted for the kitchen door, but before I could close it behind me, Mrs. Goodall, regaining both voice and volume, began to hum the mournful melody of "Home Sweet Home."

"There he goes again, Gallipoli Goodall," Annie had loitered behind with me on the gravel drive while Mr. Goodall strutted off to join Constance Amy and Dilys in the rose garden, "with his one and only topic. I wanted to strangle him."

"The little Aussie one-armed battler." I was angry too. "The problem with that identity, which attracts most men of that generation, is that it's universal and exotic—much more manly than local heroics like footie and mateship in the bush. In war, Private Goodall was a somebody. The wife and farm back home must have been dull in comparison. No wonder he celebrates it. Even losing his mates and losing an arm was a kind of victory, I suppose."

"He lost more than an arm; he lost the best years of his life. Whoever heard of a nation that celebrates defeat! As for your father and Mr. Ross, neither of them ever went to war but they're obsessed with it, too. That's something I can't understand."

"Their obsession? Probably guilt by association—a form of nostalgic male bonding. It puts them on equal terms with the returned soldier: Harry as the fireside expert, a hearthrug hero, while Mr. Ross gets to play field marshal and warlord of my dinner table. It's disgusting. They had only one theme in common, so of course it had to dominate."

"And activate. Did you notice how the memory of war lifted the lid off their violence? I couldn't believe how angry they were. To tell you the truth, I think Ivan and Duncan rather enjoyed it."

"Maybe. At least, thank heaven, Duncan is no racist."

"Nor Ivan, but you know, if Australia declared war on Asia tomorrow, I have a suspicion our husbands would be first to enlist and to hell with the wife and the baby. Let's hope fatherhood will change them. Where are they, by the way?"

"Ivan's reviving his mother, and I hope Duncan is washing the dishes. I wish they'd all go. I'm tired." I tucked my arm in hers. "It's been a hard night, but we shan't have to repeat it for months. The Ross parents leave for Europe soon, and by the time they return, we'll be able to steer family conversations to the subject of children."

"Another nostalgic Australian theme: lost innocence." Annie laughed.

"Did we have it to lose? I used to think when I was a child that while we slept snugly down here, far away to the North Pole the grownups were already awake, busily creating and solving the next set of world problems. That's not so much lost as borrowed innocence on borrowed time. Distance and isolation have sustained the great Australian illusion that we don't have to be involved. Nostalgia excuses us from having to wake up to be responsible adults."

"Not for much longer, I'd guess." Annie pointed to the stars. "Look, there's Sputnik circling the sky. By the time our children have grown up, distance will be illusory too."

We strolled back toward the house. "Annie, I'm determined to raise this baby differently from the way we were raised. Mrs. Ross is so repressed, she sometimes seems retarded. Harry and Dilys were comparatively decent tonight, but both are crippled, not as Mr. Goodall is, but by limited horizons. As for Mr. Ross, I wish I had the courage to follow Gammy's example. She treats him like a cross spoilt child."

"If you want my professional opinion, I'd say he was a bully"—Annie opened the door for me—"in need of intensive behavioral modification. Gammy should have tried that long ago."

"It always comes back to the mother."

"Precisely. The prospect would appall me were we not in this together. Look at me, dear one. Don't forget the unspeakable mother who gave birth to *me*. That should give us hope. Come, let's see if Ivan and Duncan were trained to be good husbands in spite of their disagreeable fathers and have cleared away the mess."

In bed that night, I thought about my identity and the major theme in my life now. Would I be strong enough, and good enough, to hold it all together—the man in my arms, the child we'd begun, and others to come? How on earth would I make it all work?

Harry was the only grandparent to see my baby, Emma, soon after birth. Mr. Ross had taken a liking to my mother at the dinner party and wrote from Austria to invite her to join them. Of course she accepted. Harry had to sell his gilt-edged bank dividends to finance the flight, although Donald had offered to pay all Mother's expenses. Harry didn't want to be beholden to anyone.

He looked so crestfallen at the airport after she'd gone that I suggested he come home to live with us until

Mother's return, a date that depended on the duration of Scottish hospitality.

"We'll put a spare bed in the nursery for you," I said.

"She deserved it. Your mother deserves all the good things in life that she missed because of me." He sighed.

"You deserve it, too, Dad. Why didn't you go with her? The bank probably owes you long service leave."

"That all went in sickness benefits."

"What about early retirement, or a holiday without pay?" But he was adamant. "Do you think Donald asked Mum as a consolation prize?" I joked, for Duncan had surmised that this was Donald's way of punishing me for not travelling with them. It showed that I was replaceable.

"Small consolation for me," Harry said glumly. "How shall I survive without Mother?"

"Quite comfortably, Dad, if you come to us."

"I can't sleep in a strange bed. I'd be in the way. Duncan hasn't time for me, and with the baby coming, no sooner would I arrive than I'd have to make room for it."

"We'll bring your bed over, if that's what you want, and since I'll be breast-feeding, the baby will sleep in our bedroom for the first months." I knew that tone of voice. He'd rather starve than accept my offer of help.

"I'll be better off in Mother's home, and you can come over to cook my dinner during the day. I suppose I could heat it up when I come home from the bank. It might work."

"That's much too difficult for me, Dad, having to drive across the city every day to cook for you. I'll advertise for a temporary housekeeper if you insist on staying at home."

"I don't like strangers around. I'll manage somehow," he said without conviction, "and a new baby would keep me awake with the crying."

"I hope Mother will get to London to see Cicely and her boys." I tried a different tack. "It must be exciting to see two grandsons for the first time."

"I shan't live long enough to see any of my grandchildren."

"Oh, Dad, snap out of it!" I said wearily. "You'll meet this one in about two weeks' time."

Annie gave birth to a son, Tim, three weeks after Emma was born and in the same maternity hospital.

My contractions had begun very early. Annie thought they were only trial labor when the doctor decided the head wasn't engaged, and she told me I ought to have a brandy, read Dr. Spock, and relax. Annie looked far from relaxed herself.

I read *Saint Joan* instead. Maybe, when my profile resumed its normal lines, I could at last play Shaw's virgin martyr. I was absorbed in the second act when Emma decided to compete and the contractions began in earnest. Duncan drove me to the hospital and promised to stay and time the contractions and help with my Lamaze deep breathing and relaxation techniques.

When nurses came to offer medication, I refused. Annie and I had determined to do this naturally. When the pain became intense, I asked Duncan to turn on the bedside radio and we listened to the Test cricket together, me breathing in time with Mackenzie's fast balls and Colin Cowdrey's defensive strokes, Duncan watching the clock like a field umpire at the crease. Whenever an English batsman was bowled, I heaved in pain until the next man came to the wicket, and we resumed our delicate coordination with the rhythms of the game.

Stumps were drawn and players had left the oval before Emma chose to make her debut. There were no more timely diversions. My body was in the grip of an endless earthquake and must split asunder. Nurses wheeled me into delivery, and Duncan went back to the radio to wait. I remembered a Resistance story about a woman parachutist who plummetted into France; who later said that her one act of courage as she leapt from the plane when there was no turning back was her abandonment to fear. When I was told to push, I knew I had jumped and had lost all control and there was to be no turning back. At the last, and from fear, I refused the oxygen mask, took a deep breath, and pushed in a dying effort to be free, to be done with the marathon pain and the plunging fall.

Like every mother I had watched in Orroroo, as soon as Emma lay on my chest and I saw her clenched fist and her blank blue eyes open and the sticky and surprisingly lush hair covering her head and the thick tough cord that still attached her to my womb, I was instantly relaxed, and exhausted, and awed, and in love. I looked up to see Duncan smiling down tremulously and blissfully at both of us as we panted and quivered under the glare of lights in a room that suddenly seemed frantic with rush-hour traffic. What urgency remained, I wondered deliciously, now that my baby was in my arms?

Duncan later told me that a storm had broken outside during Emma's birth. Lightning and thunder flashed and shook the windows of the delivery room, where I was aware only of tremendous upheavals of energy inside me, of fierce waves of expulsion that threatened to obliterate me in that instant when the secret life I had for so long carried and nurtured was in the end and so suddenly released.

Harry's death was so long anticipated that I felt no exceptional emotion save slight disbelief that, when it did come, a year later, and after seventeen years of rehearsal, we had no words for it. Mother looked numb. There was a surreal sheen to the early morning light in which every familiar thing looked sharp and new.

Mother was sweeping the kitchen floor when I arrived, as if it were a day as ordinary as any other.

"Please, Morgan, do check him for me. See that the district nurse has done everything nicely, will you?"

Dad had died at the moment of waking. He'd grunted when Mother asked him if he was ready for a cup of tea.

Later, she realized it was his last sound. Then she'd telephoned for me.

I entered my parents' bedroom. Harry was laid out in his bed in new pajamas. His face looked wooden. There seemed to be wadding in his mouth as if he had not quite finished swallowing something. His smile was a padded smile. I touched his cheek. It felt rubbery and unpleasant. I wasn't sure if he had really gone or had become a hovering aura, waiting for something—a word, a sign from me—before departing.

The bedroom was a shrine. On his bedside table, turned to face him, was their portrait on their wedding day, the corners of his mouth turned upward, tenderly, excitedly. On his lowboy, the photograph of Harry on horseback at the opening of Parliament House, Canberra, in the volunteer cavalry honor guard for the Duke of Gloucester. A yellow plume fluttered in the brim of his digger's hat and he wore a jaunty grin. He must have been twenty. Then I saw the flowers. The nurse had decorated him with a floral crucifix. Posies of violets, shasta daisies, rosebuds, and maidenhair fern marked both shoulders, then trailed down to his waist, where his chilled hands folded around a single rose still wet with dew. Mother would hate it.

I looked around for a vase. There was some water in his toothmug on the dressing table between their beds. Someone had removed the teeth. Perhaps they accounted for the lumps where the skin around his jaw had tightened.

I realized I was killing time. I closed the door and tiptoed to Mother's bed opposite his. I felt I should remark, in some significant if private way, between him and me, upon his death. I recalled the last time I had seen him. I'd driven them both to a Town Hall orchestral concert three, no, four days ago. I had raced to put Emma to bed because Harry insisted on punctuality. It was a cold night. A huge crowd milled around the marble entrance. Harry had turned to salute me with his old parade ground gallantry—shoulders bunched inside his overcoat, a gray scarf up to his ears—before he disappeared into the crowd. He looked like an old Quixote, all the shining glory and the manhood gone, and most of the dreams.

We'd been much closer after Emma's birth. He'd come to the maternity hospital to see us, proud, happier than I had ever seen him. He unwrapped his gift, Emma's first teddy bear, and showed me the booklet's illustrations of a worn-out Wendy Boston bear undergoing washing, hand-wringing, and mangling until it emerged as good as new. When Matron put Emma into his arms, he looked at me as if he were seeing me properly for the first time.

One of my childhood heroes, Robert Falcon Scott, had frozen heroically in his sleeping bag, his last brave words to his wife, to his baby son, and to his country open on the page with the pen still in his hand when they found him halfway home from the Pole. Dad took me to see the movie when I was twelve. There was nothing especially heroic about Harry. His death seemed almost second-hand, an anticlimax. What could I say to him now?

As I sat forward on Mother's bed and watched him, he began to dissolve into the pictures of corpses I used to study obsessively in war histories. They fascinated me when I was young. I'd turn a page over and around, trying to make out an eye, a mouth, the expression around the eyes at the moment of death, as if I wanted to recreate that moment in the hollow empty spot where moments before there'd been breath, a glance, a living response. But the features remained relentlessly closed. Pictures told nothing about that moment, no matter how hard I concentrated and tried to imagine it. When I turned to another page, I would feel I had abandoned the possibility of life.

I stared at my father's death and tried to make it personal. I kissed his cheek and forehead and pulled down the blinds to make the room seem cool and quiet like fresh earth just below the grass. I tiptoed backward to the door, a courtier unable or unwilling to withdraw, reluctant to turn from the presence. I held up my hand in salute and farewell as he had done. Then, thinking of my mother, I remembered a line of verse that I shouted once, exultantly, into the wind on a wintry beach. It suited his expression in the honor guard picture.

" 'And Death shall have no dominion,' " I whispered. Then I smiled at myself because it sounded so absurd.

Cicely flew from London the afternoon following Harry's cremation. She'd been crying. I was rueful because I had not. She looked at the empty bed, at the flowers still fresh in the toothmug. Cicely rarely showed physical affection, and when she put her head on my shoulder, I felt a surge of sadness.

"When I walked back into this house, Morgan, it had shrunk. It looked like a toy house. Does death do that to you?"

"No," I said. "Absence does. When you go away, your imagination expands things and distorts them. When you return, you're shocked to see things as they really are. Everything seems smaller. Memory itself begins to shrink."

"Will Dad shrink?" Cicely looked startled to see me cry.

"Only if he disappears from memory." It would have been tactless and unfeeling to admit that our father had always been absent for me, a portrait on a turned page. Or to tell Cicely that what made me sad was the knowledge that Harry hadn't lived to see a new grandchild. I'd just discovered I was pregnant again.

CHAPTER SIX

"Do you love me?"

"You know I do," he answered absentmindedly.

"I want to hear you say it."

"There. I've finished the trees. That only leaves the sky." Sunlight streamed through the gloryvine leaves on the terrace outside our back door. Annie and I had set up a trestle table early in the morning for our two older children, Emma and Tim, to build a cubby-house underneath with fruit crates and blankets. As soon as he saw it, Duncan commandeered the table for his new three-thousand-piece jigsaw puzzle.

"What if it rains?" I said.

"The forecast is for sun, a cloudless sky. Come on, darling, you know how much I like to solve puzzles. You can help with the easy parts—the house and haystack and the figures under the trees."

"Thank you very much. Very generous of you. What if I want to do the sky instead? What if the children upset the table or the kittens jump up to play with the bits?"

"You're trying to distract me, I know you. If you don't want to help, Emma's old enough to try."

"Darling, a two-year-old has a concentration span of about three minutes, and I've just said I want to help you. I'm so glad to have you home on a Saturday. It's like a holiday treat."

"Emma's extremely bright. This will train her to see spatial relationships and work out for herself how things are cut to fit."

"Things!" I tousled his hair. "This will take all day and all night. When Annie brings the babies back from the playground, you should ask her to help. There, a piece of your sky for a kiss."

He kissed me just as Annie wheeled the pram around the corner of the house. Duncan continued with his puzzle while I fed my Catriona, and Annie changed her Edwin's diapers and poured iced lemonade into an old camp jerrycan for the older explorers in their table-tent. For a while, I played with the little ones in the sandpit, and moved the hoses among the apricot and peach trees and the sprinkler from the roses to the lawns while Annie worked silently on Duncan's sky. The garden was busy with bees and birds and the contented sounds of children at play. Soon I curled into the hammock at the end of the vines to read my mail.

"By the way, Ivan has found the right house," Annie said.

"I didn't know you were looking—or thinking of a move. What's wrong with the present one?" Duncan asked.

"It's not that we've outgrown it yet, but we've been planning for months to buy a property large enough to have a kind of extended family," I heard Annie explain. "Morgan knows about it and thinks it's a good idea. We originally thought of separate houses, back to back, connected by a shared garden, but that still replicates the old nuclear family unit."

"Morgan never said anything to me about your house plans."

I looked up. "I didn't? I'm sure I did, Duncan. You probably don't remember."

"Ivan was dubious, too, at first. What worried him most was the thought of sharing everything. Once he saw the sense in communal cooking and dining and living rooms, and we explained that we needed a house large enough to provide the adult partners with reasonably private space for sleeping quarters, with bedrooms and a huge playroom for the four children in between the adult wings, he was as eager as we are to try it out."

"What on earth are you talking about—communal this and sharing that? Sounds idiotic to me." One of his pieces hadn't fit, and he was pulling apart a finished section of the puzzle.

"Don't be too quick to judge, darling." I rolled out of the hammock and joined them at the table. "For a long time, Annie and I have seen eye to eye on this. Why duplicate, when each of our families has similar needs and parallel development? By pooling our resources, we'd cut waste, trim consumption, reduce individual workloads, and meanwhile give the children the rare advantage of a larger family group. In terms of sheer efficiency and economic management, a merger is such an obvious benefit, I wonder that more families haven't thought of this before. As for emotional support, it's revolutionary. I think it's worth a try."

"Nothing but Marxist jargon and Communist crap— it'll never work." Duncan sounded vexed.

"Why not?"

"Because we're all individuals. I'm blessed if I'm going to pool my capital or assets with anyone else."

"We pool a lot already," Annie said. "We borrow each other's cars and consume each other's meals; Ivan's farm provides most of our combined family greens and fruit, while the Ross hens lay eggs for twenty families. Since Morgan and I replicate every day every maternal duty and task, we may as well combine forces. That way, we gain more time and energy for our professional work."

"In a way, the idea is an outgrowth from what you and Ivan already share at the Shed. Why not adapt your model to the home?"

"Little do you understand business practice, Morgan! Father would explode if he heard this."

"What's Father got to do with it?"

"Isn't that obvious? I presume you have taken financial costs into account."

"Don't be so sarcastic, Duncan. Of course we may pool some assets, like our present homes, to buy the new one and pay the mortgage . . ."

"Morgan, stop it right there—I don't want to hear another word. There's no way we can sell this house. It suits us perfectly and Father would never agree." Duncan slapped the table so vehemently that pieces of jigsaw jumped in the air and landed upside down. I noticed that the children's chatter had ceased.

"Don't shout, Duncan. This is none of your father's business."

"All our financial dealings, all of our assets are Father's business. We don't own this house for a start."

"Now there you are wrong. This was our wedding present from both of your parents. They gave it to us. Your mother said so."

"Look, I didn't mean to start a private war," Annie interrupted. "This can wait for another time. You don't have to decide anything now."

"No, you will hear me out. A Ross company bought this house, and the costs were debited to my account with that company. The deeds are in my name but I'm not free to sell or exchange it without permission from the company directors—"

"Your parents, of course—" I said.

"And me. I'm a minority vote but I will tell you now, for good and all, I have no intention of proposing any changes."

"Don't we have a house of our own, Daddy?" Emma poked her head through the blanket door beneath the table.

"Daddy and Mummy own *our* house," Tim proudly announced.

"Can't we afford a house, Daddy?" Emma persisted.

"Morgan, take the kids inside. They're too young to

understand what's going on here. You'll make them feel insecure, just as you are making me very angry. I'm going back to work. I've heard enough for one afternoon. See that you never talk about this ridiculous idea in front of the children again. I'll tell Ivan how things stand with me." He strode to the garage and started the car. When he had driven off in a hailstorm of gravel, Annie made a wry face and went to the kitchen to put on the tea.

"Well, that didn't go so well." I followed her.

"I think we'd better face it, Morgan. Duncan will never agree, no matter how hard or how logically you try to convince him. He simply isn't the cooperative type. Don't look so dejected. You'll always be part of my family, you and the girls, no matter how this works out."

"What about your plans? Do you . . . have you any other friends in mind?" I wanted it to be me, not some other friend.

"Nobody yet except old Mr. Goodall. Ever since Granny Goodall died, he's found it difficult to keep the farm commercially viable without her second pair of hands. While he doesn't get on with me particularly, he loves the boys, and it's good for children to know their grandparents. It's a start, I suppose."

"It's a very good start." One that I resented, jealously, because I should be left out of it—not only now, but forever. Then I remembered I'd left the children unattended.

I raced outside. Catriona and Edwin were not in the sandpit. There was no sign of anyone in the back garden or hiding under the trees. I ran down the drive toward the gates, fearing the worst. They'd be out on the road—they'd stray to the parklands—run over—molested! I called out to Annie when I was level with the kitchen window.

"The children have gone—can't see them anywhere!"

They were not in the front garden or on the road. I searched the dark open spaces under the veranda pilings.

Then I ran around the other side of the house toward the woodshed—funnel webs and redback spiders foremost in my mind—and bumped into Annie. She was grinning.

"You forgot the most obvious place of all. Come see." She led me back to the terrace under the vines. We bent down together to peer beneath the jigsaw table.

"There you are!" Emma clapped her hands to see me. "Catty and Ted came inside with us to make a big family. I don't care what Daddy says, I'm going to live with Tim, and the babies can live with us, too. This is our house. Do you like it, Mummy?"

"Very much. Can I join in? Annie, will you bring this family some afternoon tea? I think we're starving."

"What about the puzzle—should I pack it away?" Annie held the empty box to our blanket portal.

"No, let's leave it where it is. And I hope it bloody well rains."

"Mummy, you sweared."

"Swore, darling. Yes, I did." I huddled close to Emma, and little Catriona crawled onto my lap. We'd manage as we had before. I'd make sure Annie's boys often stayed. Whenever interstate actors came to Adelaide, we could put them up in the spare bedroom. If Cicely and Robert returned on a year's sabbatical, I'd ask them all to come to us.

And when the Ross parents died, I'd insist on moving to Kenilworth. It was so capacious—Duncan couldn't object if other families stayed with us temporarily. He'd never minded overnight visitors—it was only a permanent concept that he hadn't accepted and hadn't understood. I didn't need permission to do what was right for the kids. Rather than try to change Duncan's ideas, I could simply alter practice. That way, most likely he wouldn't even notice that we had an extended family after all.

Was it that he didn't hear me when I told him Annie's and my plans? Or was it that he didn't like what he heard in the rare times we talked about our future.

"What is a tended family, Mummy?" Emma asked.

"One big enough to include all of us, and one that cares," I replied. "Just like ours."

"Are you still mad at Daddy?"

"No, angel." Annie poked her head inside the tent. "Look, here's Annie come to join us. Make room for the other mother."

"I'm the father," Tim announced.

"No, I am—it doesn't have to be a boy," said Emma firmly.

"Yes it does."

"Not in a tended family it doesn't. We'll all take turns to be fathers and mothers, and Mummy and Annie can be our babies. Here, Mummy, put your head in my lap. Catty, feed her a biscuit. We'll take care of you both if you're quiet and don't swore."

A fastidious woman, Constance Amy had somehow managed to swallow a lifetime of everyday loathings, but not without acute discomfort. Soon after her marriage to Donald, she'd begun to suffer from flatulence. On their travels abroad, she consulted with medical experts in every port, tried every pill and prescription, obeyed all injunctions against garlic and spices, and washed down each morsel with milk, but her indigestion persisted. It sounded a feeble and distressing defense against all that threatened to invade and conquer.

With the Ross bloodline now doubly insured by two little granddaughters, Emma and Catriona, Constance Amy gave way to an inexorable decline.

She gradually retired from sensible speech. Her over-programmed memory began to splutter and misfire. The palate once cajoled by the chef at the Schweizerhof, cosseted at countless captains' tables, soothed at the Savoy, and cursed by a procession of cooks through the Kenilworth kitchen, disdained all but the dribblings of liquids— the juice of an orange, the soft-boiled yoke of an egg, the insipid flotation of arrowroot custard.

She forgot her own name and the date of her birth.

While she still dressed like Queen Mary of Teck and occasionally spoke lucidly of pleasures she missed—like the way her maid at the Connaught Hotel once teased her curls—she would toy with her pearls as if they were worry beads and crush a handkerchief to her lips while her eyes wandered distractedly over objects in a room, as if searching for an anchorage in the eddies of memory.

At first, Donald assumed she missed her trips. Every morning, after breakfast, when the nurse on duty had settled his wife on cushions in the billiard room, he read aloud to her the arrivals and departures in the daily shipping column of *The Advertiser*. Sometimes he turned the page to the vice-regal diary and recited the guest lists for garden levees and banquets, but she'd lost all appetite for society tidbits. Raw statistics no longer captivated her.

I could do nothing right as far as Mr. Ross was concerned.

Maybe it was a mistake to have them come to us for dinner every Sunday. That had been my solution to the hideous family meals at Kenilworth, when Constance Amy was refusing to eat or we'd all be served coddled eggs and Donald would yell at the children if they so much as put their fingers on his glass-fronted cabinets.

"Don't eat fish with bones," Donald grumbled. It was a Sunday in January, when tempers were already frayed by the constant heat.

"It's whiting and I know you like that and I know you can dissect fish like a brain surgeon," I countered in an even tone, "and the children love it," ignoring his petulant glare, "and what's more, Mrs. Ross is actually eating some tonight."

"Father, Mother is eating, aren't you, Mother?" Duncan sounded like a Sunday-school teacher.

"Granny can't talk," Emma chanted, and I shushed her. It was true. Constance Amy rarely spoke unless something inspired her. Now she began to recite the children's names, spelling them back as if she were repeating a telegram message.

"E as in end, M as in middle, N as in needle . . ."

"Fool. M again, not N," Donald interrupted, so that Constance Amy instantly froze and stared into space.

I tried to save her further embarrassment. "Did I tell you the fun and games we're having with the City Council, Duncan dear? Catriona, don't climb down yet, darling, you haven't finished. Yes, the town clerk slapped a contempt notice on the theatre company to try to stop us from performing at the State Theatre site. Something about building hazards and hard-hat zones."

"Fools taking on the town clerk," said Donald.

"He's only a killjoy. We're performing in the lunch hour for the Council's own builders, so no one will be working except the actors. I don't see any hazard in that. Catriona! Not yet!"

"Waste of time. Workers don't need plays."

"Nonsense." I ignored the look Duncan shot me. Why should I always have to give in? "I believe in Art for the Masses, with capitals. And we're all wearing hard hats, so it's fabulous free publicity. May even make the front page."

"A for art . . ."

"Flummery! Art, acting, self-advertisement, working-class twaddle—should have done what I said in the first place," Donald was red-faced. "Told you to choose a proper hobby—Spastics, Red Cross—something useful with a good financial record. Voluntary. Didn't I? Like Mother here. Do some good for a change instead of your arty extravagance."

"Morgan, don't you think the children have had enough?" Duncan quickly turned to me. Catriona had put her sticky fingers on Constance Amy's arm and they were beaming at each other.

"Florence Nightingale. That's who you should try to be. If you must do something, study her, be like her. Useful." Donald put his claret glass to Emma's lips.

"Grandad, stop! We don't let the children drink wine. And I'm not studying nursing. I'm an actress trying to revive Australian plays. Duncan, darling, lift Catriona down, please."

"Frogs feed babies wine. None the worse off. Next thing, you'll vote Communist."

I flushed bright pink. "As a matter of fact—" But Duncan grabbed Catriona from the high chair and stood up.

"Darling, time to clear the table. Emma, take Grandma off to the den and show her where to sit. Here, Morgan, please, have Catriona while I pack the dishes," he implored, and put Catriona on my lap. "Father, what do you want to do next?"

"Pudding. Isn't there a pudding?"

"No, fresh fruit. We'll have it in the den when I've bathed the girls." Suddenly I felt faint. "Duncan, I need to sit for a moment."

"What's up? Swallowed a bone?" Mr. Ross said sharply.

"No. I get tired, especially at the end of the day. I'm pregnant again."

"Not another girl, I hope," Donald spluttered.

"Father, that's unnecessary. We'd be very happy with three daughters, wouldn't we, Morgan—are you alright, dear?"

I nodded. I knew the word *pregnant* made Donald nauseous. He was looking at me as if I'd just stripped naked in front of a hundred construction workers. What was his word for it? *With child? In the family way?* He began to say, "Don't know when to stop, as bad as the tykes," but I left the room with Catriona to collect Emma from a mountain of jigsaw puzzles strewn all over the den floor. They'd just have to step around the pieces.

I ran the children's bath and knelt on the tiles to wash their backs. Family way! What a farce, an exhausting soap opera.

"What's wrong with Grandma, Mummy?" Emma poured water from a plastic bottle onto Catriona's hair. "She called me Anna just then."

"She's forgetful, darling, because her brain has to chug

uphill. She's like the Little Red Engine, going slower and slower, and sometimes it's too much of an effort for her. She runs short of steam and begins to forget things."

"When she dies, will she burn up like engine smoke? Pfff!" Emma blew a bubble in my face. "Do you like that, Mummy?"

"Not much. No, Grandma will slow down until one day she'll fall asleep and not wake up, and that will be dying."

"When Grandad dies, he'll make a big bang."

"Why do you think so?"

"Because he goes bang crash and makes cross noises. I don't like Grandad. Do you, Mummy? Are you crying, Mummy?"

"Not as much as I love you, silly sweetheart, and it's bedtime and I'm fine. Just fine. Come—out of the bath, into pajamas, a kiss for Daddy, and off to bed for a story." I wrapped them in fluffy towels.

Emma waggled a finger free. "And a kiss for Grandma. Toot toot, puff puff; let's be little red engines, Catty! I'll puff like Grandma and you can go bang bang like Grandad, and Mummy, you have to hold on behind us and be all the people in the train. Then will you read us *The Little Red Engine* again? Please, Mummy!"

Perhaps it was his own deteriorating health that hastened hers. Donald at first fought their decline with bursts of energy. When it dawned on him that she was neither bored nor merely forgetful but possibly, irreversibly, senile, he decided the time had come to put the record of his life in order. First, he began the tedious process of cataloguing overflowing crates of photographs and colored slides accumulated from seventeen overseas tours, a task made bearable by rediscoveries of forgotten and forbidden treats: bare breasts on the beach at Nice shot with a long-distance lens from his hotel balcony; a hot Rabelaisian scene in the window opposite his in a medieval Italian street; Angus McBain with a dead brace of pheasant.

The daily appearance of attractive young nurses traipsing through Kenilworth's gardens encouraged his mordant curiosity in matters of flesh and dress. Taken by surprise at the appearance of the miniskirt, he patted bottoms and tweaked hems from behind hidden corners of the shrubbery. The rate at which nurses gave shocked notice precipitated Donald's sacking of the loyal old staff. Cook, whom he accused of crowing when the moon was full, was fired for buying fruit that was out of season. The seamstress left in tears. A junior partner in Donald's legal advisory firm, an ambitious young man, was dismissed for proposing a merger of thirty Ross family companies into three to streamline operations and consolidate taxes. If that seemed at all harsh, Donald overreached when, with a spiteful stroke of his pen, he obliterated Duncan from the codicil to the will. Duncan only reinstated himself by reminding his father that disinheritance would benefit the Labor government treasury.

When later it was revealed that I'd marched in the Moratorium against the war in Vietnam, I, too, was removed from the Trusts and all references to Duncan's Spouse were deleted from the will. That decision held. Only our two little girls and McPhee seemed sure of tenure. In fact, it was McPhee who leaked my rebellious politics to Donald.

McPhee had never really approved of Duncan's marriage to me, and Donald's dependency on his aging gardener was too ingrained for him to imagine a Kenilworth without a McPhee. To Donald, my acts of socialist lunacy were as nothing compared with the nightmare of Kenilworth run to seed. A Culloden field of warring neighbors, with no head gardener to defend it, haunted Donald more than Gough Whitlam's Labor victories. "Over my dead body, over my bones," he repeated to himself, sunk in his leather armchair. His hair was dropping out in tufts, his shoulders were humped, and his ulcer renewed its vituperatory raids.

All that a Ross held dear was under siege. Bent double, his eyes like arrow slits, Donald took aim at historical enemies. He ranted against the four great global evils— Communism, Catholicism, Socialism, and Emancipation. He cursed the Pope for blessing multiple births. He cursed the Duke of Windsor's exile for causing pieces of Empire to abdicate. He cursed the Irish for planting Catholic convicts on colonial Australian soil. "Sacks of bad potatoes," he muttered into his Scotch.

Nearer to home and hearth, his aim was more predictible. He cursed the birds that escaped from the orchard shooting range. He cursed me for taking his name and his son. The Ross family had become a lemon, squeezed out of season, and because Constance Amy shrivelled first, Donald cursed her most of all.

She made one bid to escape. She ran off in the middle of the night. A motorist cornered her and left her at the police station where the officer on watch fossicked for an identification in the relics of her mind.

The shame was too public for Donald. He erected a high stockade around Kenilworth at a distance from the outer walls of four feet. The fortress in its ivy shroud had one gate for deliveries, and Donald kept an eye on comings and goings from his bunker in the billiard room. By the time our third daughter, Holly, was born, Constance Amy had been locked unkindly in.

I was so busy organizing preschool activities for Catriona and rushing to and from Emma's kindergarten in the gaps between Holly's four-hourly feeds that I knew little of what was happening in Duncan's life other than enormous pressures at work and demands on his highest skill as a designer.

Duncan told me his father was making all kinds of trouble for him over a mortgage he held on the Shed. He'd raised by an exorbitant amount the interest on a family loan Duncan had taken out for factory extensions.

Ivan assured me it wasn't a serious problem, more an irritant, a rather expensive adjustment which the Shed would gradually absorb, but Duncan continually complained that money was tight and we ought to rein in.

I could almost feel jealous of Annie. After Edwin's birth, she'd said two was her limit and promptly had her tubes tied. Now she had a full-time research scholarship in psychology. Since Tim was in Emma's kindergarten, and Edwin had enrolled in Catriona's play group, and I was grounded with the new baby, it made sense for me to take care of all five children while Annie worked on her rat experiments. At least, that way, I got to see her at the end of each day when she came to fetch the boys.

"Duncan's late tonight," I sighed to Annie. "He's going through a morose phase."

"Catriona, Eddie, help me stack the Lego bricks away." Annie knelt at the foot of my rocking chair to tidy the toys. "It's probably postpartum depression."

"Really? I thought only mothers got that." I smiled down at Holly's rapturous expression as she suckled my breast, oblivious to the bustle going on about her. "Not all mothers. I didn't."

"That's because you're never post. For the past five years, you've been either breeding or feeding, a contented cow. I must be more selfish than you; I'm so happy to be at my own work again. Don't you miss acting—the footlights, action, applause—your glamorous career?"

"Not its crazy hours, the roller-coaster schedules." I propped Holly against my shoulder and rhythmically stroked her back, feeling the transparent skin, the heartbeat next to mine. "It never paid much, but I miss not having my own income. It worries me that I'm doing nothing to contribute to the growing pile of bills." I settled Holly onto my other side. "It's funny you should mention my going back to work. Duncan did, too, quite recently. As if I hadn't enough to do!"

"Perhaps he feels jealous, shut out by the darling daughters, one, two, three."

"He couldn't, Annie. I have much more time for him now than when I was working, if only he'd take notice and enjoy me. I'm the neglected one." I lowered my voice. "It's—we're not getting on very well together. That is, the few times we *are* together. If I were working, it would only make matters worse. Catriona, Eddie—hop outside to the sandpit, please. We'll call when Annie is ready to leave."

"Duncan always approved of your work, Morgan dear."

I waited until the children had gone. "He approves of my independence—financially, not necessarily creatively— but if I were to return to the stage, assuming that I could, both Duncan and the children would lose some of that creativity, that energy which is there for them. No, I'm not ready to go back. The kids need me. Duncan needs me, too, dammit. I wish he'd show it more."

"You should take a holiday together—Bali, Tahiti, some faraway romantic place. You haven't been away since your honeymoon. You need to give each other some private time."

"He can't take time. He's far too busy. I can't leave the kids, especially while I'm feeding."

"Stop erecting obstacles, Morgan. I'll look after the kids, and Holly will survive a weekend on bottled milk. Why don't you persuade him? Why not try?"

Holly had finished and was ready for sleep, and I had to run the children's bath. Duncan should be home soon. A holiday was a lovely thought, but it could wait. Annie followed me into the kitchen.

"Morgan, please take my advice. Stick in there, sweet-heart—you'll make it work. What you need is a change of scene to change some old bad habits: his Ross retreats, your Evans-style anxiety."

I wanted him to touch me. I wanted to come out and reach him, his mind as well as his body, more than halfway.

Every night, since the rift with his father when I was struck from the Ross family, I'd tried to face reality,

—159—

whatever that was, sure only that reality was hard and silent. I kept hoping that if Duncan were to make love to me we might begin to talk together. As each night passed, and he did not, I imagined that I should resist him if he did turn to me, kiss me, move his hand along my thigh and stir me. Every night, when we were in bed together, I wanted him to desire me so that I could resist, until, to possess me entirely, he would have to want me irresistibly.

In daylight, I knew defeat. Sometimes, when I watched him in the early morning, I thought I hated him. Sometimes, especially in the night, I thought my memory of how we'd loved might burrow through the dark, private corridors of indifference and reach him.

I had chosen this beach. In part, because Victor Harbor was only a two-hour drive from the children who had gone to Annie's for the weekend; in part, because of the light—the clear, honest glance of sunlight on the shallow bay. I had rented a house under the brow of the Bluff, a bald round knob of rock that shut off one end of the bay where sheltered water spilled and toiled into the open sea.

Before our dinner, I'd walked up a winding, narrow path to the top to watch the sun set behind the many small islands in Encounter Bay. The water was very still. I could make out the line of the reef by a black braid of seaweed and a shimmer where the outgoing tide crossed the last row of underwater rocks. Duncan had stayed on the veranda with his pipe and newspaper.

He wasn't there when I returned. He was not in the house. I broiled two loin of lamb chops for him, and a small crayfish for myself that I'd bought down at the jetty under the Bluff, where fishermen bring in the pots at twilight and again at dawn. Duncan disliked intensely the smell of shellfish.

I ate quickly and wrapped the bright red claws and shell in the back pages of his newspaper. Later, I watched him eat. I asked if it was good, and stood nearby until he told me to sit down.

"I feel restless," I said.

"You should take another walk." He chewed on the bones, holding them in both hands, and sucked his fingers.

"I want to talk," I said.

"What about?"

"Us."

He didn't look up but pushed his wicker chair back, carried his plate to the sink, and went out by the back door. The wire screen echoed his footsteps, slap, flap, slap, like a wave slammed against rock.

Early the following morning, he coughed and stirred. I propped myself on my elbow and turned him to face me. His lips were dry. His eyes were smeared with sleep.

"We're living in a vacuum. There's a trough between us. It's intolerable to go on this way."

"Simpler to go on than to try to change anything," he muttered.

"I have changed, don't you see? It's not at all simple for me to try to explain this to you. Between us, in this pit of silence, you seem to refuse to imagine what we might become, or to admit what we are. I suppose I've tried to hope for change, I don't know what, or why, but I feel unbearably lonely."

He said nothing. I felt I must continue. "Perhaps it will be best if I leave you. I don't know what it is I need, so I can't say that you fail to meet my need, but you're never near enough for me to see if what I need concerns you or might be your concern."

He laughed then, a gruff laugh. "Morgan, you don't expect me to understand that gobbledygook, do you? You don't know what you mean, so how am I supposed to know?"

"We should try to talk together." There was an inter-mittent flash from the lighthouse at the base of the Bluff, like a chink of morning light beneath a door that might be opened.

"What about? I can't see what the matter is." He shut his eyes, but I jolted his shoulder impatiently.

"Don't go back to sleep. How can you be happy? We never make love, not since Holly was born. We don't do things together like other couples do. If we talk at all, it's limited to daily domesticity, to the children, your work, your father. There's no . . ." I searched for the right word, "no spontaneity, no possibility of something new, something unexpected that we haven't known about beforehand."

"I think . . ." he cupped his hand over a yawn. "I think you expect too much. If you could be satisfied with how things are, you'd be much happier. You're too idealistic, that's your trouble. What have you planned for us to do today? See? I do like to know beforehand."

He swung his legs out of the bed and looked around for a robe. I examined his naked body, the legs dangling over the bedside, his toes touching the mat. He'd begun to thicken at the waist. The skin near his nipples, feathered with fine blond hairs, was soft, spongy, like a chicken. When he stood up, his penis hung limply between his legs, its foreskin folded back like a plucked pink drumstick. He grinned self-consciously.

"Well?"

I stood up, too. Then his eyes roved down my body, and for a moment he looked greedy again, not with desire but with satisfaction to see everything in its place and in the scheme of things.

"I want to leave this marriage. I have to." I formed each word distinctly, like a signal sent across a no-man's-land toward certain hazards. "I'm not asking you to leave. I wouldn't give up if I thought you'd struggle with me, if you'd see the challenge, if you felt anything. Since you won't stand up to it, it's over. Isn't it?" I held out my hands, the palms open.

He answered slowly. "If you leave me, there's no point in going on. I have no intention of changing anything. If you go," he said point-blank, "I'll kill myself."

I sat rigidly on the bed while he took a shower.

I thought of the children. I couldn't do it. Rather than

imagine him capable of destroying himself, I imagined only the massive tidal destruction my leaving him would wreck upon the children.

We went on separate walks until late afternoon when we could leave for home. He drove. He chose the coast road first, but unexpectedly detoured onto a narrow dirt track that wound into the steep hills of Rapid Bay. He slammed the gearstick down to accelerate through the upgrade. He avoided using the brakes and throttled back downhill again, the engine screaming in revolt. The rear tires spun on loose gravel around corners. The cockpit shook, but he clenched the wheel fiercely and steered ever more tightly into the curves.

Once I would have found the ride exhilarating. Now I felt curiously unafraid. He wouldn't choose this way. He was too clever, too experienced a driver. I looked out the window so that he couldn't see my face. The noise of the engine saved us both from the humiliating obligation to speak.

When he stopped at Annie's gate, he left the engine running. I opened my door and turned to him. "What can we possibly do now?"

He shook his head. "Pull yourself together. There's Annie at the door, with Holly. I'll wait out here."

Holly held out her arms for me and I buried my face against her. Baby, I breathed; I'll never abandon you.

Annie crooked a protective arm around us. "What is it, sweetheart? Here, tell old Annie. What did that beast just say to upset you—something unthinking, something cruel?"

"He doesn't love me, Annie," I said. "He doesn't want me."

"Of course he does. He doesn't know how to show it, that's all. Remember, he was an emotionally deprived child. He'll learn, dearest, just from being with you. Try to be patient; give it time. So what if the weekend didn't quite work as you wanted . . ."

"I wanted to leave him, Annie. He won't let me go."

"There—that proves it, doesn't it! Let's have none of this talk about quitting—remember the magic circle—you and Duncan, Ivan and me. We'll all try harder to make the magic work because it's to everyone's benefit. Since Ivan has started the barbecue, let's eat and rally around and plan for a happier future. Go ahead—I'll fetch the grump from his cage. He won't bite an old friend like me, will he? See, you're smiling again."

It was Duncan's fortieth birthday. He'd come home early to open his presents: a new pipe and a posy of orange blossoms for his bedside picked from our trees by Emma; a dozen mysteries from me; a triumphant hug from Holly after the miracle of her first solo steps to greet him and grab his hand; his favorite cake planned by Catriona—a chocolate sponge filled with caramel cream and iced with forty forget-me-nots inside the shape of a star.

We'd made a birthday card for him. On our way home from shopping, I had swerved to avoid a dog on the road and Catriona was flung against the basket. The cake, unpacked, had collapsed under the imprint of her elbow, plum in the middle of the star. To console her, I drew a picture of the squashed cake which she colored in and surrounded with XXX's and OOO's and curlicue D's. Duncan hugged her when he saw it. He cut the cake very carefully to make sure he served himself the hollow center, insisting to a round-eyed Catriona that it was the most delicious slice of all.

I was washing up after dinner when I heard shrieks from the bathroom. I ran to open the door and met my whole family in the bath together. They were up to their ears in bright red bubbles.

"What was that yell for? Your tents are surrounded, I've got you covered. Don't move, or I'll shoot without mercy. How in heaven's name did you make those blood bubbles?"

"Catriona threw the entire contents of a tin of finger-paint powder in my bath," Duncan began, while Emma and Catriona yelped with delight, and Holly, who sat in his lap, churned whirlpools with her hands and feet.

Emma stood up in a froth of bubbles that quickly burst and dripped red dye down her short brown legs. I collapsed on the tiled floor, splitting with laughter.

"Mummy, we came in your bathroom to spy on Daddy, and Catty tipped the paint on him and he went red everywhere, so he put us all in the bath. Isn't it funny?"

Then Duncan stood up with Holly, a great goose with its gosling, both covered in red feathers. The bubbles began to slide off his shoulders. At any moment there'd be an avalanche.

"Oh Great Earth Mother," Duncan said with a giggle, "behold your children with Great Father Duncan." The bubbles were now in a slippery belt around his waist. His skin at neck and breast was streaked a lurid red. "See, little creatures, how the big Earth Mother laughs to hear your story!"

With a rush and a slither, the last attached bubbles finally slid straight down his legs and subsided into the bath water. "Yes, darlings, it's really very funny." I felt aroused, unable to take my eyes off Duncan. "So funny, I'm tempted to anoint myself in your river-red bath. Does this ritual permit a sibyl among satyrs and spies?" Duncan's eyes twinkled brightly. "Can I hop in and get red with you?" Emma and Catriona nodded excitedly.

"There were five in the boat and the middle one said, 'Roll over, roll over,'" I sang, and they all joined in, each taking turns to climb out of the bath, until the floor was awash and only Duncan and I were left in the water. When I stood up to crown him the last survivor, I saw that Duncan was aroused as well.

"Father Duncan, I will grant your reward." I kissed him on the lips. The girls clapped hands and sang "Happy Birthday" again until Duncan hustled them off to bed.

I turned down the bedspread and waited impatiently for him to join me, thinking fiercely of his long limbs streaming with bubbles, the feel of his skin against mine as we splashed in the lukewarm water, and the childlike laughter in his eyes when he smiled at me.

"That was fun, wasn't it—Mmm, your skin smells like a peach," he said, sliding in next to me.

"Or a rosy dawn," I tumbled on top of him, "to celebrate your new year and my birthday gift to you. Guess what it is."

"Show me," he smiled.

I licked the palm of his hand, softened from the bath. "It's a midsummer night's dream." I kissed his lips lightly.

"What do you mean? Summer's nearly over."

"Hush! We're going to play tonight. Close your eyes. First, I am anointing you . . ." I kissed his eyelids . . . "with nodding violet and eglantine . . ." I kissed both his ears . . . "and here are oxlips and luscious woodbine . . ." kissing the dimpled hollow under his throat . . . "to pluck for your delight." I paused.

"Go on." His eyes were tightly shut like the children's when I sang them to sleep, and the muscles of his face quivered in expectation.

"I shall wander everywhere, swifter than the moon's sphere . . . seek dewdrops here . . . hang pearls there . . . Do you like this game? Are you enchanted?"

"It feels wonderful—don't stop."

"Remember how the play proceeds, my darling—the juice of love-in-idleness that makes you dote on the first living creature that you see. Come, you've been idle long enough. Are you going to open your eyes and play your part with me?"

"If I remember rightly, this play goes out of control and takes a nasty turn. Doesn't Bottom make an ass of himself?"

"Don't prevaricate! Besides, I'm Puck tonight, and you're the mighty Oberon, and I have you in my power. Look at me."

I sat astride him and gazed into his eyes, wanting to remember the exact lines. Then I sang:

" 'Jack shall have Jill; nought shall go ill;
The man shall have . . .' "
But he was kissing me with abandon, and I fell forward
onto him, thinking all was well again, and very well.

Ironically, the midsummer revival of passion between us
did take an unexpected turn.

Faced with an urgent deadline of his own, Duncan
said it was unfortunate and badly timed and retreated to
his blueprints, but Annie called it an act of utter lunacy
when I told them, for the fourth time, I was pregnant.

Secretly, I hoped it was a son—not because there was
any exceptional magic to a son, but because I wanted my
girls to grow up coeducationally, as I had not; to know
men—boys—realistically, as ordinary brothers and friends,
before they knew them romantically—as, I reminded a
skeptical Annie, I had not.

A son, I reasoned when alone with myself, would
surely please Donald Ross. A son might bring Duncan
closer to his father. A son could be the means of reconciliation between Mr. Ross and me.

Duncan disagreed when I suggested he should inform
his parents immediately, since I was no longer welcome
at Kenilworth.

"I'd rather leave that until after the birth." He shrugged.
"Father refuses to see me, too, until the Shed repays his
loan, and since Mother no longer understands the simplest
conversation, I can't see the point."

I tried not to feel disappointed. What counted, after
all, was my relationship with Duncan. Although I knew it
was foolish to invest this love-child, born of reunion, with
magical powers, I wanted to believe that our marriage was
alive again, to the possibility of growth.

Constance Amy lingered on but never knew our Nicholas
had been born. She died the night I was locked inside the
archives.

I had just turned thirty, and had a crazy feeling that came with the end of producing children that I was running out of time.

At the start of the seventies, a new generation of Australian artists had surfaced under Gough Whitlam's Labor leadership, with a new spirit of activism and national pride. Old imitative, second-hand ways of doing art had begun to recede with the shades of British influence as we made both a new and radical art, and explored our colonial past. It was a fine time to be Australian, and I wanted to be a part of it. When a producer from my former acting days offered me a small annual grant to research historical plays, I accepted eagerly. It was a perfect job: I'd find suitable materials; the resident playwright would adapt and shape them for the stage; I could fit the work to my own and the children's schedules, and help pay Duncan's bills.

I'd gone to read newspapers in the public library and was partway through the 1880s. The archivist soon wearied of bringing the heavy bound volumes one by one to my desk and invited me to descend to the vaults and help myself.

I'd found the plots and cast lists for *Queen Venus* and *Our Village,* but reviews looked unflattering: "an inscrutable mystery and an insoluble enigma." I began to make notes on two more local satires by Marcus Clarke, *The Happy Land* and *Forbidden Fruit,* when my eye caught a headline in the Melbourne *Argus* on page five, column three, July 26, 1880: MURDER IN MEYERBEER'S LES HUGUENOTS AT THEATRE ROYAL.

I perched on a stepladder to read the article.

Mr. Greer shot his wife at close range, together with M. Soudray, a member of the French Committee attending the opening of the Melbourne International Exhibition, during the intermission before Act IV of Meyerbeer's Grand Opera. Mr. Greer then fatally shot himself. A member of the audience received a glancing wound to his right temple but had not required medical attention.

I sped through bulletins for July and August written by an *Argus* reporter whose observation post was the entrance to the Royal Melbourne Hospital. Soudray recovered rapidly. The bullet, fired at four feet, had entered his left cheek and exited at his right ear. A clean trajectory. He was discharged from hospital after being refused permission to visit Mrs. Greer.

I searched anxiously for news of Mrs. Greer. The first bullet fired had entered her head behind the left ear and come to rest on her tongue. Her condition was serious.

I clambered down to find back numbers. There she was, among the May arrivals on board the *S. S. Garonne:* Annice, a French-born actress, wife of John James MacGregor Greer of Ireland. Other passengers? I ran my finger down the list. There—the French contingent: M. Kowalski, composer; M. Commettant, of *Le Figaro;* M. Soudray, playwright.

Forward again to August 1880.

In the course of their seven-month voyage, Annice Greer had fallen in love with Soudray. On arrival at Port Melbourne, Greer left on horseback to visit the Ballarat goldfields. While he was gone, Soudray and Annice resumed their clandestine affair. But one evening, Greer returned home unannounced and discovered them together at his rented rooms in Carlton.

Greer was in a quandary. He must leave at once to clinch a land deal. So he hired a solicitor, Otto Berliner, and a housekeeper to keep Mrs. Greer under lock and key until he himself could bring her before doctors to commit her to the Kew Asylum.

The housekeeper, lacking orders to the contrary, continued to mail letters every day from Annice Greer to Louis Soudray.

Greer acquired his land and eagerly returned to Carlton. Berliner proposed that they celebrate his new status as landed gentry by attending the first night of the Exhibition Opera together with Mrs. Greer. He was, he admitted, concerned about her health. She'd not been in fresh air for a month or more. A last outing? Before the doctors . . . it couldn't hurt. Greer reluctantly agreed.

I blinked rapidly; my eyes smarted from reading the fine worn print. What a marvellous period plot it would make: a melodrama called *Murdering Meyerbeer*—better than *Forbidden Fruit* or *Queen Venus*.

I could see myself as Annice. Gold fever; Melbourne swarming with international visitors; the colony rich and alive after the shackles of convict settlement have been cast away; our first major dramatist, Marcus Clarke, writing comedies for his wife Marian to act on the stage of the Theatre Royal; the first time Australians feel national pride, a national identity . . .

Identity! Ever since I began this search, I'd sensed I'd find a key to unlock myself—who I was, where I'd come from. If I could understand Australia . . . was that a way to understand myself? Wife and mother; head girl and hockey; bush nurse; actress; Annie Goodall; Duncan—my former roles hadn't made much sense lately—it was all wife and mother now, no time to be myself, whatever that was. It wasn't enough to be another Mrs. Ross. Of that I was sure. But what?

How long—I rested my elbows on the volume—how long had they been married? A year? More? No children? She'd been an actress like me. Did she give up her career? How had they met, and why had they married? . . . John James MacGregor Greer . . . I wonder, did she call him John or James?

They'd taken their seats in a plush red velvet box. Greer seemed restless and paid closer attention to the audience than to the opera. Shortly before the interval, Otto Berliner understood why. He, too, glimpsed Soudray seated among the French delegation. Then Soudray rose, bowed, and began to approach their box. Onstage, the tenor, Paladini, was having great difficulty reaching his top notes. Soudray reached the edge of the box and whispered something to Annice Greer.

At the precise moment that the opera's Comte de Saint

Bris aimed his muzzle at the young lovers Valentine and Raoul, shots rang out in the auditorium. Actors fell down in practiced massacre, but members of the audience stood, some pointing to the box, others rushing the exits, trampling women underfoot. Soudray was slumped over the velvet balustrade. Mrs. Greer was seen to swoon as blood spread across the bodice of her gown.

There was another wild round of shots. A bullet ricocheted, and someone in the audience fell. A stray bullet shattered a mirror on the set. Then Greer shot himself in the right temple. The house gaslights went up. The wounded were laid onstage for medical attention until someone shouted that horse-drawn ambulances had arrived.

When the last act eventually proceeded, some forty minutes later, there was another stampede when more gunshots sounded—this time according to the plot. The management hurriedly brought the curtain down in the middle of the concerted finale.

Greer's body lay in the city morgue, deluged under flowers sent by sympathizers. A capacity sermon was preached by the Reverend Dr. Gilchrist on the text, "Be sure that your sin will find you out." Police guarded Mrs. Greer's hospital bed.

As the opera season continued, news of the lovers dwindled. Soudray had gone into hiding after his discharge. Berliner wrote a letter to the editor in which he described Greer as a violent and disturbed man whom Annice had tried, repeatedly, to leave. His letter was followed by a spate of affronted citizen complaints: against the Theatre Royal management; against free immigration; and against the behavior of some men in the audience that night who bolted for their lives, hid under seats, or scampered under ladies' petticoats. "What woman now would like to trust the safety of her life to one of that crowd who cowered in fear and trembling from the first appearance of danger?" asked "a Melbourne Girl" on the thirtieth of July. "Matrimony itself must surely decline."

The final *Argus* entry was elusive. An anonymous observer reputedly saw Annice, enveloped in a heavy gray cloak and accompanied by a tall, unidentified woman who was also disguised under a hooded cape, climb the gangway to a ship bound for California. Two unnamed "gentle-women" were listed among the passengers. Had Berliner helped her escape? With Soudray? There was nothing more.

I'd lost all sense of time. I realized I was absolutely starving. I called out for the archivist, then saw that the clock showed eleven. Nobody was about. Saturday night—the archive would be closed until Monday morning. The children would have missed dinner. Had Duncan listened when I told him where I'd be all afternoon?

A door led to the upstairs reading room. That was locked. I lit a cigarette under the smoke detector, but the alarm didn't sound. I found a telephone on the wall behind 1890. I called home. No answer. I waited five minutes and called again. Still nothing. Had they gone for pizza? Were they organizing a search posse for me? With mounting desperation, I tried again.

This time, Duncan picked up the receiver.

"Help!" I laughed with relief. "I'm a prisoner of the archives, lost to history. I want to be rescued."

He sounded vague. Constance Amy was dead. A night nurse had found her lying beneath her bedroom window. At first they thought she'd been strangled by the curtain cord. No, Father was sure it was accidental. One end of the cord was tied to the bell pull. Had she tried to summon help? Had anybody heard her call? The window was open—had she tried to climb out, then, and fallen?

I sat on the top step of the ladder. Tears ran down my arm and along the curly telephone cord. Had Constance Amy tried once more to escape? I might never know; so many questions might never be answered. Were they best left unasked, the search better abandoned?

In a blur of tears, I imagined I saw a ghostly Annice Greer coming through the stacks of books toward the locked door behind me. She was leaning heavily on the veiled gray figure of my mother-in-law.

"Oh Duncan, it has been such a terrible waste. There *is* no key. I have to get out of here. Please come and take me home."

Ivan, one of the pallbearers, told Annie and me that after Constance Amy died of a choking fit, Donald had the fortress fence removed to take her coffin out, so narrow was the chink, so sturdy the bolt, so tight the passageway she'd tried to struggle through.

CHAPTER SEVEN

I was afraid on the cliff path that led down to the beach at Port Willunga. I hated dry heat and the hiking bag on my back was heavy with towels and apples, my book, a thermos, the beach toys. I carried a furled beach umbrella in my free hand. The two older girls had chosen to spend that week in Adelaide with Tim and Edwin Goodall in Annie's communal house, but Nicky, who was two years old, rode my left hip, and Holly, nearly three and a half, trailed behind me with a bucket and spade. She was grizzling because I made her wear sandals and pebbles had caught under the crisscross straps. It was too hot for bare feet on gravel.

Annie had built a summer cottage there, on the clifftop overlooking the sea, but since she'd opened a psychology clinic, she rarely had time to use it. I often took my children down in the summer months. It wasn't far from the city; sometimes Duncan drove down for a night, or Annie took a week off work to bring her two boys. Mostly the children and I were alone.

Sheer clay cliffs rose on my left, but on the right the soft shell broke into a crust that crumbled two hundred feet down to the beach below.

"Holly, stay right behind me and don't go near the edge."

The path was very narrow there, about three feet wide where the last slide fell.

Roger had told me about it. Roger lived in the converted lighthouse. He found them first. There'd been unusually heavy summer rains last year. The cliff above me had swollen and sagged until it began to burst. It had slopped over the path where we were now standing, gathered rocks and debris, and tumbled mightily down to the beach. Three people were sunbaking in the shadow of the cliff. Roger dug them out. He said they were pressed as thin and as white as parchment. Roger said the cliff could go again any time. He had old photographs on his walls of coastal shipwrecks and the horse-drawn railway that used to come down the same path with wheat and wool for the cutters that traded along the coastal ports. All that was left of the original jetty now were some charred black piles and crusty planks.

I was too afraid to look down. I grasped the boy on my hip and used the umbrella as a staff. I turned to watch Holly dawdle and urged her not to look over the edge.

It was a relief to reach the cobbled steps to the beach itself. I tethered the beachbag to a post and twirled the umbrella on its shaft until it set firmly in the sand. It billowed above our heads like a bright orange sun. The children tumbled into the shallows and giggled at their toes burrowing into the wet sand. I buried the thermos to keep the juice cool. I opened my paperback with one eye on the children.

"Holly, share that bucket. Keep your sunhats on. Not too far, Nicholas. Yes, it is very hot." I read and watched and waited.

At last I spotted her coming around the next headland. She was alone. She wore her heavy cream Mexican poncho. On a day like this, I smiled. "You look like a missionary in some foreign desert in the wrong clothes," I called to her. "Parasol, gloves, long skirt, wide raffia hat, and Bible."

She laughed. She was carrying a book and her hair was braided in a thick knot behind her ears. We greeted each other shyly. We had met a month before when she joined the theatre company as our trainee playwright. She, too, had rented a summer shack around the point.

Dan Murphy, her husband, was in London with their boy, and her daughter was away with school friends. How lucky she is, I thought, to be alone like that, with her writing.

The children had crawled into one of the caves that fishermen carved deep in the cliff decades ago to shelter their boats and nets. Now they were shrinking slowly because the cliff was contracting. They stank of fish and seagull droppings and scraps of rotten picnic food. I scrambled over the counter to pull the children out. I carried Nicky under my arm to the rocks and shells where the water was shallow.

I asked Jenny to read to me. It was a draft of her new play with a setting of roses and still waters and the sounds of nature. While she read, I gazed out over the children's heads to the sparkling sea. Sometimes I stole a look at her profile.

"Now it's your turn to read," she said.

I read from Brecht until she shuddered and said he was too intense for her. We both looked out to sea. I asked about Dan, a ceramic artist at the School of Visual Arts. The Murphys had come from London. I said I thought Dan's work was stained with sea colors but it wasn't like this sea—creamy, murky—rather than our brilliant Pacific blue. She nodded. We were silent. She shaded her eyes with her hand.

"I want to leave him," she said, "but I'm afraid. I have no money anyway. He wants the two children. He is treacherous, like the sea."

While she talked, she broke pita bread and filled the pockets with falafel and a silky sesame dressing. I called Holly and Nicky to come and eat. I watched her hands fold and unfold like gentle waves. She talked about raising two babies alone in London. Her voice sounded flat and her hands trembled absently.

"Why are you afraid?" I asked.

"I have never felt anything with him," she said. "I have smiled and worn a clean apron and cooked unusual meals.

I have learned to walk as if I were floating. I let my hair grow long. Dan likes it that way. He admires the Japanese and the way they care for natural things. I have also learned to cast down my eyes and to lie with him naked but I have never felt anything. Two babies came screaming from my body yet I felt nothing. Dan whispers in my ear at night and sweeps his fingers along my thighs and makes love to me, and still I feel nothing."

I was watching the children while she spoke. They were building huts of sand and thatching them with seaweed but the tide was turning and washed the walls away. They began all over again.

Jenny let down her hair. She swept shells into a mound in front of her. Then she chose a flat stone and began to break them into fragments. I didn't hear all of her quiet words. I was thinking about myself and feeling the sun spread over my shoulders.

"One night," she was saying, "Dan said it was time for a change. He has always had other lovers, women he invites to come and live with us. They become my friends. This one, Alison, is a musician. Dan planned something altogether new. He told me that Alison would sleep with us. We undressed. I covered myself with the sheet and Alison lay beside me. But Dan was puzzled. We were soon oblivious to him. We began to make love and he couldn't take part. For a while he said he was very excited—oh, this is wonderful, this is new, this is a real turn-on—but neither of us noticed him. Then I found I was crying. I felt something. I felt things I had never felt."

She turned to face me. "Now I want to leave him but it will be very hard for me. I am still afraid."

I said I would be afraid, too. Maybe she should find another job that made more money. That's what I'd have to do, I said.

"I am not sure I want the kids," she said.

"I'd be afraid of losing mine," I said.

"There are other fears," she said.

We stared at the turning tide. Shadows had lengthened down the cliff and were moving on the water. Jenny tugged at the neck of her poncho and said she was far too hot and must go.

We loaded the sunclothes into my bag and she helped me buckle Holly's sandals. We arranged to have dinner before rehearsals resumed at the end of the summer. I waved good-bye. I told the children we should go the long way home. We hurried past the spot where the cliff fell, where sand sprayed down, and made for the low road behind the lighthouse.

I had dinner at Jenny's home. Alison was there but Dan was away. Jenny told me they were going to a meeting later that evening. Some women had approached her to form a playwriting group at the new Women's Center. I'd never heard of it. I said that I would like to go with them.

Jenny served steamed fish with brown rice and beansprouts. I sightread the piano part for Alison's flute sonata and Jenny left the dishes in the sink to come to the doorway to listen. When I began a three-part invention by Johann Sebastian Bach, Jenny asked me to stop.

"The sound enters my head," she said, "and won't flow out again. It makes me feel claustrophobic."

It was time for the meeting anyway.

There were more women than I'd expected. We divided into two groups and Jenny and Alison went to another room. My group only wanted to talk about sex. Everyone had a story about sex and we talked for four hours. When we broke up, I couldn't find Jenny anywhere.

On the following night she called and asked me please to come and see her. I decided to walk across the parklands and through the children's playground. Horses in the park shuffled and twitched their ears when I passed them softly in the grass. I wondered if animals could hear a human heart beat under darkness.

It was a cool night. She must have been waiting behind the door because she opened it before I could knock.

She pulled the sleeves of my unbleached fishing sweater as if I were some kind of sack. She led me into her room where a fire was burning. Neither of us had said a word. She hadn't let go of me and ran her hands down my sleeves and then up inside the wool to the small of my back where she linked her fingers against my skin. I held my breath and stood quite still. She kissed me on my lips and rested her mouth lightly on my mouth. I closed my eyes and pressed on her lips in return and felt her draw back as if she held something in.

I opened my eyes because Jenny was releasing me. She left the room silently. I sat on the footstool beside the fire and read the titles of her book covers sideways on the mantelshelf and told myself to stop fluttering inside like a small unruly flame.

"I have to tell you something," she said, coming into the room. "I am not really like that. I think you should leave now. I am still afraid."

I walked home slowly by the long road that goes around the park.

I called her when I had undressed.

She said, "Please don't call again—I can't see you again—we mustn't see each other again—not until I work things out." Then she hung up. I looked down at my breasts and belly. I was sure that she had felt something, too.

I couldn't stop thinking about her. Week after week I drove my car around her corner, hoping to see her as if by accident. Then the theatre company got word that she had gone away.

The group of women I'd met invited me to become a regular member. I did, at first in the hope of seeing Jenny, later because I found myself looking forward to the meetings. I asked Annie to join. She promised to think about it, when she had time. I told her my group would never get around to the subject of plays and acting because we only talked about our lives. Annie said why not make of our lives the play. I said we needed a playwright for that and, anyway, most women's lives are depressingly undramatic, which made her laugh.

I did meet Jenny again. She had cropped her hair and wore baggy overalls and rubber boots and sat on the top of a stepladder to whitewash the garden wall. I did not immediately recognize her. I thought at first she was her son.

"Are you still with the theatre company?" she asked. She sounded different. Confident, I thought; less shy, less fearful.

"Yes. I'm a producer now." I was afraid that I sounded the same. "Where have you been?"

"London, to work things out," she said.

"There's a scar above your lip."

"When I left Dan," she explained, "he refused to believe me and said I must be ill or undernourished and probably needed vitamins. When I picked up my suitcase and walked to the door, he threw one of his colored china plates at me. He missed, but slivers flew across the room when it hit the mantelshelf and one sliced open my top lip. I felt it burn." She laughed. "He swore I would come back to him. He begged me for another chance. So I agreed to meet him when I returned from London."

Jenny climbed down and moved the ladder to a fresh position under the wall. She climbed back to the top step and smiled down at me again.

"I sent my lover instead," she said. "Dan met my lover in the Botanical Gardens. He'd driven there in a new sports car. He bought that car as soon as I'd gone, when he moved into a rent-free studio with the children. My lover arrived at the Gardens before him. She wore her best white suit and a red rose. 'Whose wedding?' Dan called when he climbed from the cockpit. 'Mine,' said Alison." Jenny dipped the brush into the tin and began to paint the wall.

"Go on," I said.

"Well, Alison took the flower from her vest and presented it to Dan. He held it for a moment and then he crushed it in his fingers and blew away the petals. Then he left. Alison later mailed him my letter. It was my claim for a share of the property. He's given me the London flat, so I'll eventually go back. Of course I lost my writing job here, and have to live on the dole, but I don't have the children, and Alison says she will live here to help with the rent until I go back to London." Jenny put the brush back in the can.

"To think I once preferred celibacy," she laughed, "until Alison cut my hair. So," she called down from the top step, "what's with you?"

"I'd like a cup of tea," I said.

"Don't you miss your children?" I asked.

"Not as much as I thought I would. They come to me for the weekends. Dan's a better mother than me."

"I think I can find a grant for you. If you'd like one, that is. I . . . the company needs you."

"Depends. What are you working on?"

"Women's lives."

"Oh. That." She took my hand and fingered my wedding ring. Her own hand, I noticed, was bare. "You still believe in marriage."

"I'm afraid to leave him. I'm afraid for the children."

"Do you still have those other fears?" she asked.

"I don't know. That was a long time ago. And you have Alison."

"I had Alison then, but Alison is not like you."

"Jenny, I was obsessed with you. I came down your street for weeks and weeks. Sometimes I saw you in the garden but I didn't come in. I wrote letters that I never sent and poems you would never read. Not very good poems either. I walked and walked in the park but I couldn't quite bring myself to walk to your door. I thought you didn't want to see me."

"You frightened me. You were too intense. I wasn't ready for that, not then."

"When I found out you had gone away . . ."

"But I came back. And all that time you lived across the park, raising your children, producing your plays, a good little mother, a good little wife . . ."

I was silent.

"I'm sorry," she said. "I meant to praise continuity and loyalty. I didn't mean to hurt you. You're not happy, are you."

"It's getting late. I must go home to cook the dinner."

"I'll come with you. We'll cook together. I'm a good cook."

"I remember." I noticed that she was still holding my hand. "Look, I don't have to go right now," I added, "but I'm finding this terribly hard. I normally have a lot to say but now I'm . . ."

"You sound very eloquent to me." She smiled. Then she stood up and pulled me after her. "I am ready now," she said, and ran her hands up inside my sweater and clasped them tightly around my waist until they felt as if they'd never gone. I shut my eyes and kissed her and she pressed herself against me.

"I want to go to bed with you, Jenny," I said at last.

Once we became lovers, my initial obsession for Jenny soon levelled, to my great relief and by mutual agreement, to a playful and joyful affection. We laughed to discover that neither of us really wanted to be the grand, eternal, ultimate passion we each had imagined the other might be or want. Once that was recognized, we could celebrate what we did have, and could be together—friends, mothers, and occasional lovers—with lives so transitional when we met that a deeper commitment was out of the question. Neither of us sought to dominate or to make demands.

Neither wanted to duplicate another form of marriage. Jenny had other lovers, and, although the idea made her sometimes impatient, I still had Duncan.

Although Duncan and I slept apart, and had long since ceased to be lovers, Jenny accepted the inevitability of Duncan in my life from the start of our affair. She had made up her own mind about marriage and children but had the grace and generosity not to insist that I make the same choices and follow her example.

Whether Duncan had an inkling of that, the little he saw of Jenny he seemed to enjoy. He appeared tacitly to have accepted her as a new component of our family life. If ever she missed her own children, mine reciprocated Jenny's warmth and laughter. So long as Jenny was there, I thought, we might all continue to coexist.

Annie met Jenny on several family occasions but didn't warm to her as much as I'd hoped. She treated Jenny like a younger sister or a vagrant daughter. I had not told Annie the intimate details of our relationship. I wasn't ready to. Annie was far too absorbed, in any case, in child behavioral problems at her clinic to pay much attention to any of us.

However much I missed my regular physical contact with Annie, we continued to consult each other via telephone briefings. Only once did Annie impatiently suggest that my habitual way of talking under and around a problem with her, picking it over and over as if the problem were a skein of yarn too knotty with impurities to be carded, was my reluctant and effective way of avoiding resolutions.

"You know what Goethe wrote," she chided me one day. " 'If you think too much about the process of thinking, you'll cease to think productively at all,' or something to that effect. Morgan, if you are feeling so mired with Duncan, why don't you follow your instincts? Why not simply leave him?"

"Because that won't be simple, even if I want to, and I'm still not sure that I do," I protested. "So long as I can continue to negotiate with Duncan, I'll continue to believe we can work things out. Anyway, I don't trust instinct. It's probably the cause of my problem."

"How?"

"Following instinct, I've managed to produce four children, a distant husband—a host of contributing and highly problematic diversions—or dependents. I don't call that very productive."

"Precisely! But you haven't been acting instinctively. You've been acting from need."

"What's the difference? They both burrow in the dark where I don't always see them clearly."

"You see well enough when you want to. Not all of your needs are self-defeating, darling, but I don't like the one that chains you to these endless negotiations with a man renowned for his unchangeable views and habits. For god's sake, Morgan, you always feel better when you *act*. That's your primary natural instinct—to act, to activate, take action against a sea . . ."

"I know, I know, but I'm finding it impossible to believe that actions I take opposed to Duncan will end the problem. It's far more likely to be exacerbated."

"If only you'd take off your blinkers, sweetheart."

"What would I see, Annie?"

"That you give Duncan too much power."

"That's cruel. I don't think I like this line of conversation. I'm afraid it will lead to trouble."

"You're *in* trouble, Morgan. Your needs—God knows I have them too—to conform, to be acceptable, to be like others or be liked by others—are at war with your instincts, not that I'm sure what they are—for life, voice, expression, action—I don't know. That's for you to work out." Annie paused. I waited. "Morgan? Are you still there?"

"Yes, I'm here." I roused myself from my thoughts. "This has been a great help. When do we talk again?"

"Whenever you want. You needn't make it sound like a clinical appointment. You know I always find time for you—that's a fundamental need of *mine*." She laughed.

"So why do I have this lurking instinct that you have somewhat less time for me these days, eh?" and she hung up without waiting for my answer.

I'd been thinking: When I've worked myself out, when I know how to act, then I'll have to tell Annie the truth about me.

CHAPTER EIGHT

"Run, Nicky, run—faster, faster—come on, boyo, run!" I cheered from the sidelines. Pamela Bodley, my new neighbor who had come to live opposite Duncan and me, was cheering, too, for her son Paul, also running in Nicky's flat-race heat.

We groaned when neither son finished first, but I hugged my Nicholas proudly when he came up to me afterward, his face flushed and eager, his heart pounding under the white school gym shirt.

"Aren't you pleased with Paul? He's really joining in today." I turned to Pamela. Paul had stayed at the finishing tape to talk with his father, Bill Bodley, one of the field umpires for the All Saints Preparatory School sports day. Pamela, standing next to me, glared up the track toward the group of small boys crowded around Bill; she apparently hadn't heard me.

"Holly, why don't you take Nick to buy an orange drink to celebrate? Here's a dollar, and bring back the change." I waved as I watched them run to the kiosk, and two blond heads disappeared in the sun.

It was a beautiful February day, not a cloud in the sky, with the rich green of the watered grass on All Saints' main oval dappled here and there by shadows from the encircling plane trees and dotted around its fringes with bright clusters of families and competing boys, house banners, and bunting.

"Will you enter the mothers' race with me, Pamela?"

She turned around, preoccupied, and then replied, "No. My running days are over."

"Oh, do run with me! It'll be fun to compete with you again. I don't care how foolish I look, or how feebly I run. Come on, Pam—remember the old days when I hit your shin at hockey? Just because *your* school always won the shield—such a smart school, the only one with perfect grass to practice on, unlike my poverty-stricken Westall team who had to struggle in the onion weed and mudslides of the parklands. I well remember how you came charging at me down the wing, dribbling the ball as if it were a live grenade, and there I was, left fullback, last line of defense, facing another of your certain goals. Hockey one, hockey two—it's a miracle we're friends. You terrified me."

"All I remember is how I felt when your stick took the front of my shin off. God, you were a brutal player, Morgan," Pamela grumbled. "What's more, I think you won that day."

"Think? That was the crowning joy of all my school-days, beating your lot four to three. If I hadn't crippled you, put your number-one right wing out of action, it might have been a draw."

"A fluke. Westall was never a top sporting school. Remember when you captained the softball team and dropped the ball? I laughed and laughed. There you were, tied at the ninth, your mitt out ready for a high ball coming straight to shortstop and—"

"Be nice, Pamela. We're not competing now, we're friends, remember. What's the matter? You look so miserable—why the frown?"

"Look at Paul, hanging on for dear life to Bill's knees, and there are your two, having a wonderful time playing with their friends. God, how boys bore me."

"Pamela, that's a dreadful thing to say."

"You don't realize how lucky you are to have daughters. Bill, Paul, even baby Sam—for the rest of my life I'll be surrounded by men, but you . . . daughters, women friends . . . I'm lonely, Morgan." Pamela looked away again.

"Be thankful for some mercies," I said. "Bill adores you. He's the kind of husband and father I'd give a daily bouquet to, he's so attentive and affectionate. I envy you Bill. Duncan wouldn't come today. Not even to see his son run a race."

Pamela shrugged and sat down on the rug I'd laid for picnic lunch. We both wore pleated skirts and Oxford shirts, the uniform for All Saints mothers. Nicholas, who would soon turn six, had begged me to wear a skirt. There are times when my children really do want me to conform; when they want me to abandon jeans and look like everyone's mother. Those times, I really try to, although I would have felt more comfortable in jeans, even among the upper crust at All Saints School Collegiate, and especially at an All Saints sports day.

When Pamela did not reply, I cracked a joke about swapping partners, and she laughed grimly.

"You're welcome to him. I hate waking up every morning, the inevitability of seeing him, feeling him wanting me. Sex, nothing but sex—that's all men really want from us." She pulled out tufts of grass to make a flimsy ball and threw it in Bill's direction. "In many ways you're better off because Duncan leaves you strictly alone. Marital celibacy, that's my ideal. Who's that calling your kids?"

Nicky and Holly had dashed around the oval to greet her. Dear God, it's my Jenny, wearing her oldest faded jeans and a shirt open to the breezes! When she ran toward us, holding my children's hands, her breasts bobbed up and down like enticing jellies. Heads turned, mouths ajar, and worse—she had no shoes! Oh, Jenny, Jenny, why do you have to turn us into a spectacle for All Saints gossip?

Pamela, who knew Jenny casually, made small talk while I squirmed in embarrassment. It wasn't shame at Jenny's appearance. I wasn't used to being seen with her in public places that belonged more to family life than to our Women's Center, where Jen and I attended meetings and dances and held our play rehearsals. There: at the school where my father went, where Duncan, Donald, even Bill Bodley were Old Scholars, where now my Nick and Pamela's Paul had started school—where I was married—and in full view of all those conservative snobs— No, I was embarrassed to be myself there.

There were egg and spoon events, and obstacle races, and the tortoise race on bicycles to follow. Nicky, who fell in the hurdling, sat in my lap on the grass to watch Holly run the big sisters' race and to yell and clap when she came in second. Bill, who was fond of Jenny, joined us for lunch. He wore his Old Scholars blazer with the brass buttons and navy striped tie. I felt more comfortable when he was there to take the edge off my awkward silences.

When the day ended at three, and we'd helped pick up rubbish and retrieve small boys and sandshoes and prizes, Jenny decided to visit her kids and, rather thankfully, I drove Pamela and the children home, as Bill was going back to the staff club for a beer with the other fathers. Bill worked hard at belonging. As a scholarship boy, like my father Harry, Bill had none of the natural affinities of other Old Boys: his family wasn't among the first fleet that anchored at Holdfast Bay; his father wasn't a gynecologist like Pamela's, knighted for bringing new generations of All Saints boys into the world, or a wealthy recluse with the right address like Duncan's father. Even though Donald and Duncan had refused membership in the gregarious matings of the Adelaide Club, they'd always be honorary fellows.

I drank a glass of white wine in Pamela's kitchen while she emptied tins of sweet corn and beans into a saucepan. If the art of cooking were an entrée to society, I'd be among the elite. Pamela hated preparing food, especially for children. She resented the fact that Bill couldn't afford a housekeeper or a casual cook.

Watching her impatient movements, I wondered, did

she also resent Bill for their daughter's sudden death last year?

Elizabeth had become my Holly's dearest friend when the Bodleys moved across the street. They played at our house every afternoon after school until five, when Pamela came home from the sporting goods store she managed in the city.

Shortly before her seventh birthday, Elizabeth became ill. She seemed listless and terribly weak. Holly toned down her exuberant energy to keep pace with her friend. She became a helpful shadow at Westall, carrying Elizabeth's bags, pairing with her in gym so that other children would not exhaust her. Then a long and confusing series of tests discovered a virulent tumor.

On the eve of her operation, Holly and I visited the hospital. I put my chair closer to the bed to read *Babar the Elephant,* so Elizabeth could reach out to turn the pages back and forth. Holly curled up in the bed beside her to study the pictures, too. Elizabeth had a blue ribbon in her hair, and her face was as white as the sheets. I saw the look of determination and terror in her eyes.

The following afternoon, I picked up Holly in my car after school and told her that Elizabeth was dead. Holly climbed into the back seat, fondled my ear for a moment, then sighed. "I thought she would die. So did she, Mummy. She promised me she'll be an angel and she'll fly above my bed at night, faster than I've ever run, higher than I can jump." Of course we cried a lot, Holly and I, and we talked incessantly about Elizabeth as if both of us wanted to keep her alive.

It was harder to talk with Pamela. At first, Nicky and Holly were a great comfort. They asked the terribly frank questions children have about death and burial, and when we visited, they cleaned out the doll's house and played with Elizabeth's toys. When Paul dreamed of huge black birds that perched at night on his windowsill, Holly helped him draw his dreams and then painted her angel with

Elizabeth's golden hair and blue ribbon high in the night sky to protect him.

Bill took the brunt of cooking and caring for Paul and baby Sam when Pamela withdrew from everyone but Holly. I tried to maintain our regular family activities: pizza at our place on Friday nights, barbecued lunch at theirs on Sundays, and I often dropped by to help Bill at mealtimes.

One day, I couldn't bear any longer to see Pamela's grief. I took her firmly in my arms the way I often hugged poor Paul.

"Let go, dammit!" I said fiercely. "You've got to cry, Pam dear, you can't bottle this up forever. Cry, dammit." And she buried her head in my shoulder and began to shake like an avalanche that gathers, yields, and tumbles.

After the tears we could talk about Elizabeth and how Pamela had felt when she signed the agreement to operate as if she knew it were a death warrant. Soon she was able to return to work, and the store preoccupied her again. Toward the end of that year, I called in to see her after work. She was lying on her bed, rumpled, tearstained. I asked what the matter was.

"Oh, this feeling of being left alone in a man's world, a woman alone. You should never have made me cry." She brushed my hand away from her shoulder.

She asked me questions about my women's group, then, to my astonishment, produced from under the bed an open copy of *Playboy* magazine and thrust it under my nose.

"Is this what you and Jenny Murphy do?" She grinned lopsidedly.

They wore the usual pornographic trappings—leather and whips and scanty lacy underwear, with lascivious baby-doll pouts and drowning eyes—and I abruptly changed the subject. I was furious with Pamela. I thought she'd fully accepted my relationship with Jenny. Of all my married friends, I thought Pamela understood.

Later, I wondered if it was I who'd misjudged her because I was offended. Maybe she did want to know and needed, simply, information. Maybe she wanted reassurance about me. About herself? Maybe I should have asked her.

I wished that Pamela and Annie had joined my women's group. Jenny and the many friends who'd worked under our guidance for the past two years had completed an original script, *The Branded,* for a musical revue about convict women in colonial Sydney. I was ready, now, to shape it with the actors while Alison prepared her musicians. It was a team effort—powerful theatre, historically accurate, highly dramatic—and exhilarating for me, to work for the first time with an all-woman cast and crew.

Now that Nicky was almost seven and settled at school and the three older girls were doing well at Westall, I'd decided to accept a travel grant that the Drama Board had offered me two years before, when I'd felt the children were too young for me to leave them. I agreed to spend six months of the following year as a visiting producer with a New York acting company.

The thought of living in New York was so terrifying that Jenny offered to teach me some basic karate moves for self-defense. I hadn't lived alone for any length of time since I was in the bush. I'd not been away from the children for longer than a night or two, and that only recently when I'd sleep with Jenny in her commune across the parklands whenever rehearsals continued past midnight. I knew the children were old enough to manage my brief absences, but six months? It was a gamble. Sometimes the risks seemed greater for me than for them.

To my surprise, Duncan didn't raise any objection to the trip. I planned how he could best run the household without me. Through Pamela's contacts I found Nannie Cashmore, who would come for the children's after-school hours and cook the evening meals. Jenny promised she'd keep an eye on them. My mother always said she never saw enough of the children, so Dilys would come every

Saturday, when Duncan was fishing with Bill Bodley. Then of course, Pamela was just across the street.

Pamela had come to mean more to me than a family friend or a confidante, and much more than a neighbor. I relied on her in many ways. She filled a special place for me, one that Miss Gordon had vacated when she moved to California to train as a seismologist and to study the San Andreas fault; one that my sister Cicely might have filled had she remained in Adelaide or had our roles as wives and mothers ever met and matched. More than a close friend, Pamela was a woman whose independent judgment I respected. Despite perennial grumblings, she was securely wedded to Bill and the boys. She had a certain distance, an objectivity, a control over her emotions that seemed especially helpful at a time when I was in danger of losing both my clarity and control.

Once before, when I was troubled, when I went on another Walkabout, it was the bush that had given me the chance to see; where I finally saw that I could act to save myself. Was New York far enough away from home to have the distance, the solitude, and the time I needed— *needed*—to decide what I should do?

Pamela was the first to say I should give it a try and go. The one friend I had yet to consult was Annie. For reasons that were too hard to explain, even to myself, I put her off until it was far too late to change my mind.

Our two families had crowded around the dining table for a surprise party lovingly conceived and choreographed by my children on the eve of my departure.

Emma had baked honey crackle in cupcakes, Catriona her favorite sticky toffee, and Holly and Nicholas had decorated the room with paper streamers, balloons, and summer flowers from our garden. They'd painted a fare-thee-well mural on butcher paper: an Adelaide sketch of our house and themselves on the left, an airplane high above a Pacific surf, and on the right America's windowed skyscrapers and TV aerials, with a wobbly figure on a crowded street way down below who was waving back at them. Everyone signed messages on the mural before we hung it like a victory banner above the fireplace.

The children had planned it all by themselves, supplemented by Annie's ossobuco, Ivan's Penfold Riesling, Duncan's mashed potatoes and bottles of Woodruffe lemonade. After we'd all helped clear away, Duncan immediately returned to the Shed, but Ivan stayed briefly to help Tim and Emma with their homework, and Annie took Holly and Nick to my room to hear their reading assignments.

Catriona and Edwin were in the bath together. I'd rinsed their hair and was returning to my room when Nick and Holly galloped past me, Nick the carthorse harnessed by his pajama cord to Duncan's old dog on wheels and Holly his charioteer, calling "Giddy-up, Neddie—whoa—slow down for a bedtime kiss. Goodnight, Mummy, see you in the morning. Off to America, Nicky."

They careened past me to their bedroom while I blew kisses and waved until they disappeared.

"The oldies will be occupied for quite some time. I was quite startled to see Catriona and Edwin in the bath together." I sat down with Annie on the foot of my bed.

"Like old times, isn't it!"

"No, I meant they're growing so fast. Catriona has started little breasts. She doesn't seem aware of them yet."

"Don't you believe it! A few months from now they'll be too self-conscious to take baths together, and we'll be banished from the bathroom."

"I hope they'll stay close like Tim and Emma."

"They will. They're practically brothers and sisters. Even going to different schools hasn't changed that. Anyway, look at us."

"That's what I want to talk about. Not us, but changes. America, and what I plan to do when I come home."

"America?" Annie looked out of the bay window at my jacaranda. It was growing dark. Duncan had left the veranda lights on; the tree made a jagged shadow like a scar across the lawn. I heard Ivan's car engine, then saw his red brakelights when he turned from our drive into Worth Place. Annie broke the silence. "I'll miss you horribly, but of course you have to go for the sake of your career. It will launch you professionally, but I'm afraid you won't want to return after you've seen New York."

"I'll be homesick. Six months is too long. It's not so much the going that worries me. I'm starting to feel excited by the contacts I'll make, the opening doors. No, Annie, it's coming home afterward, coming back to . . . the hell of continuing this life with Duncan. I doubt if hell will change in six months."

"Morgan, darling, you know he won't change."

"*It* will—the possibility of staying in this any longer. It's living a lie, Annie. I know it, he must know it, and before long the kids will, too. I can't honestly sustain it. I'm having such severe headaches, my head feels as if it will split in two. I simply have to choose before I return, before everything fractures."

"Graphic, but I'm not convinced. You've managed to juggle—your work, your kids—for a long time. I can't quite see what else will change."

"Annie, I've been trying to tell you, but you've been too busy to notice. Remember the revue . . ."

"How can anyone forget! Dear one, that wasn't your finest hour. You *were* a little cuckoo late last year, but we all sensibly put that down to the travel grant, leaving for America, your newfound adventureland. It's passed, your brief fling with rapturous irresponsibility—hasn't it?"

"What do you mean, irresponsibility?" Must we always follow each other round and around like pit ponies?

"You have to admit, Morgan, you kind of abandoned us."

"Abandoned who? What am I, *The Mother of Us All*? I was frantic with the revue. Producing a feminist revue was unlike any theatre experience before. Committees for everything; meetings instead of rehearsals; process over production; ideological battles over the meaning of feminism and the impurities of entertainment that took days off our schedule; constant cast changes; having to teach basic acting to radical separatists who challenged every gesture, every move; oh god, the strikes! I thought we'd never raise the curtain, let alone attract an audience. It was utterly exhausting, even if some moments were sheer rapture. If I hadn't had some fun out of it, I'd be a walking agitprop." I paused. "I'm sorry, I probably did neglect you and the kids a little. What I was going to say was that I may have spent too much time with Jenny."

"Well, that's over, isn't it? Now that you're going separate ways." She sounded frustrated.

"I'm trying to tell you, to explain, Annie, but it isn't easy. I don't think I've been irresponsible. I've been happy, dammit. Remember when we lived together, before marriage?"

"Go on."

"Those all-night debates with Gayle and Winnie?"

"What are you getting at?"

"Well, Annie, we were lesbians then. We had no word for who we were—it was Gayle's—but that's what we were, remember?"

"For god's sake, that was fourteen, fifteen years ago, a youthful aberration. I've never forgotten it, mind, but we did move on; we transformed that into something so resilient, it has outlasted most marriages. It's encompassed six children, our careers, our husbands—Okay—that's what we were if you must give it a name—bisexual, lesb . . . whatever. But . . ."

"I still am. I always have been. I was . . . Jenny and I have been lovers."

"So? D'you think I didn't . . . I'm not surprised." She recovered quickly. "You let yourself go last year, more than you might have otherwise. Then the intensity of working together on the revue—a close friend—knowing you were going away—oh yes, I think it's perfectly understandable." Then she stared at me. "I'm not jealous, if that's what you're driving at."

"It wasn't a farewell fling, Annie. Jenny and I became lovers some years ago. She was the first person in a long time who showed me true affection. I don't mean like ours—love like ours—but . . . physical affection."

"Why didn't you tell . . . oh damn, I suppose on some level I knew and repressed it because what seemed important to me was your marriage. It was my impression that it was for you, too."

"Annie, you know it was. I've never lied to you. But I have found it hard to convince you, at times, how dreadfully lonely it's been. You always said, 'Try harder,' and god how I tried . . ."

"I want you to know I've never been jealous of Duncan either. We've been reasonably pleasant friends—superficial, perhaps—but I think if you and Duncan had managed, like I did with Ivan, . . . well, if Duncan hadn't stopped having sex with you, this might never have happened. Maybe you're more highly sexed than me."

"Annie! I'm trying to explain that this was inevitable, not a temporary lapse, not some psychological failure of Duncan's. I'm not a slave to ravaging sexual frustration."

"Don't yell at me."

"I'm sorry! My relationship with Jenny is not another passing phase. If anything, Jenny has helped me find the courage to choose . . ." I searched for the right words.

"Choose what?" she said quietly. "To break up with Duncan? Finally?"

"That, but not only that. Look, Annie, you've always been one step ahead of me. You were the one who took the first initiative. Then it was you who decided we had to stop making love. Now I'm trying to tell you that I've made a decision, this time without you. I must make it. I have to be true to myself."

There was a longer pause. The breeze had dropped. Not a leaf stirred on the jacaranda. The house that had recently hummed with activity was surprisingly still, as if listening to me.

"This is still a difficult subject for us, isn't it! It must be the first time in memory," I continued, "that you find it hard to understand me, to accept what I am."

"I feel hurt, can't you see? It's the first time you haven't shared secrets with me. What makes this unbearable is the thought of losing you. I don't want such a drastic turnabout. I know you've tried and tried with Duncan. Of course you must leave him if that's finally failed, but . . . a lesbian? I'm sorry—I'm not being very fair. It isn't even generous of me to wish you well in America. It's obvious that you'll thrive there. You'll learn, develop, and come back a bloody marvel like all bloody Australian expatriates. If you come back. You may not want to. I'm bloody possessive. I don't want to live here without you. I don't want you to live somewhere without me, with somebody else. I'm afraid of being shut out. Already my feelings are tearing, raw, exposed. Morgan—I'm sorry." She burst into tears.

I pulled Annie against me and lay down with her on my bed. I could taste her tears and smell her hair. The dear familiar hold of her, the nearness—and the enormity of what I needed to do.

"There's something I don't understand," she was saying. "You were married all this time. At least that gave you four wonderful kids. Is it because your marriage failed? When did you decide you might be . . .?"

"As long as I can remember I've been attracted to women, but I never examined what that implied because I found it too disturbing. I'd expected marriage to change that, as it obviously had for you. In truth, there were times with Duncan when I was fulfilled. Pregnancy and feeding do have their erotic pleasures; it was then, especially, that I felt closest to Duncan and didn't have to feel guilty about desire and seduction. The other feelings—I thought I could bury them . . . willpower, self-control . . . I managed to convince myself. Until I fell in love with Jenny." I laughed to remember. "I didn't recognize it at first for what it was. When I did, ironically she turned me away. We were both too afraid of the consequences. My women's group helped me face them. Even Duncan helped when he welcomed Jenny into the family, whether because she relieved him of a burden of attention, or because he didn't care . . ."

"I'm sure he has cared, in his own peculiar way. If he'd anticipated the outcome, he might have tried to stop you."

"The thought of wounding or betraying him used to make me guilty. That was another bind. Whenever in the past I've been sexually charged, I'd turn to him, hoping that if I tried to seduce him, he might fall in love with me again. He didn't. Nothing changed emotionally between us, not even with the birth of Nicholas. Emotions rather than sexual attraction tied me to Duncan, especially through the kids; it was, as you know, emotions that he would not share, or could not, that took so long to unravel, before I could . . ."

"Choose—yes, I see. I haven't had those difficulties. With Ivan, it's mainly calm seas and a prosperous . . . well, an uneventful voyage with no visible shipwrecks. The other never came back to haunt me." She laughed, close to my ear, but her body was trembling.

"Mummy, when are you coming to say goodnight?" I hadn't heard Catriona quietly enter my room. "You've been talking for ages. Can Eddie and Tim stay for the night? Please!"

Annie sat up quickly. "No, dearest one, it's a school night and I must take the boys home. We're coming soon. Your mama and I have something important to talk about."

"Is it America?"

"That, and some other little things." Catriona smiled and bounded from the room. "Like, what about them?" Annie pointed over her shoulder. "What are you going to do about the kids?"

"Have them with me when I return, I hope, if Duncan agrees."

"If he doesn't?"

"I've seen a lawyer. She says to anticipate legal action. A custody case, the Family Court."

"I hate to say it, but surely you don't hope . . . What happens if custody is awarded to him?"

"I hardly dare think of that. I know I'll miss them terribly for six months. I can't imagine not having them at all, not ever."

"You'd better, Morgan. If Duncan knows about the sex thing—"

"Of course he does. He's known everything."

"He's bound to use it. It may be a lethal weapon: an unfit mother. We'll have to prepare a strong defense. Do you trust Jenny to handle this? I mean, she gave up on her own kids—won't that look bad if she's called as a witness?"

"I don't intend to call her. I don't want to involve her."

"Duncan may. Then where would you be? Listen, you're a mother and a professional woman. I think you should deny everything. Play it straight down the middle. I'll lie, and I think you should, and Jenny as well."

"I won't. There'd be no point, since Duncan knows, and always knew . . . and I'm tired of lying. No, we'll have to play it true."

"God help us. What did your lawyer say?"

"That this one will be very hard to win."

"But not impossible?"

"Nothing's impossible—not for us, Annie."

"Not for you. If this were to happen to me . . ."

"What would you do?"

"Leave the kids with Ivan and split. But Ivan isn't Duncan, and I'm not you. Oh, darling, I'm afraid for you." Annie reached for a pad and pencil. "Let's work out some strategies before you go away. If you have to appear in a court, we must be prepared in advance. What will you need when you first come home?"

"Somewhere to live. Money."

"You'll stay with me, of course, for as long as you need. Ask Ivan for help with money. You own shares in the Shed; maybe he can look into the Ross companies behind Duncan's back."

"I suppose I'll have to prepare documents and lists: information about the cost of raising the kids, cost of living, school fees, rent, medical insurance, transport . . ."

"For once, Morgan my love, you are talking like a businesswoman." Annie sucked the tip of the pencil. "Let me think. This approach only applies if you decide to remain here after your trip to New York. What if you want to stay there longer? What if they offer you a permanent job—what happens to the children then?"

"I'd want to take them with me. Maybe Duncan will agree to their spending a year there to see if that works."

"He's unlikely to agree, surely, to let them out of the country. That doesn't sound like Duncan to me."

"I could try being a mobile mother—fly back here between productions to spend the school holidays with them. I shan't always have to work full time."

"Expensive . . . may work in the short run, for one or two trips. I'll keep my eyes on them for you, but I doubt if Duncan can possibly substitute for you. They're terribly young still. If—"

"If it comes down the line: if my Pacific leaps don't work, if my negotiations with Duncan break down, if we have to go to court, if he wins custody . . . I have everything to lose, don't I?" I paused. "Everything."

"And so do the children. Oh, Morgan, I'm scared for you."

"Gayle was right, wasn't she!"

"How?"

"It looks like war, sooner or later. I'm sure I'd have left him years ago if there hadn't been children involved. Silly, isn't it—they're the reason I chose to be with him in the beginning; they're the reason I've taken so long to decide to leave him. I wish it wasn't happening to me."

"We're in it together, darling, thick and thin. Whatever happens, I'll stick by you. Promise. Now let's go kiss the kids and bundle mine into the Honda. When you come home from America, I want to meet this lawyer of yours to make sure you are given a fighting chance. Remember my mother, the night she tried to separate us? I've never felt closer, have you?"

"Never. Oh my god—Mother! I'll have to tell Dilys. This is starting to sound like a Coming Out Ready or Not performance."

"Must be preferable to Hide and Seek. Come, it's everyone's bedtime, and funnily enough, I actually wish, nostalgically, that it could be once again with you."

"Mum, I'll have to take the children somewhere when I return from America. Why not here? You'll be in London with Cicely in any case. This house will be empty."

"No, Morgan dear, no, I wish you'd understand. Oh, dear, this is so painful. I can't bear to see what's happening to all of us. The shame! How can I possibly tell the aunts? What am I meant to say to my friends, to people who've known our family throughout your life? Divorce! No one was ever divorced in my family, or in your father's either. What will people say! Have you thought of that, Morgan?"

"The people who still care about me, Mother, should be cheering that all the years of unhappiness and loneliness are ending. I would have thought you'd be happy."

"Dearest, you must do what you think best for you. Thank god your father's dead. Forgive me, I shouldn't swear, but he must be turning in his grave. Divorce!"

"Mum, this is about custody. We shall have to settle that first. Divorce is the least of my concerns. That will follow naturally a year from when the court agrees we're legally separated. What matters first when I come back is the kids and who is to take care of them."

"Whatever words you use, they all sound foreign to me. What can Duncan's poor father be thinking? First his wife dead, then his illness, now this. It would have killed your own father."

"I think, Mother, that if Harry were here, if I asked him for the use of his house as a safe harbor for me and the kids, he would hand me the key."

"You simply won't understand my feelings. The little things, the precious things I've saved—I can't have youngsters in the house, breaking things, making everything a mess. It's all a terrible mess in any case. I don't want to make it worse."

"Don't cry, please, don't cry. I'm only asking for help, Mum. I thought at least I could come here, for a while, with my kids."

"You're breaking my heart. I will not have my home destroyed. It's all I have left. Why haven't you asked that Westall teacher who always took you in when you ran away? That Miss Gordon, the woman you always worshiped. Why can't you go to her house again?"

"I wanted to come home. Besides, she doesn't live here."

"Or your bosom friend Annie—you always did everything together. Why doesn't she take you in—or is she breaking up her marriage and her family the same as you?"

I said nothing.

"My china, my little ornaments, my books—you do appreciate that, don't you?—they're all I have left, the corners of my memories. And now, with your marriage gone, those beautiful children I may never see again, and you—wanting to leave the country, your home, your friends, wanting to break up everything I worked for, everything your father and I believed in and wanted you to have, the things your father lived for—Don't you see? Nothing's secure anymore. I wish you'd understand, dear. Why must you always be different? Why can't you take things as they are and learn to live with them? All through your life, whatever your reasons have been, whatever terrible needs you say you have, your talk of wanting to be yourself and to live the life you choose—oh, Morgan, it's always been beyond me. You could have had everything—with your brains, your acting—opportunities you had that your father and I could never have—but you always wanted to go your own way. Why, why, why, why?"

PART III

The man is walking boundaries
measuring   He believes in what is his
the grass   the waters underneath   the air

the air   through which child and mother
are running   the boy singing
the woman   eyes sharpened in the light
heart stumbling   making for the open

Adrienne Rich

CHAPTER NINE

When I turn the corner into Worth Place, I'm thankful to see the children waiting on the footpath, watching for my car. There's no sign of Duncan. He must have gone to work. Thank god I shan't have to speak to him or go inside the house.

Emma's cast is off now; she's waving her arm like a stiff windmill. Catriona looks very pale. I think she's thinner. The younger two are as cheerful as ever. They need their hair washed. I toot the horn for joy to see them, and they pile into the back with hugs and merry laughter.

"Where are we going, Mummy?" Emma nurses the hamper I packed with sandwiches and fruit and a thermos of orange juice.

"Angel Gully." They shriek approval. It's our secret hideaway, a valley cleft between hills scattered with small dairy farms. "I thought we'd play the squatters game and pretend to be immigrants who've just arrived from Wales and have to start a new life on the land."

On the hills' highway, the back seat overflowing with chatter and hurly-burly questions, I accelerate into the Devil's Elbow and up the Crafers Road toward Mount Lofty. The children urge my old Morris up steep winding roads, and whoop when we reach the summit, to begin coasting down into Piccadilly Valley.

I park on a flat area alongside a dirt road, and we carry the rug and picnic things to the highest point overlooking the valley. The paddocks are covered in soursobs, and the children launch an assault, pelting each other with handfuls of the long wet weeds and yellow flowers, rolling halfway down the hill, racing away from grassy missiles, burning off excess energy until we all collapse in exhaustion in a heap upon the rug.

At first, the children chat about school and school friends while they take off their shoes and roll up their sleeves. Our faces warm in the sun while we munch apples and sandwiches. Then I say in a matter-of-fact way, "You know, if this court case turns out to be hard for us, we can stop. Sometimes I think you may feel as if you'll tear apart. Like a tug-o-war. If it gets to be too much for you, you only have to say so. I mean that. I want you to know."

Holly grins and says in her gruff voice, "Mummy, we don't want you to give up."

"But it may not be giving up, darling. It may just be saying that this is too hard."

"We're alright, Mum." Nicholas snuggles into my shoulder. "Don't worry about us. Did I tell you I think Dad's trying to bribe me? A few days ago, he said he'd give me his old train set. He said it was locked up in the strongroom at Kenilworth but he'd find it for me and set it up at home in your old room."

Catriona wriggles under my other arm. I hold her close to me.

"I remember, darling. Grandad gave him the Hornby set when he was only five. He was too young to understand how to make it work, so Grandad played with it and your dad had to sit and watch him. He wasn't allowed to touch it. Not for years. When he was your age, he laid an elaborate track in his bedroom, but an older, tougher boy, a cousin, came and trampled on it and wrecked it. I don't think your dad ever played with it again. Grandad packed it away with all the other things the Rosses don't use. I think it's nice that Duncan wants you to have it now. I guess he thinks you're old enough."

"You don't understand, Mummy. I think he wants to

keep me with him, and that if he gives me his things I'll want to stay with him."

"He probably wants to play with it himself and make you watch." Holly waggles her finger in the air. "Just like we have to watch his boring television stuff. Boring adult stuff. He always watches what *he* wants. He gets mad if we switch channels."

"Darlings, why not talk about that with him? See if you can make a roster: some times for him, some for you."

Catriona yawns. "Oh, Mum, you know you can't talk with Dad. He's like a big mountain. You have to sneak around him, or give up."

"Well, it isn't going to work with me," Nicholas says staunchly. "Michael Scott has an electric train set. I can play with that."

I pummel him with tender pride. Emma, who is sitting on the edge of the rug a little apart from us, says thoughtfully, "Mum, the worst part is waiting around for a lot of strangers to make decisions about us and what we're going to do—adults who don't even know us. How will they decide for us? How will they know what we want?"

"Only through the way your father and I present your wishes. Even we shall have to be spoken for by lawyers who don't know us as well as you do."

"What's the judge like?"

"I don't know. I shan't see him until the case begins."

"I want to meet him. I want to tell him myself." Emma looks at each of us earnestly. "Let's all go to court and say it for ourselves."

"I'll ask Peter if that will be possible," I answer cautiously, but they circle me on their knees, grinning and nodding. "I think you have to be fourteen for a judge to agree to have you testify, but I'll ask."

"I'm nearly fourteen, and Catriona's twelve," Emma says firmly.

"And a half. If Emma can go, I go too. Promise, Mummy?"

"We'll see, Catriona, we'll see. Wait until I know what can be done."

"What about us? I'll soon be nine, and Nicky's nearly eight," Holly insists, but the older ones fall on her and squash her.

"You're both too young, but if I see the judge, I'll tell him all about you since we all want the same thing," Catriona says.

"Well, you're not going to America without me, and that's that." Holly stands and stretches. I catch my breath, she's so young, so small, and so determined. I have not done with mothering. I'm not ready to relinquish this to anyone.

"Good. Let's start the game. Hunter Holly, bring rabbit for our supper, if you please. Nick! We need wood for the fire and water from the creek."

"I'll herd the sheep." Catriona gallops down the hill on an imaginary steed. Holly disappears over the top of the hill with a dead tree branch for her shotgun, and Nicholas takes the empty thermos to the creek. I lean against a gum tree. Emma has stayed behind with me.

"What are you thinking, darling one? You look very sad."

"Only that it's getting very hard, Mummy. Catriona had a temperature last night, but Daddy took no notice and said it was her imagination. And Holly's wetting the bed again. Nannie says the best way to fix that nonsense is to make Holly lie in it. She makes Holly change the sheets, too. Holly would still be in bed if you hadn't come to pick us up today. It isn't fair."

"It's horrible. Does Nannie really call it nonsense? I only hope we haven't long to wait, dear. I don't want to make excuses for them, but I guess that Nannie and Daddy feel the strain of waiting, too. But no one has a right to be unkind. What about you? Are you bearing up?"

"Oh, Mummy, I got used to it when you were away. I *am* the eldest. I miss hockey. The doctor said my wrist won't be strong enough to play any more matches this season."

"If Duncan will agree to it, I'll ask if I can drive you to the Saturday morning games. Would that help? At least we'd get to watch the game from the sidelines."

"He won't agree, Mummy. On Saturdays I have to help him do the shopping. I know it's not for much longer, Mummy, but I wish it was all over and something was decided. It's this waiting." Emma moves closer to where I sit, and I take her hand. My dear, brave girl with the flaxen braids and steady gaze. "Another thing," she adds. "I think Nicky's going to end up just like Daddy. He's been so quiet and serious—not little anymore—do you know, Mummy?"

"I know. I think he's withdrawing. That's one way of coping with his feelings. You see, especially for the little ones, it's very scary not to know what's going to happen to you. It's very frightening when your parents are at war like enemies. We have to hold on tight and remind ourselves that this will pass, it will be over."

"I don't let myself think how it will end, Mummy. I want to be old enough to decide about my life myself. I hate adults."

She stands, shrugs, and, like a high-strung colt, tosses her hair like a mane and canters off down the hill to join Catriona at the barn at the bottom of the valley. I open my paperback, but reading won't work. I burst into tears. I haven't cried like this since I was a child. I'm not the blubbering sort. Neither are the children.

They're cut from strong cloth, my kids. I can hear Gammy Ross's voice in Holly. There's my Port Adelaide grandmother's blue eyes in Emma; a hint of my father Harry's charm in Catriona, mixed in with Constance Amy Ross's shyness. But god, please god, don't let Nicholas grow up, as Duncan did, in the image of his father.

I know I must take care when I talk about Duncan in

—213—

front of the children. I wanted to scream a moment ago—a primitive roar from the belly of rage—to rupture this peaceful valley where we play our happy and imaginary games. But I mustn't show how hurt I am; I can't express my anger or my fears. If he wins full custody, they'll have to live with him, grow up in his control. They'll have to fight, then, for themselves. I shan't be able to negotiate on their behalf. I can't always protect them. It's too late now to coach the kids in self-defense or independence. They'll be on their own. I can't do anything, now, to increase their vulnerability or to alienate them from their father.

But what about me? If he gets them, what will happen to my relationship with them? He hasn't tried to hide his rage at me. Won't they grow more like him, and end by hating me, too?

He may prevent them from seeing me.

They may not want to.

Will I then spend the remainder of my life regretting what I'm doing now? How can I really know, or have the gall to decide, that what seems best for me is best for them? My values, my view of the world—how can I be so sure? If, by holding fast to what I believe, I have to sacrifice my kids, will I still continue to believe that it was best for me to leave him, to struggle like this, for them? For what?

Should I risk such a loss for the sake of a few principles?

I've asked the court for one year together—in my care and control—before we reconsider a longer term. That will give us the chance to see if my plans are workable. But if I lose, Duncan will have them forever. Can I endure that loss?

Can they?

I can't retreat to what I had with Duncan, not even for their sakes. I can't forfeit my life, though it hurts me terribly to see them hurt. I can't imagine my life without them.

But who will care for them, as I care, if we are torn apart?

It's unthinkable that if Duncan wins this case, Nannie Cashmore will bring up my children. She scarcely knows them. She came to us initially on a part-time basis to look after the kids and run the house while I went to America for six months, but I cut the trip short to three, came home, left Duncan, and took the children with me. Duncan went to court for a temporary order returning them to him until this coming trial decides a longer arrangement. I suppose he's asked Nannie to stay on permanently. I cannot imagine how he'd manage without her.

I think Duncan likes Nannie. She probably reminds him of his own childhood nannie—another Londoner, strict, gray-haired, a stickler for routine and discipline. Nannie's husband is dead and her sons have long since grown up and left home. Duncan will give her a home, I expect. That won't please the kids.

I thought she'd do for the short run. But a substitute for me? I don't think she likes children very much.

"Open your eyes, Mummy! Come and see our new home."

The children are standing around me, silhouetted in the sun. I shade my eyes. There, down in the valley, they've laid some sticks and stones for imaginary walls on a make-believe stage.

"We're ready for the game, Mummy. What part are you going to play?"

The office is littered with books and papers like a military command post under siege. For the past four weeks we've been planning our objectives, taking evidence, deciding witnesses, imagining the cut and thrust of the other side, the four of us—Peter Fitzpatrick, his senior partner Auden Ellsworth, their junior assistant Casey Jones, and me—bent over telephones and typewriters and dictaphones in joint strategy sessions.

I've been the amateur, really, even though it's my life and my future we're plotting.

Oh, I've been helpful—vital, of course. I've watched the tactics, spotted gaps, tried to think of every possibility. Peter and I have dredged my memory, through all its accumulations, the sedimentary layers of my life, to remember, to anticipate, to collect.

Documentary evidence. Today will be my first day in court. I'm like a trained athlete, on my mark, heart pounding, waiting for the gun.

Sometimes I've felt out of control. Every day lately, I've woken feeling sick. Last night, after Annie put me to bed on her new king-size waterbed, the brandy she made me swallow gurgled in counterpoint with the mattress whenever I turned. She held my hand to help me relax. When I awoke this morning, my hand was anchored, numbly, beneath her shoulder. She didn't stir when I withdrew it.

After my bath, I let the towel slip to the floor and cleared a patch of mist off the mirror. My eyes were pinched. Skin glistened gray like a porpoise. There were creases down the valley between my breasts like a river delta at low tide. Steam swirled across the glass. I felt dizzy, held the sides of the basin, and retched.

I dressed in the costume Annie and I decided on yesterday: the camel wool button-down sleeveless tunic over a brown turtleneck and tights. The Frye boots were a mistake; I felt like a clumping carthorse. Rummaging in Annie's hall closet, I found a jaunty pair of red pumps that fit perfectly. Fine. I stared in the mirror.

Clean and sober, anywhere between thirty and forty: this one's a schoolteacher, perhaps. A fine mother and a good wife? Or Bette Davis playing an Egyptian mummy? Then I noticed the nipples. That would never do—erect, crimped, like starched ruffs—looks like defiance. Looks like fear? I undressed. I wasn't going to let them see my body knot with fear. I found a tin of Band-Aids in the cupboard behind the mirror. I taped both nipples flat under adhesive quilts. Better. I dressed again.

I combed my straight hair and drew a line of red lipstick. My mother would have told me to use some color today, especially with all the browns. If she were here, I'd probably refuse, on principle. I adjusted the belt but the touch on my stomach made me retch again. It was only saliva. I haven't eaten properly for weeks. Mustn't be sick on the stand.

Before I left to drive to Peter's office, I checked through the contents of my briefcase in Annie's kitchen. Fresh writing pad, last night's notes, the folder of preparatory jottings. My hands shook. In the front pocket, precious memorabilia. I lingered a moment over the postcard of the Statue of Liberty swimming backstroke with her torch high and dry above the waves; the pictures of the children in their school uniforms waving to me at the airport; two Met ticket stubs—one for Meyerbeer's *Les Huguenots,* the other from my first ballgame at Shea Stadium. My portfolio.

Had I overlooked anything?

I woke Annie to say good-bye. She wanted to make me breakfast; she's taking the day off from her clinic. Not because she'll be called as a witness. Not yet. And she won't be allowed in court yet. No observers, only combatants. She promised to stand by the telephone for news. She hugged me sleepily, and waved from the kitchen window when I started the car. She looked as scared as I felt.

I drove my old Morris through the Adelaide parklands that circle the inner city. It's been a cool July. Recent rains have swamped the onion weeds and left gum trees and jacarandas in tangled puddles. A raucous flock of pink and gray gallahs cackled over the playground where I used to wheel the pram and read in the shade while the children swung and slid and patted sand igloos. A mile farther, and I turned up a wide street on the eastern side of the park, then a right on King Edward Court where Peter has his office. What an omen! Edward the Eighth lost a throne. All I have to lose are my kids. I won't give in. I won't abdicate. I wish I could have them by my side today, my talismans of courage.

I parked between Peter's new Volvo and Auden's battered station wagon in their backyard. I'm glad I drive well, even when I feel sick.

Casey was making coffee in the kitchen.

"Want some? Black, I'm afraid. Someone left the milk out last night and it's sour. Oh, you do look queasy. Here, you need a shot of adrenalin. Go on in. Peter's on the blower, and Auden brought along some breakfast for you. Bet you haven't eaten, right?"

I nodded wanly and carried the mug into this office. Peter signed for me to clear books off the swivel chair and sit down. He mouthed, "The bun is from Auden. With you in a second."

I nibbled on the Bath bun but gagged at the first taste and replaced it on its sticky paper towel on top of a stack of files. I took out my notes.

I shan't have to take the stand today. Duncan goes first. By chance, he lodged his application minutes before mine. That worried me at the time. Had he gained an initiative? Would his seem more urgent, more ardent than mine? Peter assured me it makes no difference in the end; in fact, it might be to our advantage because Duncan, going first, will show his hand. Then we'll be trackers, following their prints. But I don't trust accidental advantages. Or Duncan's trajectory.

Anyway, surely it is terribly clear to all concerned that I already took the lead. I'm the one who's asked, with the absurd, improbable demand, to share the children. He has them; he has only to continue to refuse to give them up.

Isn't that the role of the respondent? I see I'm called that on these documents. If I'm not a respondent, what am I? I mean, does Peter really know? This is his first custody case. He's almost thirty and very smart, but does he *know*?

I try to read my notes. They look rather like one of my shopping lists, with dates, names, places, numbers in neat rows. Upside down, they could be my production annotations on a play script. I start to memorize them as if I were a student cramming for finals at the last minute. The marks swim and jostle on the page like tadpoles growing legs. When I squint, they're illegible. I look over at Peter again. He needs a closer shave. I wonder if he felt sick when he woke this morning.

I think the world of Peter. I didn't at first. My first lawyer handed me over to Peter when she was promoted. She's now a judge in Criminal Court. She assured me Peter's brilliant, with a gilt-edged reputation in civil law— insurance, damages, high finance, that sort of thing. He has never appeared in a Family Court case. Why on earth choose him, then? I asked her. It's like throwing a fledgling to the wolves.

"You're going to need a financial wizard in the long run," she said. "Property is the core of custody and divorce. That's why we usually leave it for last. Once you have the children, you'll need the dollars and cents. Believe me, that's the hardest part."

"But if I don't get the children, I won't need the money," I said.

"Wrong," she said.

They all say it's a landmark case. Our special difficulties have captivated Peter, as the children did when we began work on the case. Peter has given me undivided attention. Auden says it will help make Peter's name.

I'm beginning to feel and appreciate Auden's wise, benign presence behind Peter. Auden is just as brilliant but has decades of experience. His own father was a judge. Peter says Auden will never make the bench because he joined the Communist Party in the thirties. A previous Labor Government appointed him a Queen's Counsel, and he was an adviser to the Premier. But the Liberals disposed of Auden's services when they came back to power. In South Australia, the Liberal Party tends to stay in power. It will probably outlive Auden. Among fellow lawyers, Auden is said to have the keenest analytical mind, the sharpest wit, the most incisive memory for precedent. Peter says Auden's attracted to the most apparently hopeless cases because he enjoys the role of underdog. He loves defense. He anticipates a lesser lawyer's dumb mistake, and pounces.

Perhaps that's why Peter is pleased that I'm the respondent and that Duncan will be first on the stand today.

"Ready?" Peter has come around the desk and takes my hand. "A cab is on the way. I want to arrive early in case Schorman is prepared to negotiate. You never know what might happen at the last minute. Many cases are decided at the courtroom door. If only we have such luck." He laughs, nervously I think. "You'll have time to look around the court and get your bearings."

"Eat up, lass!" Auden's deep voice sounds behind us as he lurches into the office. "Can't think on an empty stomach." He takes my other hand. "Now, my dear, I want to give you some advice from an old hand. First, remember that Schorman's no fool. Oh, yes, he usually wins his family law. We know how hard this one will be for us. He'll be overconfident. Remember the type of man he is—overbearing, pompous, conservative. Maybe a little crafty and aggressive, but you can handle that. He'll be thinking he can push you over with his leading questions. Keep calm. Breathe deeply before you answer anything. Ask for the question again if you need a breathing space. Make yourself take time. Answer briefly, giving no more information than the question needs. Yes, or no. Let Schorman do the work and all the thinking. And tell the truth."

Auden pats my hand, looks intently at me, and continues. "Another matter. You will sit there, hearing people talk about you, the events of your life, your actions, words, feelings—your most private self. They will make mistakes.

They'll forget, they'll lie. You will want to rise and shout, No, no, no—it wasn't like that—it's not true. You will feel helpless and frustrated. Only parts, fragments of your story will appear. Like dots of color on a canvas, everyone adding a daub here, a shadow there, other perspectives, other lines. It will seem distorted—and untrue.

"You will have your chance, though. Even then, you cannot add all the colors, the depths, the meanings that you want. You can only answer questions, ours and theirs, not put them. Much will be left out. You will want to turn to the judge and shake him: 'This is the real story.' But you can't.

"Now, remember this. After a while, the dabs, squiggles, and small splashes of color will begin to take shape. You can stand back and see a pattern emerge. And you will find that it begins to approximate your story after all. It will be as near the truth, as much truth, as we lawyers will probably need. You must also believe, as I do, that it will be truth enough for the judge to make a fair decision. That is the process of the law. That is what we do every day. And, old fool that I am, I still believe in it, that it works. Or I wouldn't practice it."

Auden chuckles to himself and gazes out the window. I study his profile, imagine his unruly white hair under a full wig, these discreet, compassionate eyes and the gray brows and heavyweight nose set reassuringly above the bench. I hope my judge will look like this. Auden grins down at me. "And when you come back here at the end of the day, I'll have a great big Bloody Mary waiting for you. Now, off you go, all of you."

He kisses my cheek. We file down the narrow passage past smiling clerks who have gathered to watch us leave. Peter leads with two briefcases stuffed with papers. Casey follows with the books of case studies. Then me, holding the sticky bun in its white paper flag. I feel sick again.

We take the elevator to the fourth floor. It's a new building, the tallest in the city, its all-black facade strikingly modern in contrast with the granite and marble architectural styles that dominate Victoria Square and the major thorough-fares. When the doors slide open, I immediately see Duncan in front of the reception desk in the lobby. He is biting his nails. Damn. I whip around, half hoping the elevator will slam and speed me back to street level. Peter and Casey are right behind me, and Schorman has spotted us. He bustles toward Peter.

"We will proceed straight away." He avoids me. "Mr. Ross's father died early this morning. He has a funeral to handle on top of this. I recommended a delay, but he won't do it. Maybe take a break on Thursday," Schorman raises his voice, "so the man can bury his father." Then, to Peter in an aside, "Bad timing."

"Fine with us." Peter nods. Schorman walks back to Duncan and the potted plants.

Peter suggests I should wait in a small anteroom next to the number-one court. We have to walk past Duncan. His eyes narrow to a thin line, hover guardedly down my figure, and drop to the floor. He has not wept.

In the glass room where I wait alone, a wire mesh curtain turns images into negatives. Lawyers and court officials outside murmur in conspiratorial silhouette, their conversation consumed by carpet. Farther along the corridor, I can see a group of forlorn clients behind their own spidery bars. I light a cigarette. A coffee table has back numbers of *Time* magazine. This feels like a morgue.

So Donald Ross is dead. Why today? I am tempted, right now, to go and ask Duncan. He's sitting in the cubicle next to mine, crouched in a chair, his legs crossed, hands clutching knees as if the crotch were too tight.

But, I remember, we are not speaking to each other. That's his second suit—that I bought off the rack when the first, the honeymoon suit, the tailor-made suit, no longer fit. Now he's outgrown this one. Unless it's a formal occasion, he usually wears his Harris tweed over flannel slacks.

He's scuffing the carpet with his shoes. He must hate having to wait. We used to squabble over that—appointments, waiting rooms. I'd remind him it was time for an annual dental checkup. I'd make an appointment, but he never kept it. I'd say it was a bad example to the kids, but he'd shrug.

That damned pipe.

I stub out my cigarette. Where's Peter? It must be time. I decide to wait in the courtroom itself rather than see Duncan slumped in his chair.

It's a room the size of a squash court, with the same thick golden pile of the lobby carpet. Three rows of empty yellow chairs line the back spectator wall. I take one, and sit down.

The others arrive. Peter arranges our books and papers on a long bench in front of me that faces the raised dais along the opposite wall. Casey sits beside me and behind Peter. Schorman scuffles in, his black hair on end like an aggrieved porcupine. His junior counsel follows. I know her. That's Mary Best, captain of B hockey when I captained the A team. A Westall girl. She hasn't recognized me yet but nods to Duncan, who slinks in last of all and chooses the chair farthest from where we sit.

A clerk announces in unpunctuated monotones, "Ross versus Ross number A286 of 1978 Schorman and Son for the husband and Ellsworth Ellsworth and Fitzpatrick for the wife before His Honor Mr. Justice Simpson. Will the court please rise."

He is short and wears a gray suit, white shirt, and quiet navy tie, nondescript, withdrawn, a country schoolmaster grown stale with students. The Family Court is private and informal, so he does not wear his wig or gown. He sits at the top bench and glances through the papers another clerk has put before him. His face is round, bland, smooth-shaven.

Schorman stands to read a résumé of Duncan's affidavit. He lists their witnesses. I flinch at the names: Ivan

Goodall, Pamela Bodley, William Bodley, Nannie Cashmore. Both Bodleys? I make a note for Peter. Now I remember. Mary Best was a classmate of Schorman's daughter, a dark, attractive girl. I can't recall her name. And Mary Best lived across the street from our house in Hyde Park Road when I was twelve and she was ten. I feel much better writing notes, like a field anthropologist observing the natives.

Mr. Schorman addresses Judge Simpson as if they were chatting in the club over Scotch and water. For a clubman, there's a shrill edge, an odd sneer to his tone as if he has assumed that what he has to say is distasteful. Reporters are not permitted into Family Court, but Schorman drops his voice as if there were hidden microphones.

"Mr. Goodall, Your Honor, is Mr. Ross's partner and an old family friend to both parties. He will testify as to his numerous business trips to New York where he himself saw the apartment to which the wife proposes she will take the children.

"Then the neighbors, Your Honor, are Mrs. Pamela Bodley who manages a sporting goods store, I believe, and her husband, Mr. William Bodley, an accountant in private practice. They are the parents of two children. They appear, Your Honor, under our subpoena, to give evidence as to the material circumstances of my client and the condition in which they observed the children during the absence of the wife. Finally, we will call the housekeeper, Mrs. Cashmore—'Nannie' to the children, Your Honor—who, as daily helper and confidante to the children of the marriage, will testify as to the undue influence of the mother and the substantial changes in mind and attitude effected by the mother upon the children with the consequence that they have been turned against their father. It is our contention, Your Honor, that the mother has thus induced the children to appear to wish to accompany her to New York for little more than a grand holiday. My client will tell Your Honor that this change in the attitude of the children is a result of extreme pressures on the part of the wife since her return."

The wife? The children? We sound like packages. But now it is Peter's turn. He begins slowly and quietly. We will call Dr. Susannah Goodall as a witness expert in child psychology, a mother of two sons, the former wife of Mr. Goodall, witness for the husband.

"Miss Gwenyth Adair will give evidence to support her sworn affidavit before this court that two of the children have deteriorated emotionally, intellectually, and physically during the period of time when they have been in Mr. Ross's care and without their mother's daily parenting. Miss Adair is the Headmistress of Westall Church of England Girls College where both Mrs. Ross and her daughters have attended school. In Miss Adair's opinion, the children need their mother as the primary parent."

Peter then calls for two reports to be deposed as evidence. The clerk hands documents to the judge, who lists them as Exhibits R7 and R8. I haven't seen these reports, but Schorman shifts uncomfortably in his chair while Peter describes them.

"My learned friend, Your Honor, consents to the admission of these professional reports. The first is that of Johannes Leske, a court-appointed welfare officer; the second, R8, is a case interview made by Dr. Hermione Rogers, noted psychiatrist. By order of the court made in an earlier hearing before Judge Gordon, and preliminary to this main trial, these reports are the record of separate interviews with both parties and the children concerned."

Peter adds that he reserves the right to call witnesses to the reports if necessary. Schorman leaps up to object, and both lawyers hold a whispered conference. Peter then announces that such witnesses will be called only after prior agreement is reached.

Judge Simpson peers over half-moon spectacles, first at Peter, then at Schorman, but never lifts his eyes to the back row.

"I call Mr. Ross."

I look up with a start. It has begun, just as I have been lulled into a state of reasonable receptivity by Peter's calm opening remarks. Schorman smiles to Duncan, who walks toward the witness box to the left of the judge's bench. The clerk hands Duncan a Bible.

I study him in profile while he is sworn. His pipe is tucked, stem first, into his coat's breast pocket. He used to burn holes in pockets when it smouldered. That suit has to be ten years old. Keep him at a distance. His voice squeaks. He has pitched it too high. He blinks at the judge. His eyesight has been weakening for years, but he refuses to see a doctor or to wear glasses. The last time I saw him at work, he wore a silly surgical contraption—a magnifying mirror attached to a bright light—over his eyebrows so that he could see what he was drawing. Now he faces Schorman. I wonder if he can see as far as Peter, see how young Peter is. He strokes his beard as if surprised, and comforted, to find it there.

Every word is recorded by two alternating stenographers. The silence between phrases and the pause before an answer is filled with the punctilious tap-tap-tap of their metal machines. Duncan clears his throat. His right hand, on the bench in front of him, clenches, relaxes, then clenches again, as if a live weight thrashes and tugs on the end of a line.

Schorman bends to his notes. I cannot fathom the logic behind the sequence of questions. Mary reads papers next to him like a stage prompt. I think she has rehearsed Duncan in his lines, a captain who practices moves with the team on the eve of an important game. Duncan has never remembered dates well. I found many inaccuracies in his affidavit. Oddly enough, today he sounds word perfect. He doesn't stumble over the date of our marriage, the charter of his company, the names and birthdates of our children.

His top lip curls, however, as if he doubts the meanings of things remembered. If he pauses before he answers, his hand tightens. If the question is one he enjoys, he yields to the padded bench and his facial muscles loosen. I know that body. I know its lunges and its withdrawals. I know it better than I know these words.

ROSS VERSUS ROSS
A286, 1978

Mr. Schorman, examination of Mr. Duncan Ross:
"You have told us that the marriage was happy for about eight years. What happened then?"

"She was not emotionally satisfied."

"What did you say to her about that?"

"It developed into a complaint that I did not love her. It appears, in retrospect, that we didn't have the emotional contact that she desired."

"Did that cause some disagreements between you from time to time?"

"Yes. On a number of occasions which might not have started as rows but ended up as such, and covering subjects like money and her general unhappiness."

"Did she ever make any comment to you about how you might overcome her emotional situation by telling her you loved her or something of the kind?"

"There was one occasion. Not a serious one. On the following day, she said the row would not have happened if I'd taken her in my arms and said I loved her. Personally, I very much doubted that it would have happened that way."

"What occurred at that row? Did your wife throw something at you?"

"Yes. It was a wine cask, a cardboard cask that was half empty. I was leaning against the refrigerator and it didn't do me much harm. I may have shoved her around a little in return."

"Did you say anything to her on that occasion about stopping her from leaving the house?"

"She was very upset. She told the children to pack their overnight bags because she was taking them to stay with a friend. I suppose she meant the Goodalls. I considered her to be in no fit state to take the children out of the house. I said she could go if she wanted to, by all means, but there was no way I would let her take the children out of my house with her."

"What time was this?"

"Exactly eight o'clock. I was on my way back to work. Of course I ended up staying home."

"She says here, in her affidavit, that you threatened to kill her if she took the children."

"I merely said that I would prevent her from taking them. By force if necessary."

"I see."

His Honor:

"Mr. Ross, are you by nature a violent man?"

"I beg your pardon?"

"Are you in the habit of shoving your wife?"

"No. Of course not. This time I was put under extreme pressure."

"Thank you. You may proceed."

Mr. Schorman:

"What family do you have living?"

"I have . . . I am an only child. My living relatives consist of three—no, four cousins. My mother died . . . several years ago. My father died this morning. He has been ill for some time. Mother wasn't ill. She was sen . . . of unsound mind."

"Mr. Ross, quite a bit has been said about financial matters. Would you say that your wife was extravagant with money?"

"Not extravagant, exactly. No. I would say she was unable to spend money economically."

"You made some mention, did you not, of luxuries? Did she tend to buy luxuries rather than necessities?"

"Yes. Strawberries, mushrooms, things from the green-grocer. Most likely things that were out of season."

"Casey, this is ghastly. Why doesn't Peter object? That terrible fight—he's wrong, it's all wrong—he tried to hurt me." I put my hand over my breast.

"Sh! I know, Morgan, but we can't say anything yet. Peter will get back to this through cross-examination. Right now we have to listen. Be patient. Take notes. Whatever sounds wrong, write it down. Alright?"

"No, it's not. The judge will get the wrong impression. These aren't the important issues. This is trivia. We must let Peter know."

Peter turns around inquiringly. Casey shakes her head quickly. I'm twisting my pencil between my fingers. Casey puts her hand on mine and whispers again, "It's hard. Think of it as a play: Act one, scene one—okay?"

"But, Casey, I'm used to acting, not watching."

"Well, think of it as a rehearsal. They're lousy actors with rotten lines. B-grade, right?" I nod. She pats my hand. "You're not the only one. I've got the butterflies, too."

"We have our first advantage." Peter rubs his hands happily.

I watch him prise a raw Sydney rock oyster from its shell and dip it in a piquant sauce.

I shouldn't have consented to oysters today. They taste too glutinous. The first morning session is over, but Schorman has not completed his examination of Duncan. We are having lunch in a café across the street from the court. On our way out, I saw Duncan greet Ivan Goodall and together enter a delicatessen in the basement of the court building. I imagine him ordering ham and cheese on toast and a cup of instant coffee. Separate checks. He'll stick to the basics.

"Yes," Peter continues, "now that Ivan has arrived, Schorman has decided to call him. This way, Duncan must leave the courtroom during Ivan's evidence because nei-ther Schorman nor I have finished our examination and Duncan is still under oath. Morgan, eat!"

"I can't. I still feel sick. How is that an advantage?"

"I can put questions to Ivan that Duncan will have to tackle later without the benefit of knowing Ivan's response. I may be able to trip him. In fact, it's going rather well for us."

"How?"

"Because Duncan is wearing his colors like a racing jockey. He's running true to form, don't you think?"

"Ross out of Ross, you mean—gray, red, and black—wounded, angry, and inflexible."

Peter laughs. He asks to see my notes and scans them quickly. "What's this query about the Bodleys?"

"Why are they appearing for Duncan?"

"Because they have to. Worry about them when the time comes. I want your hunch about Ivan. What will his true colors be?" Peter leans over and helps himself from my untouched plate. "May I finish these?"

"Have them all. Pompous pink, I imagine, with a bluster of purple snobbery on a field of gregarious green. How am I doing?"

"Extremely well, although you could do with some color yourself." Peter scrutinizes me. "Try not to fret. You have too much imagination. You're the sort who hears the siren and sees blood long before the plane flies overhead. They haven't dropped any bombs yet, Morgan. Duncan's evidence held no surprises."

"But Ivan? Can Ivan harm me? Remember, he did see me in New York."

"It can be worked both ways. If you really are the unfit mother Duncan would have us believe, then Ivan would never have left his son in your care, and in your New York apartment."

"Peter." He has ordered a pot of tea. I can manage that; it's strong and sweet. He looks up. His face is lean like his body, and his smile is relaxed and reassuring. "I'm finding it very confusing. There's no order, no chronology. Schorman darts about without attempting to place questions in a real time frame. It reminds me of those picture puzzles in children's books where you had to find all the things that were wrong. Like a man without a mouth. Or you had to look for real things in what appeared to be a jumble of meaningless lines. I'm sure they're setting traps, but I can't see what they are."

"Try pretending it's a paper chase. All we have to do is to follow their scraps of paper. Then you'll know how to lay your trail for Schorman to follow. Actually, that's rather good, isn't it—must remember to tell Auden. What's wrong? Are you cold?"

"I'm scared. I can't pretend. It doesn't feel like a game. When I'm sitting there in court, trying to follow what's happening, my mind jumps around with the questions, but what I remember . . . I'm not sure anymore."

"Don't try to work out what's happening. It's too soon, and it's too close to you. If it's any comfort, let's imagine Schorman puffing to catch the pieces of *your* life before you and the kids blow off on the wind to America." He folds his napkin tidily, ready to leave.

"I have an imagination for disaster, remember."

"Then better not waste it on anticipation. That's my job. Coming?"

I let him go ahead. In the bathroom, I cup water in my hand to splash my face. Nothing fits. The pieces don't add up. Duncan's narrative of our marriage was too simply told, as though he'd consented to its terminal insignificance. This isn't the way I wanted to end it. There's still something I want, something from the marriage of which I'm unsure.

"Call Mr. Ivan Goodall."

He smiles fleetingly when he lumbers past me on his way to take the oath. Ivan was six feet tall at the age of fifteen. His father, the farmer, built their farmhouse exactly to the scale of a Cornish miner's cottage, low-beamed with narrow doors and passageways. Ivan always stoops, like a dazed giant.

He's an only child like Duncan, and it shows, Annie and I think, in the stoop, in the guarded way he looks at people. He nods to the judge as if they've met before. He wears a similar suit, but brown with a vest and pearl buttons. Ivan has done well for himself. Unlike Duncan, he's an optimist. Shortly after they began their partnership, Ivan spent exorbitant amounts of money on long-distance calls. He wants them to grow to multinational proportions, but Duncan always checks Ivan's ambitions and distrusts his judgment. Since undergraduate days, Ivan rose smoothly from temporary jobs in government offices to company director, member of several boards, Junior Chamber of Commerce, and chair of the Cathedral Restoration. He's come a long way from the Cornish farm.

When he repeats the oath, his nostrils work like bellows. Schorman at once asks questions about my New York apartment. With a thrill of inspiration, I draw a quick sketch of it, then add two more rooms to extend the scale to twice its actual size. Peter offers my sketch as evidence, to help Ivan remember. Ivan glances at it, nods, and resumes a description that swells to match the new dimensions. He marks each room with a number to distinguish his route through the house. As I hoped, my drawing looks ever more substantial, like one of Duncan's blueprint designs. Ivan even adds some touches of his own, like a salesman impressing a potential buyer. I stifle incredulity and grasp my notepad as Lady Teazle did with her concealing fan. Is Ivan lying—or showing off? Surely he doesn't want to help me.

When Schorman asks him to describe his business trips to New York, we have a map ready. I've marked on it my apartment, the school where I've enrolled the children, the nearest parks and playgrounds, the bus and subway stops. I know Ivan never rode the subway nor walked along the lower west side. Ivan's Manhattan is a midtown tourist brochure. Skyscrapers awe him; doormen in uniforms excite him; yes sir, he feels as safe in New York as he does in Sydney or Melbourne or in any large metropolis.

I'm so nervous that I calm myself by sketching Ivan in the dock. I draw his head too large for the torso, his eyes too close together, but I catch exactly the slightly spoiled pout of his lips. Schorman doesn't have to encourage him. Ivan readily enjoys this experience. He is just as Annie predicted: man of the world sophisticate, teaching the judge and Schorman how big the world really is.

When he called me in New York from Kennedy Airport, he was a different man.

"Tim's with me. Annie agreed I could bring him, show him something of the world. Yes, of course the Shed pays; he's still half fare. Look, I've masses of work to do, contracts to sew up—only a week—he misses his mother. Can you? He'll like that. I'm taking a room in midtown—meetings, cocktails, that sort of thing. Do you have a washing machine? Oh, with your own load. Good. Thanks."

He dumped Tim and their travel-stained clothing on my doorstep. Not that I minded. I was missing my children horribly. While I had Tim, the nightmares ceased—the bushfire dreams, or plunging airplanes, bodies akimbo in free fall.

I didn't mind at all taking time off from work. I couldn't seem to tackle anything big; my confidence took a dive whenever I worried about the children. Pamela Bodley had hinted at home troubles in a letter—nothing precise, merely rumblings of discontent across the street, nothing serious enough to have me return immediately, she wrote—but that was enough for me. I brought forward my scheduled return. By the time Ivan and Tim arrived, I still had two weeks to opening night, four to my departure. Tim was family. We walked everywhere together. I saw miracles on the streets through Tim's eyes and hoped my children would one day discover them with me.

Ivan was wary and suspicious on the streets. We ate at

a restaurant before they left New York. Once safe inside, Ivan took charge with his usual flair, made a show of tasting the wine before it was poured, produced an American Express card like a conjuror showing me new tricks, and tipped too high.

I wanted to ask about Duncan, so while we drank espresso, I sent Tim off to buy the Sunday *Times* in Sheridan Square.

"I'm afraid of what he'll do when I leave with the children. More afraid of the emotional mess than his physical strength. He'll try to bully me into returning to him. And I have no money of my own. I'm not sure how we can survive unless I find a well-paid job in Adelaide. Ivan, they litigate, the Ross family. It won't be easy, but I can't stand it much longer. We can't talk anymore. I can't negotiate with him."

Ivan nodded but looked embarrassed. So I switched the talk to the time our families grew together, the children playing under the gloryvines outside my back porch, dappled sun and shadows on the hibiscus, the ripe loquat tree, the mulberry tree in blossom. Then he told me softly, so that no one could overhear, that he and Annie had agreed to a trial separation. I knew because Annie wrote every week; we always consulted each other first. I let Ivan tell me in his own ponderous way.

"You'll be alright," he said morosely. "Women are always alright. You have support groups. What will happen to me? I'm all alone. It's such a big house. We bought that house because Annie and I wanted an extended family, a community—friends, boarders, guests, other children— We wanted to fill it with friends. You know, like we had with you before you and Duncan grew apart. It was really Annie's idea, I suppose. She's been the one with creative ideas. We've been reasonably amicable. We agreed to share the boys, school weeks with her, weekends with me in the big house. We don't need lawyers, Annie and me. But I'm the one who ends up alone. It's the men who get stranded."

"Nonsense, Ivan, men do have groups. You have the Chamber of Commerce, Boy Scouts, Freemasonry. Even Duncan has the Shed. And both of you have money."

"That isn't the same security as family, Morgan. I don't have friends the way you have Annie. Without her, there's virtually nothing left for me." He put his hand over mine and pressed it. "Sometimes, Morgan, I've wondered, haven't you? There's always been something close between us. I mean, in a way, you made my life with Annie possible. I should never have met and married her without you. You're my oldest friend. Whatever happens now between you and Duncan, we can still have each other, can't we? We can help each other. Maybe—well, you never know, something may come of that."

I withdrew my hand. "Ivan, there's no choosing sides in this. Annie comes first with me, and always will. Of course I'm fond of you, but the children and Annie are my foundation stones. Duncan has drifted away. You may, too. I can't take care of either of you. We all have to find our own way. Can't you see? We can't go back."

"But I don't want to lose you, Morgan."

"You can't hang on to me. I've only got strength enough for one right now. Look, here's Tim. Before we go back to my apartment to pack, I want to show you both my lovely theatre. I'm a great success here, Ivan, I'm proud to say. They've asked me to come back. . . . Tim, darling, you know the way, will you be our guide? No point moping, Ivan. We have too much to do."

Peter's questions lead Ivan up and down familiar paths. His cross-examination concentrates on Ivan's relationship with Duncan, who is out of earshot in the cubicle next door.

Peter asks if Duncan's work habits have always been the same. Ivan describes Duncan as a work addict. Peter pokes at worn spots. He encourages Ivan to compare their attitudes to work and holidays, to spending time with children, to spending money. Duncan, says Ivan, is mean. One does not negotiate with Duncan, especially over company money. Ivan tells Peter how he came to my rescue and took money out of my loan account with the company to help me pay for my expenses in America.

"It was really her money, of course. Our wives were directors and earned directors' fees. But Duncan insisted that Morgan's fees should be reinvested in the company. He looked upon anything either of them earned as belonging to the Shed. He disregarded my advice on that."

"What was your advice?"

"To pay her fees direct to Morgan, as we did to my wife. My wife and I used those earnings to pay for our boys' holidays and school expenses. That's what Morgan needed, but Duncan said the Shed's needs were more important. I thought Duncan was wrong."

"Would you leave your son in Mrs. Ross's care again?"

"Of course I would, anytime, anywhere. Both boys are with her right now because she's staying with my . . . with them for the present. Morgan is like a second mother to them."

"No further questions." Peter is satisfied.

CHAPTER TEN

In his office, at the end of our first day, Peter thumbs through the interview notes he took a few weeks ago when he talked in turn with Pamela and Bill Bodley. I'm so tired, I lie in his swivel armchair and watch him numbly. Casey stayed behind at the court to collect the day's transcripts. Auden went home after the promised drinks spiced with his questions about Schorman's demeanor. I ache as if I'd run a marathon without rewards—of food and rest, of finality. Tomorrow will be the Bodleys' day in court.

"Why haven't you discussed these interviews with me before?" I ask Peter. "I'm astonished that they're appearing for Duncan. Pamela is scathing about him. She knows he's incapable of bringing up the children without me. You should hear her, Peter! When I was in America, and Holly had the measles, Duncan refused to leave his work and called Pamela to take time off herself and care for Holly, as if her own work didn't matter, as if she were some kind of nursemaid."

"I did hear her, remember, and decided not to call her."

"Why ever not?"

"I thought she could be harmful," Peter mumbles.

"How? She's an ideal witness against Duncan."

"Unfortunately, when we met, Pamela insisted on my promise not to discuss with you anything she was about to say. You see, she didn't want to get involved."

"Peter, she *is* involved. Whether she chose it or not, her involvement in our family affairs goes back three years. I don't see how she can deny that."

"I had to assure her we wouldn't call her into court. However, Schorman had already scheduled his interview with them both, to follow mine. Pamela agreed that if *they* call on either herself or Bill for evidence, only then might I tell you the substance of my interview. She doesn't want you to know what she said, unless, at the last minute—"

"Has said? Will say? What's going on? Peter, you've never held back information from me, nor I from you. What has Pamela said that she can't say to me directly? What can she say to a judge or to Schorman, or to you for that matter, that she can't tell me face to face? And you, Peter—I've trusted both of you."

"I promised, Morgan. She says she doesn't want to lose your friendship."

"A friend doesn't make such conditions. You're talking like a lawyer. Why are you so evasive?" Why do I feel betrayed, suspecting him of laying a trap, in league with Pamela Bodley?

Peter has found the handwritten pages and passes them to me. "The subpoena means that the Bodleys will appear against their will, Morgan. Schorman must be short of friendly witnesses to have to force them into testifying. Remember that. Although I've kept my promise to Pamela, now I think it's fair that you should read these notes. They may answer your questions better than I can."

I hunt through the pages and skim the derisory remarks about Duncan. Those I already know. There's a lot, too, about how cold and unfurnished our house is, how poorly the children behaved while I was in America, how in Pamela's opinion neither Duncan nor I are effective disciplinarians.

There it is: sex. "Duncan is a dry old stick." That sounds like Pamela. "Morgan wants more than Duncan is prepared to give her. Morgan has many women friends"— and that could be Schorman's sneer. I look up at Peter.

"Just tell me what can hurt me. Is it 'women friends'?"

"Perhaps my notes don't tell it all. Pamela concentrated on her version of events on the Christmas Day shortly before your trip away. Apparently you disappeared early in the morning, before the children had opened their presents. According to Pamela, you visited your 'current girlfriend,' Jenny Murphy, and after Christmas dinner with your mother and the Bodleys, again disappeared to some other afternoon party, leaving Pamela with your mother and Duncan. Pamela believes that you spent some nights away from home with other women. And that if Duncan then went back to work, the children sometimes were on their own."

"Go on." I am too tired. "Neglect, is that it? From Pamela, of all people."

"That's not all. Where I think she may be harmful is in what she has to say about Jenny. I gather you and Jenny, some time before the revue, before you went to America . . . I gather she was your special . . . your—"

"Lover." My mind races backward.

"And," Peter continues quickly, "after you left, Jenny often visited the children after school, stayed for dinner, and generally babysat for Duncan, often taking the younger ones across the road to see Pamela's family. Pamela says Jenny was your substitute, or wanted to be. Jenny took your letters and photographs to show Pamela. There were, in Pamela's words, 'intimate details' of your relationship."

Why has Peter not told me this before? I thought we'd agreed not to involve Jenny; it might look bad for me that she left her own kids. "It's over, past history. We haven't denied anything."

"We may have to. It rather depends on what Pamela chooses to say in court. And that depends on what Schorman already knows. That worries me more than your letters."

"Why? What else can Pamela say?"

"Apparently one of the pictures was of you and Jenny naked or, as Pamela describes it, in 'incriminating poses.'

Actually, I think the word she used was 'pornographic.' Let me see my notes."

"There's no need. For god's sake, Peter, we were probably splashing around with the hose on a hot summer day or sunbathing on the lawn. Pamela can't produce any pictures in court. Surely I can refute her interpretation by explaining it was all in play?"

"Morgan, anything Pamela can say to imply that you've been careless in front of the children, or that your behavior was ever brazen or irresponsible, can harm you. Imagine what Schorman can do with this!" Peter rifles through the notes. "You haven't read this part. Pamela states, here, that she saw Jenny kiss Holly. On the lips."

So that's it. Child molesting. Corruption. Whore lover mother child, transparent, larger than life. They'll feast on it. How dare she! How can . . .

"Pamela would do that? Twist innocent affection into lust?"

Peter watches me sadly. I light a cigarette and stare at him through the smoke. He reaches a decision.

"Let's drive back to Annie's place. I'll ask her to give evidence on this. She knows Jenny, doesn't she?"

"Of course."

"Annie may be able to defuse this material. I think there's a way. I'll call to say we're coming now."

I follow his Volvo, driving purely on automatic reflexes. It's a double blow: Pamela's disgust, and Peter's willingness to keep it secret from me. I've been a fool to think that sexuality is a side issue, that my frank admittance is enough, that Peter, at least, has understood and accepted that. As I drive the reverse route of this morning, scenes with Jenny and Pamela replay in rapid commotion and in disarray, as if my part, in flashback, had been cut and pasted by several crude and careless hands. Pamela's forgotten who I am and who I have been for her. Perhaps she's hurt because I'm leaving, and she'll punish me by doing what she can to keep my children here—especially

Holly—in the house opposite, in the house across her street. Perhaps she thinks I don't deserve to leave Duncan and have the children, too.

My head spins. How can I know what Pamela thinks when all I have for reference is a handful of images of brief times together, when what she had to bear must have made my disintegrating marriage seem in comparison a paltry—and endurable—affliction.

Sitting in my car in Annie's driveway, I conjure Pamela's face in the windscreen. She reminds me, still, of my sister Cicely in her skirts and twinsets and sturdy sensible shoes, with her sons and her devoted husband.

While Cicely and I have drawn apart as we age, Pamela has been a late friend to me, a friendship defined and nurtured by shared misery.

Once, at the beach where Pamela and I had taken the children for a swim, we stood together side by side in the shallows by the old jetty at Port Willunga, and I felt the ways we both had weathered, resolute and firm against the elements. I thought of her as a tough encrusted crab, and envied some of her defenses. Surrounded by swirling waves and tumbling children, she had seemed to me immutable.

Pamela had planned to train to be a doctor, but her father refused to pay for a daughter in medical school; it wasn't women's work. He also refused to attend her wedding because Bill had been a scholarship boy and his father was a butcher. Her father and mother did rally after Elizabeth died, but Pamela thought of herself as a respectable rebel and the black sheep of her family. Partly for that, I took for granted that she respected my own rebellions. She took my side in my battles with Donald Ross when he disapproved of my politics and decided to curtail my allowance. She encouraged me to take up the travel grant to spend six months in America. She even helped me train Duncan to shop and to manage the house in my absence, and she promised to keep an eye on the children and remind Duncan about haircuts and dental appointments because she knew he was unreliable.

And dear reliable Bill! Once, washing up together after Elizabeth's death, he crushed me to him and kissed me warmly.

"You're a real love," he said. "You're the only person who's got through to Pam, y'know. She won't let me comfort her. Won't talk about it. I reckon she'd have broken down without you. Honest, Morg, you're a bit of alright. Reckon I've got a bit of a thing for you."

"Oh, Bill, thanks, but take those soapy paws off me. Don't misunderstand me, Bill. I'm flattered. That's my first good bear hug for years. From a man, I mean." I laughed.

"Listen, Morg, whatever it is with you and . . . well, girls . . . that's alright with me, too. That's your own business, and it never made a scrap of difference with me because I think you're—well, Duncan needs his head read, that's all. Bloody idiot, if you ask me."

Annie has opened my car door.

"Hey, dinner's ready and waiting. Peter's already told me about our friend Pamela. I'd like to throw my garbage over her fence or scrawl indecent graffiti on her walls, I'm so angry with her. You should be angry, too, not huddled out here on your own. Come and take it out on your chopsticks and tell me every word about today's hearing. I want it all—Duncan, Ivan, Schorman—every contemptuous word and sadistic look; and then we shall slice up the handmaiden, Pamela Bodley, for sweet desserts!"

"Oh, Annie, I don't deserve you." We walk arm in arm together to her kitchen door.

"Oh, yes, indeed you do. Forget that Pamela has been your friend. Forget that you ever trusted her. Think of her as a voter in a compulsory referendum: she'll prefer the nays rather than risk your daring leaps without safety nets. That's her privilege. Ours is to eat cold sesame noodles by the fire and drink what I must admit is my very best vintage claret."

In the morning, when she passes me, Pamela Bodley avoids my eye. I want to grab her, turn her to face me, jolt recognition by physical contact. Her face is expressionless, just as it was after Elizabeth's death.

Schorman treats her gently, but it is hard to hear her reluctant answers. With his promptings, Pamela discloses how annoyed Duncan made her feel when he insulted her professional responsibilities, how resentful she was to be forced to take my place when I was away.

"The children are not the problem," she tells the judge. "It's the marriage. Morgan should never have left Duncan to take care of those children. She should have known he couldn't manage. She should have known I'd have to get involved."

Her bluntness stabs me. It's as if Pamela, forced to look through a family album, says, at the end, "No, I do not know these people at all."

It is over very quickly. Schorman has not asked any of the questions Peter asked in his private interview. Pamela has not said what Peter was afraid she would.

When Bill appears, he kisses my cheek on his way to the box. He is slightly shorter than Pamela, athletic and well-muscled, more youthful than his forty years. His answers in cross-examination are more expansive than hers. An accountant, he must be accustomed to explaining facts and interpreting choices and their consequences to other people.

"In your own words, what happened after Morgan returned from America and finally left Duncan, taking the children temporarily to Annie Goodall's home?" Peter begins an informal discussion after Schorman finishes with Bill. Even Judge Simpson appears to relax.

"Duncan saw a lot of us at first."

"Did he seem upset when Morgan left him?"

—243—

"Not upset as much as surprised. I think he was shocked to find she'd actually gone."

"How did he show this?"

"He came over on a Sunday early, soon after Morgan returned from New York. Must've been shortly after it became clear to all of us that the whole thing would have to go to court. He was real angry. He told me Morgan had taken the kids with her and refused to return them to him. He threatened to go to where she was staying and take them back by force."

"What do you think he meant by that?"

"Exactly that. I was worried for the kids' safety, and for Morgan, too. So I called up and went to see her. She agreed to let me take the kids back home to my place to talk with their father. Well, I did. But Duncan didn't really talk with them. He sat them down in my study and put the telly on. I gave him some time, then I took all the kids back to Morgan—that's what I'd promised to do, and they'd agreed to that. But I knew Duncan was following my car. His hackles were up. He was insisting she had no right to have those kids."

"Did he say that, or did you suppose it?"

"Oh, he said that and more. He had a helluva lot to say to me for once. When he arrived at Annie Goodall's house, the three of us—Duncan, Morgan, and me—sat around the kitchen table and tried to negotiate. I thought I might be able to, well, facilitate some kind of friendly discussion."

"Did you succeed?"

"There was a long discussion, but it wasn't very friendly. Well, it turned out, what with Duncan screaming the kids should go home with him, and Morgan pretty determined that they wanted to be with her, I got them to agree on one thing. I'd ask the kids to speak for themselves. These kids've got minds of their own, Your Honor. Well, then we had trouble over the wording of it."

"Please tell His Honor what was the question put to the children."

"Well, Morgan thought it wasn't fair to drag them in, but Duncan was so worked up, he got his way. I had to go downstairs, where they were waiting, to ask the four children separately, in Duncan's words, 'Would you mind going home with Daddy?'"

"Was it your understanding that this question referred only to that particular weekend, or did Mr. Ross intend it to refer to a longer period?"

"It was my understanding and, I reckon, the kids' too, that Duncan meant there and then. The two older girls went upstairs at once and told their parents they'd decided to stay with their mother. That showed a lot of guts, I thought. The two younger ones whispered their answer to me instead and asked me to tell it to their father for them."

"What was their answer?"

"Holly said she didn't want her father to stay home all alone. She was worried he'd be lonely. She and Nicholas decided they would come with him for that week, then go back to their mother the following week, and take turns like that until everything was settled."

"I see. What was Duncan Ross's reaction to their answer?"

"Objection." Schorman is on his feet. "My young friend is inviting this witness to express an opinion when he can only give the facts as he himself saw them."

"That's what I was getting at, Your Honor. This witness can say what he saw or heard. He's not being asked for an opinion."

His Honor leans forward to Bill Bodley. "Did Mr. Ross react to the children's answers?"

"He took the two younger children home with him."

"Then it was your understanding, Mr. Bodley, as you have said in evidence, that the children expressed a wish to return with their father as a short-term, not a permanent, decision. The younger ones I mean, Holly and Nicholas. Eh?"

"Yes. I thought they meant for just that week. I reckon they felt sorry for Duncan."

"However, Mr. Bodley," Peter quickly resumes, "would it not be true to say, as indeed you have expressed it to this court, that you observed the children are closer to their mother than to their father? And, again in your opinion, they would seem, especially in the case of the three daughters, to have a special need of her mothering?"

"Yes, I'd have to agree on that one. With puberty coming along, things like that."

"That is all, Your Honor. No further questions."

After the judge thanks Bill and Pamela for their appearance, he announces we shall break for lunch. While Peter puts his notes in order, ready to begin his cross-examination of Duncan, I try not to think about that Sunday morning in the kitchen when the children waited in Annie's playroom underneath our shouts and accusations.

Peter sits down beside me. "Bill was good for us. I think it's going rather better than I expected."

"It's all in bits and pieces still. It seems to have too little to do with the children."

"It has everything to do with them, you'll see. Are you hungry? No? Listen, Morgan, I can't have you fade away in front of Judge Simpson before you do your stuff. Let's give seafood a rest. I know just the place around the corner. It's smorgasbord: roast beef, ham, leg of lamb, pasta primavera, pesto, artichoke hearts—everything you adore—and you help yourself. Does that stimulate the tastebuds? Then there's pineapple, avocado, mango, pawpaw, passionfruit—"

"Stop. I'll eat. I promise. Peter, I adore you!"

"Good. It's sort of mutual, and while you eat your first food for a week, we've got some reading to do. I'm bringing Dr. Rogers's report. I think you should study it."

"There's no let-up, is there!"

"No. But this will interest you. I think you'll be surprised."

Exhibit R8 is a typed report that looks like a letter on Dr. Hermione Rogers's office notepaper. It addresses both solicitors as "Gentlemen:" and concludes with her flowery signature.

Dr. Rogers is the only woman among Adelaide's small core of psychiatrists in private practice. She is my age and height, with florid auburn coloring and a cool professional manner. I'd felt confident in that manner during our two interviews. She'd appeared in several earlier custody cases and knew what courts expected of psychiatric evidence, so her questions were to the point and seemed, to me at least, to focus only on the issues in our affidavits. Both Duncan and I had been ordered to undergo interviews. I also had to take the children twice individually to talk with her. I'd presumed she would appear in court to testify about her findings, but Peter and Schorman had simply agreed to have her report accepted without further examination.

With the report now in my hands, I ask Peter again, "Why isn't Dr. Rogers coming in to court?"

"She would if one or other side hadn't accepted her findings. Frankly, I'm relieved she won't have to take the stand. She's probably the best of the court-appointed shrinks; she was involved in both previous custody cases involving a lesbian mother . . ."

"And she seemed very positive toward me and the children . . ."

"And neither of those women gained custody. Now, I think you should read before you ask more questions."

INTERVIEW WITH
MRS. MORGAN EVANS ROSS

This covered four main topics:

a. The personalities of the four children and Mrs. Ross's perception of the changes in their personalities since her trip to the U.S.A. in January 1977.

b. Mrs. Ross's reasons for wishing to take the children to the U.S.A. with her.

c. Mrs. Ross's career and future plans.

d. Mrs. Ross's personal relationships, including the marriage, the breakdown in the marriage, and her sexuality.

a. Mrs. Ross said that when she left for the U.S.A., the children were excited that she was taking up the travel grant. She said that Emma has always been shy but wants to be a leader in her peer group. Emma enjoyed some of the aspects of being the eldest child of the family while her mother was away, and took increasing responsibilities in the family. Mrs. Ross thought that there had been problems for Catriona and Holly in particular during her absence overseas. The schoolwork of both younger girls had suffered. She described Catriona as sensitive, artistic, somewhat secretive, and lacking in confidence. She said Holly had rebelled against her father, but Mrs. Ross thought that during the past few months since her return, all the children were handling the emotional difficulties of the breakdown in their parents' relationship reasonably well in her access times with them during the weekend.

Mrs. Ross thought the youngest, Nicholas, who was close to Holly in age and interests, was reasonably accepting of the changes taking place in his life.

b. Mrs. Ross felt that her previous idea of being a "mobile mother," i.e., working in America and returning to Australia frequently to visit the children, was not feasible, as she felt the children did not relate well to their father and he could not communicate with them. She feared they would become increasingly emotionally deprived were they in his day-to-day care. She had been concerned about reports during her absence of their withdrawal and lethargy, which she thought would probably increase should their father gain full custody.

c. Mrs. Ross has accepted a job in New York which she said offers her an excellent opportunity. However, she plans to return regularly to Australia for personal and professional reasons, and she intends that the children should have annual long holidays with their father. Although she plans to take the children with her for one year at the outset, she makes it clear that she would return with them to America permanently should they so wish and should all aspects of their life with her make such a proposition manageable and successful for them.

d. Mrs. Ross said she felt her marriage had been deteriorating for several years and that she had felt dissatisfied with the relationship for some time. She described the friends she had made in New York as mature and responsible people and said she would be well-supported by them. Although she said she is not presently engaged in an intimate relationship, she said she regarded herself as now having a preference for homosexual relationships.

INTERVIEW WITH
MR. DUNCAN ROSS

This mainly covered the following topics:

a. Mr. Ross's reasons for wanting the children to stay in Adelaide and not to go to New York.

b. His relationship with the four children.

c. His relationship with Mrs. Ross.

a. Mr. Ross feels the children are well settled in Adelaide. He said the younger two are more adaptable but all the children in his opinion would suffer if removed from his stable home. He said the children were used to a large house and garden, and an inner-city atmosphere would be most unsuitable for their health and development. He felt that if the children should remain with him in his full custodial care he would be prepared to consider access periods for their mother to spend some of their school holidays with them, especially if his business remained demanding. He was particularly worried that if his wife took the children out of the country, then Australian jurisdiction would not extend internationally and the children might never return.

b. Mr. Ross said he felt his relationship with all the children was good. He said he sometimes had difficulty talking with them, but he claimed his wife had similar problems. He had initially encouraged the children to write regularly to their mother while she was away although he himself had not written letters. He said the children had told him they were going to New York, but he doubts whether they fully understand what they are saying, as they seem to be making plans for staying in Adelaide as well. He said he has not tried to persuade them to stay in Adelaide and he had not talked with them about the case as he felt that would not be fair to them. He felt their mother had "worked" on them and they had been "sold the idea of a glorious holiday." He felt no one should ask the children what they wanted to do in these circumstances.

c. Mr. Ross felt his marriage had deteriorated rapidly over the last few months. He said he was particularly angry that his wife had tried to keep the children with her after her return earlier in the year. He said his wife had been involved in acting throughout the marriage and this was more important to her than anything else. He disapproved of the behavior of some of her theatre friends and was particularly angered by what he described as their "bad language" and "heavy drinking" which he felt exposed the children to immorality. He doubted whether Mrs. Ross had made "any better" friends in America.

INTERVIEW WITH
EMMA ROSS

Emma is a tall girl approaching fourteen years of age, dressed in school uniform with long blond hair. She has a habit of flicking her head to get her hair out of the way. She wore a plaster cast on a broken left arm. She spoke with quiet confidence and warmth and understanding of her siblings and parents. She said she was very happy at school, enjoyed her friends and hobbies, liked French, English, sports, especially field hockey, and reading and writing books.

She said that last year the children had all missed their mother although she had sometimes enjoyed a greater responsibility and had got closer to her father. She had worried about the behavior of her younger sisters and felt the problem was due largely to their inability to talk with their father. She felt other adults had interfered too much with the children's freedom and they had felt stifled by "too many orders and too many bossy people" during their mother's absence.

Emma felt her parents had separated because her mother was unable to discuss her emotional needs with her father. She felt there was no hope of their reconciliation. Emma feels her mother is more perceptive and more understanding of her children's needs than her father.

I asked Emma about her understanding of her mother's sexual preference. She understands that *lesbian* means to prefer the company of women. She herself has reached the age where she is interested in boyfriends. She does not feel that her mother is hostile to men or would discourage her own interest in boys. She expressed a strong wish to go to New York for a school year and then during the following long holidays with her father to review whether she wanted to continue her schooling there or in Adelaide.

In my opinion: Emma is a feminine-looking girl of mature appearance and manner. She is intelligent and has a very good ability to express concepts relative to emotions and personal relationships.

She has a close and affectionate bond with her mother whom she perceives as being empathetic and understanding. She expressed affection for her father although she feels he is not as understanding.

Emma appeared calmly confident that she would be able to cope with a change in schooling and environment. There is no evidence she would be unduly anxious about this. Her personality is well integrated, and it is my opinion that a move to New York would not be disruptive but in fact could be beneficial to her.

Her concept of her own sexuality is clearly feminine.

INTERVIEW WITH
CATRIONA ROSS

Catriona is a young girl in early puberty aged twelve and a half years but looking more mature than would be expected for her age. In her first interview with me, she was open and confiding and I felt she showed an ability to establish a warm and trusting relationship with me. In a subsequent interview, when she came in the late afternoon in her father's company, her manner was more taciturn and unresponsive.

In the first interview, her conversation was spontaneous. She is a very intelligent, articulate girl with a good ability to express verbally her own feelings. She described her inability to communicate with her father. She feels he does not understand her and discriminates against her. She said the only times she felt close to him were when they were watching war movies on television. She felt he had expectations that she would always do very well at school, and he did not want to talk about any difficulties she felt she may have had. She said that last year she had felt depressed when her mother went away and had felt rejected by her mother. She said she had sometimes felt like a stranger at home when her mother was away. She said her parents had been unhappy for a long time and she wishes they could all be happy again.

She expressed a strong wish to go to New York with her mother and felt excited about the new environment. In any case, she wishes to be more with her mother than with her father. She understands that her mother prefers the company of women and has very close female friends, but in my opinion she does not fully understand the sexual concept of lesbianism.

In my opinion: Catriona has a warm and close relationship with her mother whom she perceives as being the parent who most constantly loves her. Her feelings toward her father are more ambivalent. She feels unsure of his affection for her.

INTERVIEW WITH
HOLLY ROSS

Holly is a bright, chatty little girl who is almost nine years old. She has an easy outgoing manner and appeared cheerful and confident.

She said she had missed her mother a lot last year and had been "in a lot of trouble at home" with her father. She expressed a strong wish to go to New York with her mother. She said that even if her mother stayed in Australia she would prefer to spend most of her time with her mother.

She said her parents had been unhappy for a long time and she wished they would get together again.

In my opinion: Holly is a confident little girl who is able to understand and empathize with the feelings of both her mother and her father. She is still finding it hard to accept the separation of her parents and is in some conflict about having to make a choice between custodial parents. She expressed warm and affectionate feelings toward both parents and she anticipates missing her father and familiar things. On balance, she seems to feel closer toward her mother. Her manner was at times frivolous and defensive, and it is my opinion that this was her reaction to anxiety over the conflict between her parents. She is loyal to them both and does not wish to hurt either.

INTERVIEW WITH NICHOLAS ROSS

Nicholas is a friendly outgoing little boy approaching eight years of age who is also intelligent and articulate. He spoke happily of his school and said he was hoping to go to New York. He compared his parents in terms appropriate to his age group. He said his "Mum knows more about kids" and "she has brought us up." He thought his mother was more willing to have his friends to play in the house than his father. He saw his mother as more willing generally to do things with him and play with him than his father. He said that even if his mother were living in Australia he would prefer to live with her.

In my opinion: Nicholas is an appealing, basically cheerful boy who has coped very well with the family difficulties. Some things he said might be in imitation of what his mother or older sisters might have said; nevertheless he does appear to have formed his own independent attitude toward the conflict. He perceives his mother as being the parent with the most ability in terms of parenting and relating emotionally to the children.

IN CONCLUSION:

Mr. Ross, on his own admission, finds it hard to express emotion. His relationship with the children was previously more distant than his wife's because of his long hours at work and away from home. During her four-month absence in America, he had the children exclusively with him, and again on weekdays recently, yet this time with them appears not significantly to have increased his emotional closeness to them. His understanding of the children's individual personalities and needs was limited. He particularly lacked insight into behavior or personality problems.

Mrs. Ross is a very articulate, persuasive, and engaging person, confident of her abilities. She is skilled in articulating emotional concepts and in her understanding of personalities. Her conceptualization of the personalities of the children was congruent with my own observations. She is, I believe, a warm and expressive parent who is able to empathize with the children's feelings. The children all express a wish to be more with her than with their father, either in America or Australia. It was my impression that they all need a firm reassurance that they will return to Australia after one school year in America, when a decision will be made concerning more permanent custodial arrangements.

I believe the children should not be separated from each other as there are close bonds among all of them. Each in an individual way has expressed a wish to be living with their mother, and they each perceive their mother as being more understanding than their father.

In my opinion, Mrs. Ross is the more capable psychological parent.

"Well? What do you think?" Peter is watching me. His expression reminds me, for a moment, of my Nicholas's eager, open, trusting face. I fling my arms around him, crushing the typed pages against his chest.

"These kids! My wonderful kids! Peter, look how brave they are. I want to go to them right now and hold and comfort them. It's terrible, putting children through this. Poor babies, poor darling bright resilient loving ba—" I pound his shoulders.

"They're marvellous children, Morgan, and it's many thanks to you, as this report confirms."

"A superb report, exactly the tonic I need, to hear somebody say I'm a good mother." I sit back and smile with joy. "Peter, she's terrific—we *must* put her on the stand—an outsider, her cool professional voice—I want that voice of authority in the court; we need that public voice, just as we need the judge." I attack the heap of crisp fresh salad vegetables on my plate while Peter sips his coffee and observes me closely.

Then he says, "It's funny about professionals, Morgan, especially medical experts. In a way, you're right. A psychiatrist, like a judge, does represent the objective world and can speak for society, and to it, in a public space like a courtroom. But a psychiatrist can also be a devastating witness. Query any of these opinions, and Hermione Rogers will most likely dither and dally and fuss over technical definitions and we'll never get a clear conclusion, especially when it comes to value judgments. It's a relief that Schorman relented on this report."

"I don't really understand why he has. I mean, here's proof that I am not unfit. It would be more in character for Schorman to attack this, wouldn't it?"

"Actually, I think Auden is right about Schorman," Peter replies. "Schorman has been convinced from the start that Duncan will romp in. In his experience, which is substantial, lesbian mothers never get custody, and nobody is awarded extradition rights to take children out of the country, beyond a court's jurisdiction. Two strikes against you."

I hold up a hand to stop him. "A lesbian won custody only last year in Sydney—"

But Peter continues. "The husband in that case was a drunken derelict, my dear. Duncan is physically fit, mentally sound, and horribly wealthy. Schorman is also ahead on the more conventional and traditional factors that help decide contested custody. Status quo, for example. Your children have effectively lived in a comfortable, if cold, family home all their lives. Should they now be moved to another home, another country? An apartment? Look at Duncan's so-called material circumstances: here he clearly has a gigantic lead. The rights of the mother? Your youngest child will soon be eight. If he were a tiny baby—even then, with recent interpretations of family law, the prior rights of the mother can no longer be taken for granted, and if the father can prove she is unfit . . . many fathers now gain custody, Morgan, even if they've done little of the parenting, providing there is evidence for family support and a stable home. Finally: conduct. Add in the fact that you left the kids with Duncan while you visited the States to pursue your own career, plus the infamous career itself—the stage—and Schorman has to be laughing all the way to the bank—to the bench, his real ambition. How can he lose?"

"And you? If it's so cut and dried?"

"Because I still think we have a slim chance. Because I believe in you and in the kids. Look, Morgan, here's perhaps the most important line: 'the more capable psychological parent.' An important trend in family law today is an increasing emphasis on three areas of interpretation: the wishes of children, the best interests of children, and parenting capability. That's our edge. That's where I intend to focus our case. Time we went back, I'm afraid. Duncan Ross: meet Peter Fitzpatrick. At last!"

ROSS VERSUS ROSS
A286, 1978

Mr. Fitzpatrick, cross-examination of Mr. Ross, continued:
"Is Annie Goodall somebody who has been closely associated with your family even before your marriage?"

"Yes."

"In fact, she and her former husband Ivan were your marriage attendants?"

"Explain what you mean by attendants."

"Bridesmaid and best man."

"It's a long time ago."

"Well then, the Goodall family has been close to your

family throughout your marriage and you would agree that the children have been particularly close to Annie Goodall?"

"Not in recent times. We saw very little of her last year when my . . . when Mrs. Ross was away."

"Would you be surprised if Annie Goodall were to say that on the occasions when she did see them, she found the children to be extremely withdrawn?"

"I'd be surprised if she'd seen enough of them to make any comments."

I can hardly bear to listen to them. All that afternoon, all the following day, Duncan denies everything we have been together. Peter jabs away at his defenses with infinite patience like a swordsman in a fencing exhibition. I stop writing notes and slump in my chair, sickened now with sadness at the pettiness and spitefulness of it all.

Do you think the children watched too much television when Morgan was away? You did not approve of some of your wife's friends? I think you said of their language? Was that the group you say taught the children songs from the revue your wife was acting in? What did you object to in your children's singing? What other aspects of your wife's behavior concern you? Do you think she would engage in any behavior that would be deleterious to the children?

The answers dragged from Duncan delay and duck, feint and parry, until persistence, with a negative force, must surely appear incredible. Judge Simpson never moves. He watches Peter outclass Duncan quite impartially until Peter executes a petty point about Duncan's inability to take care of the children when I was in America. The judge sits forward, tersely, to interject.

"Mr. Fitzpatrick, I think you are holding here a dangerously two-edged sword. You will have some diffi-culty in raising any complaints by the wife or by witnesses on her account concerning the children during the period your question refers to. The whole explanation might be put down to your client's absence."

I'm beginning to realize the joust is not about winning or losing, not a weighing of our relative merits as parents, no art whereby we learn the "best interests" of our children. There must be another way. I pick up my notebook again and write: "Have lawyers devised this ritual to grind the remnants of a marriage, the vestiges of what was once a happy partnership, into particles of dust that will bury us alive?" I cross that out and write instead, "The ordeal is not new to us. We're in our natural element, a desert storm."

I start a new page, "Is it Socratic art; a form of gentlemanly dialogue; a moral inquisition; a meaningless interrogation? (Mark one box before reading the cryptic solution as follows): It's a death struggle to suck dry the last drop of warmth between us; to strangle whatever stray or careless affection might persist." I read that phrase again. I draw arrows to the next line: "Is there affection? Can Duncan know that I am hurting? Do fangs pierce his heart? Does fear run riot through his veins? Is he sorrowing, too, for loss?" I cross that out, too.

"Has Duncan ever felt what I feel? Why should he now? For the moral," I add, "neither speaks the truth nor hears it in the other's threadbare tale, for we are opposing players in each other's lives." I doodle my name in an elaborate scrawl worthy of Shakespeare, but it's no good. I give up.

I can't ask questions. I don't have answers. Duncan's missing from my text. I don't recognize him anywhere.

"What happened at the Victor Harbor holiday?"

"She said she wanted to talk about our marriage. She said she wasn't happy. She wanted to leave me."

"What was your response?"

"I said I didn't want her to leave and that life would not be worth living if she went, something to that effect.

Then she came home with me. I presumed she had changed her mind."

"Was it after that holiday that she moved into separate sleeping quarters in the house?"

"I cannot remember. I do recall I injured my back in a fishing accident, and it was then she left my bedroom and never came back."

"Was that not approximately three years after the holiday you refer to? To be precise, in October of 1975?"

"I don't recall."

"Had you engaged in sexual activities together frequently, or hardly at all, between the years 1972 and 1975?"

His Honor:

"Mr. Fitzpatrick, I believe it is now common ground that this marriage has been over for some years. Sexual aspects in the relationship of the two parties are not matters that will affect significantly the judgment I am required to make, namely, in the best interests of the children, to ascertain their future care and control. I would have thought that raising sexual matters merely prolongs this case. There is no dispute that this man and this woman had, some considerable time ago, ceased to share conjugal intimacy of an order you appear to have raised. I do not see the relevance of this line of approach."

Mr. Fitzpatrick:

"I think it may be relevant as regards the motives of the wife, Your Honor, and as regards her present sexual preference, which is an aspect on which Your Honor is required to judge with regard to Mr. Ross's stated reasons for opposing his wife's custody and her taking the children to America."

"That may be, Mr. Fitzpatrick, that may well be. However, there may be other ways of reaching that. I would have thought it would be more appropriate to take up matters of sexuality with the wife since she is the person involved."

"There is the husband's attitude, Your Honor—"

"You can get at that in other ways. Now, I do believe this may be a good time—oh, I see that Mr. Schorman requests that tomorrow be set aside. Yes, I remember, a funeral. The court will resume on Friday, then, at ten o'clock."

In the night, unable to sleep, I remember other nights when I lay still because I did not want him to know that I was awake.

I seem to struggle with illusions spun from earlier dreams, illusions of his desire for me, in a creek bed, when I had wanted to break an intolerable silence with which he surrounded himself, to move toward him over that invisible line which divided him from me.

Even so, there were endless nights when Duncan turned away from me. After he signed his father's papers that banished me from the family, Duncan became more remote than ever. Father and son reached their agreement while war raged in Vietnam—a war that I opposed—and while Constance Amy was still alive. I doubt if any woman had a ghost of a chance to make a separate, private peace. If anything brought Duncan peace of mind, it was that capitulation to his father's will.

Is that what killed desire? Or was it that I'd produced four children—the last, triumphantly, the son to bear the Ross name? I'd completed my allotted task. Whatever the causal sequence, it doesn't matter now. Everything conspired slowly to unravel us.

After all this time, what was that later weekend to me at Victor Harbor in proportion to the fourteen years of our marriage, to the twenty-two before him, a separate part of my life? Put like that, the holiday weekend was nothing.

No wonder he didn't object when I left his bed. No wonder he was glad to see me leave for America. No wonder he encouraged me to go.

What I hadn't known or guessed was that freedom for

me was conditional. I had to leave the heirs behind. That was the unwritten bargain beneath his signature. Bounties of war; territory yielded to the victors; the children and me, victims of a peace agreement between a father and his son.

The basis is property, no matter how I examine it.

The irony is that everything, originally, belonged to his mother. Now that his father is dead, everything belongs to him.

I'll never understand the power of inheritance.

My first lawyer warned me, didn't she: "The core is property, money, ownership, control."

They'd never mattered much to me.

On Friday morning, Duncan leaves the courtroom once more, for Peter has not yet finished his cross-examination and it is Nannie's turn. Mr. Schorman is on his feet. Nannie Cashmore tucks her chin into the folds of her neck and agrees that the children's attitudes have changed since I came home from America. His tone is oily and cajoling, hers smug, her lips tightly pursed.

"I have afternoon tea ready for them when they come home from school. We talk about the things children like to chat about—homework, cookies, sweets, that sort of thing. Then I say to them, 'When you have had a little rest and done all your homework, then you can watch the television until your daddy comes home for dinner.' They always go straight to their rooms when they're told." Nanny's sigh is audible. "Of late, they hardly speak to me. They disappear into their bedrooms. I don't know what they do there. I have to get on with my work. They've changed since *she* returned."

"For better or for worse, in your opinion?"

"They are very reluctant to tell me what they do at school or what homework they have to do."

"When Mrs. Ross went to America last year, did something happen with Catriona that same day when she returned from school?"

"She came in the back door, marched into her bedroom, and slammed the door. I knew something was wrong. I went in. 'Whatever is the matter? Would you like to tell Nannie about it?' She was crying very bitterly. She said to me, 'I didn't want Mummy to go to America. I hate Mummy for leaving me.' "

"Do you also remember a few weeks before Mrs. Ross returned home from America, that Emma said something to you about her mother?"

"Emma was not actually worried. She was concerned. I think Emma was begining to realize the position between her father and mother. She said to me, 'If Mummy goes back to America, and wants us all to go too, no way will I leave my daddy. I want to stay with my dad.' "

"And what is the attitude of Holly and Nicholas toward their father?"

"They love their daddy very much. When he comes home, Holly runs down the passage, says, 'Hello, Daddy,' and jumps up and wraps her arms around his neck and kisses him. He picks her up and cuddles and kisses her. Nicholas is a man, so they treat each other man to man."

"Do you remember an occasion several weeks ago when you heard about an order made in a preliminary hearing as a result of which all the children came back to their father's home?"

"Oh, yes, because Holly came home and said, 'Mummy and Daddy were in court today because they are having an argument and they don't love one another and most probably it will end in a divorce and where we are going to stay I don't know.' I said to Holly, 'Look, in the meantime, you and I are going to be great friends and get along and wait until the end result.' She was very happy with that. She put her arms around my neck and said, 'I wish I had you for my Mummy.' "

"Now, after the children had been with their mother, and after the court order returned them to their father's home before this trial began, do you remember an occasion when Holly and Nicholas were dressing up, and the comments you heard them make?"

"Yes. Holly and Nicholas are very close to each other. They often make little plays together. On this particular day, they dressed up as two old ladies. They wore long gray cloaks, old bonnets, old shoes. Holly had a dirty old feather fan. They were going on a cruise. Their husbands had not died—they had *divorced* their husbands and had *robbed* them and *fleeced* them of every *ha'penny* their husbands had saved, and now they were sailing away to *enjoy* themselves. That's how they were discussing it all."

"What do you mean by 'discussing it all'?"

"This trial, Mr. Schorman, sir. What their mother is up to."

"I have no further questions of this witness."

Peter takes Schorman's place and looks steadily at Nannie.

"I believe you said that Mr. Ross returns from his work promptly at six-thirty and immediately drives you home before he returns to eat the dinner you prepared for him?"

"Indeed I did. That is so."

"So that the only time you yourself have seen Mr. Ross with his children is for two or three minutes a day." Peter studies his notes in silence. Nannie waits edgily for the next question. I am as surprised as she when he speaks again.

"I see. I have finished with this witness, Your Honor. Please recall Mr. Ross."

"I was worried there for a moment," says Casey, who has joined us for lunch at the fish restaurant, "when Schorman had Nannie describe Nicholas dressed as an old lady. I thought, oh hell, here's the corruption theme we've been waiting for. It was *ha'penny* that gave her away. Your kids wouldn't know the word."

"Nannie made us all unrecognizable. Man to man!

And I the wicked witch casting my evil spells. I never dreamed Nannie disliked me so."

"Whoever understands motives, especially in legal battles. Whichever way she looks at it, Nannie's bound to resent you. If you win, she loses her job. If you lose, she'll end up in full-time charge of four teenagers."

"No, Casey, I think she wants to punish me because I left my husband. I remember she told me once she'd wanted to do the same."

"When you two have finished your amateur analysis, I suggest you try these rock oysters before I eat the lot. They're grilled with a spicy sauce this time. Fire in the belly. Now, let me propose a better motive for Nannie's unexpected venom. Don't you think it's incomprehensible to her that Morgan should choose to leave Duncan on the day, almost, he inherits a fortune? Of course she thinks you've lost your sanity. Even I think you have a terrible sense of timing, Morgan. My second theory is that Nannie feels underappreciated. Duncan probably pays her a minimum wage."

"Peter, you're too practical. I suspect Nannie Cashmore dreams of reconciliation between Duncan and Morgan. She's an old frustrated romantic who likes happy endings. Who knows! Who cares?"

"Stop that, both of you, it isn't a joke. I care. Especially about the effect of Nannie's evidence on Judge Simpson. He's a father, too, with two young children. Nannie made Duncan sound an ideal father, herself a devoted servant, the children innocent victims of a revengeful, plotting, greedy mother. Sorry to get carried away, but Nannie is still in daily control of my kids. I'm angrier than I was with Pamela's evidence; Nannie has a greater capacity to hurt them. She's Duncan's handmaiden, a maternal voice he hears from his spartan childhood. Pass me your handkerchief, Peter; I can't bear to think of those Dickensian characters in charge of raising my kids."

Peter puts his arm around my shoulders and Casey

sniffs sympathetically. He gently wipes my eyes. "There, there, you must be exhausted. I don't think you need to worry too much about Nannie Cashmore. We have two child specialists to follow your evidence. They'll easily counterbalance whatever Nannie had to say. Better now?"

"I'll be alright soon. Thank you both. The kids come to me this weekend. That keeps me sane and strong. I wish I could stop dreaming, every night, about Duncan and his parents. Why on earth did I marry him in the first place?"

"Objection! That's a question I'd rather not put to you in court, if you don't mind." Peter smiles. "It's immaterial now. You never could belong to the Ross clan, but something surely drove you to try."

CHAPTER ELEVEN

ROSS VERSUS ROSS
A286, 1978

Mr. Schorman, cross-examination of Mrs. Ross:

"You have already told His Honor the marriage was reasonably happy, I think those were your words, until about 1972, and of course your husband had worked back most nights right through the marriage?"

"Yes."

"As you have said, he worked sometimes at weekends?"

"On most weekends."

"Well, what was the change that occurred that made things unhappy by about 1972?"

"I was no longer bearing children. There was no longer that bond we had shared very happily together. We'd been married ten years. Duncan's work patterns had not changed. He used to promise that things would get better, that he would have more time for me and the children. I was lonely and frustrated. Our marriage seemed not to be growing."

"Frustrated because he did not spend enough time with you?"

"We were not a close couple."

"The position had not changed over those years?"

"Initially, we'd been brought closer by having children."

"But apart from that, nothing had changed?"

Mr. Fitzpatrick:
"I cannot see much relevance in this line of questions."

His Honor:
"We will see how far it goes."

Mrs. Ross:
"I had changed."

Mr. Schorman:
"Ahha, you had changed. Perhaps you can tell His Honor in what way you had changed."

"I missed companionship. I had expected that we would grow together and share more in the marriage."

"I suppose you often talked with your husband about that?"

"I tried to."

"What did you suggest to him that he should do?"

"It was more what we could both do, to spend more time together, to develop more of a life together."

"What in effect was his answer? That work had to come first, something of that kind?"

"His work was important. I'd agreed all along that it was important because it was his career, his major creative interest which I fully supported. I still do."

"What did you do on the nights that he was home with you?"

"We sometimes talked. He liked to play solitaire in front of television. I don't watch television very much, so we didn't share those interests."

"You were interested in your stage work and acting in plays then?"

"I have always been interested in my work."

"So you really did not have much time available to share with him."

"I cannot agree with that, Mr. Schorman. No matter what I was doing, I continued to wish we could do other things together."

"Other things, or things you wanted to do?"

"Both, I suppose."

"You heard your husband describe how you refused to go on holidays with him without the children, I take it?"

"I heard that, yes."

"Well, was it not so, what he said about your refusal?"

"Let me explain. For the first seven years of our marriage, I was either pregnant or breast-feeding. I couldn't take holidays without having children present."

"I take it that you acted and worked on the stage throughout the marriage. I put it to you that this hobby of yours was more important to you than anything, even when you were, as you say, raising young children."

"I would not call my work a hobby."

"What would you call it?"

"I have a brain and some talent and years of training to use them. I believed I would be a more effective parent if I continued to use my brain and develop my professional skills."

"I would suggest that your career and your interests mattered more to you than your marriage, did they not?"

"I would not agree, Mr. Schorman. I had to fit my interests and activities within my marriage, in ways that could benefit my children, not in ways that would interfere with mothering and running the home."

"You and your husband had many arguments about money, did you not? You have heard your husband describe some of those fights?"

"Yes, I heard him."

"I suggest to you that you were insisting that you have a joint bank account, that the house should be put in your name as well as your husband's name, and that you were dissatisfied with his provisions for you."

"I did suggest joint accounts because I thought we should share more, like many of our friends did."

"I put it to you that you married your husband in the knowledge that he came from a well-to-do family and that you had expectations that his money would be to your benefit, Mrs. Ross."

"Those weren't my reasons for marrying him, Mr. Schorman."

"I put it to you that you saw the chance to pursue your hobbies and your interests at your husband's expense, and that you expected him or his father to pay for that."

"That is not true."

"Would you not agree, Mrs. Ross, that you decided to take up your career in order to make enough money so that you could put into effect your plan to leave your husband?"

"That aspect has been true only for the past year or so, when it was clear to me I should have to take a job so as to support myself and the children because my marriage was over."

"Your husband, however, has always supported you, has he not?"

"I did not anticipate that he would continue to do so once I left him."

"Did not his father also hand money over to you?"

"For a few years early in the marriage, I received some money now and then from a trust fund my father-in-law established in my name when we first married."

"I suggest that Mr. Donald Ross put a stop to paying you money because your hobbies took you away from your children."

"The trust fund stopped long before I went to America."

"I was not talking about America. I was talking about your hobbies that you pursued throughout the marriage, and it was these that upset your father-in-law."

"I have never been sure what Mr. Ross's reason was."

"You did not get along with your husband's parents, did you?"

"I was very fond of Mrs. Ross and she, I believe, of

me. I thought, until a few years ago, that I had a friendly relationship with Mr. Ross as well."

"I take it that you did not agree with your husband's close relationship with his parents."

"That is not true. In fact, it was I who invited them to our home every week for dinner and who made sure we saw them regularly and included them in our family, especially with the births of grandchildren."

"You said in evidence yesterday that one of your reasons for wanting His Honor to believe that you might return from America, should you go there again, was to see your mother. Do you remember saying that?"

"I did say that—as well as professional reasons."

"You do not get on well with your mother, do you, Mrs. Ross?"

"That is untrue."

"Your mother is presently out of the country, is she not?"

"She is staying with my sister in London."

"Would it surprise you to know, Mrs. Ross, that your mother was prepared, before her departure overseas, to assist this case as a material witness on your husband's account?"

"Yes, that would surprise me."

"You are aware, are you not, that the two eldest children, Emma and Catriona, are to be interviewed by His Honor this afternoon?"

"Yes, the girls told me so when they called me on the telephone last night."

"Was it your idea for the children to see His Honor?"

"No, it was theirs."

"I would suggest that you planted that idea in their heads in the first place."

"No, Mr. Schorman, the children expressed to me their strong wish to meet the judge in order to speak for themselves."

"Have you trained them in what they are to say to His Honor? Have you told them how to answer his questions?"

His Honor:

"Really, Mr. Schorman, I don't see how this witness can possibly tell her children what to say to me when I myself have not decided yet what questions I shall put to them. As it is now two o'clock and I shall meet the two children at four, I now adjourn this court until ten tomorrow morning. Which of you is to bring these children to my chambers?"

Mr. Schorman:

"We are, Your Honor. They should arrive soon."

"Thank you. You may stand down, Mrs. Ross, but remember you are on oath and that your cross-examination will resume tomorrow morning."

We are back in Peter's office on Tuesday afternoon. I was on the stand for six hours yesterday when Peter led me through my affidavit and laid down the outline of our case, and then again for four hours today under Schorman's barrage. "It felt like stepping through a minefield. Why does Schorman concentrate on fights and disagreements between Duncan and me? I—what upsets me is that *I* should be on trial. It's monstrous, and so confusing. I had no idea Schorman would be so hostile."

"He wants to see how you react to pressure. You've handled that magnificently so far. He's tried every way to get under your guard, but you kept your head and stayed calm. I'm awfully proud of you, Morgan, and so is Auden."

It worries me that I may not have answered the questions adequately. I was conscious of selecting phrases, tuning words to the context of the courtroom, for the ear of the judge. I know it is crucial to play by their rules in order not to lose by them; to adopt their language in order to be understood; to look and to sound like their idea of a mother in order to persuade them to judge me fit to be the mother I have always been, yet . . .

"I felt as if Schorman were picking out portions of my mind like so many morsels for a feast. With every bite, it seemed I might lose a part of myself, a self that has no business in a courtroom. And it is never enough. He keeps coming back for more. I wanted you to stop him."

"I often contemplated that, but the way you handle his questions goes in your favor. I will object only if I see you can't answer him. The more he hammers you, and you remain resolute and dignified, the better you show your character and the way you withstand stress. Do you see what a plus that is?"

"All that matters to me is the children, and Schorman avoids asking me about them or about the way I've mothered them—to and fro, from career to money, from money to arguments—bending my answers to fit his picture of me as a selfish, greedy, wicked woman, bringing into focus the past few terrible years by wiping from the record all the other years—the hard daily work, the constant attention and affection—for Duncan as well as for the children. That's what is unbearable: their refusal to admit my goodness. Hauling in my mother like that— Peter, what on earth did Schorman mean?"

"He implied, I think, that they expected that your mother would come in on their side. By suggesting you and your mother are not on good terms together, they also imply that you don't have any firm or reliable family support to fall back on. It's not an uncommon ploy."

"Perhaps it was true. It's just as well for me that Dilys is in England where she can't cause more trouble. Peter, I hope the girls weren't frightened. Thank goodness it wasn't Schorman who questioned them. If Schorman is Duncan's mouthpiece, then Schorman's hostility is really Duncan's. How he hates me. This is one hell of a way to end, isn't it—I don't know whether to be relieved that it is really over, or appalled that it ever began, or sickened that it lasted as long as it did."

"Whichever way, you'll soon be free, Morgan. Free to pick up your life where you left it."

"Yes, but with whom, and where?"

ROSS VERSUS ROSS
A286, 1978

Mr. Fitzpatrick:

"Does Your Honor wish to make any statement as to the children Emma and Catriona whom Your Honor interviewed?"

His Honor:

"Yes. I interviewed the two children in my chambers with a view to ascertain the wishes of those children, and having interviewed them, I was satisfied that both of those children wish to accompany their mother to New York. So far as I could determine during the course of that interview, it did not appear to me that those children had been influenced in any way by either parent in expressing that wish. I took detailed notes of my interview with each child, which covered other matters apart from an expression of their wishes. Each child was canvassed only with a view to determining their background knowledge of the family situation and with a view to determining that the wishes they expressed were expressed voluntarily and were not the subject of influence.

"In accordance with what I believe is the accepted practice of this court, the notes that I took were placed in a sealed envelope and have been marked with a direction to the effect that those notes are not to be opened or perused by any person except upon direction by a judge of this court."

Mr. Schorman:

"Recall Morgan Evans Ross. You have heard your husband give evidence about how he came upon you and two other women topless in the garden?"

"Yes."

"That is correct, is it not?"

"I was topless in the garden."

"And the others also?"

"I don't recall."

"You are not prepared to deny that?"

"I don't deny that I was bare-breasted. It was a very hot day. I'd just finished making a batch of apricot jam, and I stripped to hose myself down and cool off in the garden behind the terrace."

"About the other women, I mean."

"I don't remember. One was reading aloud to us from a new novel. They may have had their shirts open."

"Was it often your habit to go about with your clothes off?"

"Neither my husband nor I wore pajamas or night clothing. In summer I often sunbathed on my terrace lawn, sometimes in a bathing suit, sometimes not."

"Only when you were by yourself?"

"Or when the children were playing during summer holidays. They were often naked, too. It was my own back garden."

"You heard your husband say there were piles of empty bottles in the garden after your drinking friends were there? I mean the period of that theatre piece when all those women's libbers were around the house."

"I heard him say so."

"I suppose you are denying that also."

"I don't deny there was a pile of empty bottles in the backyard before I went overseas. There'd been a large farewell party for me which contributed bottles to that pile."

"I contend that your drinking friends consumed large amounts of liquor in the period before and after that performance, and that their empty bottles were left around the garden."

"May I say—"

"Will you answer my question!"

"I wanted to explain that my husband and I saved all our empty wine bottles behind a screen in the garden, and every year or so the local Boy Scout troop collected them on their bottle drive to help raise funds. There was a large number of bottles when I left for America, which had probably accumulated over at least the previous year."

"You heard your husband give evidence that he found you in bed with a woman in the home?"

"Yes. He came into the room with a breakfast tray he'd prepared. It was a Sunday morning."

"So you do not deny you were in bed with another woman?"

"No. The children were all in the bed, too, to play. Then we all had breakfast together, Duncan as well, in my room."

"Were you topless on that occasion as well?"

"I was not. I returned to the bed because the children were playing the squatters game."

"What is that supposed to mean?"

"It's a make-believe game. The bed was a tent, and—"

"I was asking about another woman, if you would kindly attend to my questions. Do you dispute that that woman had also slept in that room?"

"No."

"And you were in bed with her?"

"She had slept in my room. She got into bed for the game."

"You heard your husband say that the door to the room you occupied was often locked at night?"

"I did often lock it at night."

"What was your purpose in locking the door?"

"I had no sense of privacy in that house. My husband used to wander in and out of my room, but at that stage of the marriage I did not want him to come in."

There have been other times when I've felt this kind of hostility. Schorman leaves a physical impression on me— not only with his eyes and tongue, but as if he's actually touching me, with loathing.

Everything now seems to be happening faster to me.

The same themes recur, repeat, overlap, or veer away, only to come together again.

At the end of my third day in the witness box, I walked down to the river to sit on the bank and watch the water. I didn't want to go back to Annie for dinner just yet. I refused Peter's offer of a drink. I wanted to be alone here for a while.

I crossed the university footbridge to the other side near the rowing sheds and the rugby field. I've often walked here along the Torrens. Sometimes with the children to feed the black swans; sometimes, when I was an undergraduate, with students. Sometimes with a lover. There are pairs of lovers here now, lying together in the reeds at the edge of the river. An old man on the bridge bends down to peer at the slowly moving river. I can hear the drone of rush-hour traffic in the distance, but here the river is peaceful.

I wish I had the energy to be angry.

He will not crack me. I will not lose control.

I'm not crazy.

It's the break. Leaving home all over again. I must, I want to, not only Duncan, but mother, too, the whole bloody country. I have to leave it or I *will* go crazy. Were it not for Annie, and Peter, and Miss Adair; were it not for my children, I don't think I could stand much more of this.

I'll miss Annie most of all.

The sound of a magpie in the morning, the smell of a eucalypt after rain—these things I'll miss. The sight of pure white sand on a nine-mile beach, the surf rolling in over rocks. Or red sand and spinifex and the hum of bees in a paddock of purple Salvation Jane. The bush.

Schorman is coming nearer. Peter says to expect it tomorrow. Everything depends now on how I withstand this attack.

I must brace myself. I will not let them see how scared I am.

"You do realize, do you not Mrs. Ross, that in a place like Adelaide the fact that you are given to lesbianism becomes known?"

"I believe it does not have to become known."

"But in fact it does?"

"If one chooses for it to be known."

"You do not believe that the word gets around at all?"

"If one leads a private life, nothing at all need be known about one's sex life unless one wants it known."

"But people do gossip, don't they?"

"I haven't found that is necessarily the case."

"Don't you realize, if word gets around, that your children are likely to suffer?"

"I don't think I can agree with that. Since I have already discussed it with my children, I believe they are unlikely to suffer from hearing about it from others."

"Well, what is it that you have told them?"

"I have told them what I understand lesbianism to mean. I have also told them what they may hear from people who do not understand it—as I myself have heard from seven-year-old boys joking about sex in the back seat of my car when I drive them home from school. I know my children can be exposed to jokes or talk about the word, about sexuality in any terms, in any context, anywhere. I spoke with them about it and said, 'How would you feel if you heard someone tease you about this, or if you were made to feel that your mother is in some way different from other children's mothers?' We talked about that at some length. They felt they could cope with it."

"Mrs. Ross, you are aware, are you not, that if people get to know that you are a lesbian, they may well refuse to allow their children to associate with your children?"

"The friends I have are not those sorts of people."

"Other people might be, might they not?"

"Other people are less likely to associate with my children."

"Not even at school?"

"At their school, my children tend to meet children from similar backgrounds, with parents who are friends or who have a feeling of ease among themselves. So I don't believe that would necessarily happen."

"You are well aware, of course, that children tend to repeat things their parents say, even if they do not fully understand them."

"I guess they do."

"Well, has it occured to you that your children may be the subject of comments, spiteful comments, by other children, not necessarily their friends, but acquaintances who may have heard their parents talk of your lesbianism?"

"Yes, I do think children can be hurt by other adults or children on any matter to do with their own parents. That's one reason I discussed my sexuality with my children."

"You have seen Dr. Rogers's report, I take it?"

His Honor:

"I take it you refer to Exhibit R8, the psychiatric report tendered by Dr. Hermione Rogers at the request of this court, Mr. Schorman?"

"Yes, that's the one. I suggest to you, Mrs. Ross, that all you have told your children is that you prefer the company of women to that of men, is that not so?"

"Mr. Schorman, I never discuss lesbianism with my children in purely sexual terms, with intimate details, which is what I take you to mean. I discuss sexual education, sexuality, in general and in terms of information and knowledge about sexual behavior with reference to the questions my children ask me. I don't share with them the more intimate details of my private life in the way you seem to be suggesting."

"How have you discussed lesbianism with them?"

"I respond to their questions. I try to answer with respect to their age, their ability to understand concepts."

"I take it you would not like your daughters to become lesbians?"

"I think, given the nature of society, it's very much easier to be part of the norm, which is heterosexual."

"Will you answer my question?"

"That was my answer. In our society, it is easier for children to grow up in the context of what is considered normal, which is heterosexual."

"I asked about your liking. We will get along a lot faster if you will listen to me. Would you like your daughters to become lesbians?"

"I would like—May I answer you in this way? I would like my children to be able to form long and lasting attachments to people they love. I would expect these to be heterosexual, because that is more usual in our society. However, I think that what matters are the lasting relationships, not aspects of what people do in bed."

"Attachments of any kind?"

"Of their choice."

"Of any kind, no matter what they choose?"

"Mr. Schorman, I believe my children have been brought up to be marvellous human beings who are free to choose for themselves, and that's their business when they are adults, not mine."

"I take it you are not prepared to give an undertaking to His Honor to give up your lesbian activities?"

"No, I am not."

"For all you know, you may share lesbian activities with women other than this . . . this Jenny Murphy woman—in the future."

"I think it is very possible that in future years I will form a relationship with another woman."

"Is this not the position, that if you happened to fall into sexual activities with another woman, *any* other woman, you cannot be sure, *if* there were another woman, that she might not corrupt your children?"

"I don't believe that I have ever had a friend, or a close relationship with any person, that has corrupted my children. On that past basis, I will say that it is most unlikely in the future."

"As I take it you intend to continue your lesbian activities, where will you conduct them?"

"I do not describe lesbianism in purely sexual terms, which is what I presume you to mean."

"Will you answer my question! Where will you conduct them?"

"My relationships with women are not purely sexual. I have had a close and very supporting commitment with Jenny Murphy. We respect and trust one another very much."

"That's as may be. I understood you were having a lesbian relationship with her."

"We were, but we didn't have to be together or engaged in any sexual activity for that relationship to exist."

"Is it not your intention to continue your activities?"

"Jenny has returned to England to live. Should I begin a new relationship, yes, that will be my intention."

"Even if the children are in the house?"

"I don't conduct sexual activities in front of my children. I am a very private person. I use my discretion."

"There was an occasion, I cannot remember exactly where or when it was, when the children were in a tent and you and some other women were in a beach house?"

"It was Jenny Murphy, not some other women."

"Did you indulge in lesbian activities on that occasion?"

"We did."

"You have had other women staying with you on various occasions and in places where you had holidays with the children?"

"Other women and their families have stayed—"

"I do not mean married women—"

"I *do* mean married women, and their children. . . ."

Duncan, I want to step down from the witness box and talk with you. Is it you giving Mr. Schorman these terrible lines? Is this what you want to say to me?

At night, when I had to listen to the flap flap flap of your card games, the interminable rounds of solitaire, the cards cascading like the flapping of wings when you shuffled the pack, was it you, or me, slowly going mad? All that time, did you ever think I could corrupt our children?

"Duncan, the children want to go with me."

"Leave them out of it. You know damned well you're needed here." Your hands shook.

"You dropped a card. There, on the floor. The game won't come out without it. Of course they need me. We both know that. That's why I am proposing to take them with me."

You frowned, sucked on your pipe, and stared down at the cards. I turned the television off. "Do you mind? We can't hear each other over this noise."

"Of course I mind. This isn't a convenient time. In many ways, we all got along much better when you were away."

I picked up the stray card and put it on your coffee table. You turned up the volume on the program you'd not been watching. I put out my hand and you flinched. Did you loathe my touch, Duncan? Did your withdrawals cleanse you, of both your flesh and mine; of loathing; of dependence? Once, you did want me to touch you, but after the children were born, something changed in you. All the qualities in you that first attracted me were gradually distorted—magnified out of proportion—your inbred solitude and concentration—qualities I wished I'd had—your quietness, a stability I'd found so secure—what I used, fondly, to call your bushman qualities.

You forbade yourself to see me, want me, touch me.

It was a relief for me, in the early years, to discover that you desired me more than I desired you. After the children, it was the other way round. Then it was too late for me. You made that very clear. I didn't want to believe you.

That evening, barely controlling my rage, I went into

our bedroom where I no longer slept. You hadn't made the bed. On the cabinet, on your side of the bed, there was an old painted tin that belonged to your father. Inside were broken valves from some useless piece of radio equipment, and six dead sparkplugs from a truck engine. A pair of socks smelled of you; the curtain reeked of your tobacco. There was a new burn mark on the kingfisher-blue silk spread we'd brought back from our honeymoon.

It's amazing to me that you never caught fire.

In the drawer on my side of the bed, I found an old photograph of myself in the kitchen. Emma sat in her high chair and Catriona straddled my hip. I would have been pregnant with Holly. Geraniums flowered in a window box behind my shoulder. There was a tea-towel in my hand. I looked radiant.

Then I noticed something about the photograph I'd not seen before. The two girls were smiling into the camera, but I was looking away, out of the frame, into the distance.

I'd put away the things I hadn't understood about myself until Nicky started school, your old school, when it felt safe enough, or I was brave enough, or desperate, to look for them again. We talked then as we had before we married, when I lived with Annie. I told you about Jenny, and how that affair was illuminating for me the other, deeper, buried things I'd never understood before.

You had said, "I understand an affair of the heart."

I believed you. We were both free—remember, that is how we understood it before we married?—to be essentially celibate, yet to have children together. We laughed, I remember, because we thought no one else would begin to comprehend that kind of contract, the intimacy of friends. It must have been laughable.

I'm still not completely sure why you are so terribly angry now. It cannot be for losing me, because you haven't desired me. You've watched us disintegrate without lifting a finger to stop me, warn me, beckon me.

You yourself have said it isn't jealousy.

Wait. I must try to be accurate. Mr. Schorman's questions have driven needles, red-hot searing needles, into my head. It's an effort to think fairly, Duncan. I hurt, all over.

You said that evening, "Morgan, you can do whatever you damned well want, but you can't take the children with you."

Standing by your bed, holding the photograph, I knew I'd have to call a lawyer in the morning. I knew it meant the courts.

It isn't about sex, or jealousy, your anger.

On the surface of your words, it might appear to be about our children. But you and I know, deep inside, that you haven't really wanted them. You enjoy them, love them in your way, but you don't want the daily work of raising them.

Duncan, do you want, more than anything, to say No no no no you can't—stamping your foot, a petulant boy— you can't have my things, I won't let you, you shan't have what you want or I'll hurt you hurt you hurt you?

We haven't finished, have we! Now that the whole pack has come tumbling down, I think you are more involved with me than you ever were.

Surely not. Surely . . . is this the something that I once longed for, from our marriage? From you, Duncan?

CHAPTER TWELVE

"My hands are shaking. Is it like this for you, Morgan?"

Miss Gwenyth Adair faces me in the washstand mirror. We have met together by chance in the women's bathroom on the fourth floor of the Family Court.

It's almost ten. In a few minutes, Miss Adair will be called as my first witness on the tenth day of proceedings. She wears her working clothes, as it's a normal Westall school day: tweed skirt, gray angora twinset, a strand of pearls. Her gray hair is newly permed. The skin under her eyes is puffy, and she is powdering the high flush marks on her cheeks.

"Yes. I've been sick every morning. You are terribly brave to have come."

"I said I would, and I keep my word. They all warned me not to go through with this. The school lawyer, my senior mistress, the chairman of the board of trustees: they all think I've gone too far, but it's too late now. I told them: I have my eyes fixed squarely on those children."

She stares at herself, smoothes the creases around her mouth, and dampens a brow with her finger.

"I look simply dreadful. I must do this. I must do it for the children. Dear me, my voice is quavering like an old lady's."

"You can never grow old, not to me. You haven't changed since French lessons at Westall."

She laughs. Her movements and words come rapidly. "What is he like, this Mr. Schorman? I knew of him, years ago, as a father at the school, not as an inquisitor. Will he be very rude to me? Goodness, how silly of me to feel afraid of him."

I take her hand in mine. "Do you know how brave you are? With your position and prestige, always in the public eye, the epitome of respectability, you've agreed to enter the lion's den for my sake and for the children. I don't know how I can thank you." I'm afraid Schorman will savage her.

She must be nearing retirement. It's almost ludicrous to share a bathroom mirror together, to be saying words of comfort to a woman who taught me French more than twenty years ago—my teacher who is now my witness and collaborator.

"Do you remember that evening last month when you came to see me in my office at Westall? After Mr. Ross called me on the telephone?" Miss Adair collects her thoughts. "He sounded so mysterious. There was something I should know, he said. I never expected it. Oh, an affair perhaps, some waywardness, but I knew it had nothing to do with the way you have mothered those children. I know you too well for that. I took his words to be a warning, to keep me out of the court. Do you forgive me for my questions? I'm so sorry, my dear, to have pried into your private life like that."

"You would have found out eventually in any case. He was determined to make it public. Your hands gripped the desk when I said the word *lesbian*."

"Well, it came as a bombshell. I remembered, there was some talk at Westall in Mary Butler's time, in perhaps the year when you were head girl, but Miss Butler pooh-poohed the whole idea. It was unthinkable for any Westall girl. But then, so was divorce." She shivers. "I doubt that Miss Butler would wish to be here in these shoes today."

"I can't begin to tell you what it means to me. People I've known for years have recently turned their backs on me. Do you remember Phillipa Whittle? She married Toby Nettle, the winemaker. When I went to see Catriona recently in the junior school play—Pip's daughter Frances was also in it—Pip Nettle literally couldn't look at me. She turned away. And Toby called out to me so that other people could hear, 'Hey, I hear you're on the loose.' I felt like a scarlet woman."

"Well, my dear, in a way you are. Scandalous, if not scarlet. Adelaide is still a small town; people here still have small minds. I deliberately came up to speak with you after the performance because I wanted to make them think. I certainly did not feel heroic, but I wanted to show you the same courtesy I would show any other old scholar and parent at my school. Toby Nettle, you know, is one of my trustees; they're very angry with me for involving myself in a custody case. I'm not afraid of them. I can control my own trustees. It's Mr. Schorman who frightens me this morning. I'm afraid I will be forgetful—dates, conversations, important details that can help the children."

"Would you mind if I light a cigarette, Miss Adair?"

"In these circumstances, of course you may." She smiles like a conspirator. "In fact, I shall have one with you. Let's smoke in the lobby."

Duncan and Schorman have not yet arrived. Miss Adair sits down on a yellow vinyl chair.

"Morgan, let me tell you what else that husband of yours tried to do. It was just last week when your case was already underway. He sent his cousin—a woman I'd met before at a teachers' conference—as a kind of emissary. She appealed to me as a teacher. She told me this was not my business. She was very persistent. She said I would destroy your husband, an only son, his father dead now, a lonely man. I felt cross-examined, and by a schoolteacher! I replied that what concerns me are children's lives, not the messes their parents make of their own. The more she argued, the stronger my conviction that I must do my duty here."

Miss Adair puts out her cigarette and sits straight in the chair. "Then she made a foolish mistake. She insisted on taking me for a drive in her car, up and down streets, mile after mile, until I felt like a hostage. I had to order her to take me back to Westall. How badly they miscalculated! Had I needed a reminder, a timely boost to my morale, your husband gave me that. That woman tried to tamper—with a witness! That *did* it. That's why I'm here. It's like a war. But for the headmistress of Westall, a battle recharges the blood. Come, dear. Don't worry about me. At my age, I shall look upon this day as a learning experience, one I hope never to repeat."

We stand together at the door to the court, backs straight, heads high, feet together as Miss Butler drilled us. Peter and Schorman are seated. The clerks are ready at their machines.

Miss Adair squeezes my arm and whispers urgently as if we were in a Westall classroom and the teacher's back was turned, "Children! What responsibilities we have. Well, dear, to the rescue." She marches firmly to the witness box like a lifeguard entering a rough surf. I take my chair behind Peter.

ROSS VERSUS ROSS
A286, 1978

Mr. Schorman, cross-examination of
Miss Gwenyth Adair, continued:
"Late with books? Poor concentration? Surely these reports are common complaints teachers would make of any normal schoolchild?"

"I think a concerned parent would read something serious between the lines."

"Did you rely on hearsay from class teachers for such observations?"

"I saw for myself."

"Do you mean to say, while managing your own considerable duties, you have time to study individual children?"

"I visit every classroom every day."

"But only to poke your head in the door, so to speak?"

"Mr. Schorman. I make it my business to know each one of my girls and their family situations. In a matter such as this, and knowing as I did the difficulties Mr. and Mrs. Ross were having, I made doubly sure I kept my eye upon those children. They were, if you like, under my magnifying glass. They were a special case."

"Would you agree that the subject of lesbianism often comes up among schoolchildren?"

"It is not a topic I have heard my girls discuss, either in jest or in their science classes."

"When did you learn that Mrs. Ross was a lesbian?"

"On about the Friday before the last term began at school."

"Did she tell you anything further about her lesbian activities?"

"She told me something of the background, the history to it."

"Did she mention the names of people with whom she had been associated?"

"I cannot recall."

"Did she tell you when it had started?"

"No, and I did not ask her. I felt it was her private business."

"You would agree, would you not, that it is mostly mothers who deal with the school—talk with teachers, attend sports days, things like that?"

"I would not agree. I make sure that fathers come as well."

"Yes, but what percentage would be fathers—ten, twenty?"

"I expect fifty-fifty, if I can help it."

"But surely you would agree, even if you would like fifty percent of fathers to attend school functions, it is normally only about ten percent who can take that sort of time away from their work or business?"

"Let me answer you in this way. Quite a large proportion of our mothers nowadays are working mothers. I expect the same willingness to attend school functions from working fathers as I get from working mothers."

"I see. You have referred to a discussion you had with Mr. Ross about Catriona's problems when her mother was abroad. I think it was to do with stealing?"

"That was Mr. Ross's word for it, not mine. Catriona was eating a lot of sugar, keeping sweet things under her bed."

"Is that not a rather typical thing with youngsters—I mean liking sweets, hoarding them?"

"It may be, but in this instance, I thought it could be a sign of something more serious, a child's sense of deprivation, a need for comfort. That's what I suggested to Mr. Ross."

"And what was his response to that?"

"He laughed. He thought it was a very minor matter."

"Why did you consider it might have been serious?"

"I think it was a sign of psychological distress."

"Oh, and what qualifies you to be a psychologist? I thought your training was in the French language, was it not?"

"I trained in psychology when I was a university student, before I became a teacher. I would add, Mr. Schorman, that there's no better training ground in child psychology than forty years' experience as a schoolteacher and headmistress. I have tried to explain to you many other signs of distress I observed in these children: the deterioration in Catriona's powers of concentration; Holly's unkempt appearance; their teeth in poor condition with inflamed gums; both children looking very drawn as though they'd been up late at night. The homework of both girls deteriorated, too, while their mother was away. . . ."

"You are not in the classroom now, Miss Adair. May I remind you that you are a witness and your job is to answer my questions, not to deliver a lesson."

His Honor:

"I think, Mr. Schorman, we may all find something instructive in what this witness has to say. Please continue, Miss Adair."

"I am very concerned, Your Honor, about Holly and Catriona. Both have appeared in their classrooms in a state of great anxiety. Catriona has broken down and cried. When I attempted to calm her, she told me she was afraid to have to return home. Holly has become extremely withdrawn. She sits at the back of the class, bites her fingernails, talks to herself, and does not cooperate in group activities. I believe arrangements for these children must be settled as quickly as possible, as both girls are showing signs of acute anxiety."

Mr. Schorman:

"You would agree, would you not, that these signs of deterioration, as you call it, can be put down to their mother's absence overseas? You do know about Mrs. Ross's determination to go overseas again, do you?"

"Mrs. Ross has kept me fully informed as to her movements."

"I suppose Mrs. Ross has often talked to you about her career."

"Not directly. I'm aware of her career because I like to keep track of what happens to my old scholars."

"I suppose she has told you of her hobby on the stage."

"Mr. Schorman, Morgan Ross attended Westall for her entire schooling during the period of my teaching career. I became headmistress to replace Miss Butler who retired the same year that Morgan completed high school, so I have known Morgan for many, many years. She was one of our most gifted actresses at Westall. We've certainly been interested to hear of her career since she left school."

His Honor:

"Do you consider that children may be disadvantaged educationally should they spend a year away from their present schools to attend a school in another country?"

"From an educational point of view, children usually benefit from such an experience. I am also of the opinion that removal to a new environment, contact with children in other places, helps provide a healing as well as stimulating experience that these particular children need. From my experience, these children are special children—intelligent, sensitive children who are highly strung with complex personalities and needs. And I do believe, Your Honor, from my observation of both parents, that Mrs. Ross is better able to meet the special needs of these children and their personalities."

Mr. Schorman:

"I was not asking for your opinion, I was asking about Mrs. Ross's career, if we could please keep to the point. I suppose she has told you her career matters more to her than anything else?"

"Mr. Schorman, I am sure I do not need to remind you, a former Westall father, that our school has always instilled in our girls the confidence and belief that a career, that development of one's talents, is as important as marriage and motherhood can be in the fulfillment of a woman's life. Mrs. Ross has lived up to our Westall motto in every way, in her family life and in her achievements, and I am sure that both matter equally to her."

His Honor:

"And what is this motto to which you refer?"

" 'Good, better, best! Never let it rest; Until your good is better; and your better best.' "

Mr. Schorman:

"I have no further questions of this witness."

His Honor:

"I would like to thank Miss Adair for coming here today."

". . . and I saw her afterward talking animatedly to Judge Simpson about the best Catholic high schools for his own children. What a woman! If ever I have a daughter, I'll send her to Westall."

"Peter, I thought your life had been given over to Morgan. I didn't know you were contemplating marriage. Who's the lucky girl?" Annie bends down to inspect the roast in the bottom oven.

"No one. There hasn't been much time, I know, but once we pack Morgan off to America, I have some delightful skirmishes planned." Peter stretches his arms above his head expansively. "A holiday by the sea, white sand, seagulls—what do you say to Victor Harbor for a hot romantic holiday?"

I join in the laughter, too, but guiltily. The case, I know, has dominated all of us. Still, it surprises me that Peter can still joke about it, or that Annie has the energy and presence of mind to cook dinner for us all.

"Happy endings." Annie turns, carving fork in hand, flushed from the oven's heat. "Here's my fantasy, Peter. The two ex-husbands, Ivan and Duncan, take a Victor Harbor holiday to recuperate with blueprints and company profit sheets; they bump into you swimming underwater with Casey in Encounter Bay; they become totally paranoid, suspect you of company sabotage, and take you to court on charges of seditious conduct. Judge Simpson collapses when he sees the same team back in court—"

"Minus Morgan, don't forget." Peter roars with laughter. "And what about the key witnesses, Miss Adair, you—"

"Stop! Don't remind me that I'm on tomorrow. In my fantasy, Miss Adair, dear brave heroic Miss Adair, secretly replaces the company blueprints with school reports and is promptly charged with educational fraud."

"Marvellous! But I don't know about Casey in this scenario. What say I take up scuba diving with Schorman's daughter?" They both break up in gusts of laughter. Annie's two sons, Tim and Edwin, come to the kitchen doorway to see what the noise is about.

"What's that you're holding, Tim?" I ask.

"Plasticine." He lays a mummy-shaped object on the table. "See, Morgan, Mr. Schorman's a robot. This is his head; it's attached by these pipes to the life-support system here. When I turn on the power, he can walk and talk; when I turn it off, he dies."

"Timmy, how disgusting." For Tim is hacking the plasticine pipes in half with his pocketknife.

"Morgan, come here a second, do you think this is done?" I go to Annie's side and she lowers her voice. "Don't get upset. Children have their ways of working out anxieties through fantasy, too. The boys feel as closely involved as I do, perhaps more helpless than even your own kids, because something awful is happening to your lives and we can't do much about it. It helps to play; you of all people should know that." She hands me the heavy baking pan. "Okay, dinner's ready, boys. Set the table, Eddie, and Tim, clear that poor unplugged robot away and turn off all your air pumps and compressors and wash your hands. Morgan, you can carve, and Peter, mash the spuds. Action stations everyone."

Dinner is pandemonium, and Peter looks relieved when Annie allows the boys to eat their ice-cream in front of television for a *M.A.S.H.* replay.

"When I watch you and Annie together, Morgan, I wonder how Ivan or Duncan could tear themselves away night after night and miss out on all this wonderful rough-and-tumble family life. They must have lacked stamina; it's exhausting, isn't it." Peter lights up a rare cigar which he holds insecurely between forefinger and thumb. It goes out after his first draw, but he doesn't seem to notice. "You both make parenting look easy, like practiced team-work. Have you always got on so well?"

Annie snuggles against me on her couch. "We've had our difficulties in—what is it?—a friendship that has lasted almost twenty years, but we always manage to work them out. To be accurate, Morgan acts them out while I do the dull analytical backstage working-out. And parenting is a damned hard act, as I'll remind you all tomorrow on the stand. I don't think I could have done it without Morgan."

"Nor I without you."

"But then, we wouldn't have had children at all without each other there, at the core." Annie sits up. "You know, silly as it sounds, we've been the real married couple all along, like one of Tim's life-support systems at the heart of both families, pumping life into all those growing arms and legs and brains—it's a funny image." Annie's eyes shine with it, but Peter looks very thoughtful.

"Ivan let go quietly and reasonably, while Duncan has fought to hang on. Who are the dependent children, I wonder—who fears the disconnection most?"

"My god, Peter, we haven't been exhausting ourselves watching our Morgan lose ten pounds and gain a few extra wrinkles for the wrong cause, have we? I hope I'm not expected to do battle tomorrow for the custody of Duncan Ross! Talking of which, it's time we rehearsed my evidence again. I'm more nervous than I normally care to admit. Morgan, do you think my black suit will lend an authoritative air?—oh, sweetheart, if only I had your professional expertise to bolster me!"

"No previous experience counts in this scenario. I think it is best to be yourself. It's your calm, sane, poised, professional voice we need, to cut through all the days of testimony to the heart of the case—my role as a mother."

"On that, I'm *the* expert. Right, Peter, fire away. Morgan can do the good old restful washing up while we practice. Put on some music, sweetheart—something soothing, something classical—and here, Peter, catch— you need a light for that cigar if you want to convince *me* you're a competent lawyer."

On Friday evening, in Peter's office, I sip my drink and smile with the others and try not to show despondency. None of us is game to guess results and project the judge's verdict, now that the trial is over. We avoid what each of us dreads and make small talk with the camaraderie of weary troops after an inconclusive battle. Will he call a retreat? Must we gird for another advance? There's nothing left to do but wait for word.

I am trying to face what it will mean for me. I shall have to give up the idea of America; the job with the Sheridan Players—the chance, I thought, of a lifetime. After all we have suffered, the children and me, through this trial and the unhappy years that led to it, I know I shan't leave them here with him. It's Australia, then, forever. A hunt for a home where they can come . . . to visit me; and for work—maybe a change of career. . . . I'm too tired to think, but I know I must plan for the inevitable. I can hear Harry's warnings, now, as distant boundaries to the future; I sense my mother's deepest insecurities.

If this had been Annie's case, would we dare imagine a victory? She was magnificent this morning. Hearing her was like listening to my own voice, like recognizing lines that I've wanted to say in court, that I haven't been able to say for myself. Hearing Annie, I saw with pride the extraordinary ways in which our friendship has blessed each one of our children. I saw how she has always been there for me, the nearest and dearest of all my friends.

What worries me is not knowing what the judge has seen, or what he needed, still, to hear. I am surprised by what Schorman didn't present. Jenny, thank goodness, has stowed away in London, well beyond reach, but why didn't he question Annie about our life together before we married? Does he not know that we were lovers? Annie and I have been very afraid that he'd bring that out.

Does this mean Duncan forgot? How can he forget, when it was he who raised it?

Lesbian. Why do I feel that no one has really dealt with this? Other than the day Schorman cross-examined me so painfully, it is the one subject that everybody skirts around and hopes to shelve. I fear what this means; that when Judge Simpson studies his notes and the evidence, he'll discover it has lurked there all along. Duncan's irrefutable trump card: Unfit Mother.

Auden is raising his glass. I must give the first toast.

"Annie, I'm so proud of you. Today was the only time I heard a voice in court that I really knew, that told me that my experience was real, that my memory was reasonably accurate, and that I'm not crazy after all. A toast, dear friends, to Annie."

We clink our glasses together.

"I've never been so scared," she says, still flushed from the ordeal. "I doubt if I'll be in any hurry to offer my psychological expertise to another court case. I need no praise. I know you would do the same for me if tables were turned. The only reward I want is to see you win. I insist you will be in New York next year. I'm the one who wants to travel. It's my turn to fly to America, and besides, I want to see those 'arrangements' you say you've made for your children. After Schorman's dreadful questions today, about the potential damage to innocent Aussie babies from inner-city sex and drugs and rock and roll, I'm worried, myself, for their safety—it's alright, Morgan, don't blanch, I'm teasing." She takes my hand and squeezes it. Her tone of voice changes. "Auden, how long is this going to take?"

"Normally several weeks, but Judge Simpson has promised to expedite it. The case persists in breaking all the rules of precedence. Whatever his decision, he says he'll take into account Morgan's imminent deadline to take up the New York position so that she can either meet it, or give notice. . . . But let's talk of your future, Annie. Should you and Ivan ever get into hot water and need legal advice, you will come to us, won't you?—although Peter, I know, hopes never to land another case like this in Family Court."

"Whichever way this case goes now, I have no regrets we took it on, Auden."

"You've done very well for a beginner, my boy. This

young whippersnapper," he says proudly, "has managed to lay down some brilliant points of order should we have to appeal."

"Appeal?" Annie cups both hands on Peter's desk and leans forward, looking at Auden in consternation. "Oh no! Surely we don't have to go through all of this again. . . . Morgan?"

"Of course, if I have to. If Duncan wins, Peter says we'll take an appeal to the High Court in Canberra. I don't know about the children, though. They should never be put through this again." I remember my answer to the judge this afternoon, when he brought me back to the witness stand after Annie's testimony to ask long questions about my future plans. "Should we win this round, I've promised to return to the court within a year when Judge Simpson will review the case and make a fresh, and perhaps more lasting, decision. Should Duncan win—and remember, he wants sole control—I'll appeal for shared custody, or we'll wait for a year to pass and see how the children have fared. If they deteriorate, as they did last year, I'll try again. Auden, does it ever end?"

"Well, Duncan or you may always challenge any custody decision at any time—especially so long as you have children under the age of fourteen for whom the law is empowered to make decisions. The situation can change. So can parents and children and their wishes." Auden stands and walks across to a wall of books, where he turns to face us. "I think, don't you, Peter, that I should be the one to utter our last words of advice before the closing benediction?" Peter gestures modestly for Auden to take the floor, and he continues, resting one arm on the bookcase.

"Should the decision go to Duncan, or should you earn your full year with the children in America, a subsequent court hearing shan't have to cover the same familiar grounds. We have the picture now; the frame is set; only time can change that. Who knows? Duncan may soften.

You, Morgan, could decide to remain in Australia. The law, like the lives it seeks to guide, is surprisingly fluid even though we often think of it as cast in stone. It never sets, neither when it is in process, nor after some poor scribe has written it down. Yet some things do achieve a kind of permanence." Auden bends down under Peter's desk, to emerge with the book of our transcripts, high enough for a footstool, thick as a dictionary. He weighs it in both hands before he continues.

"This record, Ross versus Ross, and the eventual judgment it receives, is a little like a hieroglyphic tablet. A stranger who stumbled across it might scratch his head— more likely stub his toe—and wonder what these squiggles mean. You, Morgan, may spend the rest of your life debating it, interpreting, revising, or heaven forbid, regretfully reliving what it says. Lawyers, trained to understand this sort of thing, will mine it for their future purposes. It may even hold some truths for our learned colleague, Jacob Schorman! Every record of trial becomes another stepping stone to the next for those who can read and apply it.

"For Morgan," Auden taps the book and looks at each of us in turn, "and the witnesses to this case, no matter what you next decide to do, whatever limitations may be placed upon you by the law, whatever opportunities it may afford you, here is the record of a route already taken. Yes, only a partial one, with many different voices, imperfectly inscribed, but here are the lines, however we may choose to read them." He places the book carefully on the desk. "I wonder," he adds as an afterthought, "if Duncan will see it this way. I wonder if he'll even bother to read it."

I've been wondering if Duncan will accept the judgment if it should go against him. I can't see him ever giving up.

"The longest vow." Auden nods into his empty glass. " 'Let no man put asunder.' But when love . . ." He smiles down at me with the same compassionate sweetness he showed me the very first day. "There comes a time, my dear, when each one of us must yield and go onward.

"Now I've talked much too much. I don't know about you young folk, but I'm calling it a day. My last word of advice is to you, Annie. Put this girl into a hot tub with a good strong brandy tonight. She's had enough of these questions and answers—what she needs now is a long weekend and children in her arms. It's out of your hands, Morgan. I'll see you in court when we get the call. Goodnight all!"

After he leaves us, I silently picture the children with Duncan, finishing their dinner, the younger ones cleaning their teeth, I hope, and preparing for bed. If he didn't have the children with him tonight, I'd feel sorry for him . . . the hollow bitter draught of loneliness . . . The thought thuds down to the pit of my stomach and settles there like an immovable stone. I miss them already.

"Know what I'm thinking?" Peter interrupts my reverie. "Oysters, a rack of lamb with garden mint—what say I take you both to dinner?"

"You just read my mind!" Annie throws back her head and laughs. "But we're not going out. Your heart's desire awaits you in my refrigerator—all but your passion for oysters which you can buy en route. I'm taking Auden's advice. I know when to yield. You, Morgan, haven't left the country yet. Your turn to cook."

" 'And they lived happily together for ever and ever. The end.' " I close the book and kiss first Nicky, then Holly. "Sleep tight, darlings."

"Oh, Mummy," Holly giggles, "why do bedtime stories always have mushy endings?"

"Because everyone likes to dream they come true." I tuck her under the blankets.

"It can be true, can't it, Mum," says Nicholas sleepily from his bed under the window in Annie's playroom, "if I make a wish?"

Holly snorts. "Make a proper wish: don't let the boobook owl come and get you in the night, or he'll peck out your insides and eat you and then spit you out like a worm." She makes a loud whooping sound, then the whistles and chirrups of a distressed bird.

I laugh. "Come, you two starlings, settle down, please, because tomorrow is a school day again, and I have to take you back to Duncan first thing after breakfast. Light's going out . . . now!"

In the darkness, Nicky calls to me, "Mummy, I wished. I wished I could stay with you not just for weekends but for ever and ever."

Then Holly's muffled reply: "Drongo, don't you know if you say what you wish, it never works?"

I look in the door to Tim and Eddie's bedroom, where Emma and Catriona have mattresses on the floor. They're all talking at once. No one looks ready for sleep, despite an afternoon trek together to Waterfall Gully, at least a five-mile walk to the top of the falls. *My* legs are tired. I decide to join Annie by the fire and give the older kids some extra time.

"The boys are a great comfort, Annie. Life takes on its true chaotic adolescent colors when our kids are together." I settle on the couch with Annie and our herbal teas and light a last cigarette. "I'm sure these weekends with them have helped the girls forget, or at least to bear the waiting time."

"Gives them a sense of continuity, I guess."

"In friendship, especially when that's missing from family."

I check through a list of things to be done next week ready for departure, while Annie reads a clinical case study. There's much to organize: new luggage, tickets, passports for the children, just in case. Annie wants to throw a party for me and the old friends from my women's group, but I say, wait, it may have to be a wake. When Annie finishes her report, we both stare at the fire and talk, at first, about our work; the *Medea* I've been asked to produce in a little theatre off-off-Broadway; her application to be director of psychological services in the public schools. Just dreams, I remind myself. We're both avoiding something. There are other things we should say, I think, about the future.

"After all these years," I say, "I'm never completely sure of your feelings."

"*My* feelings? You know them as well as anyone—my ambitions, my goals—success, satisfaction . . ."

"Perhaps I should have said your affections. I've always admired your control and efficiency when it comes to passionate attraction. Unlike me."

"What is this leading to, Morgan?"

"I'm wondering about future structures if I have to remain in Australia. Not only for work and children, but the changes in my position as well. I'll be making a new start. I suppose I'm wondering how you will react, what will happen to our friendship if . . . How will you feel if I begin a new commitment?"

"I don't plan to start a new relationship, if that's what you mean. I trust friendship more than passion. As I told Ivan, I'm looking forward to some solitude. I'll have the boys some of the time, of course, but I want to try living on my own, as it was before I met you." She stretches her legs toward the hearth. Firelight heightens the bronze tints in her hair. "If you have to stay, of course, we could live together, under the same roof, and pool the work and the kids and our expenses. We could go on as we were, as we originally planned all those years ago," she adds. "What would you say to that?"

I'm thinking of the day I walked through Washington Square with Annie's Tim, when we ate hot dogs and watched old men at chess and a film crew setting up lights in front of Tisch Hall; of the runners in sweatshirts panting around the park's perimeter, and a shabby bag lady poking a trash can for scraps of food. Of the energy that city gave back to me when I discovered that time, place, work, and identity were at last connected, there, for me. Of how

I wanted my children with me to complete it. Of how I can't yet dare to hope that we'll all be there together.

When I fully realize what Annie is proposing, I'm speechless. Can she be serious? Can Annie want to stop the action, freeze the frame, cheat time of quirky and spontaneous change?

Before I can ask her, the telephone jangles in her bedroom.

"Damn, its late. Who can this be?" She runs to pick it up. "For you. It's Peter."

He sounds breathless. I'm to come to the court to-morrow morning. He's ready. Yes, the judge.

". . . but I have to return the kids to Duncan."

"Bring them with you. Duncan won't be in court."

"What does that mean, Peter—what does it mean? Say that again, very slowly. Annie's here—she wants to know—"

The words seem to come from a very long way: ". . . awarded you care and control and the court's permission to take them to America. Morgan, are you there? Can you hear me?"

Yes, I heard. That my life can begin.

88-852

F
WOO
 Wood, Elizabeth
  Mothers and lovers

DATE DUE			